W Backe

Essay on Edmund Spenser and His Fairy Queen

Especially with regard to the language

W Backe

Essay on Edmund Spenser and His Fairy Queen
Especially with regard to the language

ISBN/EAN: 9783337245832

Printed in Europe, USA, Canada, Australia, Japan

Cover: Foto ©Andreas Hilbeck / pixelio.de

More available books at **www.hansebooks.com**

Programm

der

Realschule erster Ordnung zu Stralsund

Ostern 1872.

Im Namen des Lehrercollegiums

herausgegeben

von dem Director

Dr. Ernst Brandt,

Ritter des Königlichen Hohenzollerschen Hausordens.

Inhalt:

Stralsund, 1872.

Druck der Königlichen Regierungs-Buchdruckerei.

Schüler-Verzeichniß.

Wintersemester 1871/72.

Prima.

1. Karl Behrens aus Tribsees.
2. Ferdinand Berg a. Stralsund.
3. Friedrich Danckwardt a. Rostock.
4. Otto Duchâteau aus Stralsund.
5. Albert Giermann „
6. Ernst Engelbrecht „
7. Karl Heitbaner aus Behnkenhagen.
8. Ludwig Hempel aus Stettin.
9. Julius Hübner aus Stralsund.
10. Robert Knütel aus Lüssow.
11. Paul Manke aus Stralsund.
12. Theodor Ristow aus Pastiz.
13. Paul Stoll aus Bergen.
14. Emil Zimm aus Stralsund.
15. Robert Westphal aus Barth.

Ober-Secunda.

1. Eduard Bachus aus Stralsund.
2. Otto Brandenburg aus Stralsund.
3. Reinhold Brandt „
4. Otto Darffslag aus Altsüdre.
5. Wilh. Dietrich aus Barth.
6. Paul Funk aus Stralsund.
7. Ferdinand Harde aus Stralsund.
8. Konstatin Kraan aus Bergen.
9. Hermann Näter aus Lindenein.
10. Richard Nie aus Stralsund.
11. Richard Neumann aus Lapiz.
12. Otto Hamelow aus Grancburg.
13. Karl Höcke aus Altenkirchen.
14. Gustav Rosenkranz aus Stralsund.

Unter-Secunda.

1. Karl Berg aus Stralsund.
2. August Bugel aus Stralsund.
3. Robert Ewert aus Klückewitz.
4. Max Gählsted aus Stralsund.
5. Richard Gülow aus Grapzow.
6. Hermann Gronow aus Stralsund.
7. Karl Hanow „
8. Hermann Hennigs aus Wolgast.
9. Emil Hermsdorf aus Wolgast.
10. Johannes Kaich aus Wolgast.
11. Gustav Koch „
12. Friedrich Kobbahn aus Stralsund.
13. Paul Köster aus Stralsund.
14. Franz Krüger I. aus Löbniz.
15. Franz Krüger II. aus Stralsund.
16. Robert Lübermann aus Mellniz.
17. Karl Renke aus Stralsund.
18. Emil Mäde aus „
19. Friz Peters aus Grancburg.
20. Bernhard Picht aus Poseriz.
21. Friz Vorenberg aus Siz.
22. Gustav Poelke aus Stralsund.
23. Karl Schönregge a. Neuenkirchen.
24. Otto Schulz aus Stralsund.
25. Ferdinand Sorge aus Godkin.
26. Adolf Stub aus Alt-Bleen.
27. Franz Liburtius a. Gr.-Mohrdorf.
28. Heinrich Vieth aus Stralsund.
29. Karl Wendel aus Falkenhagen.
30. Richard Werthheim a. Stralsund.
31. Ernst Hebergang aus „

Ober-Tertia.

1. Julius Uhrend aus Stralsund.
2. Wilhelm Antbons aus Barth.
3. Karl Büsell aus Stralsund.
4. Max Beier „
5. Ernst Broefmann aus Stralsund.
6. Arnold Brunst aus Vajemall.
7. Herm. Buldenhagen a. Jacobsdorf.
8. Max Busksow aus Grancburg.
9. Paul Eban aus Grancburg.
10. Paul Dalmer aus Schoriz.
11. Max Danckwardt aus Stralsund.
12. Otto Ewert aus Klückewig.
13. Johannes Gabriel aus Stralsund.
14. Karl Gülze aus Trent.
15. Karl Graue aus Stralsund.
16. Otto Gronow aus „
17. Max Harber aus Hobenort.
18. August Hezberg aus Barth.
19. Paul Güth aus Stettin.
20. Ernst v. Homeyer aus Stralsund.
21. Otto Hoffeldt aus Grimmen.
22. Hermann Jungen aus Stralsund.
23. August Kaslmann „
24. Karl Kraulkammer a. Wandsbeck.
25. Ernst Krüger aus Stralsund.
26. Eduard Krüger a. „
27. Heinrich Kühlbach aus Tribsees.
28. Heinrich Lübermann aus Mellniz.
29. Friz Lergus aus Stralsund.
30. Max Lühewiz aus Trent.
31. Max Holm aus Stralsund.
32. Reinhold Plevis a. Krummenhagen.
33. Karl Reh aus Stralsund.
34. Alfred Säger aus „
35. Richard Samuel aus Domgarten.
36. Herm. Sauerbier „
37. Otto Schulz aus Barth.
38. Richard Schulz aus Stralsund.
39. Hermann Schwing aus Lüffow.
40. Hermann Siemon a. Stralsund.
41. Hermann Tode aus „
42. Emil Warbeck „
43. Hermann Wenzel a. „
44. Otto Westphal aus Reckentin.

Unter-Tertia.

1. Max Anherled aus Stralsund.
2. Ernst Beder aus Stralsund.
3. Ernst v. Berg aus Dublewiz.
4. Paul Biblingmayer aus Stralsund.
5. Alexander Boldow „
6. Wilh. Dieletin „
7. August Dinse „
8. Robert Drews „
9. Friedrich Drews „
10. Julius Dürfow „
11. Eduard Dumohl „
12. Heinrich Hoeck aus Barth.
13. Karl Frank aus Stralsund.
14. Ernst Garlof aus „
15. Ludwig Genschow aus Stralsund.
16. Albert Gronow „
17. Friedrich Harder „
18. Gustav Harbrat aus Steinhagen.
19. Wilh. Hevernil aus Stralsund.
20. Bernhard Heinsten aus Goldberg.
21. Karl Heinborn aus Stralsund.
22. Robert Hecht aus Leplow.
23. Ernst Hübner aus Stralsund.
24. Hermann v. Köhler a. Stralsund.
25. Ernst Kobbahn aus „
26. Kurt Lambced aus Thorn.
27. Otto Liesenow aus Stralsund.
28. Emil Löbewiz „
29. Leopold Manzer „
30. David Mildebradt „
31. August Müller „
32. Frommhold Pleris aus Krummenhagen.
33. Otto Rasmus aus Stralsund.
34. Wilhelm Richardt aus Stralsund.
35. Otto Röbl aus Gingst.
36. Wilhelm Runge aus Stralsund.
37. Albrecht Scherkin „
38. Max Scheeren aus Schabtof.
39. Otto Schmidt „
40. Christian Schmidt „
41. Karl Schrode aus Lipiz.
42. Robert Schwebke aus Stralsund.
43. Max Seifert „
44. Friedrich Stuck aus Alt-Bleen.
45. Julius Faselmild aus Rostock.
46. Hans Wiebrad aus Stralsund.
47. Ernst Wernbal aus Reckentin.
48. Karl Wernher aus Sagard.
49. Johannes Wieren aus Stralsund.
50. Paul Enge aus Stralsund.

Quarta A.

1. Franz Bilbingmayer a. Stralsund.
2. Ewald Black aus Wüniz.
3. Paul Bredemfelder aus Grimmen.
4. Arnold Gühring aus Wolfsdorf.
5. Ludwig Eggert aus Löbniz.
6. Walter Spebecher aus Stralsund.
7. Otto Germann „
8. Hans Engel „
9. Wilh. Engelbrecht „
10. Heinrich Ewert „
11. Hugo Gränlamb aus Dresdenow.
12. Heinrich Harbrat a. Steinhagen.
13. Salomo Israel aus Wiek.
14. Hermann Just aus Stralsund.
15. Max Keding aus Belgast.
16. Gustav Kosbahn aus Stralsund.

Quarta B.

1. Paul Büssom aus Stralsund.
2. Walbert Drews a. „
3. Karl Gierts aus Nebbelin.
4. Franz Hartung aus Stralsund.
5. Gustav Hüler „
6. Erich Insel „
7. Albert Klein „
8. Max Kraal „
9. August Krüger „
10. Karl Letener aus Grimmen.
11. Paul Martens aus Stralsund.
12. Max Mielewiz „
13. Heinrich Müller „
14. Richard Otto aus Bielgast.
15. Friz Dietch aus Stralsund.
16. Friedrich Wörk aus Barth.
17. Richard Massow aus Lapiz.
18. Max Ridmann aus Stralsund.
19. Wilhelm Schröder aus Neu-Bleen.
20. Paul Wieth aus Stralsund.
21. Paul Wieber „
22. Friedrich Westphal aus Stralsund.
23. Hans Bieler „
24. Max Höge „

Quinta A.

1. Otto Abel aus Stralsund.
2. Gustav Baseld aus Stralsund.
3. Friedrich Berg „
4. Eduard Boettiger „
5. Ernst Brandenburg a. Stralsund.
6. Hermann Deim aus „
7. Karl Danckwardt „
8. Louis Drews „
9. Max Engel „
10. Wilhelm Gräfer „
11. William Gronow „
12. Gustav Güntel aus Richtenberg.
13. August Hartwig aus Stralsund.
14. Julius Homeyer aus Reddow.
15. Max Horn aus Stralsund.
16. Albert Köster a. „
17. Rudolph Kreienmeyer a. Stralsund.
18. Hermann Köbler aus „
19. Wilh. Maak aus Gr.-Kordshagen.
20. Emil Marquardt aus Stralsund.
21. Paul Melms aus Pobkemiz.
22. Karl Niemann aus Stralsund.
23. Paul Res „
24. Gustav Rent „
25. Paul Ritter „
26. Robert Schud „
27. Carl Schud „
28. Max Scholl „
29. Karl Scholl „
30. Karl Scholl aus Kardiz.
31. Robert Schlicher aus Stralsund.
32. Erich Riedel aus Gresien.
33. Gustav Wadelein aus Stralsund.
34. Robert Walther aus Neubel.
35. Eduard Wittchen aus Stralsund.

Quinta B.

1. Karl Arndt aus Stralsund.
2. Rob. Halter „
3. Emil Biel „

Sexta A.

1. Otto Röbkagen aus Ronnewiz.
2. Hermann Abpel aus Grimmen.
3. Wilhelm Brühgam aus Stralsund.
4. Albert Döhring „
5. Otto Buchbart „
6. Karl Dinse „
7. Paul Gärter „
8. Walbert Engel „
9. Karl Ewert „
10. Eberhard Gülschow „
11. Louis Graap „
12. August Grönlamb aus Dresdenow.
13. Eduard Grünwald aus Stralsund.
14. Wilhelm Hauer „
15. Karl Hennig „
16. Paul Holtfreter „
17. Gustav Soale „
18. Walter Kobbahn „
19. Karl Krabbe aus Geshof.
20. Gottfried Krule a. Krummenhagen.
21. August Kurth aus Stralsund.
22. Karl Nadowsky „
23. Otto Rest „
24. Herm. Peters „
25. Eduard Röhl „
26. Otto Roerberg aus Richtenberg.
27. Otto Schnurr aus Stralsund.
28. Wilh. Schnurr „
29. Otto Schröber „
30. Karl Schulz „
31. Wilhelm Schulz aus Kardiz.
32. Max Siemers aus Stralsund.
33. Herm. Becker „
34. Gustav Wied „
35. Max Wittenberg „
36. Otto Witthand „

Sexta B.

1. Karl Bartens aus Stralsund.
2. Robert Benz „
3. Richard Darffslag aus Altsüdre.
4. Friz Diehl aus Sagard.
5. Ernst Jahrbolz aus Stralsund.
6. Paul Gürstenow aus Stralsund.
7. Helmuth Heinemann a. „
8. Wilhelm Hepp aus „
9. Theodor Kemplin a. „
10. Leopold Käger aus „
11. Alaus Maurer „
12. Julius Meinel „
13. Hermann Melms aus Pobkemiz.
14. Franz Nadowsky aus Stralsund.
15. Robert Kaisde aus Wittenhagen.
16. Ludwig Schlenger aus Stralsund.
17. Hugo Schuldt „
18. Hermann Schröder a. Krummenhagen.
19. August Schulz aus Stralsund.
20. Hermann Stuck aus Alt-Bleen.
21. Karl Vogt aus Stralsund.
22. Karl Wahl „
23. Max Zehren aus Sagard.
24. Alex. Zehren „
25. Bernhard Zernow aus Stralsund.

Die mit * bezeichneten Schüler sind im Laufe des Winters abgegangen, die mit † bezeichneten gestorben.

Contents.

PREFACE.

Spenser's idiom being the chief point to be considered in our essay we treated the first and second part but shortly, whereas the third ought to contain the centre of the whole. In order to become acquainted with an author's idiom, however, it is best, indeed, to peruse his works thoroughly; but not being at leisure we preferred treating some sections of his chief work rather laboriously to skimming over all his writings superficially. Therefore, we thought it impossible to abstain from translating and commenting those Cantos of the Fairy Queen which are contained in the Tauchnitz edition. Thus, however, time passed away, and we were obliged improperly to abridge the syntactical and synonymical part as well as the conclusion, yet reserving, for the future, a deeper inquiry into this interesting theme. That those very Cantos have been chosen we think justified by their being easily to be procured by every one as well as by their being the finest of that poem.

Primary sources were not at our command. The principal books we have employed are noted down in the following catalogue.

Catalogue
of the Principal Books cited in the following dissertation.

Allibone: Critical Dictionary of English Literature, etc. London, Truebner 1870.
Ariosto, Lodovico: Orlando Furioso. Firenze 1863.
Ariosto's Rasender Roland, uebersetzt von Gries. Leipzig, 1851.
Crabb, George, A. M. — English Synonymes. London 1869.
Craik, George L., L. L. D., a Compendious History of English Literature, etc. London 1869.
Diez, Etymologisches Woerterbuch der Romanischen Sprachen. 1853. Kritischer Anhang zum Etymol. Woerterb 1859. Zweite Ausgabe des Etymol. Woerterb. 1861. — Romanische Grammatik.
Graham, G. F., English Synonymes. London 1867.
Grimm, J., Deutsche Grammatik, Göttingen 1822. Ed. 2.
Herrig, L. Wagner's Gram. der Engl. Sprache. 6. auflage. Braunschweig 1857.
Johnson, Samuel, Dictionary of th'e English Language. London 1765.
Jortin, Remarks on Spenser's Poems. London 1734.
Kitchin G. W., Spenser. Book I. II. of the Fairy Queen. Oxford 1869.
Latham, an English Grammar for Classical Schools. London 1861.
Loth, Etymologische Angelsacchsisch-Engl. Gram. Elberfeld 1870.

Maetzner, Ed., Altenglische Sprachproben. Berlin 1867.1869.
Maetzner, Ed., Englische Gram. Berlin 1864.
Mueller, Eduard, Etymol. Woerterb. d. Engl. Sprache. Cocthen 1865.
Morris, Specimens of Early English. Oxford 1867.
Nares, Robert, Glossary. Stralsund 1825.
Percy's Reliques of Ancient English Poetry. Tauchnitz Vol. 847—49.
Scheler, Dictionnaire d'Étymologie Française. 1862. Ausz. kurzgefasstes Etymolog. Woerterb. der Franz. Sprache 1865.
Scherr, Geschichte der Engl. Literatur. Leipzig 1854.
Schmitz, Engl. Gram. Berlin 1868.
Schwetschke, Fuenf Gesaenge der Feenkoenigin uebersetzt. Halle 1854.
Smart, D. H. Walker's Pronouncing Dictionary of the English Language. 7th ed. London, 1865.
Spalding, William, Hist. of Engl. Lit. Edinburgh 1868.
Spenser's Sonnete, übersetzt in's Deutsche von Ritter Joseph Hammer. Wien 1815.
Spenser, the Works of Edmund, H. J. Todd. London, Routledge 1866.
Tauchnitz Vol. CCCCC.
Warton's History of English Poetry. London 1870.
Willisius, Joannes, De Lingua Spenseriana eiusque Fontibus. Bonnae 1848.

1

Essay

on

Edmund Spenser and His Fairy Queen,

especially

with regard to the Language.

INTRODUCTION.

With pride and joy the English look back on the reign of Elizabeth, in which on the one hand Old-England once more gathered up all the splendour of her mediaeval romantic poetry, and on the other hand the future part was announced that New-England was to act by her greater influence on the European continent and on the modern world beyond the ocean. Queen Bess, still to this day, is so popular in England, that a rigorous inquiry into her often mentioned virginity would be looked upon as a blasphemy; and, without doubt, she has deserved such an attachment. The daughter of Henry the Eighth mounting the throne, carried along with her as a patrimony a strong desire for absolute power, but wisdom too, as it ripens in the school of misfortune, and moreover a deep knowledge of the character of that nation which to govern she had a call. It is particularly by virtue of the latter quality, that the monarchess wisely restrained her originally very haughty notions of royal sovereignty. She knew, she durst not oppose the English nation as much as those beyond the channel were opposed by their governors, since there was adopted that polity, the chief elements of which were Spanish bigot despotism and Italian Machiavelian falsehood and imposture. Elizabeth, when she had provoked the English spirit of liberty by her natural rashness, always understood to return to the right path at the proper time. In all matters of consequence she went hand in hand with the nation; therefore, her government was a happy one within and without, and her remembrance, in spite of single faults, is blessed by posterity.

A great and wonderful period, these hundred and sixty years from 1440 to 1600! At that time one of those phases of historical development began, where, what of honorable feeling exists in man, rebels against the customary falsehood and oppression; where human strength makes every effort to satisfy, by degrees, that eternal inborn longing for knowledge, liberty, beauty, happiness. At that time the regeneration of classical learning rises like a gleaming luminous cloud on the horizon of a world restrained and obscured by monastical awkwardness. Guttenberg's invention bestowed never resting wings on human thought, Columbus's genial perseverance joined a new half to our planet, the German humanists began their activity, and Protestantism began discovering the new sphere of unbound self-determination of man. The modern arts began to bloom; for Leonardo da Vinci, Buonarotti, Raphael, Titian, Corregio, Duerer, Palestrina were building, painting, composing: Rabelais and Cervantes were disseminating great ideas by their satire and humor; Copernicus Kepler, Galilei, Bruno, Bacon were reasoning and philosophizing; Ariosto, Tasso, Lope, Shakspeare were writing poetry.

In the triumphs which then were gained by the progress of human society, the English had

a rich share. They extended their dominion in Ireland, established their influence in Scotland, subjected some territories in America under the name of Virginia, settled in the West-Indies, supported
the Protestants in France and in the Low Countries, and, by their glorious fighting against Philipp
the Second's Armada, relieved Europe from her fears of the Spanish power. It was natural that
this great victory set in motion public life in England, swelled with confidence every heart, and
drove forwards the national genius on the path of glory and industry. Agriculture assumed heigh-
tened activity, rising commerce gave a mighty impulse to manufacture. Wealth and comfort abode
in the English towns, nay, about the year 1600, London contained three hundred thousand
inhabitants, and was filled up with copious stores. At court one lived in a great style; the
grandees did not allow themselves to be outdone by their Queen in pageantry, masquerades, tour-
naments and other spectacles, and burghers and peasants did not fall short of divers amusements,
comically contrasting with the severe earnestness of puritanism, that silently was already gathering
its active forces, patiently waiting for the moment of its being called on the stage of universal
history. To be sure, austere moralists, then, had occasion enough to criticise the life of the court. The
moral law being there in vogue was very lax, and diffused its efficacy through ample spheres. An
adored Queen, piquing herself on her personal accomplishments, and being proud of her virginity, yet
despised, even in declining age, to live without a gallant, and, thus, introduced a fashion, that could
not be elegant at a time, when delicate ladies of honour breakfasted on tough roast meat and a
pot of ale, and, though hiding their smiling and blushing features, with satisfaction attended the
performance of the most frivolous comedies. But let severe zealots cry murder, as they like, about
the mastery of Asmodeus, the lecherous God of gallantry; let luxury manifoldly degenerate into
extravagant wantonness, and gayety into intemperance — there was in the 'Elizabethan Era' something
that impressed on the whole of life an ideal character, viz. a general lively inclination for culture and
civilization. The Queen herself being mistress of the old languages nor undexterous in music and
poetry, in this too set an example, and was ardently imitated by many men. She esteemed and
honoured men of letters, though not proving very liberal to them; she knew to mingle cultivating
elements even with courtly festivities, taking care, that not only the traditions of chivalry, but also
the newly acquired views of classical poetry and mythology should become evident. To understand
Latin and Greek became fashionable, even among the young ladies; nay, the unlearned so fervently
aspired after being well versed in classical pursuits, that translations of ancient authors were num-
bered with the books in greatest favor. Long before the close of the sixteenth century there existed English versions of Homer, Vergil, Horace, Musaeus, Ovid, Martial, Euripides, Seneca, Plutarch;
and the English authors of that time, even in works which, like the dramatic ones, were made for
a large and largest public, are so abounding in classical allusions, that it is evident, they were supposed to be understood even by the unlearned. Cultivation of antiquity was spread over the
English social life of those times like a poetical glimmer. It did not obtain such an influence, as
to have endangered the national development of English literature; but it awoke a liking for graceful
forms, and considerably expanded the limits of the phantastic world.

The sterility after Chaucer invading English poetry for a long time, has been characterized
by Warton by a beautiful comparison [1]. He draws a parallel between the narrator of the Canter-
bury-Tales and a serene spring-day, whose warming sunbeam conjured forth buds and flowers, but
which were destroyed by the coldness of winter once more returning. Following this metaphor, we
may say that with the Elizabethan Era a prime began to dawn for English poetry, which never
saw any winterly reaction, and in the productive atmosphere of which all trees joyfully throve and

[1] See Scherr p. 57, note 5.

1*

blew side by side. The English call this time 'the golden age' of their literature, and, although many of its branches afterwards came to a far greater degree of development, yet this denomination is very proper at least for the drama. We have already mentioned[1]) the introduction of printing in England; now we must add that it was a principal lever of literary movement taking place in that period. It was printing that gradually brought firmness and stability into language and orthography, qualities without which a literature, as soon as it passes over from tradition by word of mouth to written expression, cannot continue in development.

Among the earliest productions of English poetry, there are to be mentioned the translations of the romances of chivalry. At Elizabeth's time the celebrated romances of Amadis[2]) and Palmerin were translated, and Emanuel Ford and Henry Roberts wrote English original romances of this kind. But already a change of taste was preparing, and, while one part of the public was still delighted with the adventures of Amadis, Tristan, Lancelot and other heroes of chivalry, another was already amused with the inventions of·Italian novelists. The acquaintance with those poets was followed by versions, and soon afterwards by imitations too, as for instance by Paynter's 'Palace of Pleasure', Whetstone's 'Heptameron', and Grimstone's 'Admirable Histories'. Early, however, the English romancers came on a strange by-way. Fashion disposed the novel-writers to compose in that baroque, nay ridiculous style, which was for a long time fashionable at Elizabeth's court[3]). The Queen's erudition incited the courtiers to emulate in elaborating elegantly learned compliments. They were fishing in foreign literatures, in order to hunt out some poetical allegories, mythological figures, harmless or satirical quibbles and witty antitheses. By such trifles every day life, then, was trimmed up, and thus, that preposterous, bombastic superfluous ornament in language, that habit of playing on quibbling words began, which is to be found even in the best English poets of that time[4]), f. i. Shakspeare, and which, under the name of 'concetti-poetry', was carried forth to the zenith of insipidity, by the Italian so called Seicenti. As example we only alledge the romance 'Euphues', appearing about the year 1580; the hero is a young Athenian of this name, who, on his travels, also repaired to England. John Lily (1553—1600)[5]), the author of this book, had many followers; but soon the 'Euphuist romance' was supplanted by a new species, the pastoral romance.

About the year 400 of the Christian era a Greek work of this kind, 'Daphnis and Chloe', came forth which is attributed to one Longos and appeared in print at first at Florence[6]. Some time ago this book had been translated into Latin, and had attracted the attention of Italian archaeologists. Nevertheless it is possible that, still in a higher degree, Vergil's bucolic poetry has exerted

---

[1]) See above p. 2.

[2]) 'Dieses berühmteste aller Ritterbücher wurde höchst wahrscheinlich zuerst in portugiesischer Sprache geschrieben und zwar von Vasio de Lobeira, welcher 1335 oder 1403 gestorben sein soll. Die älteste noch jetzt vorliegende Form gab dem bucho der Spanier Gordia Ordonez de Montalvo, der unter der regierung Ferdinand's und Isabella's lebte. Eine französische übersetzung (das 1. buch des romans enthaltend) erschien zu Paris 1540, eine italienische zu Venedig 1618, eine deutsche zu Frankfurt a, M. 1583. Vgl. über die Amadisliteratur und den Ritterroman überhaupt Brinkmeier: Abriss e. Gesh. d. span. Nationallit. S. 70 fg. und Clarus: Darstellung d. span. Lit. im Mittelalter, 1, 304 fg.' (Scherr, p. 57, Note 6.)

[3]) Cf. what has been above said p. 3.

[4]) The same had place in Germany, for which sée Herrig's Archiv f. n, Sprachen XLIV, p. 6.

[5]) Von der manier Lily's kann es schon eine vorstellung geben, wenn wir hören, dass er bei gelegenheit des erscheinens seines helden am hofe von Neapel von diesem sagt, derselbe sei eher das tabernakel der Venus, als der tempel der Vesta gewesen und habe mehr für einen Atheisten als für einen Athenienser gepasst. Drayton, ein zeitgenosse Lily's hat diesen gut kritisirt,' indem er ihn einen nannte, welcher immer
'Von steinen, stornen, fischen, fliegen spricht,
Mit worten spielt, mit müss'gen bildern ficht'. (Scherr, p. 58, n. 7.)

[6]) Anno 1598.

[7]) Cf. Demogest p. 133 sqq.

influence upon modern pastoral romance; for the 'pastorelles' of the Provençal Troubadours[1]) were existing long before. The great master in novel-writing, Boccaccio, also produced 'Ameto', an eclogue in prose, yet interwoven with numerous verses. Thenceforth, this mixed form was always employed in pastoral romance, which shortly gained a very high rank in literature, inasmuch as it made advances towards sentimental idealism, and answered that calm desire that draws modern men out of the fictitious case of human society into the open air. In Italy the pastoral romance was soon joined by the pastoral drama, the former being particularly represented by Sannazaro's 'Arcadia', the latter by Tasso's 'Aminta' and Guarini's 'Pastor fido.' The most celebrated pastoral romances, however, have been produced in Spain and France. There it was Montemayor, who wrote his 'Diana', appearing in 1560, continued by Gil Polo, and imitated by Cervantes in his 'Galatea'; here it was d'Urfé, who composed 'l'Astrée', whose first volume appeared in print in 1610, and which, the delight of the gentle readers of the seventeenth century, still in the following filled Jean Jacques Rousseau's ardent dreams of youth with the idyllic scenes and shapes of an imaginary world. It is probable that Montemayor's 'Diana' became known in England shortly after its appearance; for it was this book that offered the design of a similar fiction to the chivalrous courtier Sir Philip Sidney[2]). His pastoral romance bears the title of 'Arcadia', or, as dedicated by the author to his sister, the Countess of Pembroke, that of 'The Countess of Pembroke's Arcadia'. It is the Arcadian world, cultivated already by his predecessors, into which Sir Philipp introduced his readers. But he took care to mix the pastoral element with a very strong heroic one, which reproduced all the oddness of the chivalrous romances, and yet, at least for the later taste, was not by far exciting enough to exclude insipidity and fatigue. The principal merit of the English romance is its language, which, though sometimes snatching at euphuist[3]) stilts, yet, in general, does not want any graceful manner. Sidney, being considered as a paragon of English gentleman[4]), knew to estimate poetical talents of other men, without envy. At a time, when there was not yet a public, at least what we now use to signify by that term, and when, therefore, distinguished protectors decided on the existence or non-existence of a talented but poor man — Sir Philipp Sidney was stationed in the front-rank of the conspicuous men of his country, who, by benevolence and liberality encouraged literary production. Amongst his clients we meet a man, who generally is surnamed 'the Ariosto of England' — Edmund Spenser, whose life and works, particularly the 'Fairy Queen', shall be treated by us in the following dissertation.[5])

[1]) Cf. Demogeot p. 133 sq.
[2]) See below.   [3]) See above p. 4.
[4]) The usual description of Sir Philipp Sidney is 'the Gentle Minde.' (Todd, p. 426, v. 711, n.)
[5]) Cf. Allibone, Scherr, Todd, Kitchin, Spalding, Craik etc.

Part I.

S p e n s e r.

A. His Descent and Life.

In Allibone there are cited fifty eight English authors under the name of 'Spencer', and six under that of 'Spenser'. As for the orthography of our Spenser's name, we have found it now written with s, now with c; the most usual manner of spelling, however, is that of 'Spenser' [1].

Edmund Spenser was born in London [2]) in East Smithfield [3]) by the Tower, probably about the year 1553 [4]). He immediately descended from the Spensers of Hurstwood, Lancashire [5]), and claimed [6]) [7]) kindred with the family of Sir John Spenser of Althorp [8]).

About his childhood we have found nothing. He entered as a sizar at Pembroke-Hall in Cambridge [9]), May 20. 1569 [10]). We may conjecture from his writings, especially from his Letter

[1]) Todd (p. XXXI, n. o.) says: 'The name is spelt both ways, as well in the various publications of the poet which appeared while he lived, as in ancient deeds relating to the honourable family from which he is descended. I have followed that orthography, to which we have been accustomed in respect to the poet's name. and which is copied from both his own editions of the Faerie Queene'.

[2]) Prothal. 128 sqq. (in Todd p. 467):
'To mery London, my most kyndly nurse.
That to me gave this lifes first native sourse.
Though from another place I take my name.
An house of auncient fame'.

[3]) Oldys's manuscript additions to Winstanley's Lives of the most famous English poets, copied by Isaac Reed Esqr. (Todd p. IX; Craik I, p. 507.

[4]) Craik (I, p. 506) writes: 'Edmund Spenser has been supposed to have come before the world as a poet so early as the year 1569, when some sonnets translated from Petrarch. which long afterwards were reprinted with his name, appeared in Vander Noodt's Theatre of Worldlings' (see below.); 'on the 20th of May in that year he was entered a sizar of Pembroke-Hall, Cambridge; ' (see below.) 'and in that same year, also, an entry in the Books of the Treasurer of the Queen's Chamber records that there was 'paid upon a bill signed by Mr. Secretary, dated at Windsor 18o Octobris, to Edmund Spenser, that brought letters to the Queen's Majesty from Sir Henry Norris. (First published in Mr. Cunningham's Introduction (p. XXX) to his Extracts from the Revels at Court, printed for the Shakespeare Society, 800. Lond. 1842.) It has been supposed that this entry refers to the poet. The date 1510, given as that of the year of his birth upon his monument in Westminster Abbey, erected long after his death, is out of the question; but the above-mentioned facts make it probable that he was born some years before 1553, the date commonly assigned'.

[5]) See Allibone.

[6]) Colin Clouts come home again, v. 536 sqq. (Todd, p. 452):
'Ne lesse praisworthie are the sisters three,
The honor of the noble familie:
Of which I meanest boast my selfe to be,
And most that unto them I am so nie:
'Phyllis, Charillis, and sweet Amaryllis'.

[7]) See Todd p. 397, Muiopotmos, dedication to Lady Carey. and Todd p. XXXI.

[8]) Sir John Spencer (sic) died in 1580, and left five sons as well as six daughters. The family was soon after ennobled. At the present period, the family of Spenser is also rendered more particularly interesting in the literary history of this country, by the noble possessor of Althorpe's well-known and judicious accumulation of rare and valuable books, and by the tenderness of the old poet again awakened in the strains of a learned nephew of the Duke of Marlborough. (Todd, p. XXXI, n. o.).

[9]) See this page, n. o.

[10]) That he was an unsuccessful candidate for a fellowship in Pembroke-Hall, in competition with Andrews, afterwards the well-known prelate, the best informed biographers of the poet have long since disproved. Todd, p. IX, n. e: 'See the Life of Spenser prefixed to the Edition of the Faerie Queene, in 1751; the Biographia Britannica, vol. 6, Art. Spenser etc.').

to Sir Walter Raleigh [1]) that, while at Cambridge, he studied Aristotle and Plato as well as the Greek and Latin poets. Jan. 16. 1573, he proceeded to the degree of Bachelor of Arts, and June 26. 1576 [2]) to that of Master of Arts. That some disappointments, however, had occurred, in regard to Spenser's academical views; and that some disagreement had taken place between him and the master or tutor of the society, is rendered highly probable by a letter of Gabriel Harvey [3]), — the Hobbinol of his Shepheards Calender [4]), and the author of many ingenious poems [5]), with whom he had contracted a close friendship at the University, and whose correspondence with Spenser [6]) is the chief source for our author's life and works. — He, therefore, left Cambridge soon after taking his M. A. degree, and went into the north of England, to pay a visit to his connections in Lancashire [7]), perhaps not, as is vaguely asserted by most of his biographers, as a mere pensioner on their bounty, but perhaps as a tutor to some young friend [8]). There he found a fair damsel of no ordinary accomplishments, and immediately fell deeply in love. Who this lady was, has been a fruitful subject of debate for more than two centuries, though his college-friend E. K. [9]) gives a broad hint [10]) in the remark that Rosalinde [11]) is a feigned name, which, being well ordered (viz. per metathesin), will betray the very name of his mistress. According to a late American critic, Mr. Halpin [12]), the proper 'ordering' of Rosalinde is Rose Daniel, a sister of an historian and poet, Samuel Daniel. But this may pass. She subsequently rejected Spenser, and became the wife of another author, John Florio, the Resolute.

In 1578 [13]) he was induced by Harvey's [14]) advice [15]) to quit his obscure abode in the country, and to remove to London. Harvey, as it is generally allowed [16]), introduced him to Sir Philip Sidney, who, justly appreciating the talents of Spenser, recommended him to his uncle, the powerful Earl of Leicester [17]). The poet was also invited to the family-seat of Sidney at Penshurst in Kent, where he was probably employed in some literary service, and at least assisted, we may suppose [18]), the Platonic and chivalrous studies of the gallant and learned youth who had thus kindly noticed him [19])· Some of his biographers have asserted [20]) that, during this time, our poet was

[1]) See below.
[2]) 'Prefixed by Dr. Farmer, in his own hand-writing, to the first volume of Hughes's second edition of Spenser, in the possession of Isaac Reed Esqr. See also Chalmers's Suppl. Apology etc. p. 23.' (Todd, p. IX, note c.).
[3]) See Todd p. IX sqq. and below.   [4]) See below.   [5]) See below.   [6]) See below.
[7]) See above.   [8]) See Todd p. X.   [9]) 'Edward Kirke' (?) 'was a friend of Spenser, and compiled a 'Gloss' on the Shepheards Calender", (Kitchin, intr. p. VIII, note g.).
[10]) See what E. K. relates of this hard-hearted fair, in his notes on the first Eclogue, p. 365. The author of the Life of Spenser, prefixed to Church's edition of the Faerie Queene, observes, in consequence of E. K.'s information, 'that the name being well ordered will betray the very name of Spenser's Love and Mistress', that as Rose is a common Christian name, so in Kent among the Gentry under Henry in Fuller's Worthies', we find in Canterbury the name of John Lynde'. If Rose Lynde be the person designed, she has the honour also to have her poetical name adopted by Dr. Lodge, a contemporary poet with Spenser, who wrote a collection of Sonnets entitled 'Rosalind'; and by Shakspeare, who has presented us with a very engaging Rosalind, in 'As you like it'.
[11]) See The Shepheards Calender, Eclogues April and June, and Colin Clout's Come Home Again.
[12]) See Atlantic Monthly, Boston, Nov. 1858, 677 in Allibone.
[13]) Cf. what Mr. Ball says in his Life of Spenser prefixed to his edition of the Calender.
[14]) See above.
[15]) In Eclogue VI, v. 16 sqq. of the Shepherd's Calender, Hobbinal (Harvey) prays Colin Clout (Spenser) to 'forsake the soyle that so doth thee bewitch', and 'to the dales resort'. On this E. K. (see above) remarks: 'This is no poeticall fiction, but unfeignedly spoken of the poet selfe, who for speciall occasion of private affaires ('as I have been partly by himselfe informed') and for his more preferment, removoed out of the north partes, [and]came into the south'.
[16]) See Todd p. XI.   [17]) See below p. 8.   [18]) See Todd p. XI.
[19]) Eclogue 4, v. 21: Hob. Colin thou kenst, the southerne shepheards boye; Him love hath wonnded with a deadly darte. Glosse: Seemeth hereby that Colin pertaineth to some Southern noble man, and perhaps in Surrey or Kent, the rather because he so often names the Kentish downes, and before 'As lithe as lasse of Kent'.
[20]) See Todd p. XIX. See also the conclusion of Sp.'s letter to Harvey, dated from Leycester House 16 of Oct. 1579:
'Per mare, per terras,
Vivus mortuusq;
Tuus Immerito'   (Todd p. XVIII.)

constituted Agent for the Earl of Leicester in France and other foreign countries. If not [1]), he did not, however, remain long a stranger to the business of active life. In July 1580 [2]), or in the beginning of August [3]) in the same year, on the appointment of Arthur [4]) Lord Grey of Wilton as Lord Lieutenant [5]) or Lord Deputy [6]) of Ireland, Spenser accompanied his lordship to that country as his secretary — in all probability through Lord Leicester's influence [7]).

In March of the following year, he was appointed to the office of Clerk in the Irish Court of Chancery; but Lord Grey being recalled in 1582, Spenser probably returned with him to England [8]).

Of the manner he was employed for the next three or four years, nothing is known; but in 1586 he obtained from the crown a grant of 3028 [9]) acres (including the castle and manor of Kilcolman) in the County of Cork, part of the territories forfeited by the Earl of Desmond. The grant is said to have been dated June [10]) 27. 1586; and, if it was procured, as is not improbable, through Lord Grey of Wilton, Lord Leicester and Sir Philip Sidney, it was the last kindness of that last friend and patron, whose untimely death took place in the battle of Zutphen, in 1587 [11], [12]). And now Spenser seems to have passed a few years in literary ease and employment at Kilcolman Castle. This delightful retreat is thus described by an able topographer [13]): 'Two miles Northwest of Doneraile is Kilcolman, a ruined castle of the Earls of Desmond; but more celebrated for being the residence of the immortal Spenser, where he composed his divine poem The Faerie Queene [14]). The castle is now almost level with the ground. It was situated on the North side of a fine lake, in the midst of a vast plain, terminated to the East by the county of Waterford mountains; Ballyhowra hills to the North, or, as Spenser terms them, the mountains of Mole; Nagle mountains to the South; and the mountains of Kerry to the West. It commanded a view of above half the breadth of Ireland, and must have been, when the adjacent uplands were wooded, a most pleasant and romantic situation; from whence [15]), no doubt, Spenser drew several parts of the scenery of his poem. The river Mulla, which he more than once has introduced into his poems, ran through his grounds'. Here, indeed, the poet has described himself, as [16]) keeping his flock under

And in the answer of his friend the passage: 'As for your speedy and hasty travell, methinks I dare stil wager al the books and writings in my study, which you know I esteeme of greater value than al the golde and silver in my purse or chest, that you wil not, that you shall not, I saye, bee gone over sea, for al your saying, neither the next nor the nexte weeke'. (Todd p. XVIII.)

[1]) By the date of Sp.'s next Letter to Harvey, we find him still in London; and an interval of less than six months only had elapsed, since his mention of an appointment; a period hardly sufficient to have allowed him the exercise of such an appointment, even in a small degree. (Todd p. XIX).

[2]) Todd p. XXIII,   [3]) Craik p. 508.   [4]) See below.   [5]) Todd p. XXIII.   [6]) Craik p. 508.
[7]) Kitschin p. VI.   [8]) See Craik I. p. 508, and Todd p. XXIII.   [9]) Allibone means '3029' acres.
[10]) Craik I. p. 508 says: 'July'; but see Dr. Birch's Life of Spenser, prefixed to the edition of the Faerie Queene in 1751; and the Biograph, Brit. (Todd p. XXIV, n. d.).   [11]) See below.
[12]) Spenser tenderly bewailed Sidney's death in an elegy entitled 'Astrophel'. See below.
[13]) Smith's Nat. et Civ. Hist. of the County and City of Cork, vol. I, p. 333, edit. Dublin, 1774 (Todd p. XXIV).
[14]) See below.
[15]) See the Sonnets to the Earl of Ormond and Lord Grey; Colin Clouts come home again (Todd p. XXIV, n. h.)
Faer. Qu. IV, XI, 41:

There was the Liffy rolling downe the lea;   Of Arco-hill (who knowes not Arlo-hill?)
The sandy Slane; the stony Aubrian;   That is the highest head, in all mens sights,
The spacious Shenan spreading like a sea;   Of my old father Mole, whom shepheards quill
The pleasant Boyne; the fisty fruitfull Ban;   Renowmed hath with hymnes fit for a rurall skill.
Swift Awniduff, which of the English man
Is cal'de Blacke-water; and the Liffar deep;   [16]) Colin Clouts come home againe. v. 56 sqq:
Sad Trowis, that once his people over-ran;   One day (quoth he) I sat, (as was my trade)
Strong Allo tombling from Slewlogher steep;   Under the foote of Mole, that mountaine hore,
And Mulla mime, whose waves I whilom taught to weep.   Keeping my sheepe emongst the cooly shade
     F. Q. Cant. of Mut. VI, 36:   Of the greene alders by the Mullaes shore. etc. —
That was, to wet, upon the highest hights

the foot of the mountain Mole, amongst the cooly shades of green alders by the shore of Mulla, and sounding his oaten pipe (as his custom was) to his fellow shepherd-swains.

In 1588 being appointed Clerk of the Council of Munster[1]), he, in the next year, received a visit of Sir Walter Raleigh[2]), with whom he had formed an intimacy[3]) on his first arrival in Ireland, Raleigh[4]) being at that time a captain in the Queen's army. To him he showed the first three Books of the Fairy Queen[5]) in manuscript, and by him he was persuaded to return to England[6]). There Raleigh introduced him to Queen Elizabeth[7]), to whom the Faerie Queene was dedicated, and who in February 1591 bestowed on the author a pension of 50 £. a year[8])[9]).

Mr. Thomas Warton has, with much elegance, represented him forming the following poetical wish in regard to this pleasant plot. The lines have not appeared in the late edition of Mr. Warton's Poems. They have been communicated to Mr. Todd by his nephew, the Rev. John Warton: **Votum Spenseri:**

Hoc cecinit facili Spenserus arundine carmen,
  Qua virides saltus lucida Mulla rigat:
Dii facite, inter oves interque armenta canendo
Deficiam, et sylvis me premat atra dies;
Ut mihi muscoso fiat de cespite bustum,
  Qua recubat prono quercus opaca jugo:
Quin ipso tumuli de vertice pallatet ultro
  Laurus, et injussae prosiliant hederae:
Spissaque pascentes venerentur clausa capellae,

Et propter cineres plurima balet ovis.
Exultent alii praedivite marmore manes.
  Qua reges, validi qua iacuere duces;
Ingentis qua late operosa per atria templi
  Funereum ingeminant organa rite melos:
Qua sub fornicibus sublimibus, ordine crebro.
  Suspensum nureolis fulget aplustre notis:
Mi sat erit, veteres Rosalinda agnoscat amores,
  Conseratet vernas ante sepulchra rosas. (Todd p. XXIV, n. i.)

   [1]) See Allibone.   [2]) See below.
   [3]) See Dr. Birch's Life of Spenser prefixed to the edit, of the F. Q. 1751, and Biogr. Brit. (Todd p. XXIV, n. J).
   [4]) Raleigh, while banished from court by the Earl of Essex (see Dr. Birch's Memoirs of Q. Eliz. Vol. I, p. 55?), seems to have spent some time at Kilkolman, and his visit forms one chief topic of the poem headed 'Colin Clouts Come Home Again'; Sp. calls him 'The Shepheard of the Ocean' v. 66 sqq.
   [5]) See below.
   [6]) Raleigh had got the Queen's favour again and obtained from her the manor of Sherborne. Cf. Fair: Q. IV., VII., VIII. and Todd p. XXXVII sq.
   [7]) Spenser continues thus in Colin etc. v. 60 sqq:

'There a straunge shepheard chaunst to find me out.
Whether allured with my pipes delight,
Whose pleasing sound yshrilled far about,
Or thither led by chaunce, I know not right:
Whom when I asked from what place he came.
And how he hight, himselfe he did ycleepe
The Shepheard of the Ocean by name,
And said he came far from the main-sea deepe.
He, sitting me beside in that same shade.
Provoked me to plaie some pleasant fit;
  And Colin Clout 184 sqq:
'The which to leave, thenceforth he counseld mee,
Unmeet for man, in whom was ought regardfull,
And wend with him, his Cynthia' (sc. Elizabeth) 'to see;

  And Coulin Clout v. 358 sqq:
'The Shepheard of the Ocean (quoth he)
Unto that Goddesse grace me first enhanced.
And to mine oaten pipe enclin'd her eare,
That she thenceforth therein gan take delight.
And it desir'd at timely houres to heare,

And, when he heard the musicke which I made.
He found himselfe full greatly pleasd at it;
Yet, aemuling my pipe, he tooke in hond
My pipe, before that aemuled of many,
And plaid theron; (for well that skill he cond;)
Himselfe as skillfull in that art as any.
He pip'd, I sung; and, when he sung, I piped;
By chaunge of turnes, each making other mery;
Neither envying other, nor envied,
So piped we, untill we both were weary'.

Whose grace was great, and bounty most rewardfull.
. . . .
So what with hope of good, and hate of ill.
He me perswaded forth with him to fare'.

All were my notes but rude and roughly dight:
For not by measure of her owne great mynd,
And wondrous worth, she mott my simple song,
But joyd that country shepheard ought could fynd
Worth harkening to, emongst the learned throng'. —

   [8]) Kitchin (I, p. VII): 'Mother Hubberd's Tale v. 898 sqq. may be briefly noticed here, as having given occasion to a groundless tale about Lord Burleigh's dislike to Spenser, and his endeavour to stop his pension. Spenser, who loved and admired Archbishop Grindal (Sheph.'s Cal., Ecl. VII, 213 sqq: the good Algrind). must have disliked Burleigh, who treated the Archbishop with no little severity: and on the other hand, Burleigh, Lord Leicester's rival at court, cannot have felt much goodwill towards one who was so closely attached to the party of his antagonist. Beyond this, there seems to be no ground for the tale'.
   [9]) Todd p. XXIX: 'Malone's discovery (Life of Dryden, p. 84) refutes the calumny which (Life of Spenser prefixed to the folio edition of his Works in 1679; Wirstanley's Lives of the English Poets; Hughes's Life of Spenser; Dr. Birch's Life of Spenser; Life of Spenser in the Universal Magazine, vol. XLIX etc.) several biographers of Spenser have thrown upon the character of Lord Burleigh, in their relation of the following pretended circumstances: That Burleigh told the Queen the pension was beyond example too great to be given to a 'ballad-maker': That the payment of the pension

Spenser appears to have remained in England till the beginning of the year 1592. He, then, returned to Ireland, where he lived on his estate till 1595, dividing his time between his fields and his Fairy Queen. Here the poet met with a beautiful Irish girl, 'Elizabeth', probably Miss Nagle [1]), on whom he set his affections; and after a courtship, set forth in his 'Amoretti', or 'Sonnets', he married [2]) [3]) her in 1594 [4]). The wedding [5]) took place on St. Barnabas's Day [6]), as he tells us himself, in the city of Cork, near which Kilkolman Castle lies. He was, then, forty-one or forty-two years of age [7]) [8]). In 1595 he visited London for the purpose of attending to some business, the most agreeable part of which was the publication of Books IV., V., and VI. of his great poem, which were given to the world in 1596 [9]). He, then, returned to Ireland, as it is said [10]), early in 1597, probably with the expectation of passing his days in comfort with his family at Kil-

was intercepted by Burleigh; That when the Queen, upon Spenser's presenting some poems to her, ordered him the gratuity of an hundred pounds, his Lordship asked, with some contempt of the poet, 'What! all this for a Song?' and that the Queen replied: 'Then give him what is reason'. That Spenser, having long waited in vain for the fulfilment of the royal order, presented to her this ridiculous memorial:

'I was promis'd on a time   'From that time unto this season
'To have reason for my rhime;   'I receiv'd nor rhime nor reason'.

That these magical numbers produced the desired effect in the immediate direction of payment to the insulted poet, as well as in the reproof of the adverse Lord Treasurer! Such is the substance of this marvellous opposition to the privilege conferred on Spenser by Elizabeth, varied and improved by the biographers; of which opposition the account originates, it seems, in the facetious (Dr. Birch's Life of Spenser, p. XIII. But indeed the biographer seems not to rely implicitly on Fuller's testimony) Dr. Fuller's 'Worthies of England' (a work published at the distance of more than seventy years afterwards), unsupported by requisite authority.

The generosity of Elizabeth would, doubtless, have been the theme of Puttenham's admiration, if it had been shown a little sooner; for, in his 'Art of English Poesie', published in 1589, he has written a chapter (VIII, p. 12), evidently with a view to excite her Majesty's attention to the neglected bards of that period, entitled 'In what reputation Poesie and Poets were in old time with Princes, and otherwise generally; and how they be now become contemptible, and for what causes': The object of the author, I say, is apparent by his enumeration of the bounty of preceding English monarchs to the poets: 'In later times, how much were Johan de Mehune and Guillaume de Loris made of by the French kinges; and Geffrey Chaucer, father of our English poets, by Richard the second, who, as it was supposed, gave him the maner of new Holme in Oxfordshire. — And king Henry the S. her Maiesties father, for a few Psalmes of David turned into English meetre by Sternhold, made him groome of his privy chamber, and gave him many other good gifts. And one Gray, his good estimation did he grow unto with the same king Henry, and afterward the Duke of Sommerset, Protectour, for making certaine merry Ballades, whereof one chiefly was 'The hunte is vp, the hunte is vp'. And Queene Mary, his daughter, for one Epithalamie or nuptiall Song made by Vargas, a Spanish Poet, at her marriage with king Phillip in Winchester, gave him during his life two hundred crownes pension'. — [1]) Cf. Allibone, Todd etc.

[2]) Amoretti, or Sonnets LXVII:
'Lyke as a huntsman after weary chace,   Thinking to quench her thirst as the next brooke:
Seeing the game from him escapt away,   There she, beholding me with mylder looke,
Sits downe to rest him in some shady place,   Sought not to fly, but fearlesse still did bide;
With panting hounds beguiled of their pray: Till I in hand her yet halfe trembling tooke,
So, after long pursuit and vaine assay,   And with her owne goodwill her fyrmely tyde,
When I all weary had the chace forsooke,   Strange thing, me seemd, to see a beast so wyld,
The gentle deer returnd the self-same way,   So goodly wonne, with her owne will beguyld.' —

[3]) Allibone: 'Mr. Collier, in his edition of Spenser would have us believe that this was Sp.'s second marriage since his rejection by Rosalinde; but we imagine that the verdict of the reader will be: 'Not proven'.
[4]) Allibone: 1595.
[5]) The bridegroom celebrated his nuptials with this lovely being in those magnificent strains which have made this event for ever memorable in the chronicles of the marriages of poets: 'Spenser's Epithalamium on his own marriage. written perhaps in 1594', remarks an eminent critic, 'is of a far higher mood than any thing we have named. It is a strain redolent of a bridegroom's joy and a poet's fancy. The English language seems to expand itself with a copiousness unknown before, while he pours forth the varied imagery of this splendid little poem. I do not know any other nuptial song, ancient or modern, of equal beauty. It is an intoxication of ecstasy, ardent, noble, and pure'. Hallam: Lit. Hist. of Europe, Pt. 2, 1550—1600, 4 th ed, 1854. II. 127 (All.) —
[6]) Epithalamium v. 265. 66: 'This day the Sunne is in his chiefest hight, With Barnaby the bright'.
[7]) Am. Sonn. 60: 'So, since the winged god his planet cleare Began in me to move, one yeare is spent: The which doth longer unto me appeares, Then al those forty which my life out-went'. —
[8]) Cf. Todd, p. XLIII, and Faer. Qu. VI, X, 25. — [9]) See below.
[10]) Todd. p. XLVII, n. u: Biogr. Brit. —

colman. But the author was not entirely forgotten at court, and on the last day of September 1598[1]), Spenser, by a Letter from Queen Elizabeth to the Irish government, was appointed Sheriff of the county of Cork. In the next month, however, occurred what is called 'the rebellion of the Earl of Tyrone'[2]), and occasioned the immediate flight of Spenser and his family from Kilcolman. In the confusion and terror of flight one of his little ones by some strange oversight was left behind in the castle; and the rebels, following swiftly after, sacked and burnt the house. The child was never more heard of, and, probably, perished in the fire. With his wife and, at least, two sons[3]) Spenser reached England broken-hearted; but it seems unlikely that, with his talents and great reputation, his powerful friends[4]), his pension, and the rights he still retained, although deprived of the enjoyment of his Irish property for the moment, he could have been left to perish, as has been commonly said, for want[5]) of food.

His increasing frailty was a natural consequence of the sufferings he had lately gone through. All that we know, however, is that, after having been ill for some time, he died at a lodging house in King-Street, Westminster[6]), on the 16th of January 1598.

---

[1]) Mr. Malone has discovered this Letter (Todd. p. XLVII). —

[2]) Who 'having dispersed the forces which were sent against him by the Earl of Ormond, ravaged and spoiled the whole county of Cork; so that Spenser was forced to seek his safety, together with his wife, in his native country, leaving his estate in Ireland to be plundered by the rebels; who, it is said, having carried off his goods, burnt his house and a [his] little child in it. However that be, it is certain he did not long survive this irretrievably ruinous calamity, which, reducing him to a state of absolute dependence, with the additional weight of a family, entirely broke his heart, and he languished under it until his death.,., Thus, after this admirable Poet and worthy gentleman had struggled with poverty all his lifetime, he died in extreme indigence and want of bread. However, some amends was made to his fame at last; his corpse being interred in Westminster, near Chaucer, as he had desired, and his obsequies attended by the Poets of that time, and others, who paid the last honours to his memory, Several copies of verses were thrown after him into his grave; and Robert Devereux, Earl of Essex, who had married the widow of Sir Philip Sidney, was at the expense of the funeral. A handsome monument also, with an inscription, was erected in honour of him by Anne, Countess of Dorset'. — Biog. Brit., 3810—12. (Allibone). —

[3]) 'We think', says the author of the Life of Spenser prefixed to Mr. Church,s edition of the Faerie Queene, that Spenser could hardly leave more than one son; considering that, as before stated, one child was burnt". But this opinion is not correct'. (Todd p. LI, n. q.).

[4]) See above. — Todd, p. L. —

[5]) Allibone: 'Ben Jonson's assertion (reported by Drummond of Hawthornden) that Spenser 'died for lacke of bread', and 'refused twenty pieces sent to him by my lord of Essex, adding: He was 'sorry he had no time to spend them', has been confidently challenged by some of those sages who are always so much better informed respecting the events of preceding ages than those who lived and moved in them; but we are obliged by all rules of evidence, however unwillingly, to credit the testimony of Spenser's contemporaries that he died in poverty. The melancholy story of the day is pathetically recited in the Returne from Parnassus . . ,' — Todd p. XLVIII sq. 'Camden has said, that Sp, returned to England, poor, 'in Angliam inops reversus' . . . . . The numerous narrators of Sp.'s death, both 'in prose and rhyme', have determined to give an unbounded meaning to Camden's inops; and have accordingly represented the poet as dying in extreme indigence and want of bread. . . . The author of his Life in the Biogr. Brit. says, 'that this admirable poet and worthy gentleman had struggled with poverty all his life-time. Besides Todd and Allibone cite several passages of 'The Return from Parnassus', of 'Purple Island' by Fletcher, of Jos. Hall, Mr. Pennant, and Mr. Warton. — Capell (see Todd. p. XLVIII and below,) has omitted to notice a single circumstance of his poverty. —

[6]) Todd p. XLVIII: 'The date of Sp.'s death, together with some circumstances attending it, has often been misstated. The precise day of his death is now asserted, for the first time, on the following authority communicated by the learned and reverend, John Brand, Secretary of the Society of Antiquaries: which exists in the title-page of the second edition of the F. Q., now in his possession, and which appears to have belonged originally to Henry Capell; after whose autograph, the date of 1598 is added. After the name of Ed. Spenser in the title-page, the following invaluable anecdote is preserved: 'Qui obiit apud diversorium in platea Regia, apud Westmonasterium iuxta London, 16°. die Januarii 1598°. Juxtaq; Geffereum Chaucer, in eadem Ecclesia supradict, (Honoratissimi Comitis Essexiae impensis) sepelit [ur]' Henry Capell has added apud diversorium in the paler ink with which his own name is written. It appears then that the testimony of Camden, in regard to the place of Sp.'s death, is correct; which was in King-street Westminster, as he relates; and not, as others (Cibber, Warton, Brydges) in opposition to his authority have reported, in King-street, Dublin. It appears also that he died at an inn or lodging-house, 'apud diversorium', in which he and his family had probably been fixed from the time of their arrival in England.' — Todd p. XLVII, n. y: 'In opposition to the monumental inscription in Westminster Abbey,' says Mr. Chalmers, 'I concur with Sir James Ware, and Mr. Malone, in saying, that Spenser died in 1599, though towards the end rather than the beginning of that year: For the preface of Belvidere, or, Garden of the Muses, which wasprinted in 1600, speaks of Spenser as an extant poet etc. —'

2*

What became of the wife and children of Spenser immediately after his death, does not appear.[1]) Two sons, however, certainly survived the poet,[2]) Silvanus and Peregrine; the former married Ellen Nangle, or Nagle,[3]) by which marriage he had two sons, Edmund and William Spenser. A great-grandson of Spenser[4]) is mentioned too by the biographers, Hugolin Spenser, who, afterwards, was outlawed for treason and rebellion.

To the memory of Spenser a handsome monument,[5]) with an inscription, was erected in Westminster Abbey by Anne, Countess of Dorset. Therein, however, the poet was stated to have been born in 1510, and to have died in 1596.[6]) This interval presents a lengthened period, of which little more than half was allotted to Spenser.[7]) The circumstance of his being buried near the grave of Chaucer,[8]) which is said to have been done at his own desire,[9]) grave rise to several encomiastic epitaphs.[10]

The death of Spenser has been deeply lamented[11]) by poets who lived near his time, and probably were acquainted with him.

And, indeed, he deserves their worshipping and our veneration, too, in a high degree. This will be more evident, when we shall have made some reflections on

B. His Outward Appearance, and his Character as a Man, Statesman and Author.[12])

Short curling hair, a full moustache, cut after the pattern of Lord Leicester's, close-clipped beard, heavy eyebrows, and under them thoughtful brown eyes, whose upper eyelids weigh them dreamily down; a long and straight nose, strongly developed, answering to a long and somewhat spare face, with a well-formed sensible-looking forehead; a mouth almost obscured by the moustache, but still showing rather full lips denoting feeling, well set together, so that the warmth of feeling shall not run riot, with a touch of sadness in them; such is the look of Spenser, as his portrait hands it down to us.[13]) A refined, thoughtful, warm-hearted, pure-souled Englishman. The face is of a type still current among the English; and we may read in it loyalty, ability, and simplicity. Its look is more modern in character than that of most of the portraits of the period, — more

---

[1]) Allibone says that his wife married Roger Seckerstone.   [2]) See Todd p. LII; — see above.
[3]) See Todd p. LII; — see above.
[4]) Todd p. LII, n. u. 'The biographers call him, inaccurately, the great-grandson of Spenser. See Birch, Church's edit. Faer. Qu., Biogr. Brit. etc.'
[5]) See Allibone, and Todd p. LIV sq: 'This mark of respect had been usually ascribed to the Earl of Essex, till Fenton, in his notes on Waller, related the discovery which he hade made in the manuscript diary of Stone, master-mason to King Charles the first; that the monument was set up above thirty years after the poet's death, and that the Countess of Dorset paid forty pounds for it, Obiit immatura morte' says Camden in his little treatise describing the monuments of Westminster in 1600, anno salutis 1598. The inscription as it now stands on the monument in the Abbey, is as follows: 'Heare lyes (expecting the second comminge of our Saviour Christ Jesvs) the body of Edmond Spencer the Prince of Poets in his tyme whose divine spirrit needs noe othir witnesse then the works which he left behinde him. He was borne in London in the yeare 1558, and died in the yeare 1598.'
[6]) See above.   [7]) See Todd p. LIV.   [8]) See above.
[9]) See the Lives of Spenser prefixed to the folio edition of his Works in 1679, and to Church's ed. of the F. Q. in 1758 (Todd p. LV. n. k.) —   [10]) See Todd, p. LV. —   [11]) See ibidem, note i. —
[12]) See the biographers. —   [13]) Cf. the frontispiece in Todd. —

modern, but not the Stuart gaiety, or Hanoverian heaviness, but rather, like the best type of our own age in its return to religious feeling, truthfulness and nobility of thought and character.

If our conceptions of Spenser's mind may be taken from his poetry, we shall not hesitate to pronounce him entitled to our warmest admiration and regard for his gentle disposition, for his friendly and grateful conduct, his humility, exquisite tenderness, and above all for his piety and morality. To these amiable points a fastidious reader may, perhaps, object some petty inadvertencies; yet he can never be so ungrateful as to deny the efficacy, which Spenser's general character gives to his writings, as to deny that Truth and Virtue are graceful and attractive, when the road to them is pointed out by such a guide. Let it always be remembered that this excellent poet inculcates those impressive[1]) lessons, by attending to which the gay and the thoughtless may be timely induced to treat with scorn and indignation, the allurements of intemperance and illicit pleasure. Subservient as the poetry of Spenser is to the interests of private life, let it be cited also as the vehicle to sound public spirit:

> — 'Deare Countrey! O how dearely deare
> 'Ought thy remembrannce and perpetuall band
> 'Be to thy foster childe, that from thy hand
> 'Did commun breath and nouriture receave!
> 'How brutish is it not to understand
> 'How much to Her we owe, that all us gave;
> 'That gave unto us all whatever good we have!'
> (Faer. Qu. II, X, LXIX.).

It would be necessary to compose a separate dissertation, in order to show that the same mind, the same character and feeling are conspicuous in his correspondence and in the terms on which he stood with his numerous patrons, male and female friends; but for want of time we must be satisfied with the enumeration of those persons, and some brief notes about them, for the particulars referring to the biographers cited at the bottom of the page.

His patrons: Queen Elisabeth,[2]) James VI of Scotland,[3]) — Sir Philip Sidney,[4]) the Earl of Leicester,[5]) Lord Wilton,[6]) Sir Walter Raleigh,[7]) Lord Essex,[8]) — Lord Burleigh.[9])

His male friends: Gabriel Harvey — Mr. Todd gives us six Letters from Harvey to Spenser, and four from the latter to Harvey,[10]) — John Chalkhill, Esq.[11])

His female friends: Rosalinde,[12]) Lady Carey,[13]) Mrs Kerke,[14]) the Countesses of Cumberland and Warwick,[15]) the Ladies Elizabeth and Catherine Somerset.[16])

His Wife and Children.[17])

---

[1]) 'It his worthy of remark, that John Wesley, in the plan which he offers to those Methodists who design to go through a course of ,academical learning', recommends, (together with the Historical Books of the Hebrew Bible, the Greek Testament, Homer's Odyssey, Vell. Paterculus, Euclid's Elements, etc. etc.) to students of the second year, Spenser's Faerie Queene. See the second volume of Whitehead's Life of the Rev. John Wesley, etc. 1796. (Todd p. LVIII, n. i.).'

[2]) See above.

[3]) See Craik p. 508: 'It has been conjectured that he may have been the person in a letter to Queen Elisabeth from James VI of Scotland, dated at St, Andreas, the 2d of July, 1583 (the original of which is preserved among the Cotton MSS.), where James says in the postscript, 'Madam, I have stayed Maister Spenser upon the letter quilk is written with my awin hand, quilk sall be ready within twa days.' (Note by Mr. David Laing on p. 12 of his edition of Ben Jonson's Conversations with William Drummond, printed for the Shakespeare Society. 8vo, Lond. 1842.)' —

[4]) See above p. 8; Todd; Scherr; Kitchin etc. —   [5]) Ibidem. Todd. —

[6]) Ibidem; Todd. —   [7]) See above p. 9; Todd; Warton p. 804. 806. 909.

[8]) See above p. 9 n. 4; Todd; Warton 897. —   [9]) Perhaps, however, his enemy (see above p. 9, n. 8. 9; Todd; Warton.)

[10]) See above p. 7; Todd; Warton p. 841. 872. 884. 901. 931. 940. —   [11]) See Todd p. LIX. —

[12]) See above p. 7. Todd etc. —   [13]) See Todd p. XXXI. —   [14]) See Todd. —

[15]) See Todd p. XLIII. —   [16]) See ibidem. —   [17]) See above p. 11 sqq. —

His chief worshippers immediately after his death: — The Countess of Dorset,[1]) Mason,[2]) Camden, William Browne.[3]) —

His love-affair with Rosalinde[4]) has sometimes been sneered at;[5]) but the mocker himself ought to confess that the principal fault was with the girl, though Spenser, in his modesty,[6]) finds fault only with his ambition.[7]) The same malevolent author attempts to ridicule his marriage.[8]) In like manner he has been reproached[9]) for having left behind his child in the flames, while he himself ran away. Even servility and wheedling[10]) and inordinate desire of money[11]) has been cast in his teeth — yet unjustly.[12])

More right are those who put in doubt his capacity as a statesman and politician,[13]) although seldom any one has been more, than he, inspirited by perfect and passionate patriotism.[14]) A practical statesman he was not born, that may be allowed; but the View of the State of Ireland[15]) exhibits Spenser as a politician of very extensive knowledge and profound intelligence, particularly in regard of the political design of reducing Ireland to the due obedience of the English Crown.[16])

As for his character as an author, we have ample opportunities for studying it. At Cambridge his love for poetry grew strong, though vitiated at first by the bad taste of his friends, who worshipped the English hexameter,[11]) in a rude form, as a new revelation of poetic power and promise: but the strength of the poet was not likely to be held in such bands as these, and the Shepheard's Calender, published some three years after he left Cambridge, proves how entirely he had freed himself from these unnatural trammels. His studies, by natural affinity, led him to those sources in which the highest poetry was to be found. He was full of Biblical knowledge and feeling: we can trace the influence of the Hebrew poets and of the more unconscious poetry of the New Testa-

---

[1]) See Todd p. LIV. — [2]) See Allibone. —
[3]) See Todd p. LV: In the note on Spenser's Life in the Biogr. Brit. Camden: 'Edmundus Spenser Londinensis Anglicorum Poetarum nostri seculi facile princeps, quod eius poemata fauentibus Musis et victuro genio conscripta comprobant. Obiit immatura morte anno salutis 1598, et prope Galfredum Chaucerum conditur: qui faelicissimè poesin Anglicis litteris primus illustravit.' — William Browne's eulogium:
'A dampe of wonder and amazement strooke   'Fell from each Nymph; no Sepheard's cheek was dry:
'Thetis' attendants; many a heavy looke   'A doleful Dirge, and mournefull Elegie.
'Follow'd sweet Spencer, till the thickning ayre   'Flew to te shore,' —
'Sight's further passage stopp'd. A passionate tears [tear?]   Britannia's Pastorals, edit. 1616. B. II. p. 27.
'And in another part of the same work:
'Had Colin Clout yet liv'd, (but he is gone!)   'His truest loves to his fair Rosaline,
'The best on earth could tune a lovers mone;   'Entic'd each shepheards ear to heare him play, etc.
'Whose sadder tones inforc'd the rocks to weepe.   'Heaven rest thy soule! if so a swaine may pray:
'And laid the greatest griefes in qüiet sleepe: 'And, as thy workes live here, live there for aye!'
'Who, when he sung (as I would do to mine)
[4]) See above p. 7. — [5]) Mr. Halpin in Allibone.
[6]) For instance that he subscribes himself in his letters to Harvey 'Immerito.' (Todd p. XII.) —
[7]) Colin Clouts etc. p. 935. 936: — [8]) See Allibone.
'Not then to her that scorned thing so base,
'But to my selfe the blame that lookt so hie.'
[9]) See above p. 11. — [10]) Todd. — [11]) See Craik p. 520. —
[12]) Spenser's religious character and opinions make a curious subject, which has not received much attention from his biographers. His connection with Sidney and Leicester, and afterwards with Essex, made him, no doubt, be regarded throughout his life as belonging to the puritanical party, but only to the more moderate section of it, which, although not unwilling to encourage a little grumbling at some things in the conduct of the dominant section of hierarchy, and even professing to see much reason in the objections made to certain outworks or appendages of the established system, stood still or drew back as soon as the opposition to the Church became really a war of principles. Spenser's puritanism seems almost as unnatural as his hexameters and pentameters. It was probably, for the greater part, the product of circumstances, rather than of conviction or any strong feeling, even while it lasted; and it never appears afterwards so prominent as in his Shepherd's Calendar, the first work that he published etc. (Craik I, p. 511 sq.). —
[13]) See Todd. — [14]) See above p. 13. —
[15]) 'From this opinion the editor of Sir James Ware's works in English dissents. He allows that there are some things in it very well written, yet that, in the history and antiquity of the country, he is often miserably mistaken, and seems to have indulged rather the fancy and licence of a poet than the judgement and fidelity requisite for an historian: besides his want of moderation.' (Todd p. XLVI sq.). — [16]) See ibidem. — [17]) See below.

ment in all he wrote.[1]) He knew and understood not only Plato and Aristotle, but the Homeric epics; was conversant with the chief Latin poets; studied and was master of Italian, in order that he might enjoy the free fancy of Ariosto and the more classical and colder muse of the Gerusalemme Liberata. Drawing deep draughts of poetical life from the freshest of English poets, he delighted in all ways to proclaim himself the disciple of the ancient 'Tityrus,' the father of English poetry, Chaucer himself.

By his coevals Spenser was seldom mentioned without the epithet of 'great' or 'learned.[2])' And, indeed, what poet of that period could pretend to his learning? Dr. Joseph Warton[3]) has assigned, in respect to their erudition, the first place to Milton, the second to Spenser. To Dryden Milton acknowledged that Spenser was his original.[4]) In Cowly, in Dryden, in the facetious Butler, in Prior, in Pope, in Thomson, in Shenstone, in Gray, and in Akenside obligations of importance to the 'oaten reed' and the 'trumpet stern' of Spenser may without difficulty be traced.[5]) It is, indeed, a just observation, that more poets have sprung from Spenser than from all other English writers.

Besides his epistles concerning which we refer to Mr. Todd's 'Some account of the Life of Spenser', and which are written in a most conversant and learned style, the only prose-writing, come down to us, is the above mentioned View of the State of Ireland, in which Spenser shows himself as a most interesting writer in prose, and an antiquary of various and profound erudition.[6]) Another prose-work, a monument of his art of criticism, entitled 'The English poet,' has been lost. Perhaps, as Joseph Warton means,[7]) he will have illustrated in this critical discourse, by examples drawn from the writings of his countrymen who were distinguished in either school, the manner both of the Provençal and Italian poetry.

Among the English poets he stands lower only than Shakspeare, Chaucer and Milton; and, if we extend the parallel to the continent, his masterpiece is not unworthy of companionship with its Italian model, the chivalrous epic of Ariosto. But no comparison is needed for endearing, to the pure in heart, works which unite, as few such unite, rare genius[8]) with moral purity; or for recommending, to the lovers of poetry, poems which exhibit at once exquisite sweetness and felicity

---

[1]) Cf. Todd, Kitchin.
[2]) 'See the Shepheards Content at the end of the 'Affectionate Shepheard', etc. 1594. 4to. Speaking of love:
'By the great Collin lost his libertie;
'By the sweet Astrophel forwent his ioy.' —
See also Drayton's 'Shepheards Garland,' 1593:
'For learned Collin laies his pipes to gage,
'And is to fayrie gone a pilgrimage.' —
And in the 'Lamentation of Troy etc.' 1594,he is invoked as 'the only Homer living,' and entreated to write the story 'with his fame-quickninge quill.' —
And Sir John Davies in his 'Orchestra' 1596, exclaims:
'O that I could old Gefferies Muse awake,
'Or borrow Colius fayre heroike stile,
'Or smooth my rimes with Delias servants file.'
In Camden's Remains published by Philipot, we are likewise presented with the following proof of the high estimation in which he was held while living.
'Upon Master Edmund Spencer the famous Poet.
'At Delphos shrine one did a doubt propound,
'Which by the Oracle must be released;
'Whether of Poets were the best renown'd,
'Those that survive, or those that be deceased.
'The god made answer by divine suggestion,
'While Spenser is alive, it is no question.'
Likewise William Smith etc. — (Todd p. LVI, note o.). —
[3]) Dr. Joseph Warton, Life of Pope, p. XXIV. —   [4]) Todd p. LVI. —   [5]) Ibidem.
[6]) See above p. 14, but note 15, too. —   [7]) Todd. —
[8]) 'Dryden says expressly of Spenser (prose-works vol. 3. p. 94):' No man was ever born with a greater genius,

of language a luxuriant beauty of imagination which has hardly ever been surpassed, and a tenderness of feeling never elsewhere joined with an imagination so vivid. Plato, Aristotle, Ariosto, and Chaucer[1]) were his models, and his masters. He has cultivated nearly all branches of poetry, except the dramatic. He has written pastorals, sonnets, elegies, satires, epigrams, epics etc.

C. Chronological Catalogue of His Works.

a. Those spared by time whose period of composing and moment of appearing is known.

1. The Shepheards Calender: conteining twelve aeglogues, proportionable to the twelve monethes. Entitled to the noble and vertuous gentleman, most worthie of all titles both of learning and chivalry, Maister Philip Sidney. Preceded by a letter from E. K. to G. Harvey, together with glosses of this commentator. 5 editions: 1579, 1581, 1586, 1591, 1597.

2. The Faeric Queene[2]) disposed into twelve Books, fashioning XII Moral Vertues, 1590, 4to. Contains Books I., II., and III.; differs from the later editious.

The second Part of the Faeric Queene; containing the foorth, fifth, and sixth Bookes, 1596, 4to. Both Parts, 1590—1596: Earl of Charlemont, Aug. 1865; W. N. Lettsom, Nov. 1865.

Both Parts, known as second quarto edition, 1596, 2 vols. 4to.

Faeric Queene, 1609, fol. J. Lilly's Bibl. Anglo-Curiosa, 1869. Known as first folio edition. After the six Books appears in this volume the first edition of Two Cantos of Mutabilitie.[3])

Again a folio edition 1611. Faerie Queene, new editions: Lon., 1866, 8vo; Globe ed. Book I. by Kitchin 1867, 12mo. 1869 etc.[4])

3. Muiopotmos, or the Fate of the Butterflie 1590. — Dedicated to the right worthy and vertuous Ladie, the La: Carey.

4. Complaints, containing sundrie small Poems of the Worlds Vanitie, 1591, 4to, 92 leaves. Contents: a) The Ruines of Time.   b) The Teares of the Muses.   c) Virgils Gnat.
d) Prosopopeia; or, Mother Hubberds Tale.   e) The Ruines of Rome by Bellay.[5])
f) Muiopotmos, or the Tale of the Butterflie (dated 1590, in its title.)
g) Vision of the Worlds Vanitie.   h) Bellayes Visions.[6])   i) Petrarche's Visions.[7])

---

or had more knowledge to support it.' And it has been well observed by a very judicious critic (Neve's Cursory Remarks on the ancient English Poets), that 'where the works of Spenser are original, they shew that he possessed energy, copiousness, and sublimity sufficient, if he had taken no model to follow, that would rank him with Homer and Tasso and Milton; for his greatest excellence is in those images which are the immediate foundation of the sublime. Fear, confusion and astonishment, are delineated by him with a most masterly pen.' To these marks of elevated powers I may add the attractive minuteness of Spenser's descriptions, which rarely terminate in the object described, but give an agreeable activity to the mind in tracing the resemblance between the type and anti-type. This, as the learned translator (The Rev. Henry Boyd) of Dante has observed, is an excellency possessed by Spenser in an eminent degree; and hence may be deduced the superiority of his descriptions over those of Thomson, Akenside, and almost all other modern poets." (Todd p. LVIII.).

   ¹) See Allibone. —   ²) See below. —   ³) See below.   ⁴) See Allibone and below.
   ⁵) Joachim Bellay obtained the appellation of the French Ovid. He was also called 'Pater elegantiarum, Pater omnium leporum.' He died in 1860. (Todd p. 485, L'Envoy 1.)
   ⁶) Already in 1569 they had appeared in the 'Theatre for Wordlings' (see Todd p. X, and Allibone).
   ⁷) ibidem.

5. Prosopopeia; or, Mother Hubberds Tale, 1591, 4to.
6. Teares of the Muses, 1591, 4to.   7. Daphnaida, 1591, 4to; 1592, 4to.
8. Amoretti, or Sonnets, and Epithalamion, 1595, 12 mo.[1])
9. Colin Clovts Come Home Againe, 1595, 4to. Astrophel and other pieces are annexed to Colin Clovt.[2])
10. Prothalamion, or a Spousall Verse, Lon., 1596, 4to.[3])
11. Fowre Hymnes, Daphnaida, and Epithalamion, 1596, 4to.[4])
          After his death appeared
12. A View of the State of Ireland, 1633.[5])

b. Works, whose time of appearing is unknown.

13. His Letters to Harvey 1580. (?)[6])
14. Astrophel. A pastoral elegie upon the death of the most noble and valorous Knight, Sir Philip Sidney. Dedicated to the most beautifull and vertuous Ladie the Countess of Essex. 1586. (?)[7])
15. The Dolefull Lay of Clorinda.[8])   16. The Mourning Muse of Thestylis 1587?[9])
17. A Pastorall Aeglogue, upon the death of Sir Phillip Sidney, Knight, etc.[10])
18. Sonnets. Collected from the original publications in which they appeared.[11]) 19. Poems.[12])
20. Loose verses to be found in Mr. Todd's Account etc.
     α. p. XV in a Letter to Harvey:

Jambicum Trimetrum.

Unhappie Verse! the witnesse of my unhappie state,
Make thy selfe fluttring wings of thy last flying
Thought , and fly forth unto my Love whersoever
                         she be:
Whether lying reastlesse in heavy bedde, or else
Sitting so cheerelesse at the cheerfull boorde, or else
Playing alone carelesse on hir heavenlie virginals.

If in bed; tell hir, that my eyes can take no reste:
If at boorde; tell hir, that my mouth can eate no
                         meate:
If at hir virginals; tel hir, I can hoare no mirth.

Asked why? say, Waking love suffereth no sleope:

Say, that raging love dothe appall the weake stomacke:
Say, that lamenting love marreth the musicall.

Tell hir, that hir pleasures were wonte to lull me
                         asleepe
Tell hir, that hir beautie was wonte to feede mine eyes:
Tell hir, that hir sweete tongue was wonte to make
                         me mirth.

Now doe I nightly waste, wanting my kindely reste:
Now doe I dayly starve, wanting my lively foode:
Now doe I alwayes dye, wanting my timely mirth.

And if I waste, who will bewaile my heavy chaunce?
And if I starve, who will record my cursed end?
And if I dye, who will saye, 'This was Imperito'?

     β. in the same Letter, Todd p. XVI sq.
Ad Ornatissimum virum, multis jam diu nominibus Clarissimum, G. H., Immerito sui, mox in Gallias Navigaturi, Ἐυτυχεῖν (sic!).

Sic malus egregium, sic non inimicus amicum,
Sicq; novus votorem jubet ipse Poeta Poetam

Salvere; ac cœlo, post sæcula multa, secundo
Jam reducem, cœlo magè quàm nunc ipso, secundo

---

[1]) See Allibone.   [2]) Ibidem.   [3]) Ibidem.   [4]) Ibidem.
[5]) See above p. 14; Allibone, and Todd.   [6]) See Todd.   [7]) See Todd p. XXIV.
[8]) See Todd p. LI.
[9]) In 1587 the following licence, among others, was granted by the Stationer's Company to John Wolf, printer, viz. 'The mourning Muses of Lod. Brysket upon the death of the most noble Sir Philip Sidney Knight etc.' (Todd p. 458, note.)   [10]) See Todd p. 461.   [11]) See Todd p. 430.   [12]) See Todd 481, and above.

Utier; Ecce deus (modo sit deus ille, renixum
Qui vocet in scelus, et juratos perdat amores,)
Ecce deus mihi clara dedit modo signa marinus,
Et sua veligero lenis parat æquora ligno:
Mox sulcando suas etiam pater Æolus iras
Ponit, et ingentes animos Aquilonis ——
Cuncta vijs sic apta meis; ego solus ineptus.
Nam mihi nescio quo mens saucia vulnere, dudum
Fluctuat ancipiti pelago, dum navita proram
Invalidam validus rapit, huc Amor et rapit illuc;
Consilijs Ratio melioribus usa decusq;
Immortale levi diflissu Cupidinis arcu,
Angimur hoc dubio, et portu vexamur in ipso.
Magno pharetrati nunc tu contemptor Amoris
(Id tibi dij nomen precor hand impune remittant)
Hos nodos exsolve, et oris mihi magnus Apollo:
Spiritus ad summos, scio, te generosus honores
Existimulat, (sic!) majusq; docet spirare Poëtam.
Quàm levis est Amor, et tamen haud levis est amor omnis.
Ergo nihil laudi reputas æquale perenni,
Præq; sacro sanctâ splendoris imagine, tanti
Cætera quæ vecors uti numina vulgus adorat;
Prædia, Amicitias, Urbana peculia, Nummos,
Quæq, placent oculis, Formas, Spectacula, Amores,
Conculcare soles ut humum, et ludibria sensûs;
Digna meo certe Harveio, sententia digna
Oratore Amplo, et generoso pectore, quam non
Stoica formidet veterum sapientia, vinclis
Sancire æternis; sapor haud tamen omnibus idem.
Dicitur effœti proles facunda Laërtæ,
Quamlibet ignoti jactata per æquora cœli,
Inq; procelloso longum exsul gurgite, ponto
Præ tamen amplexu lachrymosæ conjugis, ortus
Cœlestes, divûmq; thoros sprevisse beatos:
Tantûm Amor, et Mulier, vel amore potentior, Illum;
Tu tamen illudis (tua Magnificentia tanta est)
Præq; subumbratâ splendoris imagine, tanti
Præq; illo, meritis famosis, nomine parto;
Cætera quæ vecors uti numina vulgus adorat,
Prædia, Amicitias, Armenta, Peculia, Nummos,
Quæq; placent oculis, Formas, Spectacula, Amores,
Quæq; placent ori, quæq; auribus, omnia temnis;
Næ tu grande sapis! ('sapor at sapientia non est,')
Omnis et in parvis bene qui scit desipuisse,
Sæpe superciliis palmam sapientibus aufert;
Ludit Aristippum modo tetrica turba sophorûm;
Mitia purpureo moderantem verba tyranno,
Ludit Aristippus dictamina vana sophorum,
Quos levis emensi male torquet culicis umbra.
Et quisquis placuisse studet heroibus actis,
Desipuisse studet; sic gratia crescit ineptis.
Deniq; laurigeris quisquis sua tempora vittis
Insignire volet, populoq; placere faventi,
Desipere insanus dicit, turpemq; pudendæ
Stultitiæ laudem quærit. Pater Ennius unus
Dictus, innumeris sapiens; laudatur at ipse

Carmina vesano fudisse loquentia vino:
Nec tu, (pace tuâ,) nostri Cato maxime sêcli,
Nomen honorati sacrum mereare Poëtae,
Quantumvis illustre canas, et nobile carmen,
Ni stultire velis; sic 'stultorum omnia plena'!
Tuta sed in medio superest via gurgite; nam qui
Nec reliquis nimium vult desipuisse videri,
Nec sapuisse nimis, sapientem dixeris, unum
Hinc te merserit unda, illinc combusserit ignis;
Nec tu delicias nimis aspernare fluentes,
Nec serò Dominam venientem in vota, nec aurum,
Si sapis, oblatum: Curijs ea Fabricijsq;
Linque, viris miseris miseranda sophismata, quondam
Grande sui decus ij, nostri sed dedecus ævi;
Nec soctare nimis; res utraq; crimine plena.
Hoc bene qui callet (si quis tamen hoc bene callet)
Scribe vel invito sapientem hunc Socrate solum.
Vis facit una pios; justos facit altera, et alt'ra
Egregie cordata, ac fortia pectora; verùm
'Omne tulit punctum qui miscuit utile dulci.'
Dij mihi dulce diu dederant, verùm utile nunquam;
Utile nunc etiam, ò utinam quoq; dulce dedissent!
Dij mihi, quippe dijs æqualia maxima parvis,
Ni nimis invideant mortalibus esse beatis,
Dulce simul tribuisse queant, simul utile; tanta
Sed Fortuna tua est, pariter quæq; utile quæq;
Dulce dat ad placitum: saevo nos sydere nati
Quæsitum imus eam per inhospita Caucasa longè,
Perq; Pyrenaeos montes, Babylonáq; turpem;
Quod si quæsitum nec ibi invenerimus, ingens
Æquor inexhaustis permensi erroribus ultra
Fluctibus in medijs socij quæremus Ulyssis:
Passibus inde dum fessis comitabimur ægram,
Nobile cui furtum quaerenti defuit orbis:
Namq; sinu pudet in patrio, tenebrisq; pudendis,
Non nimis ingenio Juvenem infœlice virentes
Officijs frustrà deperdere vilibus annos;
Frugibus et vacuas speratis cernere spicas.
Ibimus ergò statim; (quis eunti fausta precetur?)
Et pede clivosas fesso calcabimus Alpes.
Quis dabit intereà conditas rore Iliritanno,
Quis tibi Litterulas, quis carmen amore petulcum!
Musa sub Oebalij desueta cacum ne(sic pro cacumine!?)
montis,
Flebit inexhausto tam longa silentia planctu,
Lugebitq; sacrum lacrymis Helicona tacentem;
Harveiusq; bonus (charus licet omnibus idem)
Idq; suo merito prope suavior omnibus, unus
Angelus et Gabriel, quamvis comitatus amicis
Innumeris, Geniûmq; choro stipatus amœno,
'Immerito' tamen unum absentem sæpè requiret;
Optabitq; 'Utinam meus his E d m u n d u s adesset,
Qui nova scripsisset, nec amores conticuisset
Ipse suos;' et sæpe animo verbisq; bonignis
Fausta precaretur, 'Deus illum aliquando reducat!' etc.

γ. Todd. p. XIX, hexameters¹) and pentameters:
'See yee the blindefoulded pretie god, that feathered archer
Of lovers miseries which maketh his bloodie game?
Wote ye why, hit moother with a veale hath covered his face?
Truste me, least he my Loove happely chaunce to beholde'. —

Todd p. XX:
'That which I eate, did I joy, and that which I greedily gorged;
'As for those many goodly matsers leaft I for others'. —

δ. Todd p. XLIII, note e:
To the Countesses of Cumberland and Warwicke sisters:
'Sisters of spotlesse fame! of whom alone
'Malitiouse tongues take pleasure to speake well;
'How should I you commend, when eyther one
'All things in heaven and earth so far excell.
'The highest praise that I gan give is this,
'That one of you like to the other is'.

c. Works falsely ascribed to him.

21. An Elegie,²) or Friends Passion, for his Astrophill. Written upon the death of the Right Honourable Sir Philip Sidney Knight, Lord Governour of Flushing.
22. An Epitaph, upon the Right Honourable Sir Philip Sidney Knight: Lord Governour of Flushing.³) 23. Another of the same.⁴)
24. Brittain's Ida. London: printed for Thomas Walkley. 1628.⁵)

d. The Lost Works of Spenser.⁶)

25. His translation of Ecclesiastes. 26. His translation of Canticum Canticorum.
27. The Dying Pelican. 28. The Hours of our Lord. 29. The Sacrifice of a Sinner.
30. The Seven Psalms. 31. Dreams. 32 The English Poet. 33. Legends.
34. The Court of Cupid. 35. The Hell of Lovers. 36. His Purgatory.
37. A Sennights Slumber. 38. Pageants. 39. Nine Comedies.⁷)
40. Stemmata Dudleiana. 41. Epithalamion Thamesis.
42. Books VII.—XII. of the Fairy Queen, except the Two Cantos of Mutabilitie, and two stanzas of another Canto⁸).

¹) See above p. 14.
²) Todd p. 462, note: 'This poem was written by Matthew Roydon, as we are informed in Nash's Preface to Greene's Arcadia, and in Engl. Parnassus.' ³) Todd p. 464.
⁴) Todd p. 465. — 462: 'To the two following pieces I am unable to assign their authors; but no reader will imagine them the productions of Spenser.'
⁵) Todd p. 497, note: 'The printer's assertion is the only authority on which this Poem has been admitted into the editions of Spenser's Works, since its first publication in 1628. The criticks agree in believing that it was not written by Spenser.' — Cf. Allibone. ⁶) See Todd p. LX, note r.
⁷) We have above said, Spenser has not written any drama. For it is supposed, these nine comedies were not dramatic poems, but a series of lines in nine divisions like the Teares of the Muses, and that to each division was given the denomination of Comedy; the author using that term in the wide sense in which it was employed by Dante etc. (Cf. Todd p. XXII, note w.). ⁸) See below.

Part II.
The Fairy Queen.

A. When and where this Poem was composed and edited.

E. K., the commentator on the Shepheards Calender, first published in 1579,[1] informs us, that, at the same time, the Dreams,[2] the Legends[3] and the Court of Cupid[4] were then finished by Spenser; and our author himself, in his Letter to Harvey, dated Apr. 10, 1580, mentions also that 'his Dreames and Dying Pellicane were then fully finished;' and that he designed soon 'to sette forthe a booke, entitled Epithalamion Thamesis.'[5] Well then, these Legends, Court of Cupid, and Epithalamion are closely connected with circumstances admitted into the Fairy Queen;[6] and from the same Letter we see that he has really begun the Fairy Queen in 1580; for at the end of it he writes:[7] 'Nowe, my Dreames and, Dying Pellicane, being fully finished, (as I partelye signified in my laste letters) and presentlye to bee imprinted, I wil in hande forthwith with my Faerie Queene, whyche I praye you hartily send me with al expedition; and your friendly letters, and long expected judgement withal, whyche let not be shorte, but in all pointes such as you ordinarilye use, and I extraordinarily desire etc.'

But his friend's opinion of the Poem was not calculated to encourage the ardour of the poet. For in his reply Harvey writes:[8] 'In good faith I had once againe nigh forgotten your Faerie Queene: howbeit, by good chaunce I have nowe sent hir home at the laste, neither in better nor worse case than I founde hir. And must you, of necessitie, have my judgement of hir in deede? To be plaine: I am voyde of al judgement, if your nine Comœdies, whereunto, in imitation of Herodotus, you give the names of the Nine Muses, (and in one mans fansie not unworthily,) come not neerer Ariostoes Comœdies, eyther for the finenesse of plausible elocution, or the rarenesse of poetical invention, than that Elvish Queene doth to his Orlando Furioso; which, notwithstanding you wil needes seeme to emulate, and hope to overgo, as you flatly professed yourself in one of your last Letters. Besides that, you know it hath bene the usual practise of the most exquisite and odde wittes in all nations, and specially in Italie, rather to shewe and advaunce themselves that way than any other; as namely, those three dyscoursing heads, Bibiena, Machiavel, and Aretine, did, (to let Bembo and Ariosto passe,) with the great admiration and wonderment of the whole countrey; being indeede reputed matchable in all points, both for conceyt of witte and eloquent decyphering of matters, either with Aristophanes and Menander in Greek, or with Plautus and Terence in Latin, or with any other in any other tong. But I wil not stand greatly with you in your owne matters. If so be the Faery Queene be fairer in your eie than the Nine Muses, and Hobgoblin runne away with the garland from Apollo; marke what I saye; and yet I will not say that [which] I thought; but there an end for this once, and fare you well till God, or some good Aungell, putte you in a better mind.'

Spenser was not, however, to be discouraged by this injudicious ópinion. At Kilcolman

---

[1] See above p. 16. [2] See above p. 29. [3] See ibidem. [4] See ibidem.
[5] See Todd p. XI.
[6] See the Fairy Queen III., XII, 5, 6 etc. IV., II, 10, 11 etc. [7] Todd p. XX.
[8] See Todd p. XXII sq.

Castle,[1]) on the shore of a pleasant lake, with fine distant views of mountains all round, he busied himself with the composition of the first three Books of the Fairy Queen. Here he was visited[2]) by Sir Walter Raleigh, to whom he showed the manuscript. A poet himself, and the author of a poem[3]) in praise of the Queen, Raleigh could not but listen with delight to the design which Spenser had formed. Encouraged by the judgement of this accomplished person, as he had, probably, long before been by that of Sidney,[4]) Spenser, as soon as the three Books were ready for the printer, went over to England in Raleigh's company,[5]) and committed them to the press in 1590.

In 1596 Spenser visited London again,[6]) in order to print the second part of his Fairy Queen, containing the fourth, fifth and sixth Books; and a new edition of the former part accompanied it. Of the remaining six Books, which would have completed Spenser's original design, two imperfect Cantos 'Of Mutabilitie'[7]) are the only parts with which the public has been gratified.[8])

B. In what Metre the Fairy Queen is composed.

This poem has been written in the nine-lined iambic strophe, that is in the Spenserian stanza, so called after the inventor himself. Indeed, it is said to be a modification of the 'ottava rime' of Ariosto; but, although this may be partly true, the long nine-lined stanza, ending with an Alexandrine, has an entirely independent character. Ariosto's verse runs rapidly on, answering to the lively style of the poet, and his quick transitions: but Spenser's stanza, with occasional weaknesses,[9]) arising from its greater length, has a melody, a dignity, and weight, which suit his manner of handling his subject and the gravity of his mind. It may be fairly said to be all his own, and to have been accepted at his hands by poets ever since. How many English poets of name have written, often written their best works in the Spenserian stanza! We have mentioned Ariosto; it is time we take brief notice of the

C. Sources and Argument of the Fairy Queen.

As for Homer, Virgil, Aristotle, and other authors of antiquity, whose influence on this poem can often be seen in the turn of expression and the illustrations [10]) employed, Spenser writes in his Letter to Sir Walter Raleigh, as follows:

---

[1]) See above p. 8.   [2]) See above p. 9.
[3]) Entitled 'Cynthia'. See Spenser's Sonnet to Raleigh sent with the first three Books of the Faerie Queene, his Letter to him explaining the design of the Poem. Colin Clouts Come Home Again, ver. 166; and the Introduction to the third Book of the F. Q. This poem, which Spenser has higly commended, was never published. (Cf. Todd p. XXV, n. o.)
[4]) Scherr p. 61. n. q: 'Hierueber ist uns eine sehr huebsche anecdote ueberliefert worden. Sp. theilte sm. goenner Sidn. proben aus der F. Q. mit. Kaum hatte Sir Philip einige stanzen gelesen, als er seinem hausmeister befahl, dem jungen dichter 50 pfund auszuzahlen, Nachdem er weiter gelesen, befahl er die summe zu verdoppeln, u. als d. hausmeister zoegerte, dieses freigebige gebot zu erfuellen, rief ihm d. ritter zu, er solle 200 pf. auszahlen u. zwar auf der stelle; denn liesse ihm d. diener zeit, erst noch weiter zu lesen, so koennte er in versuchung gerathen, fuer ein solches gedicht sein ganzes vermoegen hinzugeben.'
[5]) See above p. 9.   [6]) See above p. 10.   [7]) See above p. 19.
[8]) Allibone: — 'which, both for forme and matter, appeare to be parcell of some following Books of the F. Q, under the legend of Constance. Doubtless this was all that was written of the intended six additional Books of the Faerie Queene, which by some credulous persons are supposed to have been lost at sea, or to have perished by the fire at Kilcolman Castle in 1598.' — Todd: — 'which was soon after unfortunately lost by the disorder and abuse of his servant, whom he had sent before him into England.' — Fenton and Dryden are of Allibone's opinion. (Todd p. XLIV.)
[9]) See below.   [10]) See below.

'The general end, therefore, of all the Booke is to fashion a gentleman or noble person in vertuous and gentle discipline. . . . In which I haue followed all the antique poets historicall; first Homere, who in the persons of Agamemnon and Ulysses hath ensampled a good gouernour and a vertuous man, the one in his Ilias, the other in his Odysseis; then Virgil, whose like intention was to doe in the person of Æneas; after them . . . I labour to pourtraict in Arthure, before he was king, the image of a braue Knight, perfected in the twelue priuate Morall Vertues, as Aristotle hath deuised; the which is the purpose of these first twelue bookes; which if I finde to be· well accepted, I may be perhaps encoraged to frame the other part of Polliticke Vertues in his person, after that hee came to be king.'

From Chaucer [1]) he drew largely, often literal imitations, though Chaucer painted persons, Spenser qualities. Still we see the influence of the Father of English poetry, which Spenser himself willingly acknowledged, in every part of his writings. He was also well read in the old romances. The fundaments, therefore, of Spenser's epic building are the tales of King Arthur. The Fairy Queen Gloriana, on the one hand the allegorical personification of true Glory, on the other hand, at the same time, very clearly referred to Queen Elizabeth, according to an established annual custom, held a magnificent feast, which continued twelve days, on each of which respectively twelve several complaints are presented before her. To redress the injuries which were the occasion of these several complaints, she despatches, with proper commissions, twelve different knights, each of whom, in the particular adventure allotted to him, proves an example of some particular virtue, as of Holiness, Temperance, Justice, Chastity, and has one complete book assigned to him, of which he is the hero. But besides these twelve knights, severally exemplifying twelve moral virtues, the Poet has constituted one principal knight or general hero, — Prince Arthur, — who represents Magnificence, the perfection of all the rest. He, moreover, appears in every book, and at the end of his actions is to discover and win Gloriana, or Glory.

There is nothing, however, so striking as the relation in which the Fairy Queen stands to the two great Italian poets of the time, Ariosto and Tasso. Although Spenser borrowed very largely from the latter, to the extent of almost translating whole scenes, still there can be no doubt he owed more to the former; for he was drawn towards the natural and fresh mind of Ariosto. It has been rightly remarked that Spenser drew literal imitations from Chaucer, artificial fictions from Ariosto: that is, forms of expression may be found in abundance which are to be traced to the English poet, while such creations as Archimago and Duessa come from the Italian.

But his design was, in several striking features, nobler and more arduous than that of the Italian poets. His deep seriousness is thoroughly unlike the mocking tone of the Orlando Furioso; he rose still higher than the Jerusalem Delivered in his earnest moral enthusiasm; and he aimed at something much beyond either of his masters, but unfortunately at something which marred the poetic effect of his work, when he framed it so that it should be really a series of ethical allegories.

The First Book, by far the finest of all, both in idea and in execution, relates the Legend of the Red-Cross Knight, who is the type of Holiness [2]). He is the appointed champion of the per-

---

[1]) See below, the notes.

[2]) Spenser, in his Letter to Raleigh, says: 'Books I., II., and III. treat: The first of the Knight of the Redcrosse, in which I express Holynes: The seconde of Sir Guyon, in whom I sette forth Temperaunce. The third of Britomartis, a Lady Knight, in whom I picture Chastity. But because the beginning of the whole Worke seemeth abrupte and as depending upon other antecedents, it needs that ye know the occasion of these three knigths' seuerall Aduentures. For the methode of a poet historicall is. not such, as of an historiographer. For an historiographer discourseth of affayres orderly as they were donne, accounting as well the times as the actions: but a poet thrusteth into the middest, even where it most

secuted Lady Una, the representative of Truth, the daughter of a king whose realm, described in obscure phrases, receives in one passage [1]) the name of Eden. In her service he penetrates into the labyrinth of Error; at last encountering Error herself, the Knight, with the aid of his heavenly armour, overcomes and destroys her [2]). But, under the temptations of the enchanter Archimago, who is the Emblem of Hypocrisy, he is enticed away by the double-faced witch, false and frivolous, fair and foul — Duessa, or Falsehood is her name; and he, whom Error could not overcome, falls a victim to flattery and dissimulation [3]). The betrayed knight is plunged into severe suffering, and the unprotected lady is exposed to many dangers. At last, she meets with Prince Arthur [4]), who slays the Antichrist, the proud giant Orgoglio, who had captured him, and delivers the Knight from his dungeon. After this spiritual deliverance, he falls into the gloomiest state of despondency, into the 'Cave of Despair' [5]), and nearly ends his own life through consciousness of his failure and sinfulness. But Una saves him again, and carries him to the 'House of Mercy', where after due spiritual discipline, all remnants of pride, all earthly tendencies, all stains contracted by his contact with the false one, are washed or burnt away; and after a glimpse of a better world, he comes forth pure and chastened and restored to his spiritual health, wearing once more the heavenly armour. Thus prepared and equipped, he encounters the grim Dragon, at last destroys the last enemy, and triumphs gloriously. Thus has he overcome the world, the flesh, and the devil; and with his betrothment to Una the book ends [6])

In the Second Book we have the Legend of Sir Guyon, illustrating the temptations and triumphs of Moral Purity, under the name of Temperance.

The Legend of Britomart, or of Chastity [7]), is the theme of the Third Book, in which, besides the heroine, are introduced Belphœbe and Amoret, two of the most beautiful of those female characters whom the poet takes such pleasure in delineating.

Next comes the Legend of Friendship, personified in the knights Cambel and Friamond. In it is the tale of Florimel, a version of an old tale of the romances [8]), embellished with an array of fine imagery, which is dwelt on with admiring delight in one of the noblest odes of Collins. Yet this Fourth Book, and the two which follow, are generally allowed to be on the whole inferior to the first three. The falling off is most perceptible when we pass to the

---

concerneth him, and there recoursing to the things forepaste, and divining of things to come, maketh a pleasing analysis of all! The beginning therefore of my History, if it were to be told by a historiographer, should be the Twelfth Booke, which is the last'.   [1]) See I, 7, 43.

[2]) By this Spenser wished to indicate the doubts and dangers which beset the soul of him who has just embraced the truth of the Gospel — the 'variations of Protestantism', in fact, and the risks of private judgement. When this danger has been safely passed, we find the Knight a prey to what may be called 'a Roman Catholic reaction'. (Cf. Todd p. XXI.)

[3]) 'The artifices of the Jesuits, which had met with so great success, and had already stopped the progress of the Reformation in most European countries, were felt in the form of underhand plots and deceits in England; and there can be no doubt that it is at these that Spenser points. Duessa is the Roman Church herself. She is described as dressed in scarlet, riding on the monster of the Apocalypse, which all reformed England regarded as the Rome of the Papacy. The guile of the magician misleads the hero, till he thinks that truth is false, and falsehood true. This is the guiding-line to all his subsequent troubles. He gives way to self-indulgence, falls into pride, and though he overcomes the Paynim Unbelief, he presently grows enervated through the false comrade who has taken Truth's place'. (Kitchin).

[4]) In whom we may recognise that spiritual help which succours man in his worst straits, when he can no longer help himself.   [5]) See Todd p. XLIX.

[6]) The Red Cross Knight, St. George, is the pattern Englishman; he cannot be called by any one name; nor is Una more than an abstract quality; but the Fairy Queen is Queen Elizabeth, as Spenser takes no small pains to let us know (see above); Duessa is Mary Queen of Scots, as we learn from a later Book; by the giant Orgoglio is probably intended Philip II, king of Spain; Prince Arthur is Lord Leicester. (Todd. Holinshed).

[7]) This part of the poem abounds, beyond all the rest, in exquisite painting of picturesque landscapes; in some of which, however, imitation of Tasso is obvious. (Spalding).

[8]) See above.

Fifth Book, containing the Legend of Sir Artegal, who is the emblem of Justice. This story, indeed, is told, not only with a strength of moral sentiment unsurpassed elsewhere by the poet, but also with some of his most striking exhibitions of personification: the interest however, is weakened by the constant anxiety to bring out that subordinate signification, in which the narrative was intended to celebrate the government of Spenser's patron Lord Grey in Ireland[1]).

The Sixth Book, the Legend of Sir Calidore, or of Courtesy, is apt to dissatify us through its want of unity; although some of the scenes and figures are inspired with the poet's warmest glow of fancy[2]).

About the two Cantos of Mutabilitie and the fragment of another (VIII) Canto see above p. 19. —

D. In what manner the Fairy Queen has been Received by the public.

When the Fairy Queen first appeared, the whole of England seems to have been moved by it. No such poet had arisen in this country for nearly two hundred years. Since Chaucer and the author of Piers Ploughman[3]) there had been no great poem. The fifteenth century had been almost a blank, the darkest period of the English literary annals; the earlier part of the sixteenth had been occupied with great theological questions, which had engrossed men's mind, till the long reign of Elizabeth[4]) gave stability to the Reformation in England, and the first fervour of the Church writers subsided. The taste of society was favourable to a work which, with a strong theological element in it, still dealt with feats of chivalry and heroes of romance. The mind of the English was filled with a sense of poetry yet unexpressed. Great deeds, great discoveries had roused the spirit of the nation. The people were proud of their Queen and their freedom; the new aristocracy was just feeling its strength; it was a time of most varied life. Nothing was wanted but a great poem to express the universal desire; and Spenser first and then Shakspeare appeared, to satisfy the national instinct. Drayton[5]), Fletcher[6]), Milton[7]), and perhaps Bunyan[8]), shew in their writings the effect of Spenser's genius. After the Restoration his influence cannot be so easily traced. Between 1650 and 1750 there are but few notices of him, and very few editions of his works[9]).

---

[1]) See above p. 8. 13.   [2]) See Spalding.
[3]) Langland.   [4]) See above.   [5]) Michael Drayton 1563—1631.
[6]) John Fletcher 1576—1625.   [7]) John Milton 1608—1674.   [8]) John Bunyan 1628—1688.
[9]) Dryden (Preface to the trans. of Juvenal, 1693 fol.): '[In Epic Poetry] the English have only to boast of Spenser and Milton, who neither of them wanted either genius or learning to have been perfect poets, and yet both of them are liable to many censures. For there is no uniformity in the design of Spenser; he aims at the accomplishment of no one action; he raises up a hero for every one of his adventures, and endows each of them with some particular moral virtue, which renders them all equal, without subordination or preference. Every one is most valiant in his own legend; only we must do him that justice to observe that magnanimity, which is the character of Prince Arthur, shines throughout the whole poem, and succours the rest, when they are in distress. The original of every knight was then living in the court of Queen Elizabeth; and he attributed to each of them that virtue which he thought was most conspicuous in them — an ingenious piece of flattery, though it turned not much to his account. Had he lived to finish the poem, in the six remaining legends, it had certainly been more of a piece, but could not have been perfect, because the model was not true. But Prince Arthur, or his chief patron, Sir Philip Sidney, whom he intended to make happy by the marriage of his Gloriana, dying before him, deprived the poet both of means and spirit to accomplish his design. For the rest, his obsolete language, and the ill choice of his stanza are faults but of the second magnitude; for, notwithstanding the first, he is still intelligible, at least after a little practise; and for the last, he is the more to be admired that, labouring under such a difficulty, his verses are so numerous, so various, and so harmonious that only Virgil, whom he professedly imitated, has surpassed him among the Romans, and only Mr. Waller among the English'. (Allibone.)
Dryden (Preface to his Fables). See also Edin. Rev., XXXVI, 7: 'Milton has acknowledged to me that Spenser was his original'. (Allibone.)
Sir William Temple (Essay on Poetry: Miscellanea, 1689—90, 2 Pts. 8vo): 'The religion of the Gentiles had

After 1750 there was a revived interest in his poetry; and between 1751 and 1758 no fewer than four different editions appeared. The classics of the period treated Spenser as an ancient to be handled according to the then popular principles of classical criticism. They tried him by their

---

been woven into the contexture of all the ancient poetry with an agreeable mixture, which made the modern affect to give that of Christianity a place also in their poems; but the true religion was not found to become fictitious so well as the false one had done, and all their attempts of this kind had seemed rather to debase religion than heighten poetry, Spenser endeavoured to supply this with morality, and make instruction, instead of story, the subject of an epic poem. His execution was excellent, and his flights of fancy rery noble and high. But his design was poor; and his moral lay so bare that it lost the effect. It is true, the pill was gilded, but so thin that the colour and the taste were easily discovered'. (Allibone.)

Thomas Rymer: on Frag., etc.: 'Spenser may be reckoned the first of our heroic poets. He had a large spirit, a sharp judgment, and a genious for heroic poetry, perhaps above any that ever wrote since Virgil; but our misfortune is, he wanted a true idea, and lost himself by following an unfaithful guide. Though besides Homer and Virgil he had read Tasso, yet he rather suffered himself to be misled by Ariosto, with whom blindly rambling on marvels and adventures, he makes no conscience of probability; all is fanciful and chimerical, without any uniformity, or without any foundation in truth: in a word, his poem is perfect Fairy land'. (Allibone.) —

David Hume: Hist. of Eng., Reign of Elizabeth, Appendix: 'Unhappily for literature, at least, for the learned of this age, the queen's vanity lay more in shining by their own learning than in encouraging men of genius by her liberality. Spenser himself, the first English writer of his age, was long neglected, and after the death of Sir Philip Sidney, his patron was allowed to die almost for want. This poet contains great beauties, a sweet and harmonious versification, easy elocution, a fine imagination: yet does the perusal of his work become so tedious, that one never finishes it from the mere pleasure which it affords. It soon becomes a kind of task reading; and it requires some effort and resolution to carry us to the end of his long performance. This effect, of which every one is conscious, is usually ascribed to the change of manners. But manners have more changed since Homer's age, and yet that poet remains still the favourite of every reader of taste and judgment. Homer copied true natural manners, which, however rough or uncultivated, will always form an agreeable and interesting picture. But the pencil of the English poet was employed in drawing the affectations and conceits and fopperies of chivalry, which appear ridiculous as soon as they lose the recommendation of the mode. The tediousness of continued allegory, and that too seldom striking and ingenuous, has also contributed to render the Fairy Queen peculiarly tiresome; not to mention the too great frequency of its descriptions, and the languor of its stanza. Upon the whole, Spenser maintains his place upon the shelves among our English classics: but he is seldom seen on the table; and there is scarcely any one, if he dares to be ingenuous, but will confess that, notwithstanding all the merit of the poet, he affords an entertainment with which the palate is soon satiated. Several writers of late have amused themselves in copying the style of Spenser; and no imitation has been so indifferent as not to bear a great resemblance to the original. His manner is so peculiar that it is almost impossible not to transfer some of it into the copy', (Allibone). —

Dr. Johnson: Rambler, No. 121, May 14, 1751: 'To imitate the fictions and sentiments of Spenser can incur no reproach; for allegory is perhaps one of the most pleasing vehicles of instruction. But I am very far from extending the same respect to his diction as his stanza. His style was in his own time allowed to be vicious, so darkened with old words and peculiarities of phrase, and so remote from common use, that Jonson boldly pronounces him to have written no language. [But did not Jonson refer to the Shepheardes Calendar?] His stanza is at once difficult and unpleasing; tiresome to the ear by its uniformity, and to the attention by its length. It was at first formed in imitation of the Italian poets, without due regard to the genius of our language'. (Allibone.) —

Viscount de Chateaubriand: Sketches of Eng. Lit. I, 246 sq.: 'The poetry of Spenser is remarkable for brilliant imagination, fertile invention, and flowing rhythm; yet, with all these recommendations, it is cold and tedious. To the English reader the 'Faerie Queene' presents the charm of antiquated style, which never fails to please us in our own language, but which we cannot appreciate in a foreign tongue . . . Spenser is the author of a sort of essay on the manners and antiquities of Ireland (vide Nr. 11, supra,) which I prefer to his Faerie Queene'. (Allibone). —

Ellis: Specimens of Eng. Poet.: 'It is scarcely possible to accompany Spenser's allegorical heroes to the end of their excursions. They want flesh and blood, — a want for which nothing can compensate. The personification of abstract ideas furnishes the most brilliant images for poetry; but these meteor forms, which startle and delight us, when our senses are flurried by passion, must not be submitted to our cool and deliberate examination', (Allibone). —

Lord Macaulay: Edin. Rev., Dec, 1831, 451—2: The Pilgrim's Progress; repub. in his Crit. and Histor. Essays: 'Even Spenser himself, though assuredly one of the greatest poets that ever lived, could not succeed in the attempt to make allegory interesting. It was in vain that he lavished the riches of his mind on the House of Pride and the House of Temperance. One unpardonable fault, the fault of tediousness, pervades the whole of the Fairy Queen. We become sick of cardinal virtues and deadly sins, and long for the society of plain men and women. Of the persons who read the first canto, not one in ten reaches the end of the first book, and not one in a hundred perseveres to the end of the poem. Very few and very weary are those who are in at the death of the Blatant Beast. If the last six books, which are said to have been destroyed in Ireland, had been preserved, we doubt whether any heart less stout than that of a commentator would have held out to the end'. (Allibone). —

Addison writes:

'Old Spenser next, warm'd with poetic rage,
In ancient times amus'd a barb'rous age;
An age, that yet uncultivate and rude,

Where'er the poet's fancy led, pursued,
Thro' pathless fields and unfrequented floods,
To dens of dragons and enchanted woods.

4

own standard, and, as a classic, he was sorely deficient. At last some persons appeared as his champions, and pointed out to an astonished age that the 'Gothick' poet could not be judged upon class-

But now the mystic tale, that pleas'd of yore,
Can charm an understanding age no more;
The long-span allegories fulsome grow,
While the dull moral lyes too plain below,
We view well pleased, at distance, all the sights,

Of arms and palfries, battles, fields, and fights,
And damsels in distress, and courteous knights;
But when we look too near, the shades decay,
And all the pleasing landscapes fade away'.

One these lines Pope comments:
'The character he gives of Spenser is false too, [as well as that of Chaucer;] and I have heard him say that he never read Spenser till fifteen years after he wrote it'. — (Spence's Anecdotes, sect. I, 1728—30).
Let us hear Pope's own opinion of Spenser:
'After reading a Canto of Spenser two or three days ago to an old lady between seventy and eighty years of age, she said that I had been showing her a gallery of pictures. I don't know how it is, but she said very right: there is something in Spenser that pleases one as strongly in one's old age as it dit in one's youth. I read the Faerie Queene, when I was about twelve, with infinite delight; and I think it gave me as much when I read it over about a year or two ago'. Ibid. 1743—44. See, also, Pope's Works, Bowles's ed., II. 289.
On another occasion he remarked:
'Spenser has ever been a favourite poet to me: he is like a mistress whose faults we see, but love her with them all'. (Allibone). —
Ashestiel MS.: Lockhart's Life of Scott, ch. I:
'But Spenser', Scott says, 'I could have read forever. Too young to trouble myself about the allegory, I considered all the knights and ladies and dragons and giants in their outward and exoteric sense; and God only knows how delighted I was to find myself in such society. As I had always a wonderful facility in retaining in my memory whatever verses pleased me, the quantity of Spenser's stanzas which I could repeat was really marvellous'.
Later in life Scott did not hesitate to say:
'No author, perhaps, ever possessed and combined in so brilliant a degree the requisite qualities of a poet, Learned, according to the learning of his times, his erudition never appears to load or incumber his powers of imagination; but even the fictions of the classics, worn out as they are by every pedant, become fresh and captivating themes when adopted by his fancy and accommodated to his plan. If that plan has now become to the reader of riper years somewhat tedious and involved, it must be allowed, on the other hand, that, from Cowley downwards, every youth of imagination has been enchanted with the splendid legends of the Faery Queen'. (Edin. Rev., Oct. 1803, 203: Todd's Edition of Spenser'.) —
Southey was one of these 'youths':
'No young lady of the present generation falls to a new novel of Sir Walter Scott's with keener relish than I did that morning to the Faery Queen. . . The delicious landscapes which he luxuriates in describing brought every thing before my eyes. I could fancy such scenes as his lakes and forests, gardens and fountains, presented; and I felt, though I did not understand, the truth and purity of his feelings, and that love of the beautiful and the good which pervades his poetry'. (Recollections: Life and Corresp. of Southey, ch. XI. See, also, Malory, Sir Thomas.) —
In his later years he writes:
'He is the great master of English versification, — incomparably the greatest master in our language. Without being insensible to the defects of the Fairy Queen, I am never weary of reading it'. (Southey to Landor, Jan. 11, 1811: Southey's Life and Corresp., ch. XVI.) —
See, also, Landor's Imaginary Conversations. Again: 'Do you love Spenser? I have him in my heart of hearts.' (To C. H. Townshend, Feb. 10, 1816: ibid., ch. XX.) —
Southey is said to have read the Faery Queene through about thirty times. It will be observed that the tide is turning strongly in Spenser's favour: — we shall not oppose it:
'I have finished the 'Faerie Queene'. I never parted from a long poem with so much regret. He is a poet of a most musical ear, — of a tender heart, — of a peculiarly soft, rich, fertile and flowery fancy. His verse always flows with ease and nature, most abundantly and sweetly; his diffusion is not only pardonable, but agreeable. Grandeur and energy are not his characteristic qualities. He seems to me a most genuine poet, and to be justly placed after Shakspeare and Milton, and above all other English poets . . . Sir Philip Sidney, Sir Walter Raleigh, Bacon, Shakspeare, and Spenser! What a glorious reign!' — (Sir James Mackintosh: Diary, April 6, 1812; see, also, April 2, 3, and 4: Life, ch. III.) —
Campbell: Specimens of Brit. Poet:
'His command of imagery is wide, easy, and luxuriant. He threw the soul of harmony into our verse, and made it more warmly, tenderly, and magnificently descriptive than it ever was before, or, with a few exceptions, than it has ever been since. It must certainly be owned that in description he exhibits nothing of the brief strokes and robust power which characterize the very greatest poets; but we shall nowhere find more airy and expansive images of visionary things, a sweeter tone of sentiment, or finer flush in the colours of language, than in this Rubens of English poetry. His fancy teems exuberantly in minuteness of circumstance, like a fertile soil sending bloom and verdure through the utmost extremities of the foliage which it nourishes'.
Hallam: Lit. Hist. of Europe, 4th. ed., 1854, II. 138—9, 142. And see Index: 'His versification is in many pass-

ical principles. And so the attack upon him for his inaccurate use of allegories, of mythologies, of metaphors, for his 'strong writing', which offended the taste of a fastidious and dissolute age, came

---

ages beautifully harmonious; but he has frequently permitted himself, whether for the sake of variety or from some other cause, to baulk the ear in the conclusion of a stanza. The inferiority of the last three books to the former is surely very manifest. His muse gives gradual signs of weariness; the imagery becomes less vivid, the vein of poetical description less rich, the digressions more frequent and verbose . . . But we must not fear to assert, with the best judges of this and of former ages, that Spenser is still the third name in the poetical literature of our country, and that he has not been surpassed, except by Dante, in any other'. (Allibone).

Horace Walpole to William Roscoe, April 4, 1795: Letters, ed. 1861, IX, 454. See, also, II, 257: 'To our tongue the sonnet is mortal, and the parent of insipidity. The imitation in some degree of it was extremely noxious to a true poet, our Spenser; and he was the more injudicious by lengthening his stanza in a language so barren of rhymes as ours, and in which several words whose terminations are of similar sounds are so rugged, uncouth, and unmusical. The consequence was, that many lines which he forced into the service to complete the quota of his stanza are unmeaning, or silly, or tending to weaken the thought he would express'. (Allibone).

Coleridge: Remains I, 93.:
'Spenser's descriptions are not in the true sense of the word picturesque, but are composed of a wondrous series of images, as in our dreams. (Allibone).

Headley remarks that 'Spenser's works are an inexhaustible mine of the richest materials, forming in fact the very bullion of our language; and it is to be lamented that they are so rarely explored for present use'. (Select Beauties of Anc. Eng. Poets.)

'Lord Chatham, according to Mrs. A. Pitt, was always reading Spenser . . . . She said [to Mr. Grattan] he had never read but one book, — The Fairy Queen. . . . 'He who knows Spenser', says Burke, 'has a good hold on the English tongue'. [Fox] liked a book of Spenser exceedingly, before something else'. (Recollec. by Samuel Rogers, 1859, 66, 181. — Allibone.)

The religious character of the Faerie Queene has been referred to. We revert to the subject: 'The claim of Spenser to be considered as a sacred poet does by no means rest upon his hymns alone. . . . But whoever will atten- tively consider the Fairy Queen itself will find that it is, almost throughout, such as might have been expected from the author of those truly sacred hymns. It is a continual, deliberate endeavour to enlist the restless intellect and chivalrous feelings of an inquiring and romantic age on the side of goodness and faith, of purity and justice. . . . Spenser, then, was essentially a s a c r e d poet; but the delicacy and insinuating gentleness of his disposition were better fitted to the veiled than the direct mode of instruction. . . To Spenser, therefore, upon the whole, the English reader must revert as being pre-eminently the sacred poet of his country'. (Keble: Lon. Quar. Rev., 225, 228, 231: Sacred Poetry. — Allibone).

Henry More: 'You tuned my ears to the melody of Spenser's Rhymes, a poet remarkable as well for divine moral- ity as fancy'. (Allibone).

Milton: 'Our sage and serious Spenser, whom I dare be known to think a better teacher than Scotus or Aquinas'. (Allibone).

Fletcher: 'To lackey him is all my pride's aspiring'. (Allibone).

Quarles: 'Here's that creates a poet'. (Allibone).

Ben Johnson: Masque of Queens: 'We will first honour her with a home-born testimony from the grave and diligent Spenser'. (Allibone).

William Browne: Britannia's Pastorals, 1613—15, 2 Pts. fol.
'Divinest Spenser, heav'n-bred, happy muse!
Would any power into my braine infuse
Thy worth, or all that poets had before,
I could not praise till thou deserv'st no more.'

Hazlitt: Lects. on the Eng. Poets, Lects. II, (and see Appendix II., Milton's Eve.): 'The finest things in Spenser are, the character of Una, in the first Book; the Cave of Mammon, and the Cave of Despair; the account of Memory, of whom it is said, among other things,
'The wars he well remember'd of King Nine,·
Of old Assarachus and Inachus divine;'

the description of Belphœbe; the story of Florimel and the Witch's Son; the Gardens of Adonis, and the Bower of Bliss; the Mask of Cupid; and Colin Clout's Vision, in the last Book.

But some people will say that all this may be very fine, but that they cannot understand it on account of the allegory. They are afraid of the allegory, as if they thought it would bite them; they look at it as a child looks at a painted dragon, and think it will strangle them in its shining folds. This is very idle. If they do not meddle with the allegory, the allegory will not meddle with them. Without minding it at all, the whole is as plain as a pike-staff. It might as well be pretended that we cannot see Poussin's pictures for the allegory, as that the allegory prevents us from understanding Spenser. . . . The language of Spenser is full and copious to overflowing; it is less pure and idiomatic than Chaucer's, and is enriched and adorned with phrases borrowed from the different languages of Europe, both ancient and modern. . . His versification is at once the most smooth and the most sounding in the language . . . Spenser is the most harmonious of our stanza-writers, as Dryden is the most sounding and varied of our rhymists'.

Hallam: Lit. Hist. of Europe, 4 th. ed., 1854, II, 136: 'It has been justly observed by a living writer of the most ardent and enthusiastic genius, whose eloquence is as the rush of mighty waters . . . that no poet has ever had a more exquisite sense of the beautiful than Spenser' etc. (Allibone).

4*

at last to an end, — and Spenser returned to comparative oblivion. His position was assured, but his works have had little attention paid to them during the last century. Of late years there have been symptoms of a revived interest [1]).

Part III.

Spenser's Language, especially as we have it in the Cantos of the Fairy Queen contained in the Tauchnitz Collection Vol. CCCCC.[2])

A. These Cantos Translated and Commented.[3])

Book I. Canto I.

The patron of true Holinesse Foule Errour doth defeate; Hypocrisie, him to entrappe, Doth to his home entreate.	Der schutzherr wahrer frömmigkeit bekaempft die garstige sünde; die heuchelei empfängt ihn in ihrem hause, um ihn in ihre fallen zu verstricken.

I.

A Gentle knight was pricking on the plaine, Ycladd in mightie arms and silver shielde, Wherein old dints of deepe woundes did remaine, The cruel markes of many' a bloody fielde; Yet armes till that time did he never wield; His angry steede did chide his foming bitt, As much disdayning to the curbe to yield: Full iolly knight he seemd, and faire did sitt, As one for knightly giusts and fierce encounters fitt.	Ein edler ritter sprengte auf der ebene daher, ange- than mit maechtiger ruestung und einem silberschil- de, worin alte spuren tiefer streiche verblieben, die grausamen zeichen mancher blutigen schlacht; doch waffen fuehrte er bis zu jener zeit nimmer; sein mu- thiges streitross knirschte in sein schaeumendes ge- biss, als ob es grossen widerwillen empfaende, der kinnketto sich zu fuegen; ein gar herrlicher ritter schien er, und schoen sass er da, wie einer, der fuer ritterliche turniere und hitzige kaempfe ge- schmueckt ist.

---

[1]) Cf. Kitchin.
[2])Printing the words as they are to be found in the Tauchnitz Collection, we shall only cite the more essential variations between this edition and the two others lying before us, by Todd and Kitchin.
[3]) Cf. Todd, Kitchin, Jortin etc.
I. v. 1. A gentle Knight; — 'The Red Cross Knight, by whom is meant reformed England, (see C. X. 61, where he is called 'St, George of merry England'), has just been' equipped with the 'armour which Una brought (that is the armour of a Christian man, specified by St. Paul, V. [VI] Ephes.)' as Spenser tells Sir W. Raleigh in his Letter. The armour though now to the Knight, is old as Christendom. Thus equipped and guided by truth, he goes forth to fight against error and temptation, and above all to combat that spirit of falschood, concerning which the England of 1558 had learnt so much from Philip II of Spain and Alexander of Parma. The diplomatic lying which preceded the Armada contrasted with the simple truthfulness of the English and Dutch statesmen, and had taught Englishmen to couple the name of Spain with all that was false, as well as with all that was cruel'. (Kitchin.)

II.

And on his brest a bloodie crosse he bore, The deare remembrance of his dying Lord, For whose sweet sake that glorious badge he wore, And dead, as living, ever him ador'd: Upon his shield the like was also scor'd, For soveraine hope, which in his helpe he had. Right, faithfull, true he was in deede and word; But of his cheere did seeme to solemne sad; Yet nothing did he dread, but ever was ydrad.	Und auf seiner brust trug er ein blutiges kreuz, das theure andenken an seinen sterbenden Herrn, um dessen sanftmuth willen er dies ruehmliche ab- zeichen trug, und den er, mochte er leben oder ster- ben, immer anbetete: auf seinem schilde war dasselbe ebenfalls eingeschnitten, zum zeichen des unum- schraenkten vertrauens, das er in seine hilfe setzte. Rechtschaffen, treu, wahr war er in that und wort; nur zeigte sein antlitz zu feierlichen ernst; gleich- wohl fuerchtete er nichts, sondern ward stets ge- fuerchtet.

III.

Upon a great adventure he was bond, That greatest Gloriana to him gave, (That greatest glorious Queene of Faery lond) To winne him worshippe, and her grace to have, Which of all earthly things he most did crave. And ever as he rode, his hart did earne To prove his puissance in battell brave Upon his foe, and his new force to learne; Upon his foe, a dragon horrible and stearne.	Zu einem grossen abenteuer war er verpflichtet, das die erhabene Gloriana ihm aufgab, (jene erha- benste, ruhmvolle koenigin des Feenlandes) damit er sich auszeichnung erringe und ihre gunst erhalte, nach der er von allen irdischen dingen am meisten verlangte. Und immer wenn er ritt, schmachtete sein herz danach, seine macht in glaenzender schlacht zu erproben an seinem feinde und seine neue kraft zu erfahren an seinem feinde, einem schrecklichen und grausen drachen.

IV.

A lovely ladie rode him faire beside Upon a lowly asse more white then snow; Yet she much whiter; but the same did hide Under a vele, that wimpled was full low; And over all a blacke stole she did throw, As one that inly mournd; so was she sad,	Eine holde dame ritt ihm stattlich zur seite auf einem eselein, weisser denn schnee; doch sie viel weisser; aber dieselbe war in einen schleier gehuellt, der ganz herabgelassen war; und ueber alles hatte sie ein schwarzes gewand geworfen, wie jemand, der in tiefer trauer ist; auch war sie ernst und sass schwer-

II. Various readings: In Kitchin: v. 1. bloudie. v. 4. no commas, v. 7. no commas,
v. 4. And dead etc.; — The comma misses the sense, and the obvious allusion to Rev. I. 17. 18: Ἐγώ εἰμι
ὁ πρῶτος καὶ ἔσχατος καὶ ὁ ζῶν καὶ ἐγενόμην νεκρός, καὶ ἰδοὺ ζῶν εἰμι εἰς τοὺς αἰῶνας τῶν αἰώνων, καὶ ἔχω τὰς κλεῖς τοῦ
θανάτου καὶ τοῦ ᾅδου.
v. 6. For soveraine hope, which etc.; — 'the shield was 'scored' with a cross, as a sign of the 'sov‘reign
hope' which he had in the help to be given him by our Lord's death for him', (Kitchin.)
v. 7. Right, faithfull, true; — 'edd. 1590, 1596, have no commas, so making 'right' an adv., and giving
the meaning 'right faithfull and true', The reading 'right, faithfull, true,' is unlike Spenser; he would scarcely use 'right'
for 'righteous,' and 'right' as an adv. is common with him; as 'ight courteous,' 'right jolly'. So he also uses 'full,' and
'full soon,' etc. This form of the adverb (as in st. 4, l. 1, below) comes from the Old Engl. adverbial form which ends in
e, 'faire', 'righte', the e being dropped in modern spelling. See Morris, E. E. Specimens, Grammat. Introd. p. LV'.
(Kitchin. — See below).
v. 8. of his cheere, etc.; — 'in countenance and bearing seemed too solemnly grave'. (Kitchin.)
v. 9. ydrad; — 'p. p. of to 'dread', as 'yclad' of to 'clothe', etc. Spenser has been blamed for coining forms to suit
his rhymes. But this ts not so. He uses old, not new forms'. (Kitchin. — See below.)
III. Various readings: In Kitchin: v. 8. without parenthesis. v. 4. worship. v. 5. behind 'crave' a semicolon.
v. 2. greatest Gloriana; — 'Queen Elizabeth. So in the Letter to Sir W. Raleigh we read, 'In that Faery
Queene I mean Glory in my generall intention, but in my particular I conceive the most excellent and glorious person of
our soveraine the Queene'. It was court fashion to address the Virgin Queen under such names as Gloriana, Oriana, Diana,
etc. Spenser also calls her Belphoebe, and Britomart; Raleigh styled her his Cynthia'. (Kitchin).
v. 9. his foe, a dragon; — 'first the Devil, father of lies, then the powers of Spain and Rome, as the earthly
exponents of falsehood'. (Kitchin).
IV. Various readings: In Kitchin: v. 1 comma behind 'beside'. v. 2. comma behind 'snow'. v. 3. comma behind
'whiter'. v. 4. comma behind 'low'. v. 6. colon behind 'mournd'.

And heavie sate upon her palfrey slow;
Seemed in heart some hidden care she had;
And by her in a line a milke-white lambe sho lad.

muethig auf ihrem langsamen thiere; es schien, dass
sie im herzen irgend einen verborgenen kummer hatte;
und mit sich fuehrte sie ein milchweisses lamm an
einer leine.

V.

So pure and innocent, as that same lambe,
She was in life and every vertuous lore,
And by descent from royall lynage came
Of ancient kinges and queenes, that had of yore
Their scepters strecht from east to westerne shore,
And all the world in their subjection held;
Till that infernal feend with foule uprore
Forwasted all their land, and them expeld;
Whom to avenge, she had this knight from far compeld.

So rein und unschuldig, wie dies lamm, war sie
im leben und jedem tugendhaften werk, und war aus
dem fuerstlichen stamme alter koenige und koenigin-
nen entsprossen, deren scepter sich weiland vom osten
bis zur westkueste erstreckte, mit dem sie die ganze
welt in ihrer dienstbarkeit hielten; bis jener hoellische
feind mit scheusslichem aufruhr ihr ganzes land verwuestete und sie vertrieb. Um an ihm sich zu raechen, hatte sie diesen ritter von fernher entboten.

VI.

Behind her farre away a dwarfe did lag,
That lasie seemd, in being ever last,
Or wearied with bearing of her bag
Of needments at his backe. Thus as they past,
The day with cloudes was suddeine overcast,
And angry Jove an hideous storme of raine
Did poure into his lemans lap so fast,
That everie wight to shrowd it did constrain;
And this faire couple eke to shroud themselves were
fain.

Hinter ihr in weiter ferne bewegte sich langsam
ein zwerg, welcher traege schien, da er immer der
letzte war, oder ermuedet davon, dass er ihr gepaeck
auf seinem ruecken trug. Waehrend sie so daher-
zogen, verdunkelte sich die sonne ploetzlich durch
wolken, und Jupiter in seinem zorn stroemte einen
schrecklichen platzregen in seiner geliebten schooss
mit solcher gewalt herab, dass jedermann genoethigt
war, sich su schuetzen; und dies schoene paar war
ebenfalls gezwungen, sich zu bergen.

---

v. 7. colon behind 'slow'.   v. 9. no hyphen between 'milke' aud 'white'.
IV.   v. 1. A lovely ladie; — 'Una, or Truth. 'Truth is one, error manifold' must have been the thought of Spenser's mind when he fixed on this name. Church says, 'Mr. Llwyd (in his Irish Dict.) says that Una is a Dunish proper
name of women; and that one of that name was daughter to a king of Denmark. He adds Una is still a proper name
in Ireland' — where probably Spenser first found it in use and thence adopted it'. (Kitchin.)
     rode him faire beside; — 'rode fairly beside him'. For this adverbial form 'faire', see above, note on st.
2. 1. 7. (Kitchin.)
     v. 3. Yet she much whiter; — Hallam, Lit. of Eur. II. v. § 88, objects to this as strained. The 'asse more
white than snow' is extravagant; but there is an excuse for Una's whiteness, because Spenser wished to give the impression
of the surpassing purity and spotlessness of Truth. (Kitchin.)
     v. 4. Under a vele, that wimpled, etc.; — 'Her veil was plaited in folds, falling so as to cover her face'.
(Kitchin.)
     - 'A veil plaited. But the veil and the wimple were two different articles in the dress of a nun' (Upton
in Todd.)
     v. 6. so was she sad; — 'so grave she was'. (Kitchin.)
     v. 8. Seemed; 'impers. for 'it seemed'. Spenser very commonly omits the pronoun before impers. verbs'.
(Kitchin.   Cf. below.)
     v. 9. lad; 'led'. 'An old form'. (Kitchin. — Cf. below.)
V.   Various readings: In Kitchin: v. 4. 'Kings and Queenes.'   v. 7. 'infernall.'
     v. 3. from royall lynage; — an allusion to Isaiah 49, 23: וְהָיוּ מְלָכִים אֹמְנַיִךְ וְשָׂרוֹתֵיהֶם מֵינִיקֹתַיִךְ
אַפַּיִם אֶרֶץ יִשְׁתַּחֲווּ־לָךְ וַעֲפַר רַגְלַיִךְ יְלַחֵכוּ וְיָדַעַתְּ כִּי־אֲנִי יְהוָֹה אֲשֶׁר לֹא־יֵבֹשׁוּ קֹוָי :
'Spenser's meaning is that Una, Truth, or the Reformed Church, derives her lineage from the Church Universal, not from
the Papacy'. (Kitchin).
VI.   v. 1. a dwarfe; — 'the dwarf is probably intended to represent common sense, or common prudence of
humble life. 'Such an one as might be attendant on Truth - cautious, nay timid, yet not afraid - feeble, but faithful, and in
all his dangers devoted to his Lady and his Lord'. (Blackwood's Mag., Nov. 1834 in Kitchin).
     v. 4 sqq: Cf. Vergil, Georg. II. 325 sqq:
Tum pater omnipotens fecundis imbribus Aether Coniugis in gremium laetae descendit, et omnes Magnus alit,
magno commixtus corpore, fetus.
         Lucretius, de Rerum Natura I, 251 sq:
Postremo pereunt imbres, ubi eos pater Aether In gremium matris Terrai praecipitavit.
     v. 9: Todd: '— were fain — glad. Church'.

— 31 —

VII.

Enforst to seeke some covert nigh at hand,
A shadie grove not farr away they spide,
That promist ayde the tempest to withstand;
Whoso loftie trees, yclad with sommers pride
Did spred so broad, that heavens light did hide,
Not perceable with power of any starr;
And all within were pathes and alleies wide,
With footing worne, and leading inward farr:
Faire harbour that them seems; so in they entred ar.

Gezwungen, irgend einen zufluchtsort zu suchen, der
nahe bei der hand war, erspachten sie einen schatti-
gen hain in nicht weiter ferne, welcher hilfe ver-
sprach, dem sturm zu widerstehen; denn seine stattlichen baeume, mit des sommers schmuck bekleidet,
breiteten ihre aeste so weit aus, dass des himmels
licht sich verbarg und keines sternes strahl hin-
durchzudringen vermochte; und ganz im innern waren
fussptade und breite laubgaenge, von fussspuren betreten und weit nach innen fuehrend. Ein schoener
zufluchtsort scheint ihnen das zu sein, und so treten
sie ein.

VIII.

And foorth they passe, with pleasure forward led,
Ioying to heare the birdes sweete harmony,
Which therein shrouded from the tempest dred,
Seomd in their song to scorne the cruell sky.
Much can they praise the trees so straight and hy:
The sayling pine, the cedar proud and tall;
The vine-propp elme, the poplar never dry;
The builder oake, sole king of forrests all;
The aspine good for staves, the cypresse funerall;

Und lustig setzen sie ihren weg fort, an der voe-
gel suessen harmonien sich erfreuend, welche, vor
dem schrecklichen sturm geborgen, mit ihrem gesange
das grause wetter zu schmaehen schienen. Laut preisen sie die baeume, so grade und hoch: die segelnde
fichte, die stolze und schlanke ceder; die wein-stuet-
zende ulme, die nimmer trockne pappel; die bauende
eiche, die alleiniger koenig aller waelder ist, die
zu staeben geeignete espe, die die graeber zierende
cypresse;

VII. Various readings: v. 3. Kitchin has a colon. v. 4. Kitchin has no comma behind 'trees'.
    v. 6. 8. 9. Kitchin has 'starre', 'farre', 'arre', and behind 'starre' a colon.
    v. 2. A shadie grove; — 'the wood of Error, which is at first enchanting, but soon leads those astray who
wander in it. By it Spenser shadows forth the dangers surrounding the mind that escapes from the bondage of Roman
authority, and thinks for itself; and also the ultimate triumph of the man who, with help of God's armour, tracks Error to
its den, and slays it there'. (Kitchin).
    v. 5. that heavens light did hide; — So Ariosto, Orl. Fur. I, 37:
          'E la foglia coi rami in modo ħ mista,
          Che 'l Sol non v'entra, non che minor vista'.
    v. 6. Not perceable with power of any starr; — 'Warton notices here that stars were supposed to have
a malign influence on trees. But Spenser only wishes to convey an impression of great closeness and gloom in the
grove'. (Kitchin).
        Cp. Statius Theb. X. 85 sq:
        '— — — nulli penetrabilis astro
        Lucus iners — — — —'.
    VIII. Various readings: v. 2. Kitchin has J instead of I. Kitchin has a comma at the end of the four last lines.
    v. 3. Todd: 'the rein', and a comma before these words. v. 7. Kitchin has 'vine prop'.
    v. 5. Todd: 'Much can they praise — The reader will find this expression very often, Much can they
praise i. e. Much they praised. Upton'. (Cf. below.)
        Kitchin: ='much they began to praise'. Spenser sometimes writes 'can' for 'gan'. So Church quotes
Chaucer:
          'Yet half for drede I can my visage hide'.
Or perhaps 'can' is used as an auxiliary verb=do: then 'can praise' will=do praise.
    This description of trees is expanded from Chaucer's Assembly of Foules, 176. It has been objected to with
some justice as not true to nature, and laboured, as so many different kinds of trees could not have grown together in a
thick wood. But the passage suits well the general conception, as it causes a feeling of bewilderment of details, leading
us on to the 'cave of Error'. (Kitchin).
    v. 6. The sayling pine; — 'the pine whence sailing ships are made'. Chaucer, Assembly, 179, 'the saylynge
firre'. The Latin poets use pinus 'per συνεκδοχήν' for ship, as — Hor. Epod. 16, 57 sq:
        'Non huc Argoo contendit remige pinus,
        Neque inpudica Colchis intulit pedem'.
    the cedar proud and tall; — Ezekiel 31, 3: הִנֵּה אַשּׁוּר אֶרֶז בַּלְּבָנוֹן יְפֵה עָנָף וְחֹרֶשׁ מֵצַל וּגְבַהּ

IX.

The laurell, meed of mightie conquerours
And poets sage; the firre that weepeth still;
The willow, worne of forlorne paramours;
The eugh, obedient to the benders will;
The birch for shaftes, the sallow for the mill;
The mirrhe sweete-bleeding in the bitter wound;
Tho warlike beech, the ash for nothing ill;
The fruitful olive, and the platane round;
The carver holme, the maple, seldom inward sound.

Den lorbeerbaum, den preis maechtiger eroberer
und weiser dichter; die immer weinende tanne; die
von verlassenen liebhabern getragene weide; den
eibenbaum, des beugers willen gehorsam; die zu
wurfspiessen brauchbare birke; die fuĕr die muehle
geeignete saalweide; die in die bittere wunde sucss
blutende myrrhe; die kriegerische buche, die fuer
nichts untaugliche esche; den fruchtreichen oelbaum,
und die runde platane; die zum schnitzen geeignete
steineiche, den ahorn, der selten inuen gesund ist.

קוֹמָה וּבֵין עֲבֹתִים הָיְתָה צַמַּרְתּוֹ ׃

and Ez. 31, 10: לָכֵן כֹּה אָמַר אֲדֹנָי יְהוִה יַעַן אֲשֶׁר גָּבַהְתָּ בְּקוֹמָה וַיִּתֵּן צַמַּרְתּוֹ אֶל־בֵּין עֲבוֹתִים יָרָם לְבָבוֹ בְּגָבְהוֹ ׃

Isaiah 2, 13: וְעַל כָּל־אַרְזֵי הַלְּבָנוֹן הָרָמִים וְהַנִּשָּׂאִים וְעַל כָּל־אַלּוֹנֵי הַבָּשָׁן ׃ (Kitchin).

Chaucer, Complaynte of a Loveres Lyfe, 67: 'the cedres high'. (Kitchin).

    v. 7, the vine-propp elme; 'i. e. the elm that props up and supports the vine'. (Upton in Todd.)
      Kitchin: the elm in ancient Italy was largely used to train up the vine. So Chaucer, Assembly, 177,
      has 'the peler elme'.
      Ovid, Met, 10, 100:   'Pampineas vites, et amictae vitibus ulmi'.
    the poplar never dry; 'from its flourishing in damp spots, on river banks, etc.' (Kitchin).
    v. 8, the builder oake; — 'Chaucor, Assembly, 176, hat the same epithet'. (Kitchin).
    v. 9, the cypresse funerall, Chaucer, Assembly, 179, 'The ciprosse deth to pleyne'. Sir P. Sidney in his
Arcadia has 'Cypress branches; wherewith in old time they were wont to dress graves'. There was a tradition that the
Cross was made of cypress-wood. See the Squyre of Lowe Degree (quoted by Warton on Spenser; I. 139):
      'Cypresse the first tre that Jesu chase (chose)'.

Cp. also:

    Pliny, Nat. Hist, 16, 60: 'Cupressus advena, et difficillime nascentium fuit . . . . Natu morosa, fructu super-
vacua, baccis torva, folio amara, odore violenta, ac ne umbra quidem gratiosa, materie rara, ut paene fruticosi generis,
Diti sacra, et ideo funebri signo ad domos posita'.

    Seneca, Œd. 530 sqq:

        'Cr. Est procul ab urbe lucus ilicibus niger,
        Dircea circa vallis irriguae loca.
        Cupressus altis exserens silvis caput
        Virente semper alligat trunco nemus; etc.'

    Lucan, III, 440 sqq:

        'Procumbunt orni, nodosa inpellitur ilex,
        Silvaque Dodones, et fluctibus aptior alnus,
        Et non plebeios luctus testata cupressus:
        Tunc primum posuere comas'.

    Claudian, De Raptu Proserp. 107 sqq:

        'Apta frotis abies, bellis accommoda cornus,
        Quercus amica Jovi, tumulos tectura cupressus,
        Ilex plena favis, venturi praescia laurus:
        Fluctuat hic denso crispata cacumine buxus,
        Hic ederae serpunt, hic pampinus induit ulmos'.

    Statius, Theb. VI, 96 sqq:

'— — — Aderat miserabile luco
Excidium. Fugere ferae, nidosque tepentes
Absiliunt (metus urget) aves. Cadit ardua fagus:
Chaoniumque nemus, brumaeque illaesa cupressus,
Procumbunt piceae, flammis alimenta supremis,
Ornique, ilicesoque trabes, metuendaque succo

Taxus, et infandos belli potura cruores
Fraxinus, atque situ non expugnabile robur.
Hinc audax abies, et odoro vulnere pinus
Scinditur, acclinant intonsa cacumina terrae
Alnus amica fretis, nec inhospita vitibus ulmus'.

IX.   Various readings: In Kitchin v. 6: 'sweete bleeding'.
    v. 2, the firre that weepeth still; — 'distils resin' (Kitchin).
    v. 3, the willow, worne of forlorne paramours; — 'the badge of deserted lovers. See Percy's Reliques,
I, 156, and John Heywood's Song of the Green Willow:

'All a green willow, willow,
All a green willow is my garland.
Alas! by what means may I make ye to know
The unkindness for kindness that to me doth grow?

That one who most kind love on me should bestow,
Most unkind unkindness to me she doth show,
For all a green willow is my garland'.

    So too Shakespeare, in Othello, puts this refrain into Desdemona's song. Beaumont and Fletcher, The Night
Walker, Act. I,:

X.

Led with delight, they thus beguile the way,
Untill the blustring storme is overblowne;
When, weening to returne, whence they did stray,
They cannot finde that path, which first was showne,
But wander too and fro in waies unknowne,
Furthest from end then, when they neerest weene,
That makes them doubt their wits be not their owne.
So many paths, so many turnings seene,
That which of them to take in diverse doubt they
                     been.

Von wonne geleitet, betruegen sie in dieser weise
den weg, bis der brausende sturm ausgetobt hat. Als
sie, in der hoffnung, dahin zurueckzukehren, von wo
aus sie sich verirrten, jenen pfad nicht finden koennen, welcher ihnen zuerst erschienen war, sondern
hin und her wandern in unbekannten wegen, dann
gerade am weitesten vom ziele entfernt, wenn sie
sich am naechsten waehnen: da ueberfaellt sie die
furcht, sie seien nicht mehr bei verstande. So viele
pfade, so viele windungen sehen sie, dass sie in mancherlei zweifel sind, welche von ihnen sie einschla-
gen sollen.

XI.

At last resolving forward still to fare,
Till that some end they finde, or in or out,
That path they take, that beaten seemd most bare,
And like to lead the labyrinth about;
Which when by tract they hunted had throughout,
At length it brought them to a hollowe cave
Amid the thickest woods. The champion stout
Eftsoones dismounted from his courser brave,
And to the dwarfe awhile his needlesse spere he gave.

Endlich beschliessen sie, immer vorwaerts zu ziehen,
bis sie irgend ein ende faenden, innerhalb oder aus-
serhalb, und schlagen jenen pfad ein, der am meisten
kahl getreten schien und sie scheinbar aus dem irr-
garten hinausfuehrte; als sie ihn allmählig in seiner
ganzen laenge durcheilt hatten, brachte er sie schliesslich zu einer tiefen grube mitten im dichtesten walde.
Der wackre held stieg sogleich von seinem edlen
renner hinab und gab dem zwerg einstweilen seine
nutzlose lanze.

XII.

'Be well aware,' quoth then that ladie milde,
'Least suddaine mischiefe ye too rash provoke:
The danger hid, the place unknowne and wilde,
Breedes dreadfull doubts: oft fire is without smoke,
And perill without show; therefore your stroke,
Sir Knight, with-hold, till further tryall made.'
'Ah, Ladie,' sayd he, 'shame were to revoke
The forward footing for an hidden shade:
Vertue gives her selfe light trough darknesse for to
                     wade.'

'Seid wohl auf der hut,' sagte da die dame mild,
'dass ihr nicht ploetzliches unheil zu tollkuehn her-
ausfordert: Die verborgene gefahr, der unbekannte
und wilde ort erzeugt schreckliche besorgnisse: oft
ist feuer ohne rauch und gefahr ohne sichtbares an-
zeichen; darum lasst ab von eurem unternehmen,
Herr Ritter, bis fernere untersuchung angestellt ist'.
'Ach, Dame,' sagte er, 'schande waere es, den kecken
schritt zurueckzuhalten wegen eines verborgenen
schattens: tugend giebt selbst licht, um durch fin-
sterniss zu dringen.'

'Here comes poor Frank; —
  We see your willow, and are sorry for't'. (Kitchin).
    v. 4. The eugh obedient to the benders will; — 'referring to the bows made of yew. Chaucer has it
'the sheter (shooter) ewe'. (Kitchin.)
    v. 5. The sallow for the mill; — Ovid, Met. 10. 96 has
        'Amnicolacque simul salices, et aquatica lotos etc.'
    v. 6. The mirrhe etc.; — 'the myrrh has a bitter taste, but the exudation from its bark is sweet of smell.
Chaucer, Complaynte of a Loveres Lyfe, 66:
        'The myrre also that wepeth ever of kynde'. (Kitchin).
    v. 7. The warlike beech; — 'suitable for warlike arms, or because the war-chariots of the ancients were made
of it'. (Kitchin.)
    v. 9. The carver holme; — 'good for carving. Chaucer, Assembly, 178, has 'holme to whippes lasshe'. (Kit.).
  X.   Various readings: In Kitchin v. 4: 'find'.   v. 5: 'wayes'.
  XI.   Various readings: In Kitchin: v. 6. 'hollow'.
    v. 2. or in or out; — 'either on the inside or the outside of the maze'. (Kitchin).
    v. 4. like to lead etc.; — 'likely to lead them out of the labyrinth'. (Kitchin).
  XII. Various readings: In Kitchin: v. 6. 'triall'; no inverted commas.
    v. 7. 8. 'It would be shame (shameful) to recall our forward movement for (fear of) a concealed shadow of evil'.
Here again Spenser uses the impersonal verb without the neut. pron.; — shame were = 'it were shame'. (Kitchin.
— See below.)

XIII.

'Yea, but,' quoth she; 'the perill of this place
I better wot then you: Though nowe too late
To wish you backe returne with foule disgrace,
Yet wisedome warnes, whilest foot is in the gate,
To stay the steppe, ere forced to retrate.
This is the Wandring Wood, this Errours Den,
A monster vile, whom God and man does hate:
Therefore I read beware.' 'Fly, fly,' quoth then
'The fearefull dwarfe; 'this is'no place for living
men.'

'Freilich,' sagte sie, 'aber die gefahr dieses platzes
kenne ich besser, als ihr: Obgleich es jetzt zu spaet
ist, zu wuenschen, dass ihr mit haesslichem schimpfe
zurueckkehrt, so warnt doch weisheit, so lange der
fuss noch im thore weilt, den schritt zu hemmen,
ehe man gezwungen ist, sich zurueckzuziehen. Dies
ist der Irr-Wald, dies der Luege Hoehle, eines
ruchlosen ungeheuers, welches Gott und menschen
hassen: 'seid auf eurer hut.' 'Flieht, flieht,' sprach
dann der furchtsame zwerg; 'dies ist kein ort fuer
lebende menschen.'

XIV.

But, full of fire and greedy hardiment,
The youthfull knight could not for ought be staide;
But forth unto the darksome hole he went,
And looked in: his glistring armor made
A· litle glooming light, much like a shade;
By which he saw the ugly monster plaine:
Halfe like a serpent horribly displaide,
But th' other halfe did womans shape retaine,
Most lothsom, filthie, foule, and full of vile disdaine.

Aber voll feuer und ehrsuechtiger kuehnheit konnte
der jugendliche ritter durch nichts zurueckgehalten
werden; sondern vorwaerts zur dunkeln hoehle ging
er und blickte hinein: seine glaenzende ruestung
verursachte einen schwachen duestern schein, fast
gleich einem schatten, bei welchem er das haessliche
unthier deutlich sah: halb gleich einer schlange in
scheusslicher entringelung, halb frauengestalt, im
hoechsten grade ekelhaft, abscheulich, graesslich und
voll ruchlosen uebermuths.

XV.

And, as she lay upon the durtie ground,
Her huge long taile her den all overspred,
Yet was in knots and many boughtes upwound,
Pointed with mortall sting; of her there bred
A thousand young ones, which she dayly fed,
Sucking upon her poisnous dugs; each one
Of sundrie shapes, yet all ill-favored:
Soone as that uncouth light upon them shone,
Into her mouth they crept, and suddain all were
gone.

Und wie sie da lag auf dem schmutzigen boden,
bedeckte ihr riesig langer schweif ihre hoehle ganz
und gar; doch war er in knoten und vielen windungen aufgeringelt und ausserdem an der spitze mit
toedtlichem stachel versehen; an tausend junge hatte
sie, die sie taeglich an ihren giftigen bruesten
saeugte; ein jedes von verschiedener gestalt, doch
alle ungestalt: Sobald das ungewohnte licht sie be-
schien, krochen sie in ihren rachen und waren ploetzlich alle verschwunden.

XIII. Various readings: In Kitchin and Todd: v. 9. 'is no'; 'is'no', probably, is a misprint.
    v. 6. W a n d r i n g W o o d; — 'the wood of wandering'. (Kitchin).
    v. 8. '— therefore I advise you to be cautious'. (Kitchin).
XIV. v. 2. for o u g h t; — 'by any arguments', or 'for any reasons'. (Kitchin).
    v. 4. — 'a passage worthy of Rembraudt's most gloomy pencil. The image of Error should be compared with
Milton's delineation of Sin. P. I., 2. 650.' (Kitchin).
    v. 9. full of v i l e d i s d a i n e; — 'full of vileness breeding disdain'. She is Falsehood, half human, half bestial,
half true and half untrue; parent of a countless brood of lies. Her shape is taken partly from Hesiod's Echidna, Theog,
301'. (Kitchin), and partly from the locusts in Rev. 9. 7. sqq:

*Καὶ τὰ ὁμοιώματα τῶν ἀκρίδων ὅμοια ἵπποις ἡτοιμασμένοις εἰς πόλεμον, καὶ ἐπὶ τὰς κεφαλὰς αὐτῶν ὡς στέφανοι
ὅμοιοι χρυσῷ, καὶ τὰ πρόσωπα αὐτῶν ὡς πρόσωπα ἀνθρώπων, Καὶ εἶχον τρίχας ὡς τρίχας γυναικῶν, καὶ οἱ ὀδόντες αὐτῶν
ὡς λεόντων ἦσαν, Καὶ εἶχον θώρακας ὡς θώρακας σιδηροῦς, καὶ ἡ φωνὴ τῶν πτερύγων αὐτῶν ὡς φωνὴ ἁρμάτων ἵππων
πολλῶν τρεχόντων εἰς πόλεμον. Καὶ ἔχουσιν οὐρὰς ὁμοίας σκορπίοις, καὶ κέντρα ἦν ἐν ταῖς οὐραῖς αὐτῶν ἀδικῆσαι τοὺς
ἀνθρώπους μῆνας πέντε.*

XV. Various readings: In Kitchin: v. 6. 'eachone'.   v. 7. 'ill favored'.
    v. 3. Todd: 'Many b o u g h t s, i. e. many circular folds. Upton'.
    v. 4. o f h e r t h e r e b r e d; — 'there sprung from her as a mother;' 'she had a b r o o d of. (Kitchin).
    v. 7. Of s u n d r i e s h a p e s; — 'i. e. each of a shape different from all the rest; or each one able to vary its
shape — lies and rumours being many-formed'. (Kitchin).

XVI.

Their dam upstart out of her den effraide,
And rushed forth, hurling her hideous taile
About her cursed head; whose folds displaid
Were stretcht now forth at length without entraile.
She lookt about, and seing one in mayle,
Armed to point, sought backe to turne againe;
For light she hated as the deadly bale,
Ay wont in desert darkness to remaine,
Where plain none might her see, nor she see any
plaine.

Ihre mutter fuhr erschreckt aus ihrer hoehle heraus und stuerzte vorwaerts, ihren scheusslichen schweif
um ihr fluchwuerdiges haupt wirbelnd; dessen ringel
waren jetzt aufgerollt, und ohne verschlingung streckte
sie ihn der laenge nach aus. Sie blickte umher,
und da sie einen sah, der in voller ruestung und
bis an die zaehne bewaffnet war, suchte sie wieder
umzukehren; denn licht hasste sie wie das toedtliche
unheil, da sie stets in oeder dunkelheit zu weilen
pflegte, wo sie niemand deutlich sehen noch von je-
mandem gesehen werden konnte.

XVII.

Which when the valiant Elfe perceiv'd, he lept
As lyon fierce upon the flying pray,
And with his trenchand blade her boldly kept
From turning backe and forced her to stay:
Therewith enrag'd she loudly gan to bray,
And turning fierce her speckled taile advaunst,
Threatning her angrie sting, him to dismay;
Who, nought aghast, his mightie hand enhaunst;
The stroke down from her head unto her shoulder
glaunst.

Als dies der wackere Elfe gewahrte, sprang er
gleich einem wuethenden loewen auf die fliehende
beute, hielt sie mit seiner scharfen klinge kuehn vom
zurueckweichen ab und zwang sie zu bleiben. Aus
wuth hierueber begann sie laut zu bruellen, und indem sie voller grimm ihrem gefleckten schweif eine
andre richtung gab, stuerzte sie vor, ihren zornigen
stachel schwingend, um ihn in schrecken zu setzen;
doch er, durchaus nicht entmuthigt, erhob seine
maechtige hand; der streich glitt von ihrem haupt
zu ihrer schulter hernieder.

XVIII.

Much daunted with that dint her sence was dazd;
Yet kindling rage her selfe she gathered round,
And all attonce her beastly bodie raizd
With doubled forces high above the ground:
Tho, wrapping up her wrethed sterne arownd,
Lept fierce upon his shield, and her huge traine

Gar sehr entsetzt war sie ueber diesen hieb, und
ihre sinne wurden betaeubt; doch selbst ihre wuth
anfachend schwoll sie rund auf und erhob auf einmal
ihren thierleib mit verdoppelten kraeften hoch ueber
den boden: dann rollte sie ihren ringelschweif ringsum zusammen, sprang wuethend auf seinen schild

XVI. v. 1. upstart, out of her den effraide; — 'pret. of to upstart, to start up. Ed. 1590 puts a comma after 'upstart', so connecting 'out of her den' with 'effraide', — she started up, frightened out of her den. Later edd. seem to have preferred the meaning 'started up (and rushed) out of her den, quite frightened'. (Kitchin. — As for 'upstart' see below.)
  v. 4. without entraile; — 'untwisted'. (Kitchin).
  v. 6. Armed to point; — 'armed cap-à-pie', at every point. Bailey in his Dict. says 'to point, completely; — as armed to point, Spenser'. The Fr. phrase à point = to a nicety, is probably the real origin of the phrase.' (Kit.).
  v. 7. the deadly bale; -- 'Bale is here used literally for poison, its genuine signification.' (T. Warton in Todd.) —
XVII. Various readings: v. 7. Kitchin has 'angry'.
  v. 1. the valiant Elfe; — 'the Knight is described as coming from Faerie Land, C. X, 60. 61. The word 'elfe' is A. S. ælf, an elf. The A. S. had Dun-ælfen = mountain (or down) fairy; wæter-ælfen = water-baby; whence the word usually is taken to signify a small sprite, like the Teut. Kobold, etc. E. K., the ingenious commen- tator on the Shepheards Calender, declares that elfs and goblins were originally Guelfs and Ghibelines; the coincidence is curious, but the derivation absurd.' (Kitchin).
  v. 1. 2. he lept As lyon fierce; — cp. Hom. Il. E, 299: Ἀμφὶ δ᾽ἄρ᾽ αὐτῷ βαῖνε λέων ὡς ἀλκὶ πεποιθώς; etc.'
  v. 3. trenchand; — 'the older participial form; so glitterand. It is used in the Northumbrian dialect of early English. See Morris, E. E. Specimens, Grammat. Introd. p. XIV. It may be a relic of Spenser's life in the Northern Counties rather than of French origin (as if from trenchant, etc.)' (Kitchin. — See below.)
    Church in Todd: 'Fr. Trancher, cutting'.
  v. 7. Threatning her angrie sting; —\'a Latin phrase; 'threatening' being used as 'brandishing'. (Kitchin.)
XVIII. Various readings: In Kitchin: v. 8. 'stirre'.
  v. 5. 'i. e. Then wrapping all around her wreathed tail' (Upton in Todd).
  v. 6 sqq: 'Traine in the former verses signifies tail, in the latter deceit.' (Upton in Todd).
  Kitchin: 'traine; — used in l. 6 as = long trailing tail, and in l. 9 as = snare. Spenser (like Chaucer) often allows words exactly alike in form to rhyme together, so long as their meaning differs'. — (See below p. 253.)
5*

All suddenly about his body wound,
That hand or foot to stirr he strove in vaine.
God helpe the man so wrapt in Errours endlesse
        traine!

und schlang ihn dann in seiner ganzen unermesslichen
laenge urploetzlich um seinen koerper, so dass er
vergeblich sich abmuehte, hand oder fuss zu ruehren.
Gott helfe dem menschen, der so verstrickt ist in der
Luege endlose raenke!

XIX.

His lady, sad to see his sore constraint,
Cride out, 'Now, now, Sir Knight, shew what ye bee;
Add faith unto your force, and be not faint;
Strangle her, els she sure will strangle thee.'
That when he heard, in great perplexitie,
His gall did grate for griefe and high disdaine,
And, knitting all his force, got one hand free,
Wherewith he grypt her gorge with so great paine,
That soone to loose her wicked bands did her cons-
        traine.

Voller betruebniss, ihn so schmerzhaft umgarnt zu
sehen, rief seine gebieterin: 'Jetzt, Herr Ritter, jetzt
zeigt, was ihr seid; fuegt glauben zu eurer kraft
und seid nicht schwach; erwuergt sie, sonst wird sie
sicherlich euch erwuergen.' Als er das in seiner
grossen noth hoerte, begann sich sein zorn in ihm
zu regen vor schmerz und hohem unwillen, und, alle
seine kraft zusammennehmend, bekam er eine hand
frei, womit er so gewaltig ihre kehle packte, dass
sie bald gezwungen wurde, ihre verruchten bande zu
loesen.

XX.

Therewith she spewd out of her filthie maw
A floud of poyson horrible and blacke,
Full of great lumps of flosh and gobbets raw,
Which stunk so vildly, that it forst him slacke
His grasping hold, and from her turne him backe:
Her vomit full of bookes and papers was,
With loathly frogs and toades, which eyes did lacke,
And creeping sought way in the weedy gras,
Her filthie parbreake all the place defiled has.

Dabei spie sie aus ihrem unflaethigen magen eine
fluth von schrecklichem, schwarzem gifte aus, voll
von grossen fleischklumpen und unverdauten bissen,
welche einen so abscheulichen geruch verbreiteten,
dass er gezwungen ward, seinen packenden griff matter werden zu lassen und sich von ihr abzuwenden:
ihr auswurf war voll von buechern und schriften, be-
gleitet von scheusslichen froeschen und kroeten, welche
keine augen hatten und kriechend einen weg suchten
in dem grase voller unkraut; ihr garstiger auswurf
hat den ganzen platz besudelt.

XXI.

As when old father Nilus gins to swell
With timely pride above the Aegyptian vale,
His fattie waves doe fertile slime outwell,
And overflow each plaine and lowly dale;
But, when his later spring gins to avale,
Huge heapes of mudd he leaves, wherin there breed

Wie wenn der alte vater Nil zu bestimmter zeit
uebermuethig das Aegyptische thal zu ueberschwem-
men beginnt, seine fetten wogen fruchtbaren schlamm
auswerfen und jede ebene und jedes tiefe thal ueber-
fluthen; wie er aber spaeter beim sinken der wasser un-
geheure schlammmassen zurucckklaesst, worin sich

XIX. Various readings: v. 4. Kitchin has 'else'.
   v. 6. His g a l l d i d g r a t e; — 'the gall was supposed to be the seat of anger (so Greek χόλος and χολή and
Latin b i l i s, used for both), and the sense is 'his anger began to be stirred within him'. (Kitchin).
 XX. v. 1. T h e r e w i t h etc.; — 'this passage is far too coarsely drawn to please the classical critics, who condemn
it with averted faces'. (Kitchin).
   Thus, Dr. John Jortin, the author of the Remarks on Spenser's Poems says: 'Our Poet paints very strong here,
as he does also in this Book, C a n t o VIII. 47, 48. where he describes D u e s s a.
   v. 6. 'The latter end of the sixteenth century was a time of great activity in polemical pamphleteering; and Spenser hints at the writings which sprang from the Roman Catholic reaction. He probably had in mind Cardinal Allen's book
on Queen Elizabeth, and the famous Bull of Sixtus V, both of which had but just appeared, in the year 1588; — if he
alludes at all to particular works. At any rate, he refers to the scurrilous attacks on the Queen, which had of late been
published in great numbers by the English Jesuit refugees'. (Kitchin).
   v. 9. 'Parbreake is vomit' (Todd).
 XXI. Various readings: v. 3. Kitchin has: 'do'.
   v. 5. To a v a l e is to a b a t e, to s i n k d o w n, Ital. a v a l l a r e. (Upton in Todd. — See below.)
   Kitchin: 'When the inundation, towards the end, begins to abate'. In ed. 1590 the passage runs 'his later ebbe.'
But Spenser himself corrected it, in the Errata, to 'spring'. — ·

Ten thousand kindes of creatures, partly male
And partly female, of his fruitful seed:
Such ugly monstrous shapes elswhere may no man
    reed.

zehntausend arten von geschoepfen, theils maennlichen
theils weiblichen geschlechts, aus seinem fruchtbaren
saamen erzeugen, von so haesslicher, ungeheuerlicher
gestalt, wie sie anderswo kein mensch sich vorstellen kann.

XXII.

The same so sore annoyed has the knight,
That, wel-nigh choked with the deadly stinke,
His forces faile, ne can no lenger fight.
Whose corage when the feend perceivd to shrinke,
She poured forth out of her hellish sinke
Her fruitfull cursed spawne of serpents small,
(Deformed monsters, fowle, and blacke as inke,)
Which swarming all about his legs did crall,
And him encombred sore, but could not hurt at all.

Dies plagte den ritter so gruesslich, dass er, fast
erstickt von dem toedtlichen gestank, seine kraefte
schwinden fuehlt und nicht laenger zn kaempfen vermag. Als die feindinn seinen muth sinken sah,
schuettete sie aus ihrer hoellischen kloake ihre zahlreiche verfluchte brut kleiner schlangen aus, (missgestalte ungeheuer, kothig und schwarz wie dinte,)
welche schwaermend rings um seine beine kroch
und ihn zwar arg belaestigte, aber nicht im geringsten verletzen konnte.

XXIII.

As gentle shepheard in sweete eventide,
When ruddy Phebus gins to welke in west,
High on an hill, his flocke to vewen wide,
Markes which doe·byte their hasty supper best;
A cloud of cumbrous gnattes doe him molest,
All striving to infixe their feeble stings,
That from their noyance he no where can rest,
But with his clownish hands their tender wings
He brusheth oft, and oft doth mar their murmurings:

Wie ein anmuthiger schaefer in lieblicher abendstunde, wenn der goldgelbe Phoebus im westen zu
sinken beginnt, hoch auf cinem huegel, um seine
heerde in der ferne zn ueberschauen, acht giebt,
welche ihr eiliges abendessen am besten abweiden;
und dann eine wolke laestiger muecken ihn plagen,
welche alle danach streben, ihren schwachen stachel
ihm einzustossen, so dass er vor ihrer zudringlichkeit nirgends ruhe hat, sondern mit seinen plumpen
haenden ihre zarten fluegel abkehrt und oft ihr
gesumme stoert:

---

v, 7. 'A poetical figure, not a fact; though it was generally believed and related in Spenser's day by both historians and poets'. — (Kitchin). —
    Cp. B. III. Canto VI, 8:
        So after Nilus' inundation
        Infinite shapes of creatures men do find,
        Informed in the mud, on which the sun hath shin'd.
    Ovid. Met. I. 422.
Sic ubi deseruit madidos septemfluus agros   Inveniunt, et In his quaedam modo coepta per ipsum
Nilus, et antiquo sua flumina reddidit alveo,   Nascendi spatium, quaedam imperfecta, suisque
Aethereeque recens exarsit sidere limus.   Trunca vident humeris: et eodem corpore saepe
Plurima cultores versis animalia glebis   Altera pars vivit: rudis est pars altera tellus.
    Mela I. 9. Nilus — adeo efficacibus aquis ad generandum, ut — glebis etiam infundat animas, ex ipsaque humo
vitalia effingat, etc.
    Macrobius VII. 16. Perfecta autem in exordio fieri potuisse testimonio sunt nunc quoque non pauca animantia,
quae de terra et imbre perfecta nascuntur: ut in Aegypto mures, et aliis in locis ranae, serpentesque, etc.
    'Spenser rightly calls the Nile Father. Pater is an appellation common to all Rivers, but more particularly to the Nile, as Broukhusius has observed on Tibullus I. VIII. 23. and many before him'. (Jortin). —
    XXII. Various readings: In Kitchin v. 2: 'welnigh'.   v. 4. 'perceiv'd'.   v. 7. no parenthesis.
    XXIII. Various readings: In Kitchin v. 1: 'even-tide'.   v. 2. 'Phoebus'.
    v. 1. Cp. Hom. II. B, 469 sqq:
        Ἥυτε μυιάων ἀδινάων ἔθνεα πολλά,
        Ἅἵ τε κατὰ σταθμὸν ποιμήνιον ἠλάσκουσιν
        Ὥρῃ ἐν εἰαρινῇ, ὅτε τε γλάγος ἄγγεα·δεύει,
        Τόσσοι ἐπὶ Τρώεσσι καρηκομόωντες Ἀχαιοί
        Ἐν πεδίῳ ἵσταντο, διαρραῖσαι μεμαῶτες.
    v. 4. their hasty supper; — So Milton, Comus, 541:
        'The chewing flocks
        Had ta'en their supper on the savoury herb'.

XXIV.

Thus ill bestedd, and fearefull more of shame
Then of the certeine perill he stood in,
Halfe furious unto his foe he came,
Resolvd in minde all suddenly to win,
Or soone to lose, before he once would lin;
And stroke at her with more than manly force,
That from her body, full of filthie sin,
He raft her hatefull heade without remorse;
A streame of cole-black blood forth gushed from her
corse.

So uebel berathen, und mehr die schmach als die
unzweifelhafte gefahr fuerchtend, in der er sich befand, stuerzte er sich halb rasend auf seinen feind,
entschlossen, mit einem schlage den sieg davonzutra-
gen oder lieber bald zu unterliegen, als noch einmal abzulassen; und fuehrte auf sie einen streich
mit mehr als menschlicher kraft, so dass er von ihrem
rumpfe, voll von garstiger suende, ihr verhasstes
haupt ohne mitleid trennte; ein strom kohlschwarzen
blutes stroemte aus ihrem koerper hervor.

XXV.

Her scattred brood, soone as their parent deare
They saw so rudely falling to the ground,
Groning full deadly all with troublous feare
Gathred themselves about her body round,
Weening their wonted entrance to have found
At her wide mouth; but, being there withstood,
They flocked all about her bleeding wound,
And sucked up their dying mothers bloud,
Making her death their life, and eke her hurt their
good.

Sobald die zerstreute brut ihre theure mutter so
ungestuem zu boden fallen sah, schaarte sie sich ins-
gesammt, vor wirrer furcht ein ganz moerderisches
geheul erhebend, rings um ihren leichnam, im wahne,
ihren gewohnten eingang in den weiten rachen ge-
funden • zu haben; da sie aber dort ein hinderniss
trafen, sammelten sie sich um ihre blutende wunde
herum und sogen ihrer sterbenden mutter blut ein,
deren tod zu ihrem leben und selbst deren verderben
zu ihrem vortheile verwendend.

XXVI.

That détestable sight him much amazde,
To see th'unkindly impes, of heaven accurst,
Devoure their dam; on whom while so he gazde,
Having all satisfide their bloudy thurst,
Their bellies swolne he saw with fulnesse burst,
And bowels gushing forth: well worthy end
Of such, as drunke her life tho which them nurst.
Now needeth him no lenger labour spend,
His foes have slaine themselves, with whom he should
contend.

Dieser abscheuliche anblick, zu sehen wie die unnatuerlichen, vom himmel verfluchten sprossen ihre mutter
verschlangen, erfuellte ihn mit starrem entsetzen; wie er
so auf sie hinsah, gewahrte er, dass, nachdem sie
alle ihren durst nach blut gestillt hatten, ihre vor
fuelle geschwollenen baeuche bursten und eingeweide
hervorquoll: ein tod, den sie wohl verdienten, sie,
die das leben derjenigen tranken, die sie saeugte.
Nun braucht er nicht laenger sich abzumueden; seine
feinde, mit denen er sonst haette kaempfen muessen,
haben sich selbst getoedtet. .

XXVII.

His lady seeing all, that chaunst, from farre,
Approcht in hast to greet his victorie,
And saide: 'Faire knight, borne under happie starre,

Seine Herrin hatte alles, was sich zutrug, von
ferne gesehen; sie nahte in eile, seinen sieg zu be-
glueckwuenschen, und sprach: 'Edler Ritter, der ihr

XXIV. Various readings: In Kitchin: v. 4. 'resolv'd'.　　　v. 8. 'head'.　　v. 9. 'cole black'.　　'bloud'.
XXVI. Various readings: In Kitchin: v. 1. The accent upon 'detestable' is not marked.　　　v. 3. 'gazd'.
　　v. 3. on whom etc.; — 'a cumbrous sentence='while he thus gazed on them, who had all satisfied their thirst
for blood, he saw their bellies, swollen with fullness, burst etc.' (Kitchin.)
　　v. 7. her life, the which them nurst; — 'the life of her who nursed them'. 'Which', in Spenser's day
was used equivalently with 'who', and the article was not unfrequently placed before it. In this place it is relative to 'her',
not to 'life'. The Fr. lequel answers exactly to this usage of 'the which'. In the Spectator, No. 78, there is a criticism
on the Lord's Prayer, in which the writer is clearly unaware of this propriety of usage. 'In the first and best prayer children are taught, they learn to misuse us (who and which): 'Our Father, which art in heaven', should be 'Our Father,
who etc.' (Kitchin. — See below.)
　　v. 9. with whom he should contend; — 'should'='should have had to'; — 'his foes, with whom he
otherwise would have had to contend, have slain themselves'. (Kitchin.) —
XXVII. Various readings: In Kitchin: v. 3. 'happy'.
　　v. 1. that chaunst; — 'that had happened'. (Kitchin).

Who see your vanquisht foes before you lye;
Well worthie be you of that armory,
Wherein ye have great glory wonne this day,
And proov'd your strength on a strong enimie,
Your first adventure; many, such I pray,
And henceforth ever wish that like succeed it may!'

unter gluecklichem stern geboren seid und eure besiegten feinde vor euch liegen seht; gar wuerdig seid
ihr des waffenschmuckes, worin ihr heute grossen ruhm
geerndtet und eure kraft an einem starken feinde erprobt habt. Dies war euer erstes abenteuer; viele
solcher erfolge noch, so bete ich und wuensche, moe-
get ihr in zukunft erringen'.

XXVIII.

Then mounted he upon his steede againe,
And with the lady backward sought to wend:
That path he kept, which beaten was most plaine,
Ne ever would to any by-way bend;
But still did follow one unto the end,
The which at last out of the wood them brought.
So forward on his way (with God to frend)
He passed forth, and new adventure sought;
Long way he traveiled, before he heard of ought.

Darauf stieg er wieder auf sein streitross und
suchte, mit der dame umzukehren: den pfad hielt er
inne, welcher am meisten glatt getreten war, und
wollte niemals in irgend einen nebenweg abbiegen;
sondern immer den einen verfolgte er bis zum ende,
der sie denn auch zuletzt aus dem walde heraus-
fuehrte. So zog er denn mit Gottes beistand weiter
auf seinem wege und suchte ein neues abenteuer;
eine lange strecke ritt er dahin, bevor er von irgend
etwas hoerte.

XXIX.

At length they chaunst to met upon the way
An aged sire, in long blacke weedes yclad,
His feete all bare, his beard all hoarie gray,
And by his belt his booke he hanging had;
Sober he seemde, and very sagely sad;
And to the ground his eyes were lowly bent.
Simple in shew, and voide of malice bad;
And all the way he prayed, as he went,
And often knockt his brest, as one that did repent.

Schliesslich trafen sie zufaellig auf dem wege einen
bejahrten mann, in lange schwarze gewaender gekleidet, seine fuesse ganz nackt, sein bart eisgrau, und
in seinem guertel hatte er sein gebetbuch hangen;
ruhig schien er, sehr weise und ernst, und seine augen waren demuethig auf die erde gerichtet, ohne
falsch und ohne tueckische bosheit, dem anscheine
nach; und den ganzen weg ueber betete er, wenn er
ging, und schlug oft an seine brust, wie einer, der
reue empfand.

---

v. 3. borne under happy starre; — refers to the astrological belief, in nativities:
Stat. Silv. III. 4. 63;

— — — 'O sidere dextro
'Edite, multa tibi Divûm indulgentia favit'.
v. 5, that armory; — the armour of a Christian man. —
Eph. 6. 13 sqq:

Διὰ τοῦτο ἀναλάβετε τὴν πανοπλίαν τοῦ θεοῦ, ἵνα δυνηθῆτε ἀντιστῆναι ἐν τῇ ἡμέρᾳ τῇ πονηρᾷ καὶ ἅπαντα κατεργασάμενοι στῆναι. Στῆτε οὖν περιζωσάμενοι τὴν ὀσφὺν ὑμῶν ἐν ἀληθείᾳ, καὶ ἐνδυσάμενοι τὸν θώρακα τῆς δικαιοσύνης, καὶ ὑποδησάμενοι τοὺς πόδας ἐν ἑτοιμασίᾳ τοῦ εὐαγγελίου τῆς εἰρήνης, ἐπὶ πᾶσιν ἀναλαβόντες τὸν θυρεὸν τῆς πίστεως, ἐν ᾧ δυνήσεσθε πάντα τὰ βέλη τοῦ πονηροῦ τὰ πεπυρωμένα σβέσαι. Καὶ τὴν περικεφαλαίαν τοῦ σωτηρίου δέξασθε, καὶ τὴν μάχαιραν τοῦ πνεύματος, ὅ ἐστι ῥῆμα θεοῦ.

v. 9. = 'and I wish that like (similar) success may henceforth follow it'; literally, 'that like may succeed it'. Another instance of infringement of the natural order of words'. (Kitchin. — See below.)
XXVIII. v. 7. Todd: 'with God to frend: To befriend him'.
   Kitchin: 'with God for a friend'. An O. Eng. idiom corresponding 'to have one to my friend to my foe; or 'freud'
may be a verb and = 'to befriend'. — (See below.)
XXIX. v. 2. An aged sire; — 'Archimago, the chief enchanter; who is also called Hypocrisy. From his connection
with Duessa he may be intended either for the Pope, or the Spanish King (Philip II), or for the general spirit of lying
and false religion. The whole adventure is drawn from Ariosto, Orl. Fur. 2. 12'.

'Volta il cavallo, e ne la selva lieta
Lo caccia per un aspro e stretto callo;
E spesso il viso smorto addietro volta,
Chè le par che Rinaldo abbia alle spalle.
Fuggendo non avea fatto via molta.
Che scontrò un eremita in una valle,
Ch'avea lunga la barba a mezzo il petto,
Devoto e venerabile d'aspetto'.

'Sie schwenkt den gaul und treibt auf engem rauben
Holzweg ihn eiligst durch den dichten wald,
Indem gar oft die augen rueckwaerts schauen;
Denn immer glaubt sie hinter sich Rinald.
Nicht lang' ist sie geflohn voll angst und grauen
Da kommt durch's thal ein eremit gewallt,
Sein langer bart reicht auf die brust hernieder,
Und wuerdig ist sein ansehn, fromm und bieder'.

XXX.

He faire the knight saluted, louting low,
Who faire him quited, as that courteous was;
And after asked him, if he did know
Of straunge adventures, which abroad did pas.
'Ah! my dear sonne', quoth he, 'how should, alas!
Silly old man, that lives in hidden cell,
Bidding his beades all day for his trespás,
Tydings of warre and worldly trouble tell?
With holy father sits not with such thinges to mell.

Er gruesste den ritter artig, indem er sich demuethig verneigte, und dieser erwiderte seinen gruss,
wie es schicklich war; und darauf fragte er ihn, ob
er von fremden abenteuern wuesste, die sich in der
fremde zutruegen. 'Ach! mein theurer Sohn', sagte
er, 'ach, wie sollte ich schlichter alter mann, der in
verborgener zelle lebt und um seiner suenden willen
den ganzen tag seinen rosenkranz betet, nachrichten
von krieg und weltlicher truebsal melden? einem heiligen vater ziemt es nicht, sich in solche dinge zu
mischen'.

XXXI.

'But if of daunger, which hereby doth dwell,
And homebrodd evil ye desire to heare,
Of a straunge man I can you tidings tell,
That wasteth all this countrie farre and neare'.
'Of such', saide he, 'I chiefly doe inquere;
And shall thee well rewarde to shew the place,
In which that wicked wight his dayes doth weare:
For to all knighthood it is foule disgrace,
That such a cursed creature lives so long a space'.

'Aber wenn ihr von einer gefahr, die hier in der
naehe weilt, und von heimischem elend zu hoeren
wuenscht, so kann ich euch von einem seltsamen
manne berichten, der dies ganze land nah und fern ver-
wuestet'. 'Nach solchen', antwortete jener, 'forsche
ich hauptsaechlich, und ich werde dich gut belohnen,
wenn du uns den ort zeigen willst, an welchem jener
gottlose boesewicht seine tage hinbringt: denn fuer
die ganze ritterschaft ist es ein schimpf, dass ein so
verfluchtes geschoepf so lange zeit lebt'.

XXXII.

'Far hence', quoth he, 'in wastful wildernesse
His dwelling is, by which no living wight
May ever passe, but thorough great distresse'.
'Now', saide the ladie, 'draweth toward night;
And well I wote, that of your later fight
Ye all forwearied be; for what so strong,
But, wanting rest, will also want of might?
The sunne, that measures heaven all day long,
At night doth baite his steedes the ocean waves
emong.

'Fern von hier', sagte er, 'in oeder wildniss ist
seine wohnstaette, bei welcher kein sterblicher jemals ohne grosses ungemach vorbeiziehen kann'.
'Jetzt', sagte die dame, 'neigt sich der tag; und ich
weiss wohl, dass ihr von eurem letzten kampfe sehr
ermuedet seid; denn was ist so stark, das nicht bei
mangelnder ruhe auch der kraft entbehren wird?
Selbst der sonnengott, der den ganzen tag ueber den
himmel durcheilt, fuettert des abends seine rosse in
den wellen des oceans'.

XXX. Various readings: In Kitchin: v. 7. the accent is not marked. v. 9. 'things'.
v. 1. 2. Todd: 'louting low; — This seems to have been a proverbial expression. 'They were very low in
their lowtings:' Ray. The word is used in the cause of servilely bowing often in Spenser, and in Chaucer and
Skelton'.
'— Who faire him quited; — Requited, payed him back his salutations again'. (Upton in Todd.)
Kitchin: 'bowing humbly' (as a rustic, in sign of deep humility) to the knight, who returned his salute fairly,
as was courteous from a superior'. 'As that' is exactly equivalent to our present use of 'as'. — (See below.)
v. 6. Silly old man; — 'harmless, simple'. (Kitchin).
v. 7. Bidding his beades; — 'saying his prayers'. (Kitchin).
v. 9. Kitchin: '—it sits not' — 'it is not seemly'. Also in Chaucer. So the French 'il ne sied pas'. Some edi-
tors, following ed. 1609, read 'fits'. — Todd: 'It sits not — 'tis not becoming. Il sied, it sits well, 'tis becoming. So we
say: it sits well on a person, Upton'.
XXXI. Various readings: In Kitchin v. 2. 'homebred'. v. 4. 'countrey'.
v. 5. 'said', and a parenthesis. 'do'. v. 6. 'yon' instead of 'thee'.
v. 6. to shew the place; — 'for shewing', or 'if you will shew'. Like the Greek article with the inf. τοῦ
ποιεῖν, 'for doing', 'for shewing'. (Kitchin. — See below.)
XXXII. Various readings: In Kitchin v. 1. 'quoth he' in a parenthesis. 'wastfull'. v. 4. '(sayd the lady)'.

— 41 —

XXXIII.

'Then with the sunne take, sir, your timely rest,
And with new day new worke at once begin;
Untroubled night, they say, gives counsell best'.
'Right well, Sir Knight, ye have advised hin',
Quoth then that aged man; 'the way to win
Is wisely to advise. Now day is spent:
Therefore with me ye may take up your in
For this same night'. The knight was well content:
So with that godly father to his home they went.

'Goennt euch also, o Ritter, mit dem sonnengotte
eure rechtzeitige ruhe und beginnt mit dem neuen
tage zugleich die neue arbeit; guter rath kommt ueber
nacht, sagt man'. 'Ein sehr guter rath, Herr Ritter,
ist euch gegeben worden', sagte darauf der alte
mann; 'weiser rath ist der weg zum ziele. Nun ist
der tag dahin: daher moegt ihr bei mir fuer diese
nacht eure wohnung aufschlagen'. Der ritter war es
wohl zufrieden, und so giugen sie mit dem gottseligen vater nach seinem hause.

XXXIV.

A little lowly hermitage it was,
Downe in a dale, hard by a forest's side,
Far from resort of people, that did pas
In traveill to and froe: a little wyde
There was an holy chappell edifyde,
Wherein the hermite dewly wont to say
His holy things each morne and eventyde:
Thereby a christall streame did gently play,
Which from a sacred fountaine welled forth alway.

Eine kleine bescheidene klause war es, tief in
einem thal, dicht bei dem saume eines waldes, fern
vom gewoehle der menschen, die reisend hin- und
herzogen; in geringer entfernung war eine heilige
kapelle erbaut, worin der klausner regelmaessig jeden
morgen und abend seine heiligen gebete herzusagen
pflegte: in der naehe trieb ein crystallner strom sein
liebliches spiel, der aus einer heiligen quelle bestaendig hervorwallte.

XXXIII. Various readings: v. 5. Kitchin has '(Quoth then that aged man)'.
    v. 3. night they say gives counsell best; — 'this is a proverb — Ἐν νυκτὶ βουλή, or 'La nuit donne
conseil', or 'La notte ò madre di pensieri'. Upton. Dryden refers to this passage when he writes:
        'Well might the ancient poets then confer
        On Night the honored name of Counseller'. (Kitchin).
XXXIV. Various readings: v. 2. Kitchin has 'forests'.   v. 4. Kitchin has 'travell'.
    v. 4. a little wyde; — 'a little apart', or 'at a little distance'. (Kitchin).
    v. 5. edifyde; — 'Built'. (Todd.)
    Kitchin: 'built; a Latinism (aedificare) — shewing, that in the sixteenth century the terms 'edi-
fy', 'edification', had not caught their modern technical and exclusive signification; and that in the time of the translators
of the Bible the word conveyed St. Paul's meaning more exactly than it does now. Mr. Wright, in his Bible Word-Book,
in referring to this passage says that 'Spenser affects archaisms'; perhaps it would be more exact to say that he here affects
Latinisms; for 'to edify', and 'edification', are used by others of his age in their first sense'. (See below).
    v. 6. wont to say; — '(was) wont'. (Kitchin).
    v. 9. 'So sacri fontes frequently occur in the ancient poets, they are call'd divini in some In-
scriptions.
        Καὶ ποταμῶν ζαθέων κελαδήματα, —   (Aristophanes, Nub. 282).
    Heads of Rivers, and Fountains had temples and altars erected to them, and other divine honours paid to
them. See Grutor's Inscript. No. 94. 1072. Fabretti, p. 432. Spon. Misc. Erud. Ant. p. 31. Frontinus, de Aquaed. p.
225. Pausanias VI, 22.
    Cicero de Nat. Deor. XX: — ergo et flumina et fontes. Itaque et Fontis delubrum Maso ex Corsica dedicavit
et in augurum precatione Tiberinum, Spinonem, Almonem, Nodinum, alia propinquorum fluminum nomina videmus.
    Tacitus, Annal. XIV, 22; Iisdem diebus nimia luxus cupido infamiam' et periculum Neroni tulit, quia fontem
aquae Marciae (Marsyae? in the notes), ad urbem deductae, nando incesserat; videbaturque potus sacros, et caerimoniam
loci corpore loto polluisse. Secutaque anceps valetudo iram Deum affirmavit.
    Seneca, Epist. XLI: Magnorum fluminum capita veneramur: subita et ex abdito vasti amnis eruptio aras habet;
coluntur aquarum calentium fontes: et stagna quaedam, vel opacitas vel immensa altitudo sacravit.
    Homer, Il. E, 77: — ὅς ῥα Σκαμάνδρου Ἀρητῆρ ἐτέτυκτο.
    Horat. Carm. III, XIII; O fons Bandusiae, splendidior vitro etc.
    This was part of the religion of the Persians:
    Herodotus 1. 138: Ἐς ποταμὸν δὲ οὔτε ἐνουρέουσι, οὔτε ἐμπτύουσι οἱ χεῖρας ἐναπονίζονται, οὐδὲ ἄλλον οὐδένα
περιορῶσι, ἀλλὰ σέβονται ποταμοὺς μάλιστα.
    Strabo: Εἰς τὸν ποταμὸν οὔτ' οὐροῦσιν, οὔτε νίπτονται Πέρσαι, οὐδὲ λούονται, οὐδὲ νεκρὸν ἐμβάλλουσι, οὐδ᾽ ἄλλα
τῶν δοκούντων εἶναι μυσαρῶν. Vid. Herodot. p. 588. Ed. Gronov.

6

XXXV.

Arrived there, the litle house they fill,
Ne looke for entertainement, where none was;
Rest is their feast, and all thinges at their will:
The noblest mind the best contentment has.
With faire discourse the evening so they pas;
For that olde man of pleasing wordes had store,
And well could file his tongue, as smooth as glas:
He told of saintes and popes, and evermore
He strowd an Ave-Mary after and before.

Dort angelangt, fuellen sie das kleine haus und
suchen keine bewirthung, wo keine war; ruhe ist ihr
labsal und so gut als haetten sie alles, was sie
wuenschten; je edler der Sinn, desto zufriedener.
Mit freundlichem gespraech bringen sie so den abend
hin; denn jenem alten manne stand eine fuelle hol-
der worte zu gebote, und wohl konnte er seine zunge
glaetten, so glatt wie glas: er erzaehlte von heiligen und paepsten, und stets streute er vorher und
nachher ein Ave-Maria ein.

XXXVI.

The drouping night thus creepeth on them fast;
And the sad humor loading their eye-liddes,
As messenger of Morpheus, on them cast
Sweet slombring deaw, the which to sleep them biddes.
Unto their lodgings then his guestes he riddes,
Where when all drownd in deadly sleepe he findes.
He to his studie goes; and there amiddes
His magick bookes, and artes of sundrie kindes,
He seeks out mighty charmes to trouble sleepy minds.

Die hereinbrechende nacht beschleicht sie auf diese
weise schnell; und die truebe fluessiggeit beschwerte
ihre augenlieder, als bote des Morpheus, und senkte
suessen schlummertau auf sie herab, der sie zum
schlafen einladet. Zu ihren gemaechern geleitet er
sodann seine gaeste; und als er dort alles in todes-
aehnlichen schlummer versenkt findet, geht er in sein
studierzimmer; und dort sucht er, inmitten seiner
zauberbuecher und kuenste mancherlei art, maechtige
zaubermittel aus, um schlafende seelen zu quaelen.

Book II. Canto IX.[1]

The House of Temperance, in which
Doth sober Alma dwell,
Besieged of many foes, whom straunge-
er knightes to flight compell.

Das Haus der Maessigkeit, in welchem die
besonnene Alma wohnt, belagert von vielen
feinden, die fremde ritter zur flucht zwingen.

I.

Of all Gods workes, which doo this worlde adorne,
There is no one more faire and excellent
Then is mans body, both for powre and forme,
Whiles it is kept in sober government;
But none then it more fowle and indecent,
Distempred through misrule and passions bace;
It grows a monster, and incontinent
Doth lose his dignity and native grace.
Behold, who list, both one und other in this place.

Von allen Gotteswerken, welche diese welt schmuck-
en, giebt es nicht eines, das schoener und herrlicher waere als der mensch, an kraft sowohl als
an schoenheit, so lange er sich in besonnener
beherrschung haelt; aber keines abscheulicher und
haesslicher, wenn er durch unfug und niedrige
leidenschaft entstellt ist; er wird ein ungeheuer
und verliert unverzueglich seine wuerde und natuerliche anmuth. Wem es beliebt, kann beides an dieser stelle schauen.

XXXV. v. 3. Kitchin: 'rest is a good as the having all things as they might wish'.
v. 7. Todd: 'This expression we often find both in our poet, and in those old poets whom he imitated'. 'Tis a Gal-
licism: Avoir la langue bien affilée. Upton'.
XXXVI. Various readings: v. 2. Kitchin has: 'humour'; 'eye liddes'.
v. 3. Morpheus; — 'the god of sleep, who sprinkles the 'slombring deaw' of sleep from his horn, or off his
wings, or from the branch he carries, dipped in Lethean stream. He is the god of dreams, as his name indicates; — the
formative power in sleep'. (Kitchin. Cp. μαρμάω, μορφή.)
Motto. Various readings: In Kitchin: v. 3. 'Besiegd'; 'straunger'. v. 4: ed. 1596 reads 'fight'.
I. Various readings: In Kitchin: v. 8. 'dignitie'.
[1] 'This Canto contains a special allegory within the main one. It shadows out, with many quaint fancies, the

II.

After the Paynim brethren conquer'd were,
The Briton prince recov'ring his stolne sword, .
And Guyon his lost shield, they both yfere
Forth passed on their way in fayre accord.
Till him the prince with gentle court did bord;
'Sir knight, mote I of you this court'sy read,
To weet why on your shield, so goodly scord,
Beare ye the picture of that ladies head!
Full lively is the semblaunt. though the substance
dead'.

Nachdem die Heidnischen brueder besiegt waren,
der Britische fuerst sein gestohlenes schwert und
Guyon seinen verlornen schild wiedererlangt hatten,
zogen sie beide fort auf ihrem wege zusammen in
schoener eintracht, bis letzterer von dem fuersten mit
artiger hoeflichkeit also angeredet wurde: 'Herr Ritter,
darf ich euch um die gefaelligkeit ersuchen, mich
wissen zu lassen, warum ihr auf eurem so praechtig
gezierten schilde das bildniss von dieser dame haupt
tragt? gar lebhaft ist der ausdruck, wenn auch das
original todt ist'.

III.[1])

'Fayre sir', sayd he, 'if in that picture dead
Such life ye read, and vertue in vaine shew;
What mote ye weene, if the trew lively-head
Of that most glorious visage he[2]) did vew!
But yf the beauty of her mind ye knew,
That is, her bounty, and imperiall powre,
Thousand times fairer then her mortall hew,
O! how great wonder would your thoughts devoure,
And infinite desire into your spirite poure!

'Edler Herr', sagte er, 'wenn ihr in disem todten
gemaelde solches leben findet und tugend in einem
unbedeutenden schaustueck; was muesstet ihr meinen,
wenn ihr das wahre lebendige haupt dieses herrlich-
sten aller antlitze saehet! Aber wenn ihr die schoenheit ihres gemuethes konntet, d. h. ihre guete und
herrschermacht, tausendmal herrlicher, als ihre sterbliche huelle, — o! wie grosse bewunderung wuerde
sich eurer gedanken bemeistern und unendliches seh-
nen in euer gemueth ausstroemen!

IV.

'She is the mighty Queene of Faëry,
Whose faire retraitt I in my shield doe beare;
Shee is the flowre of grace and chastity,
Throughout the world renowmed far and neare,
My life, my liege, my soveraine. my deare.

'Es ist die maechtige Feenkoeniginn, deren holdes bildniss ich auf meinem schilde trage; sie ist
die blume des liebreizes und der keuschheit, durch
die ganze welt weit und nah beruehmt, mein leben,
meine herrinn, meine fuerstinn, meine liebe, deren

---

soul (Alma, anima) dwelling in the body (the House of Temperance). Body and soul are assaulted by many foes, who
strive to occupy the senses, and so to get footing within, and to lead captive the soul. The subject became a favourite one
with religious writers, and others. Fletcher's Purple Island is an allegorical poem on man; Bunyan's Mansoul is a spiritu-
alised, or perhaps rather a Puritanised, form of the struggle here pourtrayed. The enemies here drawn are moral (according to
Spenser's general conception of this Book): in Bunyan they are spiritual. The soul displays her dwelling-place to her visit-
ors. The frame of it, described in stanzas 21—32, gives us the 'dwelling of clay' (st. 21), the mystical harmonies of body
and soul (st. 22), the mouth (st. 23), the lips (st. 24), the tongue (st. 25), the teeth (st. 26), then eating and appetite
(st. 27, 28), then the stomach, lungs, digestion, etc. (st. 29—32), After that come various moral qualities, seated in the
breast (st. 33 - 43). especially Praps-desire, or love of approbation (st. 36—39), and Modesty (st. 40—43). Then the men-
tal qualities, seated in the brain. The head is first described, with the hair and eyes (st. 45, 46). Lastly are pourtrayed
the three dwellers in the brain, Imagination (st. 49—52), Judgment)st. 53), and Memory (st. 54—58)'. (Kitchin).
   v. 9. in this place; — 'That is, in the opposite characters of Prince Arthur and the Two Brethren'. (Church
in Todd).
   Kitchin: 'i. e. in Book II, and especially in Canto VIII, we have 'both one and other' in the dignity and chiv-
alric purity of Arthur and Guyon, and in the ungoverned baseness of Pyrochles and Cymocles'.
   II.   In Kitchin: v. 4. 'faire'.   v. 6. curt'sie.
   v. 9. the substance dead; — 'i. e. it is only a picture of the living lady'. (Kitchin).
   [1]) St. 3—5. 'The praises of Queen Elizabeth'; they run through the usual scale, but none the less express the
genuine feeling of the time. Men were willing to erect her into a kind of Protestant Madonna, and to dedicate themselves
to her service; that service being also felt to be the service of truth and liberty'. (Kitchin.)
   [2]) A misprint. Kitchin and Todd have 'ye'.
   III.   Various readings: In Kitchin: v. 1. 'Faire'; '(sayd he)'.   v. 6. 'bountie'.   v. 7. 'than'.
   IV.   Various readings: In Kitchin: v. 1. 'Faerie'.   v. 2. 'retrait'.   v. 3. 'chastitie'.
   v. 5. 'soveraigne'.   v. 8. 'prayses'.

6*

Whoso glory shineth as the morning starre,
And with her light the earth enlumines cleare;
Far reach her mercies, and her praises farre,
As well in state of peace, as puissaunce in warre'.

ruhm glaenzt wie der morgenstern, und die mit ihrem
glanze die erde hell erleuchtet; fern reicht ihre gnade
und ihre ehre weit im frieden, wie ihre macht im
kriege'.

V.

'Thrise happy man', said then the Briton knight,
'Whom gracious lott and thy great valiaunce
Have made thee soldier of that princesse bright,
Which with her bounty and glad countenaunce
Doth blesse her servaunts, and them high advaunce!
How may straunge knight hope ever to aspire,
By faithfull service and meete amenaunce
Unto such blisse? sufficient were that hire
For losse of thousand lives, to die at her desire'.

'Dreimal gluecklicher mensch', sagte darauf der
Britische ritter, 'den das guetige geschick und seine
grosse tapferkeit zum kaempfer jener hehren fuerstinn
gemacht hat, welche durch ihre guete und erfreuende
gunst ihre diener segnet und sie hoch erhoeht! Wie
darf ein unbekannter ritter hoffen, durch treuen dienst
und schickliche fuehrung zu solcher seeligkeit zu ge-
langen? auf ihren wunsch zu sterben, das waere hin-
reichender lohn fuer den verlust von tausend leben.

VI.

Said Guyon: 'Noble lord, what meed so great,
Or grace of earthly prince so soveraine,
But by your wondrous worth and warlike feat
Ye well may hope, and easily attaine?
But were your will her sold to entertaine,
And numbred be mongst Knights of Maydenhed,
Great guerdon, well I wote, should you remaine,
And in her favor high bee reckoned,
As Arthegall and Sophy now beene honored'.

Sprach Guyon: 'Edler gebieter, welcher preis ist
so gross, oder welche gunst eines irdischen fuersten
so unumschraenkt, die ihr nicht durch euer wunder-
sames verdienst und eure kriegerischen heldenthaten
wohl hoffen moegt und leicht erlangen? Waere es
vielmehr euer wille, in ihren sold zu treten und unter
die ritter der jungfraeulichkeit gezaehlt zu werden, so
wuerde, das weiss ich wohl, euch grosser lohn zu theil
werden, und ihr wuerdet hoch in ihrer gunst stehen,
wie Arthegall und Sophy jetzt geehrt werden'.

VII.

'Certes', then said the prince, 'I God avow,
That sith I armes and knighthood first did plight,
My whole desire hath beene, and yet is now,
To serve that queene with al my powre and might.
Now hath the sunne with his lamp-burning light

'Fuerwahr', sagte darauf der fuerst, 'ich bekenne
bei Gott, dass, seit ich zum ersten male den waffen
und dem ritterthum mich angelobte, mein ganzes seh-
nen gewesen ist und noch jetzt ist, jener koeniginn
mit aller meiner macht und kraft zu dienen. Jetzt

---

v. 2. — 'retraitt; Picture, portrait. Ital. ritratto'. (Church in Todd).
V. Various readings: In Kitchin: v. 1. '(said then the Briton knight)'. v. 2. 'lot.'
v. 3. 'souldier'. v. 4. 'countenaunce'. v. 7. 'amenaunce'. v. 9. 'dye'.
VI. v. 5. '= To receive her pay. Fr. solde, a soldier's pay'. Church in Todd.)
v. 6. mongst Knights of Maydenhed; — 'the Order of the Garter may here be signified: but Spenser probably only meant that all who entered the Queen's service became champions of her purity'. (Kitchin.)
v. 9. Arthegall; — 'the hero of Book V, 'the legend of Artegall or of Justice'. Under his person is probably
intended Arthur, Lord Grey of Wilton, Lord Deputy of Ireland, Spenser's honoured lord and patron'. (Kitchin. — See
above.)
Sophy; — 'would doubtless have been the hero of one of the later unwritten books. We may conjecture from
the name that the book would have treated of the struggle between Wisdom (σοφία) and Folly'. (Kitchin.)
VII. Various readings: In Kitchin: v. 1. a parenthesis. v. 4. 'all'.
v. 1. Certes, etc.; — 'there are two movements throughout the Faery Queene: 1) that of the several knights,
the servants of the Queen, fulfilling each his own task of resisting some force of malignant evil; and 2) that of Prince
Arthur, who is gradually and very skilfully displayed before us, as the Briton Prince, in search for Gloriana, whom he had
seen in a vision only. This latter movement forms the under-current, but was doubtless designed to become more and more
clear as the action of the poem proceeded'. (Kitchin).
v. 5. 6. 'Ed. 1590 reads:
'Seven times the sunne with his lamp-burning light
Hath walkte about the world;'

— 45 —

Walkt round about the world, and I no lesse,
Sith of that goddesse I have sought the sight,
Yet no where can her find: such happinesse
Heven doth to me envy and fortune favourlesse'.

ist die sonne mit ihrem leuchtenden glanze rund um
die welt gewandert, und ich nicht minder, seit ich
jene koeniginn zu erschauen suchte; dennoch kann
ich sie nirgend finden: ein solches glueck beneidet
mir der himmel und das unguenstige geschick'.

VIII.

'Fortune, the foe of famous chevisaunce,
Seldom', said Guyon, 'yields to vertue aide,
But in her way throwes mischiefe and mischaunce,
Whereby her course is stopt and passage staid.
But you, faire sir, be not herewith dismaid,
But constant keepe the way in which ye stand;
Which were it not that I am els delaid
With hard adventure, which I have in hand,
I labour would to guide you through al Faery-land'.

'Das schicksal, der feind ruhmreicher unterneh-
mung', sagte Guyon, 'gewaehrt der tugend selten
hilfe; vielmehr wirft es ihr unheil und missgeschick
in den weg, wodurch ihr lauf gehemmt und ihr gang
behindert wird. Seid aber nicht verzagt hierueber,
tapfrer herr, sondern bleibt bestaendig in dem wege,
in dem ihr euch befindet; waere ich nicht durch ein
beschwerliches abenteuer behindert, das ich vorhabe,
wuerde ich mich bemuehen, euch durch das ganze
Feenland zu leiten'.

IX.

'Gramercy, sir', said he, 'but mote I woete
What straunge adventure doe ye now pursew?
Perhaps my succour or advizement meete
Mote stead you much your purpose to subdew'.
Then gan Sir Guyon all the story shew
Of false Acrasia, and her wicked wiles;
Which to avenge, the palmer him forth drew
From Faery court. So talked they, the whiles
They wasted had much way, and mesurd many miles.

'Besten dank, herr', sagte er, 'aber darf ich wissen, welches seltsame abenteuer ihr jetzt vorhabt?
vielleicht mag meine hilfe oder ein nuetzlicher rath
euch dabei ganz dienlich sein, euer vorhaben auszu-
fuehren'. Darauf begann Herr Guyon die ganze geschichte zu erzaehlen von der gottlosen Acrasia und
ihren gottlosen raenken, und wie ihn der pilger vom
Feenhof fortzog, diese zu raechen. So sprachen sie,
waehreud sie eine grosse strecke zuruecklegten und
viele meilen durcheilten.

X.

And now faire Phoebus gan decline in haste
His weary wagon to the westerne vale,
Whenas they spide a goodly castle, plaste
Foreby a river in a pleasaunt dale;
Which choosing for that evenings hospitale,
They thether marcht: but when they came in sight,
And from their sweaty coursers did avale,
They found the gates fast barred long ere night,
And every loup fast lockt, as fearing foes despight.

Und nun begann der herrliche Phoebus in eile
seinen mueden wagen zum westlichen thale zu neigen,
als sie ein huebsches schloss erspaehten, welches dicht
an einem fluss in einem gefaelligen thale lag; dies
waehlten sie zur herberge fuer jene nacht und zogen
dorthin: aber als sie ankamen und von ihren schweiss-
triefenden rennern stiegen, fanden sie die thore fest
verriegelt, obgleich es lange noch nicht nacht war,
und jede spalte fest verschlossen, als wenn man fein-
destuecke fuerchtete.

shewing that Spenser at first meant to describe Prince Arthur as having already spent seven years in his quest of the Faery
Queene; but that on second thoughts he considered that too long a space, and altered it to one year'. (Kitchin.)
    VIII. Various readings: In Kitchin: v. 2. 'Seldome (said Guyon).'   v. 9. 'Faery land'.
        v. 1. Todd: 'Chevisaunce is enterprise, from the Fr. chevissaunce'.
        Kitchin: 'Fortune the foe, etc.; — 'cp. Seneca, Herc. Fur. 523: 'O Fortuna, viris invida fortibus'. (Upton).
There is probably an allusion to the popular old ballad of 'Fortune, my foe', of which the first verse has been preserved by
Malone, beginning
                    'Fortune, my foe, why dost thou frown on me,
                    And will my fortune never better be?'
    IX.   v. 1. weete; — 'edd. 1590, 1596 read 'wote', but the cotemporary marginal corrector of ed. 1590 writes 'weete',
which is required by the rhyme'. (Kitchin.)
    X.   Various readings: In Kitchin: v. 1. 'hast'.   v. 3. 'plast'.   v. 6. 'thither'.
        v. 5. hospitale; — 'Inn. Lat. hospitiolum'. (Church in Todd.)
        v. 7. avale; — 'Come down, dismount. Fr. avaller'. (Todd. — See below.)

XI.

Which when they saw, they weened fowle reproch
Was to them doen, their entraunce to forestall;
Till that the squire gan nigher to approch,
And wind his horne under the castle wall,
That with the noise it shooke as it would fall.
Eftsoones forth looked from the highest spire
The watch, and lowd unto the knights did call,
To weete what they so rudely did require?
Who gently answered, they entraunce did desire.

Als sie das sahen, meinten sie, schimpfliche schmach
wuerde ihnen angethan, da man ihren eintritt von
vorn herein hinderte; bis der ritter naeher heran-
kam und unter der schlossmauer in sein horn stiess,
so dass sie bei dem schalle erbebte, als wollte sie
einstuerzen. Zu wiederholten malen spaehte der waechter vom hoechsten thurme aus und rief laut den rittern zu, um zu erfahren, was sie so ungestuem begehrten. Diese antworteten hoeflich, sie wuenschten
einlass.

XII.

'Fly, fly, good knights', said he, 'fly fast away,
If that your lives you love, as meete ye should!
Fly fast, and save yourselves from neare decay;
Here may ye not have entraunce, though we would.
We would and would againe, if that we could;
But thousand enemies about us rave,
And with long siege us in this castle hould;
Seven yeares this wize they us besieged have,
And many good knights slaine that have us sought
to save'.

'Flieht, flieht, gute ritter', sagte er, 'flieht schnell
weg, wenn ihr euer leben liebt, wie ihr es eigentlich
solltet! Flieht schnell und rettet euch vor nahem
missgeschick; hier koennt ihr nicht eintreten, wenn
wir auch wollten. Wir wuerden es sicherlich wollen,
wenn wir koennten, aber tausend feinde rasen um
uns herum und halten uns schon lange in diesem
schlosse belagert; sieben jahre haben sie uns in dieser weise eingeschlossen und viele tapfre ritter erschlagen, die uns zu erloesen versuchten'.

XIII.

Thus as he spoke, loe! with outragious cry
A thousand villeins rownd about them swarmd
Out of the rockes and caves adioyning nye;
Vile caitive wretches, ragged, rude, deformd,
All threatning death, all in straunge manner armd;
Some with unweldy clubs, some with long speares,
Some rusty knives, some staves in fier warmd:
Sterne was their looke, like wild amazed steares,
Staring with hollow eies and stiff upstanding heares.

Als er so sprach, siehe da schwaermten mit wue-
thendem geschrei tausend kerle rund um sie her
aus den felsen und nahe angrenzenden hoehlen heraus; erbaermliche arme schelme, zerlumpt, roh, ungestalt, alle tod drohend, alle in seltsamer weise bewaffnet; einige mit unbehuelflichen knitteln, andre
mit langen speeren, wieder andre hatten rostige mes-
ser oder in feuer gehaertete staebe: starr war ihr
blick, gleich dem wilder, rasender stiere, glotzend
mit hohlen augen und steifen aufrecht stehenden
haaren.

XI. Various readings: In Kitchin: v. 2. 'forstall'. v. 9. 'entrance'.
XIII. Various readings: In Kitchin: v. 2. 'round'. v. 3. 'adjoining'. v. 9. 'eyes'.

v. 2. A thousand villeins; — 'these are the evil desires, vices, temptations, which beset man's moral nature.
There is also a bye allusion to the outbreak of the 'villenage', jacquerie, etc., that with rude assault, and weapons of the
field, attacked the feudal castles; possibly also a slight allusion to the wild Irish, of whom Spenser was presently to have
such sad experiences. As, in Spenser's mind, the castle and its lord represented knowledge, virtue, civilisation, the part of
the gentleman; so the rude clown and serfs represented ignorance, brutality, the ungentle character. We must not forget
that Spenser was full of contempt for the 'raskall rout', and had no sympathy for any but the gentleman-class'. (Kitchin. —
See above.)

v. 7. staves in fier warmd; — cp. Statius, Theb. IV, 64:
'— Pars gesa manu, pars robora flammis
Indurata diu' etc.'
Q. Curtius, III, 2: 'Invicta bello manus, fundis, credo, et hastis igne duratis repelluntur'.
Vergil Aen. VII, 523:
'— — Non jam certamine agresti,
Stipitibus duris agitur, sudibusve praeustis'.
Arrian Indica, c. 24: 'Λόγχας δὲ ἐφόρεον παχέας, μέγεθος, ὡς ἐξαπήχεας ἀκμὴ δὲ οὐκ ἐπῆν σιδηρέη, ἀλλὰ τὸ ὀξὺ
αὐτῇσι πεπυρακτωμένον τὸ αὐτὸ ἐποίει'.

XIV.

Fiersly at first those knights they did assayle,
And drove them to recoile: but, when againe
They gave fresh charge, their forces gan to fayle,
Unhable their encounter to sustaine;
For with much puissaunce and impetuous maine
Those champions broke on them, that forst them fly,
Like scattered sheepe, whenas the shepherds swaine
A lion and a tigre doth espye
With greedy pace forth rushing from the forest nye.

Grimmig griffen sie zuerst die ritter an und zwangen sie, sich zurueckzuziehen: aber als sie wiederum einen erneuten angriff machten, begannen ihre kraefte zu schwinden, und sie waren nicht im stande, den zusammenstoss mit ihnen zu ertragen; denn mit grosser macht und ungestuemer gewalt stuerzten unsere helden auf sie ein, so dass sie sie zur flucht zwangen, gleich zerstreuten schafen, wenn der schaefer einen loewen und einen tiger erspaeht, der in gierigem laufe aus dem nahen walde hervorbricht.

XV.

A while they fled, but soon retournd againe
With greater fury then before was found;
And evermore their cruell capitaine
Sought with his raskall routs t'enclose them rownd,
And overronne to tread them to the grownd:
But soone the knights with their bright-burning
blades
Broke their rude troupes, and orders did confownd,
Hewing and slashing at their idle shades;
For though they bodies seem, yet substaunce from
them fades.

Eine zeit lang flohen sie, kehrten aber bald mit groesserer wuth wieder zurueck, als vorher; und immer mehr suchte sie ihr grausamer anfuehrer mit seinen schuftigen rotten ringsum einzuschliessen, sie zu ueberwaeltigen und zu boden zu treten: aber bald brachen die ritter mit ihren hell leuchtenden klingen ihre rohen schaaren und zerstoerten ihre reihen, indem sie auf ihre traegen schattengestalten mit aller gewalt einhieben; denn obgleich sie koerper scheinen, schwindet ihnen doch die kraft.

XVI.

As when a swarm of gnats at eventide
Out of the fennes of Allan doe arise,
Their murmuring small trompetts sownden wide,
Whiles in the aire their clustring army flies,
That as a cloud doth seeme to dim the skies;
Ne man nor beast may rest or take repast
For their sharpe wounds and noyous iniuries,
Till the fierce northerne wind with blustring blast
Doth blow them quite away, and in the ocean cast:

Wie wenn ein mueckenschwarm zur abendzeit aus den suempfen von Allan sich erhebt und ihr gesumme weithin kleine trompetenstoesse hoeren laesst, waehrend in der luft ihre zusammengeballte schaar fliegt, welche, wie eine wolke, den himmel zu verdunkeln scheint; und weder mensch noch thier rasten oder ein mahl einnehmen kann vor ihren schmerzhaften stichen und ihrer laestigen zudringlichkeit, bis der ungestueme nordwind mit brausendem wehen sie ganz wegblaest und in den ocean wirft:

XIV. Various readings: In Kitchin: v. 1. 'assaile'.   v. 3. 'faile'.   v. 5. 'such' instead of 'much'.
v. 8. 'lyon'.
XV. Various readings: In Kitchin: v. 1. 'returnd'.   v. 4. 'round'.
v. 5. 'overrun'. 'ground'.   v. 7. 'confound'.
v. 3. their cruell capitaine; — 'Maleger, afterwards described in c. XI. 20—22. He is the incarnation of evil and malignant passions, lord of all temptations, the moral aspect of Satan'. (Kitchin).
v. 4. his raskall routs; — 'This expression appears to have been common for a mob of the lowest kind'. (Todd.)
v. 5. overronne to tread them, etc.; — 'a Latin use, 'Superatos ad terram dejicere'.
v. 6. bright-burning blades; — 'the metaphor is the same as that of the subst. 'brand', because a sword flashes like a blazing torch'. (Kitchin.)
XVI. Various readings: In Kitchin: v. 2. 'do'.   v. 3. 'trompets'.   v. 7. 'injuries.'
v. 1. a swarm of gnats; — cp. above Hom. Il. B, 469.
v. 4. their clustring army; — cp. Il. B, 89:
     'Βοτρυδὸν δὲ πέτονται ἐπ' ἄνθεσιν εἰαρινοῖσιν'.
v. 2. the fennes of Allan; — 'an Irish experience of the poet. The 'Bog of Allen' is the general name for a set of turbaries, spread over a wide surface, across the centre of the country, from Wicklow Head to Galway, and from Howth Head to Sligo, all on the east bank of the Shannon'. (Kitchin.)

XVII.

Thus when they had that troublous rout disperst,
Unto the castle gate they come againe,
And entraunce crav'd, which was denied erst.
Now when report of that their perlous paine,
And combrous conflict which they did sustaine,
Came to the ladies eare which there did dwell,
Shee forth isséwed with a goodly traine
Of squires and ladies equipaged well,
And entertained them right fairely, as befell.

So kamen sie, als sie jene laestige rotte zerstreut
hatten, wieder zum schlossthor und begehrten einlass,
der ihnen bisher abgeschlagen war. Jetzt, als die
nachricht von ihrer gefahrvollen anstrengung und
dem beschwerlichen kampfe, dem sie sich unterzogen
hatten, zum ohre der dame gelangte, die dort wohnte,
kam sie heraus mit einem stattlichen gefolge von
rittern und edeldamen in praechtiger kleidung und
bewirthete sie gar herrlich, wie es sich geziemte.

XVIII.

Alma she called was; a virgin bright,
That had not yet felt Cupides wanton rage;
Yet was shee woo'd of many a gentle knight,
And many a lord of noble parentage,
That sought with her to lincke in marriage:
For shee was faire, as faire mote ever bee,
And in the flowre now of her freshest age;
Yet full of grace and goodly modestee,
That even heven reioyced her sweete face to see.

Alma ward sie genannt; eine herrliche jungfrau,
die noch Cupido's muthwilliges treiben nicht gefuehlt
hatte; doch war sie umworben von manchem feinen
ritter und manchem herrn aus edler familie, welche
sich mit ihr durch heirath zu verbinden begehrten:
denn sie war schoen, so schoen man immer sein
kann, und jetzt gerade in der bluethe ihres zarte-
sten alters, doch voll von anmuth und lieblicher bescheidenheit, so dass selbst der himmel innige freudo
empfand, ihr holdes antlitz zu schauen.

XIX.

In robe of lilly white she was arayd,
That from her shoulder to her heele downe raught:
The traine whereof loose far behind her strayd,
Braunched with gold and perle most richly wrought,
And borne of two faire damsels which were taught
That service well: her yellow golden heare
Was trimly woven, and in tresses wrought,
No other tire she on her head did weare,
But crowned with a garland of sweete rosiere.

In ein lilienweisses gewand war sie gekleidet, welches von der schulter bis zur ferse hinabreichte;
dessen schleppe rauschte lose weit hinter ihr her,
war mit gold und hoechst kostbar gearbeiteten perlen
besetzt und wurde von zwei schoenen zofen getragen,
die indessen dienst wohl unterwiesen waren: ihr goldgel-
bes haar war kunstvoll geflochten und in locken gelegt, und keinen andern schmuck trug sie auf ihrem
haupte, als einen kranz lieblicher rosen.

XX.

Goodly shee entertaind those noble knights,
And brought them up into her castle hall;
Where gentle court and gracious delight
Shee to them made, with mildnesse virginall,
Showing herselfe both wise and liberall.
There when they restod had a season dew,
They her besought of favour speciall
Of that faire castle to affoord them vew:
Shee graunted; and, them leading forth, the same
                                          did shew.

Trefflich bewirthete sie die edlen ritter und fuehrte
sie dann hinauf in ihre schlosshalle, wo sie ihnen
feine unterhaltung und wonniges entzuecken beroitete,
indem sie bei ihrer jungfraeulichen sanftmuth sich
sowohl weise als freisinnig zeigte. Als sie sich dort
eine angemessene zeit ausgeruht hatten, erbaten sie
von ihr als besondere gunst, dass sie ihnen die be-
sichtigung jenes schoenen schlosses gestatten moechte:
sie gewaehrte die bitte und zeigte es ihnen, indem
sie selbst ihnen zur fuehrerinn diente.

XVII. Various readings: In Kitchin: v. 7. no accent.
    v. 9. as befell; — 'as was proper and seemly', answering to the German phrase, 'Wie befohlen ist'. (Kitchin. —
See below).
XVIII. Various readings: In Kitchin: v. 3. 'she'.
    v. 1. Alma; — 'That is, The Mind'. (Church in Todd. — See above).
XIX. v. 5. two faire damsels; — 'the commentators suggest Plato's ἐπιθυμητική and θυμητική under proper govern-
ance. But this is doubtful'. (Kitchin.)
    v. 9. — rosiere; — 'The rose-tree'. (Church in Todd.)

XXI.

First she them led up to the castle wall,
That was so high as foe might not it clime
And all so faire and fensible withall;
Not built of bricke, ne yet of stone and lime,
But of thing like to that Ægyptian slimo,
Whereof king Nine whilome built Babell towre;
But, O great pitty! that no lenger time
So goodly workmanship should not endure!
Soone it must turne to earth; no earthly thing is
sure.

Zuerst geleitete sie sie auf die schlossmauer; die
war so hoch, dass ein feind sie nicht erklimmen
konnte, und alles so schoen und vertheidigungsfaehig
dabei; nicht aus backstein war sie gebaut noch selbst
aus stein und lehm, sondern aus einer masse, die
jenem Aegyptischen erdharze aehnlich war, woraus
koenig Ninus weiland den thurm zu Babel baute;
aber, o jammer, dass so treffliche arbeit nicht laenger
dauern solltel bald sollte er zu staub werden; denn
kein irdisches ding ist unvergaenglich.

XXII.

The frame thereof soemd partly circulare,
And part triangulare: O worke divine!
Those two the first and last proportions are;
The one imperfect, mortall, fœminine;
Th'othor immortall, perfect, masculine;
And twixt them both a quadrate was the base,
Proportiond equally by seven and nine;
Nine was the circle sett in heavens place:
All which compacted, made a goodly diapase.

Der bau davon erschien theils kreisfoermig und
theils dreieckig: O goettlich werk! Diese beiden
verhaeltnisse sind das erste und letzte: das eine ist
unvollkommen, vergaenglich, weiblich; das andre un-
sterblich, vollkommen, maennlich; und zwischen ihnen
beiden war ein viereck die basis, auf gleiche weise
durch sieben und neun in 'verhaeltniss gebracht; neun
war der kreis, der an stelle des himmels angebracht
war; alles zusammen gab eine schoene harmonie.

XXI. Various readings: In Kitchin: v. 5. 'Aegytian'.
v. 5. of thing like: — the 'clay' of which man is made.
Gen. 2, 7: וַיִּיצֶר יְהֹוָה אֱלֹהִים אֶת־הָאָדָם עָפָר מִן־הָאֲדָמָה וַיִּפַּח בְּאַפָּיו נִשְׁמַת חַיִּים וַיְהִי הָאָדָם לְנֶפֶשׁ חַיָּה׃
that Ægyptian slime; — here Spenser wrote Aegyptian for Assyrian. Herodotus speaks of the bitumen
or 'slime' found in the Cissian territory, and of that used for the walls of Babylon.
Her. I, 179: ὀρύσσοντες ἅμα τὴν τάφρον, ἐπλίνθευον τὴν γῆν ἐκ τοῦ ὀρύγματος ἐκφερομένην· ἐλκύσαντες δὲ
πλίνθους ἱκανάς, ὤπτησαν αὐτὰς ἐν καμίνοισι· μετὰ δὲ τέλματι χρεώμενοι ἀσφάλτῳ θερμῇ, καὶ διὰ τριηκοντα δόμων πλίνθου
ταρσοὺς καλάμων διαστοιβάζοντες, ἐδειμαν πρῶτα μὲν τῆς τάφρου τὰ χείλεα· δεύτερα δὲ αὐτὸ τὸ τεῖχος τὸν αὐτὸν τρόπον.
v. 6. Whereof king Nine; — 'Ninus, the eponymic and mythical founder of Nineveh, is nowhere spoken of
as being the builder of 'Babell towre', unless he be regarded as the same with Nimrod, the Scriptural founder of Babylon'. (Kitchin.)
XXII. Various readings: In Kitchin: v. 4. 'fæminine'. v. 8. 'set'. v. 9. 'Dyapase'.
v. 1. The frame thereof etc. — 'this quasi-Platonic passage has much exercised the ingenuity of expoun-
ders. Sir Kenelm Digby made it the subject of a long letter addressed — it is a curious illustration of the age — to a sea-
captain, 'To Sir E. Esterling (or Stradling), aboard his ship'.
He holds that the circle is man's soul; the triangle, his body; the quadrate, the four principal 'humours' of
man's body, viz. choler, blood, phlegm, melancholy; the seven, the seven planets; the nine, the nine orders of angels, which
have to do with man's soul.
There are those who less crudely imagine the circle to be man's head; the triangle, to be formed by his legs
and the ground; the square, 'twixt them both', to be the trunk of the body, of a rough square form. But this gives no
explanation of the three last lines of the stanza.
The just explanation seems to be that 1) the circle is (as Sir Kenelm says) the soul, the most perfect figure,
and, according to Pythagorean language, of the masculine gender; 2) the triangle, also, is the body, the least perfect figure,
as including least amount of space. and so fulfilling worst the special function of a figure; and also feminine by reason of
its feebleness and inferiority; 3) But the quadrate, betwixt them both, is the ancient τετρακτύς or fountain of perpetual
nature: a sacred quaternion. embracing all the members, elements, powers and euergies of man, as Hierocles says, ἁπλῶς
τὰ ὄντα πάντα ἡ τέτρας ἀπεδήσατο. (Hier. p. 169.) Cp. also Cic. de Nat. Deor. 2, 33:
'Et quum quattuor sint genera corporum, vicissitudine eorum mundi continuata natura est'.
In the proportion by 'seven and nine' 4) 'seven' relates to the seven planets, whose influences on man's life and
nature are mysteriously great: see the treatment of the subject in the first book of the Astronomica of Manilius. The subject is also handled in the same way in Cicero's Somnium Scipionis (from the sixth book of his De Republica). Macrob.
I. 6. It forms an usual part of the speculations of the Neo-Platonists as to the relations between mind and matter.

XXIII.

Therein two gates were placed seemly well:
The one before, by which all in did pas,
Did th'other far in workmanship excell;
For not of wood, nor of enduring bras,
But of more worthy substance fram'd it was:
Doubly disparted, it did locke and close,
That, when it locked, none might thorough pas,
And, when it opened, no man might it close;
Still opened to their friendes, and closed to their foes.

Darin waren zwei thore gar schicklich angebracht:
das vordere, durch das alles hineinging, uebertraf
das andre bei weitem an arbeit; denn nicht von holz
noch aus dauerhaftem messing, sondern aus werthvollerem stoffe war es gebildet: doppelt getheilt, griff
es so in einander und schloss so, dass, wenn es zu-
geschlossen wurde, niemand hindurchgehen konnte,
und wenn es geoeffnet war, kein mensch es zu schliessen vermochte; ihren freunden hielten sie es stets
offen, ihren feinden verschlossen.

XXIV.

Of hewen stone the porch was fayrely wrought,
Stone more of valew, and more smooth and fine,
Then iett or marble far from Ireland brought;
Over the which was cast a wandring vine,
Enchaced with a wanton yvie twine:
And over it a fayre portcullis hong,
Which to the gate directly did incline
With comely compasse and compacture strong,
Nether unseemly short, nor yet exceeding long.

Von behauenem gestein war die vorhalle praechtig
gebaut, von werthvollerem und glatterem und zarte-
rem gestein, als gagat oder marmor, der weither von
Irland geholt wird; darueber war ein rankender wein-
stock gepflanzt, eingefasst mit einem ueppigen epheu-
gewinde: ueber diesem schwebte ein schoenes fall-
gatter, welches sich in gerader linie nach dem thore
zu neigte, mit schicklicher rundung und starkem ge-
fuege, weder unziemlich kurz, noch auch uebertrie-
ben lang.

XXV.

Within the barbican a porter sate,
Day and night duely keeping·watch and ward;
Nor wight nor word mote passe out of the gate,
But in good order, and with dew regard;
Utterers of secrets he from thence debard,
Bablers of folly, and blazers of cryme:
His larum-bell might lowd and wyde be hard
When cause requyrd, but never out of time;
Early and late it rong, at evening and at prime.

Im thurm sass ein waechter, der tag und nacht
pflichtgetreu wache hielt und auf der hut war; weder
ein lebendes wesen noch ein wort durften aus dem
thore gehen, wenn nicht in guter absicht und mit
gebuehrlicher ruecksicht; geheimnisskraemer schloss
er von dort aus, ebenso narrenschwaetzer und solche,
die verbrechen anstiften: seine laermglocke konnte
laut und weithin gehoert werden, wenn die sache es
erforderte, aber nie zur unrechten zeit; frueh und spaet
erscholl sie, am abend und am morgen.

---

5) 'Nine', 'the circle set in heaven's place', is obviously the ninth orb of the heavenly sphere, enfolding all things, the 'Summus ipse Deus'. And 6) the whole 'compacted made a goodly Dyapase', i. e. the διἀ πασὦν or octave, the harmony of all the members and elements was goodly. In other words, Man, the microcosm, like the great world, and acted on by that great world, is, according to this philosophy, that 'noblest work of God', afterwards alluded to by Dryden in his Ode on St. Cecilia's Day: 'The Diapason closing full in man'. Cp. also Pliny, Nat. Hist. 2, 22, where, speaking of the Pyth. system, he sums it up thus: 'Ita septem tonos effici, quam diapason harmoniam vocant, hoc est, universitatem concentus'. (Kitchin.)

XXIII. Various readings: In Kitchin: v. 9. 'friends'.
p. 2. The one; — 'so, the mouth. With this fanciful description of the parts of man's body cp. Eccles. 12. 4. Upton also quotes Plato, Timaeus I, 4, and Cic. de Nat. Deor. 2. 54 etc.' (Kitchin.)

XXIV. Various readings: In Kitchin: v. 1. 'fairely'. v. 3. 'jet'. v. 6. 'faire'.
v. 9. 'Neither'.
v. 1. the porch; — 'the lips'. (Kitchin).
v. 3. Marble far from Ireland brought; — 'Todd says, 'Near Kilcolman (the poet's seat) there was, it seems, a red and grey marble quarry: see Smith's Hist. of Cork, 1, 343'. (Kitchin).
v. 4. a wandring vine; — 'probably the beard and moustache'. (Kitchin.)
v. 6. a faire portcullis; — 'the nose'. (Kitchin.)

XXV. Various readings: v. 7. Pitchin has: 'larum-bell', 'wide'. v. 8. Kitchin has: 'requird'.
v. 1. a porter; — 'the tongue, kept in due restraint'. (Kitchin).
barbican; — 'The watch-tower, generally meaning a strong and lofty wall with turrets, intended for the defence of the gate and drawbridge of the old castles'. (Todd.)

XXVI.

And rownd about the porch on every syde
Twise sixteene warders sett, all armed bright
In glistring steele, and strongly fortifyde;
Tall yeomen seemed they and of great might,
And were enraunged ready still for fight.
By them as Alma passed with her guestes,
They did obeysaunce, as beseemed right.
And then againe retourned to their restes:
The porter eke to her did lout with humble gestes.

Und rings herum in der saeuleuhalle sassen an
jeder seite zweiwal sechszohn waechter, alle glaenzend
geruestet mit blitzendem stahl und stark bewaffnet;
kuehne mannen schienen sie und von grosser macht
und waren immer schlachtfertig aufgestellt. Als Alma
bei ihnen mit ihren gaesten vorbeiging, machten sie
eine verbeugung, wie es sich ziemte, und setzten sich
dann wieder nieder: der pfoertner verbeugte sich
gleichfalls mit demuethigen geberden gegen sie.

XXVII.

Thence she them brought into a stately hall,
Wherein were many tables fayre dispred,
And ready dight with drapets festivall,
Against the viaundes should be ministred.
At th'upper end there sate, yclad in red
Downe to the ground, a comely personage,
That in his hand a white rod menaged;
He steward was, hight Diet; rype of age,
And in demeanure sober and in counsell sage.

Von dort brachte sie sie in eine stattliche halle,
worin viele tische sauber aufgestellt waren und schon
geschmueckt mit festlichen wollenen decken, in er-
wartung der speisen, die aufgetragen werden sollten.
An dem oberen ende, da sass, bis auf die erde in
roth gekleidet, eine anmuthige persoenlichkeit, welche
in ihrer hand einen weissen stab hielt; es war der
haushofmeister, mit namen Diet, in reifem alter, im
benehmen besonnen und im rathe weise.

XXVIII.

And through the hall there walked to and fro
A iolly yeoman, marshall of the same,
Whose name was Appetite; he did bestow
Both guestes and meate, whenever in they came,
And knew them how to order without blame,
As him the steward badd. They both attone
Did dewty to their lady, as became;
Who, passing by, forth ledd her guestes anone
Into the kitchin rowme, ne spard for nicenesse none.

Und durch die halle ging der ceremonienmeister
desselben, ein froehlicher bursche, hin und her; dessen name war Appetite: er wies sowohl den gaesten
als den gerichten ihren platz an, so oft sie hinein-
kamen, und wusste sie ohne tadel zu ordnen, wie
der haushofmeister es ihm gebot. Beide erwiesen
ihrer herrinn die gebuehrende ehrerbietung; doch
diese fuehrte ihre gaeste sogleich weiter in den kue-
chenraum, der an keiner zierlichkeit mangel litt.

XXIX.

It was a vaut ybuilt for great dispence,
With many raunges reard along the wall,
And one great chimney, whose long tonnell thence
The smoke forth threw: and in the midst of all

Es war ein mit vielen kosten erbautes gewoelbe,
mit vielen rosten, die sich laengs der mauer erhoben,
und einem grossen schornstein, dessen lange roehre
von dort den rauch hinausliess: und in der mitte von

XXVI. Various readings: In Kitchin: v. 1. 'round'.   v. 2. 'sat'.   v. 3. 'fortifide'.
    v. 2. Twise sixteene warders; — 'the teeth on the upper and lower jaw'. (Kitchin.)
XXVII. Various readings: In Kitchin: v. 2. 'faire'.
    v. 3. drapets; — 'Linen cloths. Ital. drappo'. (Upton in Todd.)
    v. 8. hight Diet; — 'the proper requirement of man's diet, etc., and the connection of health with moral life,
were much pondered in Spenser's time. We see this in Bacon, who, a few years later, busied himself much with specula-
tions and experiments on different kinds of food, etc.' (Kitchin.)
XXVIII. Various readings: In Kitchin: v. 2. 'jolly'.   v. 6. 'bad'.
    v. 2. a jolly yeoman; — 'appetite, vigorous and healthy, like a yeoman fresh from his fields'. (Kitchin).
XXIX. Various readings: In Kitchin: v. 6. 'mighty'. 'furnace'. 'whot'.   v. 7. 9. 'whot'. 'got'.
    v. 1. — dispence; — 'Consumption. He uses it for expence, F. Q. II. XII, 42.' (Church in Todd.)
    It was a vaut, etc.; — 'the kitchens of the time were often large vaulted rooms, built for a great con-
sumption of provender'. (Kitchin.)
    v. 3. one great chimney; — 'as may still be seen in the Glastonbury kitchen'. (Kitchin.)
7*

There placed was a caudron wide and tall
Upon a mightie fornace, burning whott,
More whott then Aetn', or flaming Montgiball;
For day and night it brent, ne ceased not,
So long as any thing it in the caudron gott.

allem war ein geraeumiger grosser kessel auf einen
maechtigen ofen gestellt, der heiss gluehte, heisser
als Aetna oder der flammende Montgiball; tag und
nacht gluehte er und hoerte nicht auf zu gluehen,
so lange irgend etwas in den kessel kam.

XXX.

But to delay the heat, least by mischaunce
It might breake out and set the whole on fyre,
There added was by goodly ordinaunce
An huge great payre of bellowes, which did styre
Continually, and cooling breath inspyre.
About the caudron many cookes accoyld
With hookes and ladles, as need did requyre;
The whyles the viaundes in the vessell boyld,
They did about their businesse sweat, and sorely toyld.

Aber um die hitze zu mildern, damit sie nicht durch
ein unglueck ausbraeche und das ganze in brand
steckte, war dort durch trefliche anordnung ein ungeheuer grosser blasebalg hinzugefuegt, der bestaendig in bewegung war und kuehlende luft zuwehte.
Um den kessel herum waren viele koeche versam-
melt mit gabeln und loeffeln, wie es die nothwendig-
keit erheischte; waehrend die speisen in dem gefaesse
kochten, schwitzten sie bei ihrem geschaefte und ar-
beiteten hart.

XXXI.

The maister cooke was cald Concoction;
A carefull man, and full of comely guyse;
The kitchin clerke, that hight Digestion,
Did order all th' achátes in seemely wise,
And set them forth, as well he could devise.
The rest had severall offices assynd;
Some to remove the scum as it did rise;
Others to beare the same away did mynd;
And others it to use according to his kynd.

Der kuechenmeister ward Concoction genannt, ein
sorgsamer mann und von schicklichem benehmen;
der kuechenschreiber, welcher Digestion hiess, ordnete
alle einkaeufe an in geziemender weise und wandte
sie nach bestem ermessen an. Den uebrigen waren
verschiedene aemter zugewiesen; einige hatten den
schaum zu entfernen, sobald er sich erhob; andre
mussten ihn wegtragen, noch andre ihn entsprechend
verwenden.

XXXII.[1])

But all the liquour, which was fowle and waste,
Not good nor serviceable elles for ought,
They in another great rownd vessell plaste,
Till by a conduit pipe it thence wore brought;
And all the rest, that noyous was and nought,

Aber alle fluessigkeit, welche verdorben und ueber-
fluessig war, nicht gut noch tauglich zu irgend etwas
sonst, brachten sie in einem andern grossen behael-
ter unter, bis sie durch eine abfallsroehre von dort
weggefuehrt wuerde; und alles uebrige, was stoerend

---

v. 5. a caudron; — 'the digestive process. The Hindus hold that one of the functions of fire is digestion. One Hindu writer bids the reader press his hands on his ears, and he will then hear the inward roaring of this fire'. (Kitchin).
    v. 7. flaming Montgiball; — 'Upton quotes L'Adone del Marino, 'Fumar Etna si vede e Mongibello', adding that 'or' is not a disjunctive particle, but that Etna and Montgibel are two names for the same mountain. Montgibel is the Arabic name for Etna; jebel being Arabic for a mountain'. (Kitchin.)
    'Aetna, or, as it is likewise called, Montgibel. Or is not a disjunctive particle'. (Upton in Todd.)
XXX. Various readings: In Kitchin: v. 4. 'paire'.   v. 7. 'require'.   v. 8. 'whiles'.
    v. 1. delay; — Temper. Wine it said to be delayed, when it is tempered with water'. (Church in Todd.)
v. 4. an huge great payre of bellowes; — 'the lungs', (Kitchin).
    v. 5. inspyre; — 'Blow, or breathe'. (Todd.)
    v. 6. accoyld; — 'Stood around, coiled up together, gathered together. Ital. accogliere, from ad and colligere'. (Upton in Todd.)
XXXI. Various readings: In Kitchin: v. 2. 'guise'.   v. 4. no accent marked.   v. 6. 'assind'.
v. 7, 8. 'mind'. 'kind'.
    v. 4. Did order all th' achates; — 'Provisions, old French. achet, a thing bought'. (Todd.)
XXXII. [1]) In Kitchin this stanza is omitted, probably because his edition is made for scholars.
v. 3. vesica urinaria.   v. 4. urethra.   v. 6. intestinum: duodenum, jejunum, caecum etc.
v. 7. rectum.

By secret wayes, that none might it espy,
Was close convaid, and to the backgate brought,
That cleped was Port Esquiline, whereby
It was avoided quite, and thrown out privily.

und zu nichts nuetze war, wurde auf geheimen wegen, damit niemand es sehen moechte, unbemerkt
hinweggeleitet und nach dem hinterthor gebracht,
welches Porta Esquilina hiess, durch welches es
voellig entfernt und heimlich hinausbefoerdert wurde.

XXXIII.

Which goodly order and great workmans skill
Whenas those knights beheld, with rare delight
And gazing wonder they their mindes did fill;
For never had they seene so straunge a sight.
Thence backe againe faire Alma led them right,
And soone into a goodly parlour brought,
That was with royall arras richly dight,
In which was nothing pourtrahed nor wrought;
Not wrought nor pourtrahed, but easie to be thought:

Als die ritter diese koestliche ordnung und grosse
kuenstler-geschicklichkeit sahen, ward ihr gemueth
voll von seltenem entzuecken und staunender bewunderung; denn nie hatten sie ein so wunderbares
schauspiel gehabt. Von dort fuehrte sie die schoene
Alma in passender weise wieder zurueck und leitete
sie bald in ein reizendes wohnzimmer, welches mit
praechtiger tapisserie reich geschmueckt war; hier
war nichts gemalt noch gestickt, nichts gestickt
noch gemalt, was nicht leicht zu denken ist.

XXXIV.

And in the midst thereof upon the floure
A lovely bevy of faire ladies sate,
Courted of many a iolly paramoure,
The which them did in modest wise amate,
And each one sought his lady to aggrate:
And eke emongst the little Cupid playd
His wanton sportes, being retourned late
From his fierce warres, and having from him layd
His cruell bow, wherewith he thousands hath dismayd.

Und in dessen mitte sass auf dem fussboden eine
liebliche gesellschaft schoener damen, umworben von
vielen froehlichen liebhabern, die ihnen in bescheidener weise gesellschaft leisteten, und von denen
ein jeglicher die gunst seiner dame zu erwerben
suchte: und auch der kleine Cupido trieb unter
ihnen seine muthwillige kurzweil, der soeben von
seinen heissen kaempfen zurueckgekehrt war und
seinen grausamen bogen abgelegt hatte, womit er
schon tausende in schrecken versetzt hat.

XXXV.

Diverse delights they fownd themselves to please;
Some song in sweet consórt, some laught for ioy;
Some plaid with strawes; some ydly sett at ease;
But other some could not abide to toy,
All pleasaunce was to them griefe and annoy;
This frownd; that faund; the third for shame did
          blush;
Another seemd envious, or coy;
Another in her teeth did gnaw a rush;
But at these straungers presence every one did hush.

Verschiedenen zeitvertreib erfanden sie, um sich
zu vergnuegen; einige sangen in lieblichem verein,
andre lachten vor freude; noch andre spielten mit
strohhalmen oder sassen in gemaechlichem nichtsthun
da; manche aber mochten nicht taendeln, alle lust
war fuer sie kummer und verdruss; diese runzelte
die stirn; jene schmeichelte; die dritte erroethete vor
scham; eine andre schien neidisch oder sproede; wieder
eine andre nagte mit ihren zaehnen eine binse; aber
in gegenwart dieser fremden wurde jeder still.

XXXIII. Various readings: In Kitchin: v. 3. 'minds'.   v. 8. no accent marked; the like v, 9.
     v. 6. a goodly parlour; — 'the heart, abode of the affections and moral qualities'. (Kitchin.)
XXXIV. Various readings: In Kitchin: v. 3. 'jolly'.   v. 7. 'returned'.
     v. 2. Todd: 'A lovely bevy; — Company'.
     . Kitchin: 'the feelings, tastes, etc., of the heart — music, laughter and joy, flattery, envy, etc.'
XXXV. Various readings: In Kitchin: v. 1, 'found'.   v. 2. no accent'; 'joy',   v. 3. 'idly'.
     v. 7. Kitchin: 'seemed'. — probably a misprint in Tauchnitz.
     v. 8. 'A curious picture of manners, intended to express anger or moroseness. In a letter to Thomas à Becket
(Giles, Patres Eccl. Angl. vol. 39, p. 260) we find a curious description of the passion of Henry II. 'Rex itaque solito
furore succensus pileum de capite proiecit, . . . stratum sericum quod erat supra lectum manu propria removit, et,
quasi in sterquilinio sedens, coepit straminis masticare festucas' — began to gnaw the rushes of the floor'. (Kitchin.)

XXXVI.

Soone as the gracious Alma came in place,
They all attonce out of their seates arose,
And to her homage made with humble grace;
Whom when the knights behold, they gan dispose
Themselves to court, and each a damzell chose:
The prince by chaunce did on a lady light,
That was right faire aud fresh as morning rose,
But somwhat sad and solemne cke in sight,
As if some pensive thought constraind her gentle
spright.

Sobald die huldreiche Alma erschien, erhobon sie
sich alle auf einmal von ihren sitzen und brachten
ihr in bescheidener anmuth ihre huldigung dar; als
die ritter, sie erblickten, begannen sie sich zu artiger
unterhaltung anzuschicken, und jeder waehlte eine
jungfrau: der fuerst traf zufaellig auf eine dame, die
wunderlieblich und frisch wie eine morgenrose war;
aber sie hatte dabei etwas ernstes und feierliches im
blick, als wenn ein tiefer gedanke ihren edlen geist
beschaeftigte.

XXXVII.

In a long purple pall, whose skirt with gold
Was frotted all about, she was arayd;
And in her hand a poplar braunch did hold,
To whom the prince in courteous maner sayd:
'Gentle Madáme, why beene ye thus dismayd,
And your faire beautie doe with sadnes spill?
Lives any that you hath this ill apayd?
Or docn you love, or docn you lack your will?
Whatever bce the cause, it sure beseemes you ill'.

In ein langes purpurgewand, dessen saum mit gold
ueberall durchwirkt war, war sie gekleidet, und in
ihrer hand hielt sie einen pappelzweig. Zu dieser
sagte der fuerst in hoeflicher weise: 'Schoene Dame,
warum seid ihr so verzagt und truebt eure blenden-
de schoenheit durch traurigkeit? Giebt es irgend jemand, der euch dies uebel, oder der euch liebe angethan hat, oder der eurem willen gewalt angethan
hat? Was immer der grund soin mag, es steht
euch sicherlich schlecht an'.

XXXVIII.

'Fayre sir', said she, halfe in disdaineful wise,
'How is it that this word in me ye blame,
And in yourselfe doe not the same advise?
Him ill beseemes anothers fault to name,
That may unwares be blotted with the same:
Pensive 1 yeeld I am, and sad in mind,
Through groat desire of glory and of famo:
Ne ought I weene are ye therein behynd,
That have twelve months sought one, yet no where
cau her find'.

'Edler Herr', sagte sie, halb in geringschaetziger
weise, 'wie kommt es, dass ihr an mir dies weson tadelt
und an euch nicht ebendasselbe wahrnehmt? dem
geziemt es schlecht, eines anderen fehler namhaft zu
machen, der wider vermuthen mit ebendemselben be-
haftet sein mag: nachdenkend bin ich, das gestehe
ich, und ernsten sinnes aus grossor begier nach ruhm
und ehre; aber nicht im geringsten, meine ich, steht
ihr darin mir nach, der ihr zwoelf monate lang je-
manden suchtet und doch nirgends finden koennt'.

XXXIX.

The prince was inly moved at her speach,
Well weeting trew what she had rashly told;
Yet with faire semblaunt sought to byde the breach,
Which chaunge of colour did perforce unfold,
Now seeming flaming whott, now stony cold:

Der fuerst war tief bewegt bei ihren worten, da er
wohl wusste, dass wahr war, was sie auf's gerathe-
wohl gesagt hatte, suchte jedoch mit guter miene
seine errogung zu verbergen, welche indess durch seinen farbenwechsel sich verrathen musste, indem

---

XXXVI. v. 5. themselves to court; — 'to act in courteous style, according to the proper and polite ways of knights at court'. (Kitchin.)
    v. 8. sad and solemne; — 'Prays-desire, or love of the approbation of the good, is dressed in purple and gold, imperially, and is staid and solemn, as one who has noble aims and high desires'. (Kitchin).
XXXVII. Various readings: In Kitchin: v. 5. no accent marked.   v. 9. 'be'.
    v. 3. a poplar branch; — 'Spenser is still thinking of the tree sacred to Hercules, and therefore symbolical of high adventure. Possibly he also thought that victors in the games were crowned with it'. (Kitchin.)
XXXVIII. Various readings: In Kitchin: v. 1. 'Faire'.   v. 3. 'your selfe'.   v. 8. 'behind'.
    v. 9. sought one; — 'i. e. the Faery Queens, in whose presence he desired to be honoured. See also stanza 7 of this canto'. (Kitchin.)
XXXIX. Various readings: In Kitchin: v. 3. 'hide'.   v. 5. 'whot'.
    v. 2. rashly; — 'At a venture, that is, without knowing that she spake true'. (Church in Todd.)

Tho, turning soft aside, he did inquyre
What wight she was that poplar braunch did hold:
It answered was, her name was Prays-desire,
That by well doing sought to honour to aspyre.

or bald gluehend heiss, bald steinkalt erschien: Dann
wandte er sich sanft zur seite und fragte, wer
sie sei, da sie einen pappelzweig halte: es ward
geantwortet, ihr name sei Prays - desire, und
sie suche durch gute handlungen nach ehre zu
streben.

XL.

The whiles the Faery knight did entertaine
Another damsell of that gentle crew,
That was right fayre and modest of demayne,
But that too oft she chaung'd her native hew:
Straunge was her tyre, and all her garment blew,
Close rownd about her tuckt with many a plight;
Upon her fist the bird which shonneth vew
And keeps in coverts close from living wight,
Did sitt, as yet ashamd how rude Pan did her dight.

Waehrend dessen unterhielt der Feenritter eine
andre jungfrau aus jener edlen schaar, welche gar
schoen und bescheiden von benehmen war, nur dass
sie zu oft ihre natuerliche farbe veraenderte: seltsam
war ihr kopfputz und ihro ganze kleidung blau,
dicht um sie herum mit vielen falten aufgeschuerzt;
auf ihrer hand sass der vogel, der den anblick scheut
und sich in schlupfwinkeln versteckt haelt vor lebenden wesen, als wenn er noch sich schaemte, wie
kunstlos ihn Pan schmueckte.

XLI.

So long as Guyon with her communed,
Unto the grownd she cast her modest eye,
And ever and anone with rosy red
The bashfull blood her snowy cheekes did dye,
That her became as polisht yvory,
Which cunning craftesman hand hath overlayd
With fayre vermilion or pure castory.
Great wonder had the knight to see the mayd
So straungely passioned, and to her gently said:

So lange sich Guyon mit ihr unterhielt, schlug sie
ihr sittsames auge zu boden, und ununterbrochen
faerbte mit rosenroth das schamhafte blut ihre schnee-
igen wangen; das stand ihr an wie geglaettetes elfen-
bein, das kundige kuenstlerhand ueberzogen hat mit
herrlichem carmesin oder reinem castoroel. Es nahm
den ritter sehr wunder, die jungfrau so auffallend
erregt zu sehen, und er sagte zu ihr hoeflich:

XL. Various readings: In Kitchin: v. 3. 'faire'; 'demaine'.　　v. 8. 'keepes'.　　v. 9. 'sit'.
　　v. 7. th e b i r d; — 'the owl; symbolical here of a retiring disposition. It does not appear from mythology how
Pan maltreated her. There is a story that Pan had a daughter named Iynx, who was afterwards changed by Juno into a
bird. But I know of no tale of Pan and the owl'. (Kitchin.) — Some say, Iynx was the daughter of Peitho, some that
of Echo.
　　v. 1. The whiles; — 'Sir Guyon's characteristic is moderation and modesty. The strong and true knight is also
bashful and shy'. (Kitchin.)
XLI. Various readings: In Kitchin: v. 1. 'commoned'.　v. 2. 'ground'.　v. 3. 'rosie'.　v. 4. 'bloud'.　v. 7. 'faire'.
　　v. 7. c a s t o r y; — 'edd. 1590, 1596 read 'lastery'; but it is corrected to 'castory' in 'Faults Escaped' at end
of ed. 1590'. (Kitchin.)
　　v. 9. p a s s i o n e d; — 'Disordered'. (Church in Todd.)
　　Cp. Vergil, Aen. XII, 64 sqq:
　　　　Accepit vocem lacrimis Lavinia matris
　　　　Flagrantes perfusa genas, cui plurimus ignem
　　　　Subiecit rubor, et calefacta per ora cucurrit.
　　　　Indum sanguineo veluti violaverit ostro
　　　　Si quis ebur, aut mixta rubent ubi lilia multa
　　　　Alba rosa: tales virgo dabat ore colores.

Cp. F. Q. V, III. 23.

　　　　Whereto her bashful shamefastness ywrought
　　　　A great increase in her fair blushing face;
　　　　As roses did with lillies interlace.

Homer Il. Δ, 141.

　　　　Ὡς δ᾽ ὅτε τίς τ᾽ ἐλέφαντα γυνὴ φοίνικι μιήνη
　　　　Μηονὶς ἠὲ Κάειρα, παρήιον ἔμμεναι ἵππων
　　　　Κεῖται δ᾽ ἐν θαλάμῳ, πολλές τέ μιν ἠρήσαντο
　　　　Ἱππῆες φορέειν. — —

XLII.

'Fayre damzell, seemeth by your troubled cheare,
That either me too bold ye weene, this wise
You to molest, or other ill to feare
That in the secret of your hart close lyes,
From whence it doth, as cloud from sea, aryse:
If it be I, of pardon I you pray;
But, if ought else that I mote not devyse,
I will, if please you it discure, assay
To ease you of that ill, so wisely as I may'.

'Schoene jungfrau, durch euren getruebten frohsinn
gewinnt es den anschein, dass ihr mich entweder fuer
zu kuehn haltet, weil ich euch in dieser weise be-
hellige, oder dass ihr ein andres uebel fuerchtet, das
als geheimniss in der tiefe eures herzens verborgen
liegt, von wo es sich, wie eine wolke von der see,
erhebt: wenn ich die ursache bin, so bitte ich euch
um verzeihung; aber wenn es sonst irgend etwas ist,
das ich nicht errathen kann, so will ich, falls es
euch beliebt es zu enthuellen, versuchen, euch von jenem uebel zu befreien, so gut ich kann'.

XLIII.

She answerd nought, but more abasht for shame
Held downe her head, the whiles her lovely face
The flashing blood with blushing did inflame,
And the strong passion mard her modest grace,
That Guyon mervayld at her uncouth cace;
Till Alma him bespake; 'Why wonder yee,
Faire sir, at that which ye so much embrace?
She is the fountaine of your modestee;
You shamefast are, but Shamefastnes itselfe is shee'.

Sie antwortete nichts, sondern, noch mehr bestuerzt,
hielt sie ihr haupt vor scham gesenkt, waehrend das
siedende blut ihr liebliches antlitz mit schamroethe
entflammte; und die starke erregung that ihrer sitt-
samen anmuth abbruch, so dass Guyon ueber ihr son-
derbares benehmen staunte, bis Alma zu ihm sagte:
'Warum wundert ihr euch, Edler Ritter, ueber das,
was ihr in so hohem grade besitzet? sie ist die
quelle eurer bescheidenheit: ihr seid schamhaft, aber
die schamhaftigkeit selbst ist sie'.

XLIV.

Thereat the Elfe did blush in privitee,
And turnd his face away; but she the same
Dissembled faire, and faynd to oversee.
Thus they awhile with court and goodly game

Darueber erroethete der Elfe im geheimen und
wandte sein antlitz weg; aber sie verstellte das ihre
artig und that, als wenn sie es nicht bemerkte. So
troesteten sie sich eine zeit lang mit hoeflichkeit und

Claudian, R. Pros. I. 269 sqq.
  Coeperat et vitreis summo iam margine texti
  Oceanum sinuare vadis: sed cardine verso
  Sensit adesse Deas, imperfectamque laborem
  Deserit, et niveos infecit purpura vultus
  Per liquidas succensa genas: castaeque pudoris
  Illuxere faces. Non sic decus ardet eburnum,
  Lydia Sidonio quod femina tinxerit ostro.
Statius, Achill. I, 304 sqq:
  Nec latet haustus amor, sed fax vibrata medullis
  In vultus aique ora redit, lucemque genarum
  Tingit, et impulsum tenui sudore pererrat.
  Lactea Massagetae veluti cum pocula fuscant
  Sanguine puniceo, vel ebur corrumpitur ostro.
Ovid. Amor. II, V. 34:
Hoc ego; quaeque dolor linguae dictavit: at illi
  Conscia purpureus venit in ora pudor.
Quale coloratum Tithoni coniuge coelum
  Subrubet, aut sponso visa puella novo.
Ovid Met. IV, 330 sqq:

Quae rosae fulgent inter sua lilia mixtae:
  Aut ubi cantatis Luna laborat equis:
Aut quod, ne longis flavescere possit ab annis,
  Maeonis Assyrium femina tinxit ebur.

  Nescit quid sit amor: sed et erubuisse decebat.
  Hic color aprica pendentibus arbore malis,
  Aut ebori tincto est. — —
Many more passages of ancient writers might be added where these favourite comparisons occur.
XLII. Various readings: In Kitchin: v. 1. 'Faire'.   v. 5. 'arise'.   v. 7. 'devise'.
XLIII. Various readings: In Kitchin: v. 3. 'blond'.   v. 9. 'Shamefastness'.

Themselves did solace each one with his dame,
Till that great lady thence away them sought
To vew her castles other wondrous frame:
Up to a stately turret she them brought,
Accending by ten steps of alabaster wrought.

angenehmem spiele, jeder mit seiner dame, bis jene
erhabene gebieteriu sie von dort wegholte, damit sie
auch die andern herrlichen baulichkeiten ihres schlosses in augenschein nachmen: auf einen stattlichen
thurm fuehrte sie dieselben, indem sie auf zehn ala-
basterstufen hinanstieg.

XLV.

That turrets frame most admirable was,
Like highest heaven compassed around,
And lifted high above this earthly masse,
Which it survewd, as hils doen lower ground:
But not on ground mote like to this be found;
Not that, which antique Cadmus whylome built
In Thebes, which Alexander did confound;
Nor that proud towre of Troy, though richly guilt,
From which young Hectors blood by cruell Greekes
was spilt.

Jenes thurmes bau war hoechst wunderbar, gleich
dem hoechsten himmel rund herum gewoelbt und
hoch erhaben ueber diese irdische masse, die er ueber-
schaute, wie huegel niedriges erdreich ueberragen.
Aber nicht moechte auf dem erdenrund einer gefun-
den werden, der diesem gliche; weder der, den der
alte Cadmus weiland in Theben baute und den Alexander zerstoerte, noch jener stolze thurm von Troja,
obgleich er reich vergoldet war, von dem aus des
jungen Hector's blut durch die gransamen griechen
vergossen ward.

XLVI.

The roofe hereof was arched over head,
And deckt with flowres and herbars daintily;
Two goodly beacons, set in watches stead,
Therein gave light, and flamd continually:

Das dach hievon war oben gewoelbt und mit blu-
men und kraeutern zierlich bedeckt; zwei herrliche
leuchtthuerme, die an stelle von waechtern aufgestellt waren, guben darin licht und brannten bestaen-

---

XLIV. v. 7. other wondrous frame; — the head.
   v. 8. a stately turret; — so Cicero, Tusc. I, 10, says: 'Eius doctor Plato triplicem finxit animum: cuius
principatum, id est rationem, in capite, sicut in arce, posuit; et duas partes parere voluit, iram et cupiditatem: quas
locis disclusit; iram in pectore, cupiditatem subter praecordia locavit'.
   v. 9. ten steps of alabaster; — 'the neck, though why 'ten steps' does not appear.' (Kitchin.)
   XLV. Various readings: In Kitchin: v. 9. 'bloud'.
   v. 6. antique Cadmus whylome built; — 'the acropolis of Thebes, called Cadmeia, named after Cadmus
the Phoenician (or Egyptian).' (Kitchin.)
   v. 7. which Alexander did confound; — 'in the year 335 B. C. Alexander marched upon Thebes, which
had recovered her independence for a moment after Philip's death, took the city with great carnage, and then razed it to
the ground, with the exception of the Cadmeia, which was held by a Macedonian garrison as a stronghold. So that Spenser
is not quite accurate.' (Kitchin.)
   v. 8. though richly guilt; — 'these words have been pointed out as an instance of an unnecessary filling up
of a line. But they are quite defensible when we recollect that Oriental cities sometimes had coloured walls, and even
gilded ones'. (Kit.) — So Herodotus I, 98, describes the seven walls of Ecbatana as all having coloured battlements; the sixth
silvered, the seventh gilt: 'Δύο δὲ οἱ τελευταῖοί εἰσι, ὁ μὲν κατηργυρωμένους, ὁ δὲ κατακεχρυσωμένους ἔχων τοὺς προμαχεῶνας'.
   v. 9. From which young Hectors blood, etc.; — 'referring probably to the fate of young Astyanax, Hector's son, whom the Greeks hurled headlong from the battlements of Ilium.' (Kitchin.)
   Hom. Il. Z, 401 sqq:
                          Ἑκτορίδην ἀγαπητόν, ἀλίγκιον ἀστέρι καλῷ,
                     Τὸν ῥ᾽ Ἕκτωρ καλέεσκε Σκαμάνδριον, αὐτὰρ οἱ ἄλλοι
                     Ἀστυάνακτ᾽ οἶος γὰρ ἐρύετο Ἴλιον Ἕκτωρ. —
   Ovid. Met. XIII, 416 sqq:
                          Mittitur Astyanax illis de turribus, unde
                          Pugnantem pro se, proavitaque regna tuentem,
                          Saepe videre patrem monstratum a matre solebat.
   XLVI. Various readings: In Kitchin: v. 4. 'flam'd'.
   v. 1. The roofe; — 'the upper part of the skull.' (Kitchin.)
   v. 2. deckt with flowres and herbars; — 'hair and eyebrows.' (Kitchin.)
   v. 3. set in watches stead; — 'in the stead or place of watches.' (Upton in Todd. — Cp. below.) 'in the
place of watchmen'. (Kitchin.)
   So Cic. de Nat. Deor. II, 56:
   'Oculi tamquam speculatores altissimum locum obtinent, ex quo plurima conspicientes fungantur suo munere'.

8

For they of living fire most subtilly
Were made, and set in silver sockets bright,
Cover'd with lids deviz'd of substance sly,
That readily they shut and open might.
O, who can tell the praysee of that makers might!

dig: denn sie waren aus lebensfeuer hoechst kuenst-
lich bereitet und in glaenzende silberhoehlen gestellt,
bedeckt mit schirmen, die aus feiner substanz ersonnen waren, so dass sie sich leicht schliessen und oeff-
nen konnten. O, wer kann das lob von jenes kuenst-
lers macht verkuenden! .

XLVII.

Ne can I tell, ne can I stay to tell,
This parts great workemanship and wondrous powre,
That all this other worldes worke doth excell,
And likest is unto that heavenly towre
That God hath built for his owne blessed bowre.
Therein were divers rowmes, and divers stages;
But three the chiefest and of greatest powre,
In which there dwelt three honorable sages,
The wisest men, I weene, that lived in their ages.

Weder vermag ich zu erzaehlen, noch darf ich
schweigen von der grossen kunst und wundersamen
pracht dieses gebaeudetheiles, der die ganze uebrige
welt uebertrifft und am besten zu vergleichen ist
jenem himmlischen dom, den gott zu seiner eignen gesegneten wohnung erbaut hat. Darin waren
verschiedene raeume und verschiedene abtheilungen,
von denen jedoch drei die hauptsaechlichsten und
maechtigsten waren; in diesen wohnten drei ehr-
bare weise, die weisesten maenner, meine ich, ihres
zeitalters.

XLVIII.

Not he, whom Greece, the nourse of all good arts,
By Phœbus doome the wisest thought alive,
Might be compar'd to these by many parts:
Nor that sage Pylian syre, which did survive
Three ages, such as mortall men contrive,
By whose advise old Priams cittie fell,
With these in praise of pollicies mote strive.
These three in these three rowmes did sondry dwell,
And counselled faire Alma how to governe well.

Nicht der, den Griechenland, die pflegerinn aller
schoenen kuenste, nach des Phoebus ausspruch fuer
den weisesten der lebenden hielt, koennte mit diesen
in vielen punkten verglichen werden: noch jener
weise mann aus Pylos, der drei zeitalter durchlebte,
wie sie sterbliche menschen verleben, und durch dessen rath des alten Priam's veste fiel, koennte mit
diesen im ruhme der klugheit wetteifern. Diese drei
wohnten in diesen drei raeumen, jeder fuer sich, und
ertheilten der holden Alma rath, wie man gut regieren muesse. .

XLIX.

The first of them could things to come foresee;
The next could of thinges present best advize;
The third things past could keep in memoree:

Der erste von ihnen konnte zukuenftige dinge vor-
hersehen; der andre konnte ueber gegenwaertige
dinge am besten rath ertheilen; der dritte konnte

---

v. 7. 'Sly' is here used in the sense of 'thin', 'fine'. (Todd.)
XLVII. v. 4. likest is; — allusion to Gen. I. 27: וַיִּבְרָא אֱלֹהִים אֶת־הָאָדָם בְּצַלְמוֹ בְּצֶלֶם אֱלֹהִים בָּרָא אֹתוֹ
v. 8. three honorable sages; — 'these are:
1) Imagination, looking on to the future; youthful, poetical,
2) Judgment, deciding calmly on the present; manly, philosophical,
3) Memory, looking back to the past; aged, historical.' (Kitchin.)
XLVIII. Various readings: In Kitchin: v. 8. 'roomes'. 'sundry'.
v. 1. Not he, whom; — 'Socrates, whom the Delphic Oracle declared to be the wisest man alive. This, he
says, was because he knew how ignorant he was.' (Kitchin.)
v. 4. that sage Pylian syre; — 'Pylian Nestor, τριγέρων; he had ruled over three generations of men, and
was appealed to throughout the siege of Troy as an oracle. His opinion was equal to that of the gods. His mediation reconciled Agamemnon and Achilles, and his advice helped greatly towards the fall of Ilium.' (Kitchin.)
v. 5. contrive; — 'Spenser abounds with Latinisms, which makes me think that contrive may be from conterere, to wear out.' (Jortin in Todd.)
XLIX. Various readings: In Kitchin: v. 6. 'For thy' — at any rate, a misprint, v. 7. 'prejudize'.
v. 1. The first of them; — 'The allegorical persons here spoken of, are Imagination, Judgement, Memory.'
(Church in Todd.)

So that no time nor reason could arize,
But that the same could one of these comprize.
Forthy the first did in the forepart sit,
That nought mote hinder his quicke preiudize;
He had a sharpe foresight and working wit
That never idle was, ne once would rest a whit.

vergangene dinge im gedaechtniss bewahren: so dass
weder eine zeit noch ein verhaeltniss entstehen konnte,
ohne dass einer von diesen das .verstaendniss davon
hatte. Daher sass der erste in dem vorderen raume,
damit nichts seine schnelle einbildungskraft hindern
moechte; er hatte eine scharfe sehergabe und einen
durchdringenden verstand, der nimmer traege war
noch je im geringsten rastete.

L.

His chamber was dispainted all within
With sondry colours, in the which were writ
Infinite shapes of thinges dispersed thin;
Some such as in the world were never yit,
Ne can devized be of mortall wit;
Some daily seene and knowen by their names,
Such as in idle fantasies do flit:
Infernall hags, centaurs, feendes, hippodames,
Apes, lyons, aegles, owles, fooles, lovers, children,
dames.

Sein zimmer war innen ueberall mit absonderlichen
farben bemalt, und es waren darin unendlich viele figuren der verschiedenartigsten gegenstaende zu sehen;
zum theil von solchen, die noch nie in der welt waren noch von sterblichem verstande ersonnen werden
koennen; zum theil von solchen, die taeglich zu sehen
und deren namen bekannt sind, so wie sie in unbe-
schaeftigter phantasie umherflattern: hoellische hexen,
centauren, teufel, nilpferde, affen, loewen, adler, eulen,
narren, liebhaber, kinder, damen.

LI.

And all the chamber filled was with flyes
Which buzzed all about, and made such sound
That they encombred all mens eares and eyes;
Like many swarmes of bees assembled round,
After their hives with honny do abound.
All those were idle thoughtes and fantasies,
Devices, dreames, opinions unsound,
Shewes, visions, sooth-sayes, and prophesies;
And all that fained is, as leasings, tales, and lies.

Und das ganze zimmer war mit fliegen angefuellt,
welche ueberall umhersummten und solchen laerm
machten, dass sie aller ohren und augen belaestig-
ten; in gleicher weise tummeln sich viele schwaerme
im kreise versammelter bienen hinter ihren mit honig
gefuellten stoecken. Alles dies waren muessige go-
danken und phantasieen, einfaelle, traeume, krank-
hafte wahngebilde, schaustuecke, visionen, weissagun-
gen und prophezeiungen; und alles, was erdichtet ist,
als aufschneidereien, maehrchen und luegen.

LII.

Emongst them all sate he which wonned there,
That hight Phantastes by his nature trew;
A man of yeares yet fresh, as mote appere,
Of swarth complexion, and of crabbed hew,
That him full of melancholy did shew;
Bent hollow beetle browes, sharpe staring eyes
That mad or foolish seemd: one by his vew
Mote deeme him borne with ill-disposed skyes,
When oblique Saturne sate in th'house of agonyes.

Unter ihnen allen sass der, welcher dort wohnte,
seinem eigentlichen wesen gemaess Phantastes genannt; ein noch junger mann, aber von dunkler farbe
und muerrischem aussehen, was bewies, dass er voller
melancholie war; mit gebogenen, tiefliegenden, her-
abhaengenden augenbrauen und scharfen starrenden
augen, die wahnwitzig oder wenigstens naerrisch erschienen: man moechte bei seinem anblick meinen,
er sei unter unguenstiger constellation geboren, als
der tueckische Saturn im hause der kaempfe sich
befand.

---

v. 7. quicke preiudize; — 'the Imagination does not really judge, it prejudges; moving too fast for the Reason.' (Kitchin.)
    L.   v. 3. Infinite shapes; — 'the creations of the imagination.' (Kitchin.)
       v. 8. hippodames; — Sea-horses. (Todd.)
    LI. v. 1. 2. flyes Which buzzed; — 'the idle thoughts and fantasies of imagination.' (Kitchin.)
    LII. Various readings: In Kitchin: v. 8. 'ill disposed'.
       v. 2. Phantastes; — The Imagination. (Church in Todd.)
      'φαντάστης, from φαντασία, the 'fantastic' or imaginative faculty. Note the melancholy side of the qual-
ity; what we call the 'sadness of youth'. (Kitchin.)
      v. 8. with ill-disposed skyes; — 'with the stars arranged unluckily; so — 'borne under evill starre', (Kitchin. —
Cp. above.)

LIII.

Whom Alma having shewed to her guestes,
Thence brought them to the second rowme, whose wals
Were painted faire with memorable gestes
Of famous wisards ; and with picturals
Of magistrates, of courts, of tribunals,
Of commen wealthes, of states, of pollicy,
Of lawes, of iudgementes, and of décretals,
All artes, all science, all philosophy,
And all that in the world· was ay thought wittily.

Nachdem ihn Alma ihren gaesten gezeigt hatte,
brachte sie sie von dort in das zweite gemach, dessen
waende herrlich bemalt waren mit denkwuerdigen thaten beruehmter weisen und mit bildern von obrigkeiten,
hoefen, tribunalen, republiken, staaten, politik, ge-
setzen, richterspruechen und verordnungen, allen
kuensten, aller wissenschaft, aller weltweisheit und
allem, was je in der welt fuer sinnreich gehalten
ward.

LIV.

Of those that rowme was full; and them among
There sate a man of ripe and perfect age,
Who did them meditate all his life long,
That through continual practise and uságe
He now was growne right wise and wondrous sage;
Great plesure had those straunger knightes to see
His goodly reason and grave personage,
That his disciples both desyrd to bee:
But Alma thence them led to th'hindmost rowme of
three.

Hiemit war das gemach angefuellt; und mitten
darunter sass ein mann von reifem, vollendetem alter,
der diese bilder sein ganzes leben hindurch betrach-
tete, so dass er durch bestaendige uebung und ge-
wohnheit nunmehr gar weise und wunderbar klug
geworden war; grosses gefallen fanden die fremden
ritter daran, seinen trefflichen verstand und ernste
erscheinung zu sehen, so dass beide seine schueler
zu sein wuenschten; aber Alma fuehrte sie von dort
fort in das hinterste der drei gemaecher.

LV.

That chamber seemed ruinous and old,
And therefore was removed far behind,

Dies zimmer schien verfallen und alt und war daher weit nach hinten gelegt; doch waren die waende,

---

v. 9. 'Oblique Saturne' was of all planets the most malign; Propertius, El. 4. 1. 84:
'Est grave Saturni sidus in omne caput'.
He was considered oold and blighting;
Virg. Georg. I, 336:
'Frigida Saturni sese quo stella receptet'.
Lucan I, 650 sq:
'— — summo si frigida cælo
Stella nocens nigros Saturni accenderet ignes'.
So Chaucer, Knightes Tale, l. 1577, has 'pale Saturnes the colde'. Saturn goes on to say,
'Myn is the drenchyng in the see so waw; The Iallyng of the toures and the walles
Myn is the prisoun in the derke cote;· Upon the mynour or the carpenter.
Myn is the stranglyng and hangyng by the throte; I slowh Sampsoun in schakyng the piler.
The murmur, and the cherles rebellyng; And myne ben the maladies colde,
The groynyng, and the pryvé enpoysonyng, The derke tresoun, and the castes olde;
I do vengance and pleyn correctioun, Myn lokyng is the Iadir of pestilens'.
Whyles I dwelle in the signe of the lyoun, (Knightes Tale, 1590—1604.)
Myn is the ruen of the hilie halles,
    th 'house of agonyes; — 'in astrology 'house' is the τέμενος ούρανοΰ, the district of the heavens in which a
planet rises. 'Agonyes' refers to the belief (alluded to in the Knightes Tale, 1592, 1593) that under Saturn strife and con-
tention (ἀγῶνες) largely prevail. So the almanack called 'the Compost of Ptholomeus' tells us that 'the children of the sayd
Saturne shall be great jangeleres and chyders . . . they will never Iorgyve tyll they be revenged of theyr quarell'; and
again, 'When he doth reygne, there is moche debate'. (Quoted by Mr. Morris, on Chaucer's Knightes Tale, I, 1535).'
(Kitchin.)
    LIII. Various readings: In Kitchin: v. 2. 'roome'.
        v. 2. second rowme; — 'the seat of the Judgment (or Reason); all civil, political, or philosophical learning.' (Kit,)
        v. 7. decretals; — 'Spenser probably only means 'decrees'; he would hardly allude to the Papal decretals; un-
less he means by 'lawes', 'judgements', 'decretals' to signify all law civil or canon.' (Kitchin.)
    LIV. Various readings: In Kitchin: v. 4, no accent marked. v. 6. 'straunger knights'. v. 8. 'desir'd'. v. 9. 'roome'.
        v. 2. There sate a man; — The Judgement. (Church in Todd.)
        v. 9. hindmost rowme; — 'seat of memory.' (Kitchin.)

Yet were the wals, that did the same uphold,
Right firme and strong, though somwhat they declind;
And therein sat an old old man, halfe blind,
And all decrépit in his feeble corsé,
Yet lively vigour rested in his mind,
And recompenst them with a better scorse:
Weake body well is chang'd for minds redoubled forse.

die dasselbe stuetzten, recht fest und stark, obgleich
sie sich etwas neigten. Und darin sass ein alter
alter mann, halb blind, mit ganz .abgelebtem, schwa-
chem koerper; doch lebendige kraft war seinem geiste
geblieben und ersetzte die koerperkraefte durch einen
bessern tausch: denn, wenn ein schwacher koerper
gegen doppelte geisteskraft eingetauscht wird, so ist
das ein guter tausch.

LVI.

This man of infinite remembraunce was,
And things foregone through many ages held,
Which he recorded still as they did pas,
Ne suffred them to perish through long eld,
As all things els the which this world doth weld;
But laid them up in his immortall scrine,
Where they for ever incorrupted dweld.
The warres he well remembred of king Nine,
Of old Assaracus, and Inachus divine.

Dieser mann hatte ein unbegrenztes gedaechtniss;
er behielt die vergangenen begebenheiten vieler zeitalter und erinnerte sich ihrer noch so, wie sie sich
zutrugen, duldete auch nicht, dass sie durch die
laenge der zeit untergingen, wie alle sonstigen dinge
dieser welt; sondern hob sie auf in seinem ewigen
schrein, wo sie fuer immer in unverdorbenem zustande verblieben. So erinnerte er sich auch noch
recht wohl der kriege des koenigs Ninus, des alten
Assaracus und des goettlichen Inachus.

LVII.

The yeares of Nestor nothing were to his,
Ne yet Mathusalem, though longest liv'd;
For he remembred both their infancis:
No wonder then if that he were depriv'd
Of native strength now that he them surviv'd.
His chamber all was hangd about with rolls
And old records from auncient times derivd,
Some made in books, some in long parchment scrolls,
That were all worm-eaten and full of canker holes.

Die jahre Nestor's waren nichts im vergleich zu
seinen, noch die Methusalem's, der doch am laeng-
sten lebte; denn er erinnerte sich ihrer beider kind-
heit: kein wunder also, dass er seiner urspruenng-
lichen kraft beraubt war, da er sie jetzt noch ueber-
lebte. Sein zimmer war ueberall mit jahrbuechern
und alten denkschriften behaengt, die aus uralten
zeiten herstammten, und von denen einige in buc-
chern, andre in langen pergamentrollen gearbeitet
waren, die alle wurmstichig und voller mottenloecher
waren.

LVIII.

Amidst them all he in a chaire was sett,
Tossing and turning them withouten end;
But for he was unhable them to fett,
A little boy did on him still attend

Unter ihnen allen sass er auf einem stuhle, sie
unaufhoerlich hin- und herwerfend und umwendend;
aber da er nicht im stande war, sie alle selbst her-
beizuholen, so war immer ein kleiner knabe bei ihm,

LV.   Various readings: In Kitchin: v. 5. 'an old oldman'.
      v. 3. scorse: — Exchange. (Church in Todd,)
LVI. Various readings: In Kitchin: v. 1. 'remembrance'.
      v. 8. The warres . . . of King Nine; — 'these 'warres' exist only in imagination.' (Kitchin.)
      v. 9. old Assaracus; — mythical king of Troy, son of Tros, father of Capys, great-grandfather of Aeneas.
(Luebker, p. 63.)
      Inachus divine: a river god, and also king of Argos.   He is called son of Oceanus and Tethys, and
gives his name to the river Inachus. (Luebker, p. 453.)
LVII. Various readings: In Kitchin: v. 7. 'records' without the accent.   'deriv'd'.   v. 3. 'infancies'.
LVIII. Various readings: In Kitchin: v. 1. 'set'.   v. 3. 'fet'.
      v. 3. But for; — But because. (Church in Todd.)
      — 'but for that', 'but inasmuch'. (Kitchin.)
      v. 8. 9. Todd: 'These two are known 'by their properties'. The old man, being of infinite remembrance,
was hence called Eumnestes, from ἐν, bene, and μνήμη, memoria, μνησθῆναι, meminisse. And the boy,
that attended on this old man was called Anamnestes, from ἀναμνάω, or ἀναμιμνήσκω, reminiscor, recordor.
Upton'. A mistake, as it seems; Upton, probably, means: 'moneo'.

To reach, whenever he for ought did send;
And oft when thinges were lost, or laid amis,
That boy them sought and unto him did lend:
Therefore he Anamnestes cleped is;
And that old man Eumnestes, by their propertis.

um, sobald er nach etwas ihn schickte, es ihm zu rei-
chen; und oft, wenn etwas verloren oder verlegt war,
suchte es jener knabe und brachte es ihm: daher
ist sein name Anamnestes, und jener alte mann
heisst Eumnestes, nach ihren eigenthuemlichkeiten.

LIX.

The knightes there entring did him reverence dew,
And wondred at his endlesse exercise.
Then as they gan his library to vew,
And antique regesters for to avise,
There chaunced to the princes hand to rize
An auncient booke, hight *Briton Moniments*
That of this lands first conquest did devize,
And old division into regiments,
Till it reduced was to one mans governments.

Dort eintretend erwiesen ihm die ritter die gebuehrende ehrerbietung und wunderten sich ueber
sein endloses studium. Als sie darauf anfingen seine
bibliothek zu besichtigen und alte urkunden in augenschein zu nehmen, da gerieth zufaellig ein altes buch
dem fuersten in die haende, das den titel 'Britische
Denkmaeler' fuehrte; dies berichtete von der ersten
eroberung jenes landes und von der alten eintheilung
in verschiedene reiche, bis es unter Eines mannes
herrschaft gebracht ward.

LX.

Sir Guyon chaunst eke on another booke,
That hight *Antiquitee of Faery Lond:*
In which whenas he greedily did looke,
Th'ofspring of Elves and Faryes there he fond,
As it delivered was from hond to hond:
Whereat they, burning both with fervent fire
Their countreys auncestry to understond,
Crav'd leave of Alma and that aged sire
To read those bookes; who gladly graunted their
desire.

Herr Guyon stiess auch auf ein andres buch, be-
titelt: 'Des Feenlandes Vorzeit': Als er begierig
hineinblickte, fand er dort den ursprung der Elfen
und Feen, wie er von hand zu hand ueberliefert
war: Da sie hiebei von gluehendem eifer entbrann-
ten, ihres vaterlandes voreltern kennen zu lernen, so
baten sie Alma und jenen bejahrten herrn um er-
laubniss, jone buecher zu lesen; und mit vergnuegen
ward ihrem begehr gewillfahrt.

Kitchin: 'Anamnestes; — the Reminder, ἀναμνήστης, from ἀνάμνησις, the faculty by which the lost links of memory are recovered (see Plato, Phaed. 72, E.). Ingenious critics suggest that Memory ought to need no helper, and propose to read 'Anagnostes', or the 'Reader'; alleging that ancient libraries used to have a 'Lector' or ἀναγνώστης appointed as an official in them. But Spenser knew well that aged Memory always does need a 'reminder', to bring out hidden stores of knowledge'. 'Eumnestes'; — of good memory, ἀνάμνησις, εὐ, μέμνημαι, of infinite remembrance'.

LIX. Various readings: In Kitchin: v. 3. 'librarie'. v. 4. 'registers'.
  v. 4. avise; — To look upon. (Church in Todd.) — As for 'for to' — see below.
  v. 6. Briton Moniments; — 'That is, Briton's monuments, or, The antiquities of Britain'. (Church in Todd.)

Kitchin: 'the 'Monumenta Britannica', or a fabulous chronicle of the earliest times. Spenser made large use of Holinshed's Chronicle. It is often drawn almost literally from Hardyng's Chronicle. Partly, perhaps, from Geoffry of Mon-mouth, though this is not so clear.
  v. 8. 'That is, independent governments.' (Upton in Todd.)
  v. 9. 'one mans governments; — 'this does not relate, as might seem at first sight, to the so-called Heptarchy, and its end; but to the division of Britain into small kingdoms, united at last under King Arthur, who, accor-ding to the chroniclers, reduced the whole of Britain under his own rule'. (Kitchin.)

LX. Various readings: In Kitchin: v. 2. 'Antiquitie'. 'Faerie'. v. 3. 'when as'. v. 4. 'off-spring'. 'Faries'. v. 7. 'countries'.
  v. 2. Antiquitee of Faery Lond; — 'a still more imaginative chronicle; whose aim is to glorify the paren-tage and character of Queen Elizabeth. Spenser breaks off the 'Moniments' just before the account of Prince Arthur's birth, in order that the hero may not too soon become aware of his parentage.' (Kitchin.)
  v. 4. Th' ofspring: — 'i. e. the origin, not the descendants. So confirming the view taken in note on Bk. I. VII. 30.' (Kitchin.)

Canto X.

A chronicle of Briton kings,
From Brute to Uthers rayne;
. . . .

Eine chronik der Britischen koenige, von
Brute bis zu Uther's regierung;
. . . .

I.

Who now shall give unto me words and sound
Equall unto this haughty enterprise?
Or who shall lend me wings, with which from ground
My lowly verse may loftily arise,
And lift itselfe unto the highest skyes?
More ample spirit than hetherto was wount
Here needes mo, whiles the famous auncestryes
Of my most dreadred soveraigne I recount,
By which all earthly princes she doth far surmount.

Wer wird mir jetzt worte und klang verleihen, die
diesem kuehnen unternehmen angemessen sind? oder
wer wird mir schwingen leihen, mit denen mein bescheidener vers sich stolz von der erde erheben
und sich in die hoechsten sphaeren schwingen kann?
Eine erhabenere begeisterung, als mir bis jetzt zu
werden pflegte, ist mir hier noethig, indem ich von
den beruehmten vorfahren meiner hoechst erhabenen
herrscherinn ausfuehrlich berichte, durch die sie alle
irdischen fuersten weit uebertrifft.

II.

Ne under sunne that shines so wide and faire,
Whence all that lives does borrow life and light,
Lives ought that to her linage may compaire;
Which though from earth it be derived right,
Yet doth itselfe stretch forth to hevens hight,
And all the world with wonder overspred;
A labor huge, exceeding far my might!
How shall fraile pen, with fear disparaged,
Conceive such soveraine glory and great bountyhed?

Auch lebt unter der sonne, die so weit und herrlich leuchtet, von der alles, was lebt, leben und licht
entlehnt, nichts, das mit ihrem stammbaume wetteifern koennte; denn dieser leitet zwar natuerlicher-
weise seinen ursprung von der erde her, reicht aber
dennoch empor zu des himmels hoehen und erfuellt
alle welt mit erstaunen. Eine gewaltige arbeit, die
meine macht weit uebersteigt! Wie soll meine
schwache feder, durch furcht getruebt, so erhabenen
ruhm und so grosse guete fassen!

I. Various readings: In Kitchin: v. 2. 'haughtie'.
v. 6. 'hitherto'. v. 7. 'auncestries'.
v. 9. 'farre'.
v. 1. Straight from Ariosto, Orl. Fur. 3, 1:
Chi mi darà la voce e le parole
Convenienti a sì nobil suggetto?
Chi l'ale al verso presterà, che vole
Tanto, che arrivi all' alto mio concetto?
Molto maggior di quel furor che suole,
Ben or 'convien, che mi riscaldi il petto;
Chè questa parte al mio Signor si debbe,
Che canta gli avi onde l'origin' ebbe:
Cp. Ovid, Fast. II. 119 sqq:

v. 3. 'shal'. v. 5. 'it selfe'. 'skies'.
v. 8. 'dreaded'. Todd: the same (A misprint in Tauchnitz.)

Wo soll ich stimme jetzt und worte fodern,
Wie sie erheischt so edlen stolles rang?
Wo schwingen leihn dem lied, wie sie eisodern
Die stolzen hoeh'n, da mein begriff entsprang?
Von dichterwuth muss meine brust entlodern,
Weit maecht'ger, glueh'nder, als bis durchdrang;
Denn dieses lied wird meinem Herrn gesungen,
Es singt den stamm, von welchem er entsprungen.

Nunc mihi mille sonos, quoque est memoratus Achilles,
Vellem, Maeonide, pectus inesse tuum.
Dum canimus sacras alterno carmine Nonas;
Maximus hinc Fastis accumlatur honos.
Deficit ingenium, maioraque viribus urgent.
Haec mihi praecipuo est ore canenda dies.

Kitchin: 'This canto, by far the dullest of all, has for its real aim the praises of Elizabeth. It is however interesting as shewing the attention given at that time in literary circles to archæological questions; an attention altogether
uncritical, but giving evidence of the newly aroused national life and feeling. Men were moved to look at the origin of
their race, and 'ad Deos referre auctores', as Livy says. Holinshed's Chronicle had not long been published (first ed, is dated
1587): Camden's Britannia was also new (first ed. 1586), and Stowe had appeared in 1574: but the influence of Holinshed
was clearly very great on Spenser's mind'.
II. Various readings: In Kitchin: v. 5. 'it selfe'. 'heavens'. v. 8. 'feare'. v. 9. 'bountihed'.

III.

Argument worthy of Mæonian quill;
Or rather worthy of great Phoebus rote,
Whereon the ruines of great Ossa 'hill,
And triumphes of Phlegræan Jove, he wrote,
That all the gods admird his lofty note.
But, if some relish of that hevenly lay
His learned daughters would to me report
To decke my song withall, I would assay
Thy name, O soveraine Queene, to blazon far away.

Ein thema, wuerdig der Maeonischen feder oder
vielmehr wuerdig des grossen Phoebus' leier, auf der
er den sturz des hohen Ossaberges und die triumphe
des Phlegraeischen Jupiters besang, so dass alle goet-
ter sein erhabenes lied bewunderten. Aber, wenn
mir seine gelehrten toechter einen beigeschmack von
jenem himmlischen liede verleihen wollten, meinen
gesang damit zu schmuecken, so wollte ich versuchen,
o gewaltige koeniginn, deinen namen weithin zu
preisen.

IV.

Thy name, O soveraine Queene, thy realm, and
race,
From this renowmed prince derived arre,
Who mightily upheld that royall mace
Which now thou bear'st, to thee descended farre
From mighty kings and conquerours in warre,
Thy fathers and great grandfathers of old,
Whose noble deeds above the northern starre
Immortall Fame for ever hath enrold;
As in that old mans booke they were in order told.

Dein name, erhabene Koeniginn, dein reich, dein
stamm, ruehren von jenem beruehmten fuersten her,
welcher maechtig das koenigliche scepter fuehrte, das
nun du traegst, das zu dir fernher hinabgelangt ist
von maechtigen koenigen und eroberern im kriege,
deinen vaetern und ur-urgrossvaetern, deren den
polarstern ueberragende edle thaten die unsterbliche
Fama fuer immer verzeichnet hat, wie sie in jenes
alten mannes buch der reihe nach berichtet waren.

V.

The land which warlike Britons now possesse,
And therein have their mighty empire raysd,
In antique times was salvage wildernesse,
Unpeopled, unmanurd, unprovd, unpraysd;
Ne was it island then, ne was it paysd

Das land, welches die kriegerischen Briten jetzt
besitzen, und worin sie ihr maechtiges reich gegruen-
det haben, war in alter zeit wilde wueste, unbevoel-
kert, unbebaut, unbewaehrt, unberuehmt; auch war
es damals keine insel, und schwebte nicht inmitten

III.   Various readings: In Kitchin: v. 5. 'loftie'.   v. 6. 'heavenly'.   v. 9. 'farre'.
        v. 1. Maeonian quill; — the pen of Homer, called Maeonian, or Maeonides, from the ancient name of Lydia,
to which country Homer was supposed by some to belong.
        v. 2. great Phoebus rote; — 'a musical instrument.' (Todd.)
        Apollo's lyre, the god of music and poetry. He was supposed to be the inspirer of poets. So Odysseus tells
Demodocus the bard, that either the Muse has taught him, or Apollo.
        Homer, Od. Θ, 486 sqq:
                Δὴ τότε Δημόδοκον προσέφη πολύμητις Ὀδυσσεύς
                Δημόδοκ᾽, ἔξοχα δή σε βροτῶν αἰνίζομ᾽ ἁπάντων.
                Ἤ σέ γε μοῦσ᾽ ἐδίδαξε Διὸς παῖς, ἤ σέ γ᾽ Ἀπόλλων.
        v. 3. the ruines of great Ossa hill; — 'the assault of the giants upon heaven, and their defeat by Zeus.'
(Kitchin.)
        Virg. Georg I, 280:
                                Ter sunt conati imponere Pelio Ossam
                                Scilicet, atque Ossae frondosum involvere Olympum;
                                Ter Pater exstructos disiecit fulmine montes.
        v. 4. Phlegræan Jove; — 'rightly so styled in this place, as the conflict between him and the giants was said
to have taken place at Phlegra (Pallene.)' (Kitchin.)
        he wrote; — 'a bold usage of the verb as — 'he described' or sung'. (Kitchin.)
        v. 7. His learned daughters; — 'the Muses. These are attributed to many parents: 1) Zeus and Mnemosyne
(Memory); 2) Uranus and Gaia (Heaven and Earth); 3) Pierus and a Nymph; 4) Zeus and Plusia, or Zeus and Moneta,
or Zeus and Athene; 5) or Aethor and Gaia (Air and Earth), as well as 6) Apollo. In the mixture of mythology and poetry
this was inevitable.' (Kitchin.)
IV.   Various readings: In Kitchin: v. 1. 'realme'.   v. 5. 'mightie'.   v. 7. 'deedes'. 'northerne'.
        v. 2. this renowmed prince; — 'does Spenser mean Arthur?' (Kitchin.) — We think so.
V.   Various readings: In Kitchin: v. 2. 'mightie'.
        v. 5. paysd; — 'Poised. Fr. peser, To paise is thus used in Scotland.' (Todd.)

Amid the occan wavos, ne was it sought
Of merchants farre for profits therein praysd;
But was all desolate, and of some thought
By sea to have bene from the Celticke mayn-land
brought.

der wogen des oceans; noch ward es von fernen kauf-
leuten wegen darin geruehmten gewinnes besucht;
sondern es war voellig oede und, wie einige meinen,
durch die soe vom Coltischen festlande heruebergc-
schwemmt.

VI.

Ne did it then deserve a name to have,
Till that the venturous mariner that way
Learning his ship from those white rocks to save,
Which all along the southerne sea-coast lay
Threatning unheedy wrecke and rash decay,
For saftéty that same his sea-marke made,
And nam'd it *Albion;* but later day,
Finding in it fit ports for fishers trade,
Gan more the same frequent, and further to invade.

Auch verdiente es damals nicht, einen namen zu
haben, bis der verwegeno scefahrer dadurch sein
schiff vor jenen weissen felsen bergen lernte, welche
ueberall laengs der suedkueste lagen, unvermuthetes
scheitern und raschen untergang drohend, und bis
er ebendies land zu seiner scekennung machte und
es 'Albion' nannte, spacter aber, als er in ihm zum
fischergewerbe geeignete haefen fand, dasselbe hacu-
figer zu besuchen und weiter zu betreten begann.

VII.

But far in land a salvage nation dwelt
Of hideous giaunts, and halfe-beastly men,
That never tasted grace, nor goodness felt;
But wild like hcastes lurking in loathsome den,
And flying fast as roebucke through the fen,
All naked without shame or care of cold,
By hunting and by spoiling livedon;
Of stature huge, and eke of corage bold,
That sonnes of men amazd their sternesse to behold.

Aber fern im lande wohnte ein wildes volk von
schrecklichen riesen und halb thierischen menschen,
die nimmer barmherzigkeit empfanden noch guete
fuehlten, sondern, gleich wilden thieren in ekelhaften
hoehlen lauernd und schnell wie ein reh ueber das
marschland dahin fliehend, ganz nackt, ohne scham
oder sorge um die kaelte, von der jagd und vom
raube lebten; von ungeheurer koerpergroesse und
auch von kuehnem muthe, so dass menschenkinder er-
staunten, wenn sie ihre staerke sahen.

VIII.

But whence they sprong, or how they were begott,
Uneath is to assure; uneath to wone

Aber wie sie entsprangen, oder wie sie erzeugt
wurden, ist schwer zu sagen; schwer, den graessli-

No was it island then; — 'a curious forecast of a geological truth. Sammes (Britannia, c. 4) says, 'That this Island hath been joyned to the opposite continent, by a narrow isthmus between Dover and Bullen, or thereabouts, hath been the opinion of many: As of Antonius Volsius, Dom. Marius Niger, Servius Honoratus, our countryman John Twine, and the French poet Du Bartas'. And Camden, Brit. (publ. 1586) writes, 'Inter Cantium enim, et Caletum Galliae ita in altum se evehit, et adeo in arctum mare agitur, ut perfossas ibi terras antea exclusa admisisse maria opinentur non-uulli'. The same was thought to have been the case with Sicily, as Virgil notes, 'Hesperium Siculo latus abscidit', (Kit.) v. 9. the Colticke mayn-land; — 'properly so called, 'Gallia Celtica'.* (Kitchin.)
VI.   Various readings: In Kitchin: v. 5. 'unheedie'.   v. 6. 'For safeties'. — Todd: 'For safety'.
    v. 3. those white rocks; — 'there are cretaceous cliffs 1) on the coast of Yorkshire (Flamborough Head); 2) on the Norfolk coast (Hunstanton Cliff to Cromer); 3) at the North Foreland in Kent; 4) at the South Foreland, from Deal to Hythe (to which district Spenser probably alludes more particularly); 5) in Essex (Benchy Head to Brighton); 6) the Isle of Wight (at St. Helen's on the east and at the west to the Needles); 7) along a portion of the Dorset coast (ending at Weymouth); and 8) on the Devonshire shore (about Sidmouth).' (Kitchin.)
    v. 6. For saftüty; — 'ed. 1590, 'safety' (as a trisyllable).' (Kitchin.); — probably a misprint in Tauchnitz.
    v. 7. nam'd it Albion; — 'So called from the white rocks.' (Church in Todd.)
    'The chroniclers hold that this name comes from the giant Albion (ep. st. 11), Or from alb, white, or from alp, a pasture or hill, or from Albine, daughter of the mythical Dioclesian.' (Kitchin.)
VII.   Various readings: In Kitchin: v. 1. 'farre'.   v. 2. 'giaunts'.   'halfe beastly'.   v. 3. 'goodnesse'.
    v. 4. 'beasts'.   v. 7. 'lived then'.   v. 8. 'corage'.
    v. 2. hideous giants; — 'so Geoffry of Monmouth has it, c. 9: 'Erat tunc nomen insulae Albion, quae nomine exceptis paucis gigantibus inhabitabatur'. (Kitchin.)
    v. 7. lived then; — 'ed. 1590 reads 'liveden', an old pret. inflexion which Spenser seems to have thought too archaic.' (Kitchin.) Cp. below
VIII.   Various readings: In Kitchin: v. 1. 'begot'.   v. 3. 'assot'.   v. 4 'fiftie'.

9

That monstrous error which doth some assott,
That Dioclesians fifty daughters shene
Into this land by chaunce have driven bene;
Where, companing with feends and filthy sprights
Through vaine illusion of their lust unclene,
They brought forth geaunts, and such dreadful wights
As far exceeded men in their immeasurd mights.

chen irrthum zu glauben, der einige bethoert, dass
Dioclesian's fuenfzig schoene toechter zufaellig in dies
land verschlagen worden sind, wo sie aus eitler taeu-
schung ihrer unreinen lust sich mit teufeln und gar-
stigen geistern einliessen und riesen gebaren und so
schreckliche wesen, dass sie durch ihre unerhoerten
kraefte menschen weit uebertrafen.

IX.

They held this land, and with their filthinesse
Polluted this same gentle soyle long time;
That their owne mother loathd their beastlinesse,
And gan abhorre her broods unkindly crime,
All were they borne of her owne native slime:
Until that Brutus, anciently deriv'd
From roiall stocke of old Assaracs line,
Driven by fatall error here arriv'd,
And them of their unjust possession depriv'd.

Sie blieben im besitz dieses landes und besudel-
ten mit ihrer unflaethigkeit lange zeit unsern edlen
boden, so dass ihre eigne mutter ueber ihre rohheit
ekel empfand und die unnatuerlichen laster ihrer
kinder zu verabscheuen begann, die alle aus ihrem
eignen mutterschlamme geboren waren: bis Brutus,
der von alters her aus dem koeniglichen stamme der
dynastie des alten Assaracus herstammte, durch ver-
haengnissvolle irrfahrt hieher verschlagen wurd und
sie ihres unrechtmaessigen besitzes beraubte.

X.

But ere he had established his throne,
And spred his empire to the utmost shore,
He fought great batteils with his salvage fone;
In which he them defeated evermore,
And many giaunts left on groning flore,
That well can witnes yet unto this day
The westerne Hogh, besprincled with the gore
Of mighty Goëmot, whome in stout fray
Corineus conquered, and cruelly did slay.

Aber ehe er seinen thron befestigt und seine herrschaft bis zur aeussersten kueste ausgebreitet hatte,
schlug er grosse schlachten mit seinen wilden feinden, in welchen er sie stets besiegte und viele riesen auf dem aechzenden boden liess, was noch bis
zum heutigen tage die westliche anhoehe bezeugen
kann, die mit dem blut des maechtigen Goëmot be-
spritzt ist, den in mannhaftem kampfe Corineus besiegte und grausam umbrachte.

---

v. 7 is erased by Kitchin, because his edition is for scholars.   v. 8. 'giants'.   'dreadfull'.   v. 9. 'farre'.
   v. 3. That monstrous error. etc.; — 'all this is direct from Hardyng's Chronicle, c. 1 and 5. He gives the
tale (describing the daughters of 'Dioclesian, King of Greece', as thirty, not fifty); and adds also that he considers it
to be false and without foundation. In the legend these 'thirty daughters' are described as performing the feat of Danaides,
with whom they are evidently confounded. Holinshed (Hist. of Engl. I. 3.) explains how the name of 'Dioclesian' got into
the legend. He gravely rebukes the ignorance of the chroniclers, saying that they took 'Danaus' to be as short way of
writing 'Dioclesianus'. (Kitchin.)
     assott; — 'Beguile, bewitch, or deceive; a word frequent in romance.' (Todd.)
   IX.   v. 3. their owne mother; — 'i. e. Albion. Spenser hints that, like the classical Gigantes, these British giants
were earth-born (γηγενεῖς).' (Kitchin.)
   v. 6. Brutus; — 'this legendary Brutus is always described as descended from Aeneas. His coming to Albion
is described by Hardyng, c. 11. Robert of Gloucester fixes his date of arriving at 1132 B. C. Holinshed puts it at 1116.
Stow at 1108. He is said to have landed at Totnes in Devon, with his comrade Corineus.
   v. 7. old Assaracs line; — cp. above IX. 56 and
Virg. Georg. III. 34 sqq:
                'Stabunt et Parii lapides, spirantia signa,
                Assaraci proles, demissaeque ab Jove gentis
                Nomina, Trosque parens, et Troiae Cynthius auctor'.
   v. 8. Driven by fatall error; — 'That is, by wandering (Lat. error) as the fates directed.' (Church
in Todd.)
   X.   Various readings: In Kitchin: v. 3. 'battels'.   v. 5. 'giants'.
   v. 3. He fought great batteils; — Hardyng says:
             'The giauntes als he sleugh doune beelive
             Through all the lande in battaile mannely:
             And lefte no moo but Gogmagog onely'. (Kitchin.)
   v. 7. The westerne Hogh; — 'That is, as Camden calls it, the Haw.' (Church in Todd.)
     Kitchin: 'Camden calls it 'the Haw' in his Britannia (under Devonshire). It is now 'the Hoe', near Ply-

XI.

And eke that ample pitt, yet far renownd
For the large leape which Debon did compell
Coulin to make, being eight lugs of grownd,
Into the which retourning backe he fell;
But those three monstrous stones doo most excell,
Which that huge sonne of hideous Albion,
Whose father Hercules in Fraunce did quell,
Great Godmer threw, in fierce contention,
At bold Canutus; but of him was slaine anon.

Und auch jene grosse grube (sc. kann es bezeugen), die noch jetzt weithin beruehmt ist wegen des
weiten sprunges, welchen Debon den Coulin zu machen zwang, obgleich sie acht ruthen landes breit
war, in die er denn auch beim zuruecksprungen hineinfiel.
Jene drei ungeheuren steine aber zeichnen sich besonders aus, welche jener riesenhafte sohn des scheusslichen Albion — dessen vater, Hercules, starb in
Frankreich —; der grosse Godmer in wildem streit
auf den kuehnen Canutus warf, von dem er aber
gleich darauf erschlagen wurde.

XII.

In meed of those great conquests by them gett,
Corineus had that province utmost west
To him assigned for his worthy lott,
Which of his name and memorable gest
He called Cornwaile, yet so called best :
And Debons shayre was, that is Devonshyre;
But Canute had his portion from the rest,
The which he cald Canutium, for his hyre;
Now Cantium, which Kent we comouly inquyre.

Als lohn fuer diese grossen durch sie bewerkstel-
ligten eroberungen hatte sich Corineus die provinz
im· aeussersten westen zu seinem wohlverdienten antheil bestimmt, die er nach seinem namen und sei-
·ner denkwuerdigen heldenthat Cornwaile nannte, wie
sie denn auch jetzt noch am besten so genannt wird :
und Debon's antheil war, was jetzt Devonshire ist;
aber Canute bekam, was uebrig blieb, zu seinem erb-
lichen antheil und hiess es Canutium, jetzt Cantium,
das wir gewoehnlich Kent nennen.

XIII.

Thus Brute this realme unto his rule subdewd,
And raignod long in great felicity,
Lov'd of his froends, and of his foes eschewd:
He left three sonnes, his famous progeny,
Borne of fayre Inogene of Italy;
Mongst whom he parted his imperiall state,
And Locrine left chiefe lord of Britany.
At last ripe age bad him surrender late
His life, and long good fortune, unto finall fate.

So unterjochte Brutus dies reich seiner herrschaft
und regierte lange in grosser gluockseligkeit, geliebt
von seinen freunden und gemieden von seinen feinden: er hinterliess drei soehne, seine beruchmte
nachkommenschaft, geboren von der schoenen Inogene
aus Italien. Unter diese theilte er seinen herrscher-
staat, und Locrine hinterliess er als oberherrn von
Britannien. Endlich hiess ihn sein hohes alter, wenn
auch erst spaet, sein leben und langes gluock dem
schliesslichen vorhaengniss uebergeben.

mouth. Geoffry of Monmouth (c. 9) says, 'ille (Goemagot) per abrupta saxa cadens in multa frusta dilaceratus est, et flu-
ctus sanguine maculavit'. Cp. also Hardyng, c. 12, for this conquest of Corineus. Holinshed says Gogmagog was thrown
over the cliffs near Dover. (Hist. of Eng., 2. 4.)
     XI.   Various readings; In Kitchin: v. 1. 'pit'. 'farre'.   v. 4. 'returning'.
          v. 3. l u g s; — 'A l u g is a pearch or rod with which land is measured, containing sixteen feet and an half.'
(Church in Todd.)
          v. 6, h i d e o u s A l b i o n; — 'a legendary giant, whose history is given in Holinshed, 1. 3.' (Kitchin.)
          v. 7. H e r c u l e s i n F r a u n c e d i d q u e l l; — 'a curious mixture of classical with mediæval legend. Hercules
is mentioned as being in France with Brutus, by Robert of Gloucester. Holinshed tells us that Hercules fought a terrific
battle with Albion on the Rhone, and eventually defeated him by showers of stones, which still lie there, in the district
called the Crau. (Hist. of Eng, 1. 3.)' (Kitchin.)
          v. 9. C a n u t u s; — 'another of the legendary companions of Brutus, eponymous of Cantium or Kent.' (Kitchin.)
     XII.   Various readings: In Kitchin: v. 1. 'got'.   v. 3. 'lot'.   v. 5. 'Cornewaile'.   v. 9. 'comuonly'.
          v. 5. H e c a l l e d C o r n w a i l e; — 'so stated in Geoffry of Monmouth, c. 3.' (Kitchin.)
          v. 6. t h a t i s D e v o n s h y r e; — 'I have not succeeded in finding the legends of Godmer, Debon, and Canutus.'
(Kitchin.)
     XIII.   Various readings: In Kitchin: v. 2. 'felicitie'.   v. 3. 'friends'.   v. 5. 'faire'.
          v. 5. f a y r e I n o g e n e o f I t a l y; — 'Robert of Gloucester (who spells the name 'Innogen'), describes her as the
wife of Brute, daughter of Pandras, king of Greece, not Italy.' (Kitchin.)

XIV.

Locrine was left the soveraine lord of all;
But Albanact had all the northerne part,
Which of himselfe Albania he did call;
And Camber did possesse the westerne quart,
Which Severne now from Logris doth depart:
And each his portion peaceably enioyd,
Ne was there outward breach, nor grudge in hart,
That once their quiet government annoyd;
But each his paynes to others profit still employd.

Locrine also wurde als der oberherr aller hinterlassen; Albanact aber hatte den ganzen noerdlichen theil, den er nach sich Albania benannte; und Camber besass das westliche gebiet, welches jetzt Severne von Logris trennt: jeder genoss friedlich, was er hatte; weder fand ein aeusserer bruch noch groll im herzen statt, der jemals ihre ruhige regierung gestoert haette; vielmehr verwendete stets jeder seine muehe zu des andern vortheil.

XV.

Untill a nation straung, with visage swart
And corage fierce that all men did affray,
Which through the world then swarmd in every part,
And overflowd all countries far away,
Like Noyes great flood, with their impórtune sway,
This land invaded with like violence,
And did themvelves through all the north display:
Untill that Locrine for his realmes defence,
Did head against them make and strong muníficence.

Bis eine fremde nation mit dunkelbraunem gesichte und wildem, alle menschen in schrecken setzonden muthe, welche damals in jeder richtung durch die welt schwaermte und gleich Noah's grosser fluth alle laender mit ihrer laestigen macht ueberstroemte, dies land mit gleichem ungestuem ueberfiel und sich ueber den ganzen norden hin verbreitete: bis endlich Locrine zur Vertheidigung seines reiches ihnen die spitze bot und starke befestigungen anlegte.

XVI.

He them encountred, a confused rout,
Foreby the river that whylóme was hight
The ancient Abus, where with courage stout
He them defeated in victorious fight,
And chaste so fiercely after fearefull flight,
That forst their chiefetain, for his safeties sake,
(Their chiefetain Humber named was aright,)
Unto the mighty streame him to betake,
Where he an end of batteill and of life did make.

Er traf sie als einen verworrnen haufen dicht bei dem flusse, der weiland der alte Abus genannt ward, wo er sie mit mannhaftem muthe in siegreichem gefecht besiegte und sie auf ihrer wilden flucht so ungestuem verfolgte, dass er ihren anfuehrer (er ward in wirklichkeit Humber genannt) zwang, sich zu seiner rettung in den maechtigen strom zu stuerzen, wo er schlacht und leben beendete.

---

v. 7. Locrine . . . chiefe lord of Britany; — 'Hardyng, c. 15 and 17:
'On Locryne it should ever be homage'.
Britany here means Britain.' (Kitchin.)
XIV. Various readings: In Kitchin: v. 6. 'enjoyd'. v. 9. 'paines'.
v. 2, 3, Albanact . . . Albania; — 'Hardyng, c. 15:
'Fro Humber north unto the Northwest sea
Of all Britaine, which he called Albanye
For Albanacte the kyng thereof to be'. (Kitchin.)
v. 4. quart; — 'Division, the fourth part, Fr. quart.' (Upton in Todd.)
v. 5. depart; — Separate. (Church in Todd.)
Logris; — 'all to the east of Severn, and 'from the south sea unto the river of Humber'. (Holinshed, Hist.
of Eng. 2. 5.)' (Kitchin.)
v. 6. each his portion peaceably enjoyd; — 'so Hardyng, c. 17:
'And reyned so bylyfe in one assente', etc. (Kitchin.)
XV. Various readings: In Kitchin: v. 2. 'courage'. v. 5. no accent marked. v. 9. 'munifience'.
v. 1. Untill, etc.; — 'this incursion of Huns or Scythians is described in full in Hardyng, c. 18.' (Kitchin.)
v. 9. munificence; — 'ed. 1596 has 'munificence'. (Kitchin.)
Jortin: 'Quaere, whether by making strong munificence he means, he fortified himself against them'.
Todd: 'By munificence our author signifies defence, or fortification; from munio and facio.
T. Warton'.
XVI. Various readings: In Kitchin: v. 2. accent not marked. v. 3. 'auncient'. v. 6. 'chieftaine'.
v. 7. 'chieftaine'. v. 8. 'mightie'. v. 9. 'battell'.

XVII.

The king retourned proud of victory
And insolent wox through unwonted ease,
That shortly he forgot the ieopardy,
Which in his land he lately did appease,
And fell to vaine voluptuous disease:
He lov'd faire Ladie Estrild, leudly lov'd,
Whose wanton pleasures him too much did please,
That quite his hart from Guendolene remov'd,
From Guendolene his wife, though alwaies faithful
prov'd.

Der koenig kehrte siegesstolz zurueck und wurde
durch ungewohnte ruhe uebermuethig, so dass er in
kurzem die gefahr vergass, die er juengst in seinem
lande daempfte, und in thoerichte, lasterhafte wollust
verfiel; er liebte, straeflich liebte er die schoene
Dame Estrild, deren ueppige reize ihm zu sehr ge-
fielen, so dass sein herz sich gaenzlich von Guendolene entfernte, von Guendolene, seinem weibe, obgleich
sie sich immer als treu erwiesen hatte.

XVIII.

The noble daughter of Corinêus
Would not endure to bee so vile disdaind,
But, gathering force and corage valorous,
Encountred him in batteill well ordaind,
In which him vanquisht she to fly constraind;
But she so fast pursewd, that him she tooke
And threw in bands, whore he till death remaind;
Als his faire leman flying through a brooke
She overhent, nought moved with her piteous looke,

Die edle tochter des Corineus wollte nicht dulden,
dass sie so schnoede verachtet ward, sondern, kraft
und kuehnen muth sammelnd, griff sie ihn in wohl-
geordneter schlacht an, in der sie ihn besiegte und
zur flucht zwang; aber sie verfolgte ihn so schnell,
dass sie ihn gefangen nahm und in's gefaengniss
warf, in dem er bis zum tode verblieb; auch sein
schoenes schaetzchen holte sie ein, als es gerade
durch einen bach floh. Sie liess sich durchaus nicht
durch ihr klaegliches aussehn ruehren,

XIX.

But both herselfe, and eke her daughter deare
Begotten by her kingly paramoure,
The faire Sabrina, almost dead with feare,
She there attached, far from all succoúre:
The one she slew in that impatient stoure;
But the sad virgin innocent of all
Adqwne the rolling river she did poure,
Which of her name now Severne men do call:
Such was the end that to disloyall love did fall.

Sondern sowohl sie selbst als auch ihre theure
tochter, die von ihrem koeniglichen buhlen gezeugt
war, die schoene Sabrina, fast todt vor furcht, nahm
sie dort fest, fern von aller hilfe: die eine erschlug
sie in jonem erbitterten kampfe, die arme jungfrau
aber, die an allem unschuldig war, stuerzte sie in
den rollenden strom hinab, den man jetzt nach ihrem
namen Severne nennt. So war das ende, das un-
treuer liebe zu theil wurde.

XX.

Then for her sonne, which she to Locrin bore,
(Madan was young, unmeet the rule to sway,)

Darauf behielt sie fuer ihren sohn, den sie dem
Locrin geboren hatte, (Madan war jung und nicht

---

v. 3. The ancient Abus; — 'The Humber in Yorkshire. Abus is from the British Aber, which signifies
the mouth of a river.' (Church in Todd.)
    Kitchin says the same.
XVII. Various readings: In Kitchin: v. 1. 'returned'. 'victorie'.   v. 3. 'jeopardie'.   v. 6. 'lewdly'.
    v. 6. 8. faire . . . Estrild . . . Guendolene; — 'see Hardyng. c. 18. Estrild is described as a 'young
damsel of excellent beauty', daughter of a certain king of Scythia, taken captive in the battle on the Humber. (Holinshed,
Hist. of Engl. 2. 5.)' (Kitchin.)
XVIII. Various readings: In Kitchin: v. 2. 'be'.   v. 3. 'courage'.   v. 4. 'battell'.
    v. 4. in batteil well ordaind; — 'This is a Latinism, Proelio bene ordinato.' (Upton in Todd.)
    Kitchin quotes the same.
XIX. Various readings: In Kitchin: v. 1. 'her selfe'.   v. 4. accent not marked.
    v. 3. Sabrina; — 'daughter of Estrild, drowned in the Severn; narrated by Hardyng, c. 18.' (Kitchin.)
    v. 5. Todd reads: 'The one she slew upon she present floure', and adds in the notes: 'That is, upon
the spot'.
    Kitchin says: 'ed. 1590 reads 'upon the present stoure'.
XX. Various readings: In Kitchin: v. 2. no parenthesis. 'of sway'.   .v. 6. 'glorie'.

In her owne hand the crowne she kept in store,
Till ryper years he raught and stronger stay;
During which time her powre she did display
Through all this realme, the glory of her sex,
And first taught men a woman to obay;
But, when her sonne to mans estate did wex,
She it surrendred, ne her selfe would lenger vex.

geeignet, die herrschaft zu fuehren,) die krone einstweilen in ihrer eignen hand, bis er zu reiferen jah-
ren und groesserer festigkeit gelangt war. Waehrend dieser zeit entfaltete sie ihre macht durch dies
ganze reich, der stolz ihres geschlechts, und war
die erste, die maenner einer frau gehorchen lehrte;
aber als ihr sohn zur manneswuerde heranwuchs,
trat sie ihm die herrschaft ab und wollte sich nicht
laenger damit plagen.

XXI.

Tho Madan raignd, unworthie of his race;
For with all shame that sacred throne he fild.
Next Memprise, as unworthy of that place,
In which being consorted with Mamild,
For thirst of single kingdom him he kild.
But Ebranck salved both their infamies
With noble deedes, and warreyd on Brunchild
In Henault, where yet of his victories
Brave moniments remaine, which yet that land envies.

Darauf regierte Madan, unwuerdig seines stammes;
denn mit aller schande erfuellte er den geheiligten
thron. Unmittelbar darauf herrschte Memprise, ebenso
unwuerdig jener stellung: denn er hatte Manild zum
mitregenten und toedtete denselben aus begierde nach
alleinherrschaft. Aber Ebranck machte ihre greuel
wieder gut durch edle thaten und bekriegte Brunchild
in Henault, wo noch denkmaeler tapfrer siege uebrig
sind, die noch jenes land beneidet.

XXII.

An happy man in his first dayes he was,
And happy father of faire progeny:
For all so many weekes, as the yeare has,
So many children he did multiply;
Of which were twentie sonnes, which did apply
Their mindes to prayse and chevalrous desyre:
Those germans did subdew all Germany,
Of whom it hight; but in the end their syre
With foule repulse from Fraunce was forced to
retyre.

Ein gluecklicher mann war er in seinen ersten
tagen und gluecklicher vater einer herrlichen nachkommenschaft: denn, gerade sovicle wochen das jahr
hat, sovicle kinder erzeugte er; von diesen waren
zwanzig soehne, die nach ruhm und ritterlicher lust
strebten. Jene brueder unterjochten ganz Germanien,
das nach ihnen den namen hat; aber schliesslich
wurde ihr vater gezwungen, mit schimpflicher abwei-
sung aus Frankreich sich zurueckzuziehen.

XXIII.

Which blott his sonne succeeding in his seat,
The second Brute, the second both in name

Diesen fleck tilgte derjenige seiner soehne, der
ihm in der regierung folgte, der zweite Brute, der

---

v. 2. Madan; — 'Hardyng c. 20, who says she governed for him fifteen years.' (Kitchin.)
rule to sway; — 'ed. 1590 reads so'. (Kitchin.)
Todd:'Rule is here used for realm, as in st. 66. The sense is thus perspicuous: Madan was young, unfit
to sway the realm'.
XXI. v. 3. Memprise; — 'Hardyng, c. 20; Holinshed, History of England 2. 5. Manild, his brother, is called 'Man-
lius by Holinshed, 'Maulyne' by Hardyng.' (Kitchin.)
v. 6. Ebranck! — 'the legendary founder of Eber-wik (or Caer-Ebrank), Everwyk (Eber's town), i. e. York.
See Hardyng, c. 21. He had twenty wives, twenty sons and thirty daughters; so that 'as many weekes', etc., is no strictly
true, unless we take the fifty lunar weeks in the solar year. According to Hardyng, he 'warred in Gaule', which would do,
perhaps, for Henault, Hainault. His sons, according to this same authority, conquered Germany. There is no trace of his
warring on Brunchild.' (Kitchin.)
XXII. Various readings: In Kitchin: v. 2. 'happie'. v. 6. 'minds'. 'praise'. 'desire'. v. 3. 'sire'. v. 9. 'retire'.
v. 7. germans ... Germany: — 'the derivation is on a par with the rest of the history.' (Kitchin).
XXIII. Various readings: In Kitchin: v. 1. 'blot'. v. 3. 'semblance'. 'puissance'. v. 9. 'sundrie'.
v. 2. The second Brute; — 'this was Brutus Greneschilde. See Hardyng, c. 22. It is this prince who is said
by Holinshed to have gone over into 'Henaud', and to have warred with 'king Brinchild', who gave him a sore repulse.

And eke in semblaunce of his puissaunce great,
Right well recur'd and did away that blame
With recompence of everlasting fame:
He with his victour sword first opened
The bowels of wide Fraunce, a forlorne dame,
And taught her first how to be conquered;
Since which with sondrie spoiles she hath been ran-
          sacked.

zweite sowohl dem namen nach als auch in betreff
der aehnlichkeit seiner grossen macht, auf gar schickliche weise und that jenen makel hinweg, indem er
ihn durch ewigen ruhm ersetzte. Er oeffnete zuerst
mit seinem schwert das innere des grossen Frankreich's, das nun verloren war, und zeigte ihm zuerst,
was erobert werden heisst; seit dieser zeit aber ist
es von verschiedenen verwuestungen heimgesucht
worden.

XXIV.

Let Scaldis tell, and let tell Hania,
And let the marsh of Esthambruges tell,
What colour were their waters that same day,
And all the moore twixt Elversham and Dell,
With blood of Henalois which therein fell.
How of that day did sad Brunchildis see
The *greene shielde* dyde in dolorous vermell?
That not *scuith guiridh* it mote seeme to bee,
But rather *y scuith gogh*, signe of sad crueltee.

Moege der Scaldis, moege Hania und die marsch
von Esthambruges erzachlen, von welcher farbe an
jenem tage ihre wasser waren und das ganze sumpf-
land zwischen Elversham und Dell von dem blute
der Henaler, die dort ihren untergang fanden. Wie
sah an jenem tage der duestere Brunchildis den
'gruenen schild' mit schmerzlichem purpur gefaerbt?
so, dass er nicht mehr 'der gruene schild' zu sein
schien, sondern vielmehr 'der rothe schild', ein zeichen grimmer grausamkeit.

XXV.

His sonne king Leill, by fathers labour long,
Enioyd an heritage of lasting peace,
And built Cairleill, and built Cairleon strong.
Next Huddibras his realme did not encrease,
But taught the land from wearie wars to cease.
Whose footsteps Bladud following, in artes
Exceld at Athens all the learned preace,
From whence he brought them to there salvage parts,
And with sweet science mollifide their stubborne harts.

Sein solm, koenig Leill, genoss in folge von seines vaters langer anstrengung ein erbe dauernden
friedens und baute Cairleill und das starke Cairleon.
Der naechste, Huddibras, vergroesserte sein reich
nicht, sondern lehrte das land, von ermuedenden krie-
gen abzulassen. In dessen fusstapfen trat Illadud,
der zu Athen in den schoenen kuensten die ganze
gesellschaft der gelehrten uebertraf, jene von dort in
diese wilden gegenden brachte und mit suesser wissenschaft die harten herzen der bewohner erweichte.

(Hist. of Engl. 2. 5.) Milton. Hist. of Britain, Bk. I, says that Jacobus Bergomas and Lassabeus, in their account of Hainault, give these fables.' (Kitchin.)
    v. 6. first opened The bowels of wide Fraunce; — 'he is said to have passed into Armorica, and to
have given to that district a name derived from his own, i, e' Brittany.' (Kitchin.)
        With v. 2. 3 cp. Virgil. Aen. VI, 768 sqq.:
               '— — — et qui te nomine reddet
               Silvius Aeneas, pariter pietate vel armis
               Egregius, — — — — —'
XXIV. Various readings: In Kitchin: v. 2. 'Estham bruges'.   v. 5. 'bloud'.   v. 6. 'How oft'.
        'The quaint proper names heaped together in this stanza remind us of Milton's delight in such displays; e. g. Par.
Lost, 5. 268.' (Kitchin.)
    v. 1. Scaldis; — the river Scheldt. (Kitchin.)
        Hania; — 'the country of Hainault in Belgium. Milton says it is a river. The Henalois below are the
men of Hainault.' (Kitchin.)
    v. 2. Esthambruges; — 'Bruges, in Belgium.' (Kitchin.)
    v. 8. 9. scuith guiridh; — 'Welsh for a 'green shield'; y scuith gogh, 'the red shield'. It had been green,
but was dyed red in the blood of the men of Hainault.' (Kitchin.)
        'The sense is, Insomuch that it might then not so properly have been called 'scuith guiridh', green shield, as
'y scuith gogh', The red shield.' (Church in Todd.)
XXV. Various readings: In Kitchin: v. 5. 'warres'.   v. 6. 'arts'.
    v. 1. Leill; — 'see Hardyng. c. 23: founder of Caerleill (Carlisle) and Cairleon (Chester, otherwise called Leou-
cester, Leicester, 'Legionum castra'.) Caer, British for 'city'. (Kitchin.)
    v. 4. Huddibras; — 'called 'Ludhurdibras' by Holinshed, 'Rudhudebras' by Hardyng. c. 24.' (Kitchin.)
    v. 6. Bladud following; — 'famed for his learning, as Hardyng says, c. 25:

XXVI.

Ensample of his wondrous faculty,
Behold the boyling baths at Cairdabon,
Which seeth with secret fire eternally,
And in their entrailles, full of quick brimston,
Nourish the flames which they are warmd upon,
That to their people wealth they forth do well,
And health to every forreyne nation:
Yet he at last, contending to excell
The reach of men, through flight into fond mischief
fell.

Als beispiel seiner bewunderungswuerdigen faehig-
keit betrachte man die warmen baeder von Cairdabon,
welche durch verborgenes feuer immer sieden und in
ihrem von lebendigem schwefel angefuellten innern
die flammen naehren, auf denen sie erhitzt worden,
so dass sie den dortigen bewohnern reichthum und
jedem fremden volke gesundheit hervorsprudeln: doch
als er zuletzt das menschen moegliche ueberschreiten
wollte, kam er bei einem fluge auf thoericht - elende
weise um's leben.

XXVII.

Next him king Leyr in happie peace long raynd,
But had no issue male him to succeed,
But three faire daughters, which were well uptraind
In all that seemed fitt for kingly seed;
Mongst whom his realme he equally decreed
To have divided; tho, when feeble age
Nigh to his utmost date he saw proceed,
He cald his daughters, and with speeches sage
Inquyrd, which of them most did love her parentage?

Nach ihm regierte koenig Leyr lange in gluueckli-
chem frieden, hatte aber keine maennlichen sprossen
zu seiner nachfolge, wohl aber drei schoene toechter,
welche wohl aufgezogen wurden in allem, was fuer
koenigskinder passend schien; unter diese beschloss
er sein reich gleichmaessig zu theilen: als er darauf
aber das kraftlose alter immer mehr zum aeussersten
lebensziele vorschreiten sah, rief er seine toechter und
forschte mit weisen reden danach, welche von ihnen
ihren vater am meisten liebte.

XXVIII.

The eldest Gonorill gan to protest,
That she much more than her owne life him lov'd;
And Regan greater love to him profest
Then all the world, whenever it were proov'd;
But Cordeill said she loved him as behoov'd;

Die aelteste, Gonorill, begann zu betheuern, dass
sie ihn viel mehr, als ihr eignes leben, liebte; und
Regan bekannte, ihn mehr zu lieben, als die ganze welt,
wenn immer es erprobt wuerde; aber Cordelia sagte,
sie liebe ihn, wie es sich gebuehre. Diese ihre ein-

'When at Athenes he had studied clere,
He brought with hym iiii philosophiers wise
Schole to holde in Brytayne and exercyse.
Stamforde he made that Stamforde hight this daye
In whiche he made an universitee', etc.' (Kitchin.)
v. 9. Cp. the passage in Ovid:
'Adde quod ingenuas didicisse fideliter artes
Emollit mores, nec sinit esse feros'.
XXVI. Various readings: In Kitchin: v. 4. 'entraile'. 'quicke'. no accent.   v. 5. 'warm'd'.   v. 7. 'forreine'.
v. 2. the boyling baths at Cairdabon; — 'Spenser follows Geoffry of Monmouth, c. 14, 'Ædificavit urbem
Kaer-badum, quae nunc Badus nuncupatur'. See Hardyng:
'Cair Bladud, so that nowe is Bath, I rede'.
Holinshed (Descr. of Engl. 2. 23) gives a long account of the Bath waters, under the name of Caer-bledud.'
(Kitchin.) — Cairbadon, then, is the more accurate reading. So Kitchin in the notes.
v. 6. 'Forth do well, i. e. pour forth.' (Upton in Todd). — 'Notice the play on the words 'wealth' and 'well'.'
(Kitchin.)
v. 9. through flight; — 'And to shew his cunning in other points, upon a presumptuous pleasure which he
had therein, he tooke upon him to flie in the aire, but he fell upon the temple of Apollo, which stood in the citie of
Troynovant, and there was torne in peeces'. (Holinshed, 2. 5.) And Hardyng:
'And afterward a Featherham (feather-man) he dight
To flye with wynges as he could best descerne,
He flyed on high to the temple Apolyne,
And ther brake his necke, for all his great doctrine'. (Kitchin.)
XXVII. Various readings: In Kitchin: v. 1. 'raind'.   v. 4. 'fit'.
v. 1. king Leyr; — 'this legend, so familiar to us through Shakespeare, is best given by Robert of Gloucester;
also by Holinshed (Hist. Engl. 2. 5), and by Hardyng more briefly, c. 26.' (Kitchin.)
XXVIII. Various readings: In Kitchin: v. 4. 'when ever'.   v. 6. 'faire'.

Whose simple answere, wanting colours fayre
To paint it forth, him to displeasaunce moov'd,
That in his crown he counted her no hayre,
But twixt the other twain his kingdom whole did
        shayre.

fache antwort, die aller schoenen, ausschmueckenden
farben ermangelte, brachte ihn so in zorn, dass er
sie als erbin seiner krone gar nicht in anschlag
brachte, sondern unter die andern beiden sein ganzes
koenigreich theilte.

XXIX.

So wedded th' one to Maglan king of Scottes,
And th' other to the king of Cambria,
And twixt them shayrd his realme by equall lottes;
But, without dowre, the wise Cordelia
Was sent to Aganip of Celtica.
Their aged syre, thus eased of his crowne,
A private life ledd in Albania
With Gonorill, long had in great renowne,
That nought him griev'd to beene from rule deposed
        downe.

So verheirathete er die eine an Maglan, den koenig der Schotten und die andre an den koenig von
Cambria und theilte unter sie sein reich nach gleichen theilen; aber ohne mitgift wurde die ehrenhafte
Cordelia zu Aganip von Celtica geschickt. Ihr alter
vater war auf diese weise von seiner krone befreit
und lebte als privatmann in Albania bei Gonorill,
von der er lange in hohen ehren gehalten wurde, so
dass nichts ihn bereuen liess, der herrschaft entsagt
zu haben.

XXX.

But true it is that, when the oyle is spent
The light goes out, and weeke is throwne away;
So, when he had resignd his regiment,
His daughter gan despise his drouping day,
And wearie wax of his continuall stay:
Tho to his daughter Regan he repayrd,
Who him at first well used every way;
But, when of his departure she despayrd,
Her bountie she abated, and his cheare empayrd.

Aber wahr ist es, dass, wenn das oel verbraucht
ist, das licht ausgeht und der docht weggeworfen
wird; so begann seine tochter, als er auf seine regierung verzichtet hatte, seine sinkenden tage zu
verachten und seines bestaendigen aufenthalts muede
zu werden: darauf begab er sich zu seiner tochter
Regan, die ihn zuerst in jeder weise gut behandelte;
als sie aber an seiner abreise verzweifelte, minderte
sie ihre guete und truebte seinen frohsinn.

XXXI.

The wretched man gan then avise too late,
That love is not where most it is profest;
Too truely tryde in his extremest state!
At last, resolv'd likewise to prove the rest,
He to Cordelia himselfe addrest,
Who with entyre affection him receav'd,
As for her syre and king her seemed best;
And after all an army strong she leav'd,
To war one those which him had of his realme bereav'd.

Der unglueckliche mann fing damals zu spaet an
einzusehen, dass liebe nicht da ist, wo sie am meisten betheuert wird, was sich nur als zu wahr er-
wies in seinem so grossen unglueck. Zuletzt ent-
schloss er sich, auf gleiche weise auch die letzte zu
erproben, und wandte sich an Cordelia, die ihn mit
aufrichtiger liebe empfing, wie es ihr fuer ihren vater
und koenig am angemessensten schien; und schliesslich ruestete sie eine starke armee aus, um diejenigen
zu bekriegen, die ihn seines koenigreichs beraubt
hatten.

XXXII.

So to his crowne she him restord againe;

So setzte sie ihn in seine koenigswuerde wieder

---

v. 7. 'displeasance'.   v. 8. 'crowne'. 'haire'.   v. 9. 'twaine'. 'shaire'.
XXIX. Various readings: In Kitchin: v. 1. 'Scots'.   v. 3. 'lots'.   v. 7. 'led'.
     v. 1. Maglan; — 'Duke of Albania', or 'Albanie' (N. England), according to Holinshed and Hardyng.' (Kitchin.)
     v. 2. the king of Cambria; — 'Henninus' in Holinshed; 'Evin' in Hardyng.' (Kitchin.)
     v. 5. Aganip of Celtica; — 'Holinshed says: 'one of the princes of Gallia (which now is called France), whose
name was Aganippus, hearing of the beautie, womanhood, and good condition of the said Cordeilla, desired to have hir in
mariage', etc. This Aganippus was one of the twelve kings that ruled Gallia in those daies'. (Kitchin.)
     XXX. Various readings: In Kitchin: v. 5. 'waxe'.
     XXXI. Various readings: In Kitchin: v. 5. 'him selfe'.
     v. 8. leav'd; — 'Levied, raised. Gall. lever.' (Upton in Todd.)

10

In which he dyde, made ripe for death by eld,
And after wild it should to her remaine:
Who peaceably the same long time did weld,
And all mens harts in dew obedience held:
Till that her sisters children, woxen strong,
Through proud ambition against her robeld,
And overcommen kept in prison long,
Till weary of that wretched life herselfe she hong.

ein; er starb als koenig in reifem alter eines natuer-
lichen todes, nachdem er ihr das reich testamenta-
risch vermacht hatte; und sie regierte es lange in
frieden und hielt aller menschen herzen in pflicht-
schuldigem gehorsam; da aber empoerten sich die
inzwischen herangewachsenen kinder ihrer schwestern
aus stolzem ehrgeiz gegen sie, besiegten sie und hielten sie lange in gefangenschaft, bis sie, dieses elenden lebens muede, demselben durch den strang ein
ende machte.

XXXIII.

Then gan the bloody brethren both to.raine:
But fierce Cundah gan shortly to envy
His brother Morgan, prickt with proud disdaine
To have a pere in part of soverainty;
And, kindling coles of cruell enmity,
Raisd warre, and him in batteill overthrew;
Whence as he to those woody hilles did fly,
Which hight of him Glamorgan, there him slew:
Then did he raigne alone, when he none equal knew.

Alsdann begannen die blutigen brueder beide zu
regieren: aber der stolze Cundah beneidete bald seinen bruder Morgan, von duenkelhaftem unwillen an-
gestachelt, dass er einen genossen in der herrschaft
haette; und die flammen grausamer feindschaft schue-
rend, fing er krieg an und besiegte ihn in einer
schlacht; und als er von dort zu jenen waldigen
huegeln floh, welche nach ihm Glamorgan heissen,
schlug er ihn daselbst todt; darauf regierte er allein,
als er keinen genossen mehr hatte.

XXXIV.

His sonne Rivall' his dead rowme did supply,
In whose sad time blood did from heaven rayne.
Next great Gurgustus, then faire Cæcily,
In constant peace their kingdomes did contayne,

Sein sohn Rivalle kam an seiner stelle zur regierung, als er starb; es war eine ernste zeit, und blut
regnete vom himmel. Darauf regierte der grosse
Gurgustus, dann die schoene Caecilie in bestaendigem

XXXII. Various readings: In Kitchin: v. 1. 'restor'd'. v. 9. 'wearie'. 'her selfe'.
v. 3. after wild; — 'i. e. left the kingdom by will to Cordelia.' (Kitchin.)
v. 9. her selfe she hong; — 'Hardyng, c. 28, says:
'For sorow then she sleugh hir selfe for tene'.
We may notice that the legend, as treated by Shakespeare, differs very much from that of the chroniclers, who
restore Lear to his throne and honours, nor do they say he was blind.' (Kitchin.)
XXXIII. Various readings: In Kitchin: v. 1. 'bloudy'. v. 2. 'envie'. v. 4. 'soveraintie'. v. 5. 'enmitie'.
v. 6. 'battell'. v. 7. 'woodie'. 'hills'. 'flie'. v. 9. 'equall'.
v. 2. Cundah; — 'Condage' in Hardyng, 30; 'Cunedag' in Holinshed, 2. 6.' (Kitchin.)
v. 8. hight of him Glamorgan; — 'Holinshed says (Hist. Engl. 2. 8): 'that countrie tooke name of him,
being there slaine, and so is called to this dale Glan Margan, which is to meane in our English tong, Margans land'.
(Kitchin.)
XXXIV. Various readings: In Kitchin: v. 2. 'bloud'. 'raine'. v. 3. 'Caecily'· v. 4. 'containe'.
v. 5. 'raine'. v. 6. 'farre'. 'yeares'. v. 7. 'twaine'.
v. 2. 'A prodigy not unfrequent, if you will believe ancient poets and historians.' (Jortin.)
Kitchin: 'Hardyng, 30:
'And rayned bloodde thesame, iii dayes also,
Greate people dyed, the land to mykell woo',
So too Holinshed, 2. 7.
v. 3. great Gurgustus; — 'Why 'great'? Hardyng, 30, says of him that he reigned
'In mykill ioye and worldly selynesse,
Kepyng his landes from enemyes as a manne,
But drunken he was eche daye expresse,
Unaccordynge to a prince of worthynesse'. (Kitchin.)
v. 4. In constant peace: — 'Not so Hardyng, 30:
'In whose tyme eche man did other oppresse
The lawe and peace was exiled so indede
That ciuill warres and slaughter of men expresse,
And murderers foule throgh all his lande, dayly,
Without redres or any remedy'. (Kitchin.)

After whom Lago and Kinmarke did rayne,
And Gorbogud, till far in years he grew;
Then his ambitious sonnes unto thom twayne
Arraught the rule, and from their father drew;
Stout Ferrex and sterne Porrex him in prison threw.

frieden. Nach dieser herrschten Lago und Kinmarke und Gorbogud bis zu sehr hohem alter; worauf seine beiden ehrgeizigen soehne, der starke Ferrex und der fuerchterliche Porrex, ihrem vater die herrschaft entrissen und ihn in's gefaengniss warfen.

XXXV.

But O! the greedy thirst of royall crowne,
That knowes no kinred, nor regardes no right,
Stird Porrex up to put his brother downe;
Who, unto him assembling forreigne might,
Made warre on him, and fell himselfe in fight:
Whose death t'avenge, his mother mercilesse,
Most mercilesse of women, Wyden hight,
Her other sonne fast sleeping did oppresse,
And with most cruell hand him murdred pittilesse.

Aber ach! der unersaettliche durst nach der koenigsherrschaft, der keine verwandtschaft kennt noch irgend ein recht achtet, stachelte Porrex auf, seinen bruder zu entthronen: er sammelte gegen ihn eine fremde macht und bekriegte ihn, fiel aber selbst in der schlacht. Um seinen tod zu raechen, beruckte seine unmenschliche mutter, die unmenschlichste der frauen, ihren andern sohn in festem schlaf und mordete ihn auf's grausamste mit eigener hand erbarmungslos dahin. Ihr name war Wyden.

XXXVI.

Here ended Brutus sacred progeny,
Which had seven hundred years this sceptre borne
With high renowne and great felicity:
The noble braunch from th'ántique stocke was torne
Through discord: and the roiall throne forlorne.
Thenceforth this realme was into factions rent,
Whilest each of Brutus boasted to be borne,
That in the end was left no moniment
Of Brutus, nor of Britons glorie auncient.

Hier endete des Brutus verruchte nachkommenschaft, die sieben hundert jahre lang mit hohem ruhm und grossem glueck das scepter gefuehrt hatte; der edle zweig wurde durch zwietracht vom alten stamm gerissen und der koenigliche thron verloren. Seitdem war dies koenigreich in parteien zerrissen, indem jede sich ruehmte, von Brutus abzustammen, so dass schliesslich kein denkmal von Brutus noch von der Briten altem ruhme uebrig blieb.

XXXVII.

Then up arose a man of matchlesse might,
And wondrous wit to menage high affayres,
Who, stird with pitty of the stressed plight
Of this sad realme, cut into sondry shayres

Darauf stand ein mann auf von unvergleichlicher macht und wunderbarer gabe, hohe dinge zu vollbringen. Er ward von mitleid bewegt mit dem trostlosen zustande des armen reiches, das von solchen,

---

v. 8. Arraught the rule; — 'not according to Holinshed and Hardyng.' (Kitchin.)
Todd: 'Seized. Fr. arracher, to snatch or wrest'.
XXXV. Various readings: In Kitchin: v. 4. 'forreine'.
v. 3. Stird Porrex up, etc.; — there is a very pardonable confusion in this history; the chroniclers being uncertain whether Ferrex killed Porrex, or Porrex Ferrex. Spenser follows Geoffry of Monmouth, c. 16. But Holinshed and Hardyng make Ferrex the slayer. Geoffry also gives us their mother's name, 'Wyden', (Kitchin).
v. 9. him murdred; — 'So Hardyng, c. 30:
'Ther mother that Indon hight,
To Ferrex came, with her maydens all in ire
Slepyng in bed slew hym upon the night,
And smote hym all on peces sett on fyre,
With suche rancor that she could not ceas,
Which, for passyng yre, was mercyles'.
So Spenser call' (sic! probably a misprint) 'her his mother mercilesse'. (Kitchin.)
XXXVI. Various readings: In Kitchin: v. 1. 'progenie'.　　v. 4. accent not marked.　　v. 9. 'glory'.
v. 6. into factions rent; — 'so Hardyng, c. 31.' (Kitchin.)
XXXVII. Various readings: In Kitchin: v. 2. 'affaires'. *　　v. 4. 'sundry'. 'shaires'.　　v. 5. 'haires'.
v. 1. Then up arose; — 'finely introduced. We do not learn the name of this matchless hero till st. 40, 'Donwallo dyed.' He is called in Holinshed 'Mulmucius Dunwallo' (Hist. Engl. 3. 1), and by Hardyng (c. 31) 'Moluncius'.
'Sammes, Brit, p. 172, gives his laws, seven in number, dealing, as Spenser gives it (st. 39), with temples of the Gods, highways, and ploughlands, and restraining robbery.' (Kitchin.)

10*

By such as claymd themselves Brutes rightfull hayres,
Gathered the princes of the people loose
To taken counsell of their common cares;
Who, with his wisedom won, him streight did choose
Their king, and swore him fealty to win or loose.

die sich des Brutus rechtmaessige erben nannten, in
einzelne stuecke zerrissen war, und versammelte die
fuersten des unvereinigten volkes, um mit ihnen ueber
den gegenstand ihrer gemeinsamen sorgen rath zu
pflegen: und diese waren von seiner weisheit so ein-
genommen, dass sie ihn alsbald zu ihrem koenige
waehlten und ihm treue schwuren auf leben und tod.

XXXVIII.

Then made he head against his enimies,
And Ymner slew of Logris miscreate;
Then Ruddoc and proud Stater, both allyes,
This of Albány newly nominate,
And that of Cambry king confirmed late,
He overthrew through his owne valiaunce,
Whose countries he reduc'd to quiet state,
And shortly brought to civile governaunce,
Now one, which earst were many made through vari-
aunce.

Dann wandte er sich gegen seine feinde und toedtete Ymner, den unehelichen sohn des Logris; darauf
besiegte er durch persoenliche tapferkeit den Ruddoc
und den stolzen Stater, die sich beide mit einander
verbuendet hatten, und von denen der letztere juengst
zum koenig von Albanien und der erstere kuerzlich
zu dem von Cambray erwaehlt war; ihre laender
brachte er wieder in einen friedlichen zustand zuruock
und verschaffte ihnen in kurzem eine gesittete regierung und vereinigte, was ehedem durch feindselig-
keit getrennt wurde.

XXXIX.

Then made he sacred lawes, which some men say
Were unto him reveald in vision;
By which he freed the travelers high-way,
The churches part, and ploughmans portion,
Restraining stealth and strong extortion;
The gracious Numa of great Britany;
For, till his dayes, the chiefe dominion
By strength was wielded without pollicy:
Therefore he first wore crowne of gold for dignity.

Darauf machte er heilige gesetze, die, wie einige
sagen, ihm im traume offenbart waren; durch sie
machte er des wanderers strasse frei, gab der kirche
und dem ackerbau sicherheit, indem er diebstahl und
harte bedrueckung hemmte, — der wohlwollende Numa
Gross-Britannien's; denn bis zu seinen tagen wurde
die oberste leitung durch macht ohne staatsklugheit
gehandhabt: daher trug er zuerst eine goldne krone
als abzeichen seiner wuerde.

XL.

Donwallo dyde, (for what may live for ay?)
And left two sonnes, of pearelesse prowesse both,
That sacked Rome too dearely did assay,
The recompence of their periúred oth;
And ransackt Greece wel tryde, when they were wroth,

Donwallo starb, (denn welches wesen kann ewig
leben?) und hinterliess zwei soehne, die beide von unvergleichlicher tapferkeit waren; die brachen ihren schwur,
griffen Rom mit ungestuem an und pluenderten es, ver-
heerten Griechenland in ihrem zorn und unterwarfen

XXXVIII. Various readings: In Kitchin: v. 4. 'Albanie'.   'v. 7. 'redus'd',   v. 8. 'civill'.
XXXIX. Various readings: In Kitchin: v. 3. 'high way'.   v. 6. 'Britanie'.   v. 7. 'pollicie'.   v. 9. 'dignitie'.
     v. 6. The gracious Numa; — 'the legendary lawgiver and second king of Rome, to whom Donwallo may
well be likened.' (Kitchin.)
     v. 9. first wore crowne of gold; — 'so Holinshed says: 'He ordained him . . . a crowne of gold;
and because he was the first that bare a crowne here in Britaine, he is named the first king of Britaine'. And
Hardyng:
                    'The first he was, as chroniclers expresse,
                    That in this isle of Brytein had croune of golde,
                    For all afore copre and gilt was to beholde'. (Kitchin.)
     XL.   Various readings: In Kitchin: v. 4. no accent marked.'   v. 6. 'subjected'.   v. 9. 'Bellinus'. 'kings'.
     v. 2. two sonnes; — 'Belinus and Brennus.' (Kitchin.)
     v. 3. That sacked Rome; — 'Holinshed (Hist. Engl. 3. 2—3) tells us that after many adventures, Brennus,
who had married the daughter of the 'Duke of Allobrog', came into Britain to overthrow his brother. But being reconciled
by their mother, they both set forth against Gallia and Rome. They reached Clusium, besieged it, made treaty with the
Romans, broke it — 'their perjured oth' — and took and sacked Rome. See Livy. The date B. C. 365. (Hardyng, c.
32.)' (Kitchin.)

Besides subiected France and Germany,
Which yet their praises speake, all be they loth,
And inly tremble at the memory
Of Brennus and Belinus, kinges of Britany,

ausserdem Frankreich und Deutschland, die noch
ihren ruhm verkuenden, obgleich sie schaudern und
bis in's innerste erbeben bei dem andenken an Brennus und Belinus, die koenige von Britannien.

XLI.

Next them did Gurgunt, great Belinus sonne,
In rule succeede, and eke in fathers praise ;
He Easterland subdewd, and Denmarke wonne,
And of them both did foy and tribute raise,
The which was dew in his dead fathers dales.
He also gave to fugitives of Spayne,
Whom he at sea found wandring from their waies,
A seate in Ireland safely to remayne,
Which they should hold of him as subiect to Britáyne.

Unmittelbar auf sie folgte Gurgunt, des grossen
Belinus sohn, in der regierung und trat in des vaters
ruhmreiche fusstapfen. Er unterjochte das oestliche
land, gewann Daenemark, liess beide treue schwoe-
ren und erhob von ihnen den tribut, der schon bei
lebzeiten seines verstorbenen vaters faellig war. Er
gab auch Spanischen fluechtlingen, die er auf irr-
fahrten zur see traf, einen sitz in Irland zum sichern
aufenthalte, in welchem sie als unterthanen von Britannien verbleiben sollten.

XLII.

After him raigned Guitheline his hayre,
The iustest man and trewest in his daies,
Who had to wife Dame Mertia the fayre,
A woman worthy of immortall praise,
Which for this realme found many goodly layes,
And wholesome statutes to her husband brought;
Her many deemd to have beene of the Fayes,
As was Aegeriè that Numa tought:
Those yet of her be Mertian lawes both nam'd and
thought.

Nach ihm regierte sein erbe Guitheline, der ge-
rechteste und aufrichtigste mann seiner zeit ; zum
weibe hatte er die schoene dame Mertia, eine frau
unsterblichen ruhmes wuerdig, welche fuer dies koenigreich viele treffliche gesetze erfand und ihrem gemahl heilsame satzungen an die hand gab; viele
meinten, sie sei eine der Feen, wie Aegeria, die den
Numa lehrte: noch heute glaubt man, dass sie von
ihr herstammen und nennt sie daher die Mertiani-
schen gesetze.

XLI. Various readings: In Kitchin: v. 5. 'dayes'.   v. 7. 'wayes'.   v. 9. 'subject'. no accent.
    v. 1. Gurgunt; — 'Holinshed. Hist. Engl. 3. 5.' (Kitchin.)
    v. 3. Easterland subdewd, and Denmarke wonne; — 'i. e. the Danes and Northmen. Holinshed and
Hardyng only record his triumphs over the Danes.' (Kitchin.)
    v. 4. foy; — 'The tribute due from subjects. An expression borrowed from the old French. Homme de
foy is a vassal, or tenant, that holds by fealty.' (Todd.)
    v. 6. fugitives of Spayne; — 'Holinshed (Hist. Engl. 3. 5) says: 'he encountred with a navie of 30 ships, be-
sides the Iles of Orkenies. These ships were fraught with men and women, and had for their capteine one Bartholin, who,
being brought into the presence of King Gurguint, declared that he with his people were banished out of Spaine, and
were named Balenses, or Baselenses (? Basques), and had sailed long on the sea, to the end to find some prince that would
assigne them a place to inhabit to whom they would become subjects, and hold of him as of their sovereigne governor'.
So Spenser, l. 9:
                     'Which they should hold of him as subject to Britayne'.
    See also Robert of Gloucester, who is quoted on the praises of Ireland. This is a manifesto, to shew the right
of England over Ireland in the days of Queen Elizabeth, and to justify her severe measures, in which Spenser had necessarily taken some part.' (Kitchin. — See above.)
XLII. Various readings: In Kitchin: v. 2. 'justest'. 'dayes'.   v. 4. 'prayse'.   v. 8. no accent.
    v. 1. Guitheline, etc.; — 'So Hardyng, c. 35, whom Spenser has here followed almost literally:
                'Guytelyn his sonne gave reigne as heyre
                Of all Brytayn, aboute unto the sea,
                Who wedded was to Marcyan full fayre
                That was so wyse in her femynites,
                That lawes made of her syngularytes,
                That called were the lawes Marcyane
                In Britayne tongue, of her owne witte alone'.
    'These lawes', says Holinshed, 'Alfred . . . translated also out of the British tong into the English Saxon speech,
and then they were called after that translation, Marchen a lagh, that is to meane, the lawes of Marcia' (they were really
Border-laws.)' (Kitchin.)

XLIII.

Her sonne Sifillus after her did rayne;
And then Kimarus; and then Danius:
Next whom Morindus did the crowne sustayne;
Who, had he not with wrath outrageous
And cruell rancour dim'd his valorous
. And mightie deedes, should matched have the best
As well in that same field victorious
Against the forreine Morands he exprest;
Yet lives his memorie, though carcase sleepe in rest.

Ihr sohn Sifillus regierte nach ihr, dann Kimarus,
und darauf Danius: nach ihm trug Morindus die
krone; haette dieser nicht durch jachzorn und rach-
sucht seine tapfern und maechtigen thaten verdun-
kelt, wuerde er den besten gleichgekommen sein, wie
er es zum beispiel in der siegreichen schlacht gegen
die fremden Moriner bewies; noch lebt sein andenken, wenn auch seine sterblichen ueberreste in ruhe
schlafen.

XLIV.

Five sonnes he left begotten of one wife,
All which successively by turnes did rayne:
First Gorboman, a man of virtuous life;
Next Archigald, who for his proud disdayne
Deposed was from princedome soverayne,
And pitteous Eliduro put in his sted;
Who shortly it to him restord agayne,
Till by his death he it recovered;
But Periduro and Vigent him disthronized:

Fuenf soehne hinterliess er von Einer frau, welche
alle nach einander, wenn die reihe an sie kam, re-
gierten: zuerst Gorboman, ein mann von tugendhaf-
tem leben; danach Archigald, der wegen seines stolzen uebermuthes der fuerstenwuerde entkleidet ward,
und an dessen stelle der mitleidige Eliduro eingesetzt wurde, der ihm die herrschaft bald wiedergab,
bis er sie durch den tod desselben zum zweiten mal
erhielt; aber Periduro und Vigent entthronten ihn.

XLV.

In wretched prison long he did remaine,
Till they out-raigned had their utmost date;
And then therein reseized was againe,
And ruled long with honorable state,
Till he surrendred realme and life to fate.
Then all the sonnes of these five brethren raynd
By dew successe, and all their nephewes late;

. In elender gefangenschaft blieb er lange, bis zum
letzten augenblick ihrer regierung, wurde dann wieder eingesetzt und herrschte noch geraume zeit mit
ehrenvollem ansehen, bis er reich und leben dem
schicksal anheimgeben musste. Sodann kamen alle
soehne dieser fuenf brueder in gebuehrlicher reihen-
folge, und noch die spaeten enkel von ihnen allen;

---

v. 5. layes; — 'Laws, for the rhyme's sake.' (Church in Todd.)
XLIII. Various readings: In Kitchin: v. 3. 'sustaine'.   v. 6. 'deeds'.   v. 9. 'carcas'.
v. 8. the forreine Morands: — 'Holinshed, Hist. Engl. 3. 6; 'In his daies, a certaine king of the people
called Moriani . . . landed in Northumberland . . .' These people I take to be either those that inhabited about Terrouane
and Calice, called Morini, or some other people of tho Galles or Germaines'. (Kitchin.)
XLIV. Various readings: In Kitchin: v. 2. 'raine'.   v. 3. 'vertuous'.   v. 4. 'disdaine'.   v. 5. 'soveraine'.
v. 7. 'againe'.
v. 6. pitteous Eliduro; — 'so called because he had pity on, and abdicated in favour of, his deposed brother
Arthegal, or Archigald. (Hardyng, c. 37.) Holinshed (Hist. Engl. 3. 7) says: 'For this great good-will and brotherly love
by him shewed thus towards his brother, he was surnamed The Godly and Vertuous'. And Hardyng, c. 38:
'He was so full of all pytee
That in all thynge mercy he dyd preserve'.
v. 9. Vigent; — 'Vigenius', Holinshed; 'Iugen', Hardyng.' (Kitchin.)
XLV. Various readings: In Kitchin: v. 2. 'out raigned'.
v. 1. In wretched prison, etc.; — 'Hardyng, c. 38:
'And prisoner hym full sore and wrongfullye
All in the towre of Troynovante for thy'. (Kitchin.)
v. 3. then therein reseized was againe; — 'Hardyng, c. 39:
'Eledour was kyng all newe made againe,
Thrise crowned'. (Kitchin.)
Todd: 're seized; — Had seisin or possession again; reinstated in his kingdom. Upton.'
v. 6. Then all the sonnes; — 'Spenser closely follows Holinshed, who merely mentions these thirty-three
kings, saying that 182 years must be apportioned among them, and adding that there is no certainty among authors on the
subject.' But Hardyng goes through with them diligently by name.
Cp. F. Q. II, VIII. 29: 'from the grandsire to the nephew's son', to the third and fourth generation.
v. 7. By dew successe; — 'That is, by due succession; in their dew descents; as he expresses it, st. 74.'
(Church in Todd.)

Even thrise eleven descents the crowne retaynd,
Till aged Hely by dew heritage it gaynd.

ja dreimal eilf nachkommen trugen die krone, bis
sie der bejahrte Hely durch rechtmaessige erbschaft
erlangte.

XLVI.

He had two sonnes, whoso eldest, called Lud,
Left of his life most famous memory,
And endlesse moniments of his great good:
The ruin'd wals he did rœdifye .
Of Troynovant, gainst force of enimy,
And built that gate which of his name is hight,
By which he lyes entombed solemnly:
He left two sonnes, too young to rule aright,
Androgeus and Tenantius, picturos of his might.

Dieser hatte zwei soehne, deren aeltester, namens
Lud, ein hoechst ruhmreiches andenken seines lebens
hinterliess und endlose denkmaeler seiner grossen tugend: die verfallenen mauern von Troynovant stellte
er wieder her gegen feindliche macht und baute das
thor, das nach seinem namen genannt ist, und bei
welchem er feierlich begraben liegt: er hinterliess
zwei soehne, die noch zu jung waren, um in der rich-
tigen weise zu regieren, Androgeus und Tenantius,
ebenbilder seiner macht.

XLVII.

Whilst they were young, Cassibalane their eme
Was by the people chosen in their sted,
Who on him tooke the roiall diademe,
And goodly well long time it governed;
Till the prowde Romanes him disquieted,
And warlike Cæsar, tempted with the name
Of this sweet island never conquered,
And envying the Britons blazed fame,
(O hideous hunger of dominion!) hether came.

Fuer die zeit ihrer minderjaehrigkeit wurde Cassi-
balanus, ihr oheim, vom volke zu ihrem stellvertreter
gewaehlt, der das koenigliche diadem annahm und
vorzueglich gut lange zeit hindurch regierte; bis die
stolzen Roemer ihn beunruhigten und der kriegerische
Caesar, durch die beruehmtheit dieses herrlichen
eilands, das nie erobert worden war, angelockt und
neidisch auf den weit verbreiteten ruhm der Briten,
hieher kam. (O garstiger hunger nach herrschaft!)

XLVIII.

Yet twise they were repulsed backe againe,

Doch zweimal wurden sie zurueckgetrieben und

---

nephewes; — 'Nephews are nepotes, grand sons.' (Jortin in Todd.)
     v. 9. aged Hely; — 'eponymous of the 'Isle of Ely'. (Kitchin.)
XLVI. v. 1. Lud; — 'Holinshed, Hist. Engl. 3. 9; Hardyng, c. 40, 41.' (Kitchin.)
     v. 4. The ruin'd wals; — 'Hardyng says:
        'With walles faire, and towres fresh about
        His citie great of Troynovaunt, full fayre,
        Full well he made, and batelled throughout;
        And palays fayre, for [royalles to appeare]
        Amendyng other defectyve and unfayre,
        From London stone to his palays royall
        That now Ludgate is knowen over all'.
He says he built hard by Ludgate his palace and a temple, and then
        'He died so, and in his temple fayre
        Entombed was'. (Kitchin.)
     v. 5. Troynovant: — 'that is, London, the city of the Trinobantes, there is of course no ground for the old
derivation from 'Troia nova', New Troy, the city founded by Brutus, and named after the city of his fathers.' (Kitchin.)
     v. 8. too young to rule aright: — 'so Hardyng:
        'Which were to young to rule the heritage'. (Kitchin.)
XLVII. Various readings: In Kitchin: v. 3. 'royall'.   v. 5. 'prowd'.   v. 9. 'hither'.
     v. 1. their eme: — 'Their uncle.' (Church in Todd.)
     v. 5. Till the prowde Romanes; — '55 B. C. Hardyng, c. 42, says:
'In which tyme so came Caesar Iulius   To sayle anone into this Britayn made,
Into the lande of Fraunce that nowe so hight;   In Thamis aroue, wher he had ful sharpe shores (stow-
[And on a daye walkyng up and downe full right]   res?)
On the sea syde, wher he this lande did see,   . . . Wher, after battayle, smythen and forfought
Desyrryng sore [of it] the soverayntee,   · Iulius fled, and there preuayled nought'.
His nauye greate, with many soudyoures
     Caesar's true reason was not a mere 'hideous hunger of dominion', but a clear opinion that unless Britain, the
stronghold of Druidism, were checked, he could never hold Gaul in security.' (Kitchin.)

And twise renforst backe to their ships to fly;
The whiles with blood they all the shore did staine,
And the gray ocean into purple dy:
Ne had they footing found at last perdie,
Had not Androgeus, false to native soyle,
And envious of uncles soveraintie,
Betrayd his country unto forreine spoyle.
Nought els but treason from the first this land did
    foyle!

zweimal gezwungen, zurueck zu ihren schiffen zu fliehen; unterwegs beflockten sie mit blut die ganze
kueste und faerbten den grauen ocean purpurn: und
nicht, bei Gott, haetten sie zuletzt festen fuss ge-
fasst, haette nicht Androgeus, verraether an seinem
heimathlichen boden und neidisch auf des oheims
herrschaft, sein vaterland fremdem raube ueberliefert.
Nichts anders als verrath besiegte dies land von an-
    beginn an!

XLIX.

So by him Cæsar god the victory,
Through great bloodshed and many a sad assay,
In which himselfe was charged heavily
Of hardy Nennius, whom he yet did slay,
But lost his sword, yet to be seene this day.
Thenceforth this land was tributarie made
T'ambitious Rome, and did their rule obay,
Till Arthur all that reckoning defrayd:
Yet oft the Briton kings against them strongly swayd.

So errang Caesar durch seine vermittelung den
sieg, wenn auch durch grosses blutvergiessen und
manchen harten strauss, wobei er selbst von dem
kuehnen Nennius hart bedraengt wurde; jedoch toedtete er ihn, verlor aber sein schwerdt, das noch heutigen tages zu sehen ist. Von nun an ward dies
land dem ehrgeizigen Rom tributpflichtig gemacht
und gehorchte seiner herrschaft, bis Arthur die ganze
rechnung bezahlte: doch noch oft hatten die Britischen koenige harte kaempfe gegen sie zu bestehen.

L.

Next him Tenantius raignd; then Kimbeline,
What time th' Eternall Lord in fleshly slime

Unmittelbar nach ihm regierte Tenantius; dann
Kimbeline, zu der zeit als der Ewige Herr von

XLVIII. **Various readings:** In Kitchin: v. 8. 'countrey'.
    v. 1. **Yet twise, etc.;** — 'Hardyng give it us, c. 43:
        'came to Britayn again
        Into Thamis, where Cassibelayn the
        Great pyle of tree and yron sette hym again,
        His shippes to peryshe, and so he did certain
        Through which greate parte of his nauy was drowned
        And [some other] in batayl wer confounded.
        Then fled he eft with shippes that he had
        Into the lande of Fraunce', etc.
    . Caesar, Comment. Bk. 4. 5, only makes two descents in 55 and 54 B. C,, not into the Thames at all. He
landed both times somewhere near the South Foreland. Nor was he ever really repulsed by the Britons, though his successes were of but small value. For it is very clear, after all, that he obtained very little hold upon Britain. After his
second incursion he withdrew upon receiving the nominal submission of Cassibelan, some slaves, and a quantity of pearls.
But Britain remained as she was, and the tribute was never paid.' (Kitchin.)
    v. 2. **renforst;** — 'So all the editions. I think it should be enforst, i. e. forced, obliged.' (Church in Todd.)
    v. 6. **Androgeus;** — 'Hardyng (whom Spenser follows here) describes this in c. 44.' (Kitchin.)
    v. 9. **foyle!;** — 'Foil here signifies to defeat or conquer, as it also signifies, in F. Q. V, XI, 33, and in
other places.' (Todd.)
XLIX. **Various readings:** In Kitchin: v. 2. 'bloudshed'.   v. 3. 'him selfe'.
    v. 4. 5. **Nennius, whom he yet did slay, But lost his sword;** — 'Hardyng, c. 41:
'But Neminus, brother of Cassybalayne,   (Which of manly force and myght vigorous)
Full manly fought on Iulius tymes tweyne.   The sweardo he brought away out of the felde,
With strokes sore ayther on other bette,   As Iulius it [set faste] in his shelde.
But [at the laste this prynce ayr] Iulius   Through which stroke sir Neminus then died,
Crosea mors his swerde in sheide sette   . . . Crosea mors his swearde layde by his syde
Of the manly worthy sir Neminus;   Which he [brought from] Iulius that tyde'.
    So also the story is told by Geoffry of Monmouth. This tale is doubtless connected with that sword which Cae-
sar is said to have lost in the Gallic War.' (Kitchin.)
    v. 8. **Till Arthur;** — 'the Prince reads his owne name and noble actions unconscious that he is intended.
And, indeed, there is a certain confusion about it. Spenser means that Britain continued subject to Rome till Arthur delivered her. As to this subjection, even Holinshed, Hist. Engl. 3. 16, says, 'Cæsar might seem rather to have shewed Britaine
to the Romans than to have delivered possession of the same',. (Kitchin.)
    L. **Various readings:** In Kitchin: v. 4. 'sinfull'.   v. 7. a parenthesis.

Enwombed was, from wretched Adams line
To purge away the guilt of sinful crime.
O joyous memorie of happy time,
That heavenly grace so plenteously displayd!
O too high ditty for my simple rime! —
Soone after this the Romanes him warrayd;
For that their tribute he refusd to let be payd.

menschlichem leibe empfangen ward, um von des
elenden Adams nachkommen die schuld verbrecheri-
scher suende hinwegzuwaschen. O herrliche erinnerung an die gluockliche zeit, da die himmlische gnade
sich in solcher fuelle offenbarte! O zu hohes lied fuer
meinen einfachen reim! — Bald nachher bekriegten
ihn die Roemer dafuer, dass er sich weigerte, ihnen
den tribut zu zahlen.

LI.

Good Claudius, that next was emperour,
An army brought, and with him batteile fought,
In which the king was by a treachetour
Disguised slaine, ere any thereof thought:
Yet ceased not the bloody fight for ought:
For Arvirage his brothers place supplyde
Both in his armes and crowne, and by that draught
Did drive the Romanes to the weaker syde,
That they to peace agreed. So all was pacifyde.

Der gute Claudius, der danach kaiser war, ruockte
mit einem heere an und schlug mit ihm eine
schlacht, in der der koenig durch einen verkappten
verraether erschlagen wurde, bevor jemand daran
dachte: doch hoerte der blutige kampf dadurch durchaus nicht auf: denn Arvirage trat an seines bruders
stelle; er legte seine waffen an, setzte seine krone
auf und zwang die Roemer durch diese list zum wei-
chen, so dass sie in den frieden willigten. So war
alles wieder ruhig.

LII.

Was never king more highly magnifide,
Nor dredd of Romanes, then was Arvirage;
For which the emperour to him allide
His daughter Genuiss' in marriage:
Yet shortly he renounst the vassallage
Of Rome againe, who hether hastly sent

Nie wurde ein koenig hoeher gepriesen noch
von den Roemern mehr gefuerchtet, als Arvirage;
deshalb gab ihm der kaiser seine tochter Genuissa
zur gemahlinn: doch bald schwur er die abhaengig-
keit von Kom wieder ab, das in folge dessen eilig
den Vespasian hinsandte, der raubend und mordend

---

v. 2. What time; — 'so Holinshed and Hardyng.' (Kitchin.)
v. 9. For that their tribute, etc.; — 'this is told, not of Kimbeline, but of his son and successor Guyder.' (Kitchin.)
LI. Various readings: In Kitchin: v. 2, 'battell'.   v. 5 'bloudy'.   v. 6, 'supplide'.   v, 8. side'.
v. 9. 'pacifide'.
v. 1. Good Claudius; — 'Emperor, A. D. 41, was of Sabine origin, born at Lyons. He spoke but a barbarous Latin, and preferred Greek; he was proud of his Gallic birthplace, and hated Rome. A fragment of his speech in the Senate, advocating the claims of the Gaelic chiefs to a seat in that assembly, is still preserved in the museum at Lyons. This friend-liness for the Gael is doubtless the origin of the title 'good', which scarcely bears its proper moral significance in this case. This is probably the answer to Mr. Church's question: 'But why does he call good?' Claudius came into Britain A. D. 43.' (Kitchin.)
v. 3. In which the king, etc.; — 'so Hardyng, c. 45:
'One Hamon rode faste into the route
Havyng on him the Britains sygne of warre
Who, in the prees, slewe the Kyng Guyder'. (Kitchin.)
v. 6. Arvirage; — 'Hardyng, c. 46:
'His brothers armis upon hymself he cast;
Aud Kyng was then of all' Great Britain'.
v. 7. by that draught; — 'That is, by that resemblance, by the stratagem of putting on his Brother's armour.' (Church in Todd.)
LII. Various readings: In Kitchin: v. 2. 'dred'.   v. 6. 'hither'.
v. 4. His daughter Genuiss'; — 'so say Geoffry of Monmouth, Holinshed (Hist. Engl.), Hardyng, c. 46. All these details are wanting in the Roman histories, and are in fact incidents of romance. This must be noticed now that we have come to historic times and names.' (Kitchin.)
v. 5. Yet shortly, etc.; — 'so Hardyng:
After agayne, the Kyng truage denyed,
And none wolde paye; wherefore Vespasian
Hyther was sent'. (Kitchin.)
v. 6. who hither, etc.; — 'who' = Rome in the person of her Emperor Claudius. Vespasian came into Britain, 43 A. D., as 'legatus legionis;' the same year in which Claudius himself was here.' (Kitchin.) ·

11

Vespasian, that with great spoile and rage
Forwasted all, till Genuissa gent
Porsuaded him to ceasse, and her lord to relent.

alles verwuestete, bis die zarte Genuissa ihn ueber-
redete, abzulassen und ihren gemahl zur nachgiebig-
keit bewog.

LIII.

He dide; and him succeded Marius,
Who ioyd his dayes in great tranquillity.
Then Coyll; and after him good Lucius,
That first received Christianity,
The sacred pledge of Christes Evangely,
Yet true it is, that long before that day
Hither came Ioseph of Arimathy,
Who brought with him the Holy Grayle, :(they say,)
And preacht the truth; but since it greatly did
decay.

Er starb, und ihm folgte Marius, der in tiefer ruhe
seine tage genoss; dann Coyll, und auf ihn der gute
Lucius, der zuerst das Christenthum annahm und das
heilige pfand des Evangeliums von Christo; doch wahr
ist es, dass lange vor jenem tage Joseph von Arimathia
hieher kam, welcher, wie gesagt wird, den heiligen
Graal mitbrachte und die wahrheit predigte, die seitdem allerdings sehr in verfall gerathen ist.

LIV.

This good king shortly without issew dide,
Whereof great trouble in the kingdome grew,
That did herselfe in sondry parts divide,
And with her powre her owne selfe overthrew,
Whilest Romanes daily did the weake subdew:
Which seeing, stout Bunduca up arose,
And taking armes the Britons to her drew;
With whom she marched straight against her foes,
And them unwares besides the Severne did enclose.

Dieser gute koenig starb bald ohne nachkommen,
worueber grosse verwirrung im koenigreiche entstand,
welches sich in verschiedene parteien spaltete und
mit seiner eignen macht sich zu grunde richtete,
waehrend die Roemer taeglich die schwachen unterjochte: dies sah die starke Bunduca, erhob sich, er-
griff die waffen und brachte die Briten auf ihre seite;
mit ihnen marschirte sie stracks gegen ihre feinde
und schloss sie unvermuthet in der naehe der Severne ein.

LIII. Various readings: In Kitchin: v. 1. 'dyde'. v. 2. 'joyd'.
v. 3. 4. good Lucius, That first received Christianity; — 'The early Welsh notices and the Silurian
Catalogues of Saints state that Lleurwg, called also Lleufer Maur, 'the great light' — Lucius (lux), applied to Rome for
spiritual instruction, and that in consequence four teachers, Dyfan, Ffagan, Medwy, and Elfan, were sent to him by Pope
Eleutherius,' (Smith's Dict, of Biogr., Lucius.) Bede gives in substance the same account, giving the date A. D. 156. This
is credible enough; but he was an obvious field for legend, and has been used accordingly
So in Geoffry of Monmouth, 2. 1. This King Lucius is said by Hardyng to have received two 'holye menne,
Faggan and Dunyen', from Pope Eleutherius. Another account describes him as going a pilgrimage and suffering martyr-
dom at Chur (Coire) in the Grisons, where the cathedral is dedicated to him,' (Kitchin.)
v. 5. The sacred pledge; — 'sc. Baptism.' (Kitchin.)
v. 6. Yet true it is; — 'the very dubious legend of Joseph of Arimathea; who, according to Hardyng (c. 47)
and Holinshed (Hist, Engl. 4. 5), came into England, and made many converts. The tale runs that Joseph, carrying the
Holy Grayle with him, set forth in a boat, which guided itself through the Pillars of Hercules, across the main sea, into
the Bristol Channel. She went steadily on, till she grounded in a marshy spot, since called Glastonbury. There he landed,
and in sign of possession, planted his staff, which took root, and became the famous Glastonbury thorn ' (Kitchin.)
v. 8. the holy grayle; — 'either 1) the earthen dish off which our Lord ate the Passover; or 2) the 'sanguis
realis', or actual blood of our Saviour. The quest of the Sangreal forms a large element in the Morte d'Arthur.' (Kitchin.)
LIV. Various readings: In Kitchin: v. 3. 'her selfe'. 'soundry'.
v. 6. Bunduca; 'better known as Boadicea. Her story is handed down to us by Tacitus, 14. 31—37. She
was aroused in A. D. 62 by the infinite wrongs done her family by the Romans; and raising the Iceni and Trinobantes,
she stormed and took the Roman position of Camaloducum. Afterwards she defeated Petilius Cerealis. The Britons next
seized London, even then a great emporium, and Verulamium. These three towns were the chief Roman settlements in
Britain. Baodicea was afterwards met and utterly defeated by Suetonius Paulinus. Robert of Gloucester, Geoffry of Monmouth, Hardyng, give no account of her; but Holinshed gives her history and descripton at length, Hist, Engl. 4. 10. 11:
'Hir mightie tall personage, comelie shape, severe countenance, and sharpe voice, with hir long and yellow tresses of haire
reaching downe to hir thighes, hir brave and gorgeous apparelle also caused the people to have hir in great reverence. She
wore a chaine of gold, great and verie massie, and was clad in a lose kirtle of sundrie colours and aloft thereupon she
had a thicke Irish mantell; hereto in hir haud she bare a speare, to shew hirselfe the more dreadfull'. (Kitchin.)
v. 9. besides the Severne: — 'besides — near.' (Church in Todd.)
Kitchin: 'we do not know where the battle was fought; but it could not have been in West England. Baodicea was an eastern queen; her successes were at Camalodunum (Colchester), London, and Verulamium (St. Alban's), all in
the East of England. Her followers were Iceni and Trinobantes, eastern tribes.

LV.

There she with them a cruell batteill tryde,
Not with so good successe as shee deserv'd;
By reason that the captaines on her syde,
Corrupted by Paulinus, from her swerv'd:
Yet such, as were through former flight preserv'd,
Gathering againe, her host sho did renew,
And with fresh corage on the victor servd:
But boing all defeated, savo a few,
Rather thau fly, or bo captiv'd herselfe she slew.

Dort wagte sie mit ihnen eine fuerchterliche schlacht,
aber nicht mit so gutem erfolge, als sie es verdiente, da ihre feldherren von Paulinus bestochen
wurden und sie im stiche liessen: doch die, die zei-
tig geflohen und daher noch am leben waren, sammelte sie wieder, bildete noch einmal ein heer und
warf sich mit frischem muthe auf den feind: aber
nachdem alle, ausser einigen wenigen, niedergemacht
waren, wollte sie lieber sterben als fliehen oder gefangen werden und gab sich selbst den tod.

LVI.

O famous moniment of womens prayse!
Matchablo either to Semiramis,
Whom ántiquo history so high doth rayse,
Or to Hypsiphil', or to Thomiris:
Her host two hundred thousand numbred is,
Who, whiles good fortuno favoured her might
Triumphed oft against her enemis;
And yet, though overcome in haplesse fight,
Shee triumphed on death, in enemies despight.

O beruehmtes denkmal des frauenruhms! entweder
der Semiramis vergleichbar, welche die alte geschichte
so hoch erhebt, odor der Hypsiphile odor der Thomiris: ihre armee wird auf zweihundert tausend mann
geschaetzt, die, so lange das glueck ihre macht be-
guenstigte, oft ueber ihre feinde triumphirten; und
als sie in uuglueucklicher schlacht besiegt ward, trium-
phirte sie doch noch im todo den feinden zum trotz.

LVII.

Her reliques Fulgent having gathered,
Fought with Severus, and him overthrew;
Yet in the chace was slaino of them that fled;
So made them victors whome he did subdow.
Thon gan Carausius tirannize anew,

Nachdem Fulgent ihre storblichen reste gesammelt
hatte, kaempfto er mit Severus und besiegte ihn;
doch auf der verfolgung wurde er von den fliehenden
erschlagen; so dass auf diese weise, die er unter-
jocht hatte, sieger wurden. Darauf begann Carausius

Spenser's account differs from that given by Holinshed. He says that after her defeat by Suetonius, 'those that escaped would have fought a new battell, but in the meane time Voadicea' (sic!) 'deceased of a naturall infirmitie, as Dion Cassius writeth, but other say that she poisoned hir selfe, and so died, because she would not come into the hands of hir bloodthirsty enimies.' (Kitchin.)
    LV.   Various readings: In Kitchin: v. 1. 'battell'.   'tride'.   v. 2. 'she'.   v. 7. 'courage'.   'serv'd'.
    v. 9. 'her selfe'.
    v. 2. Not with so good success; — 'in this great battle the Romans had but 10,000 men, while Boadicea commanded (it is said) 230,000. The Romans took up a strong position, and utterly defeated the barbarians with immense slaughter; 80,000 are said to have perished.' (Kitchin.)
    LVI.   Various readings: In Kitchin: v. 3. 'antique'.   'raise'.
    v. 2. Semiramis; — 'the mythical founder of Nineveh, wife of Ninus. Her beauty and bravery placed her among most memorable women'.
    v. 4. Hypsiphil'; — 'was in the legends, Queen of Lemnos. Her one feat (Apollod. 3. 6. 4.) was that of saving her father when in the Lemniun madness the women slew all the men on the island. It is hard to see why she has been selected by Spenser among the heroic parallels to Boadicea.' (Kitchin.)
    Thomiris; — 'Tomyris is described by Herodotus (1. 205) as a heroic queen of the Massagetae, who resisted and defeated Cyrus.' (Kitchin.)
    Jortin: 'Tomyris it should be, though 'tis likely enough that Spenser might write it as it is printed.' But he surely never intended Hysiphil'. It should be Hypsiphyl', Hypsiphyle.'
    LVII.   Various readings: In Kitchin: v. 4. 'victours'.   'whom'.
    v. 1. Fulgent; — 'Hardyug, c. 52:
                            'the northern Brittons,
                    With Fulgen stode, was Kyng of Scotlande bore'. (Kitchin.)
    v. 2. Fought with Severus; — 'Iulius Severus is described by Dion Cassius (69. 13) as a legate of Hadrian, and for a time governor of Britain. He built the wall (Murus Britannicus) between the Tyne and the Solway. The chron-iclers confouud the Picts' Wall with this. Hardyng (c. 53) says:
                    'From Tynmouth to Alclud his fayre citee',
Alcluid being on the Clyde (Dumbarton), where the Picts' Wall, running from the Frith of Forth, ended'. (Kitchin.)

And gainst the Romanes bent their proper powre;
But him Allectus treacherously slew,
And tooke on him the robe of emperoure;
Nath'lesse the same enioyed but short happy howre.

von neuem den tyrannen zu spielen und richtete gegen die Roemer ihre eigne macht; aber ihn toedtete Allectus verraetherischer weise und legte das kaiserliche gewand an; nichtsdestoweniger genoss derselbe nur eine kurze glueckliche stunde.

LVIII.

For Asclepiodate him overcame,
And left inglorious on the vanquisht playne,
Without or robe or rag to hide his shame;
Then afterwards he in his stead did raigne.
But shortly was by Coyll in batteill slaine,
Who after long debate, since Lucies tyme,
Was of the Britons first crownd soveraine:
Then gan this realme renew her passed prime:
He of his name Coylchester built of stone and lime.

Denn Asclepiodatus besiegte ihn und liess ihn ruhmlos auf dem felde seiner niederlage, ohne kleid oder einen lappen, seine schande zu verbergen. Hierauf regierte er dann an seiner stelle. Aber binnen kurzem wurde er von Coyll in einer schlacht geschlagen, der nach langem kampfe seit Lucy's zeiten zuerst von den Briten zum herrscher gekroent wurde. Dann begann dies reich seinen vorigen glanz wieder zu erlangen: er baute das nach ihm genannte Coylchester von stein und kalk.

LIX.

Which when the Romanes heard, they hether sent
Constantius, a man of mickle might,
With whome king Coyll made an agreëment,
And to him gave for wife his daughter bright.

Als dies die Roemer hoerten, sandten sie den Constantius hieher, einen mann von ansehnlicher macht; mit diesem traf koenig Coyll ein uebereinkommen und gab ihm seine reizende tochter zum weibe,

---

v. 5. Then gan Carausius; — 'M. Aurelius Valerius Carausius, a native of the district of the Menapi, a poor pilot, being set by Maximinian over the cruisers who watched the pirates, swarming in and out of the mouths of the Rhine and Scheldt, fled with his fleet to Britain, gained over the legions there stationed, and assumed the title of Augustus. He was eventually recognised as colleague by Diocletian and Maximian. This resistance against Maximian Spenser refers to in saying that he
'Gainst the Romanes bent their proper powre',
though he is not very exact in saying so. He was murdered by Allectus, his chief officer (as Spenser says, l. 7), in the year A. D. 293.' (Kitchin.)
v. 8. And tooke on him, etc.; — 'Allectus did assume the purple, and wore it for three years — that was his 'short happy howre'. In 296 Constantius sent against him Asclepiodotus (sic!) with army and fleet, and subdued him.' (Kitchin.)
LVIII. Various readings: In Kitchin: v. 4. 'rayne'. v. 5. 'battell'. v. 6. 'time'.
v. 2. on the vanquisht plaine; — 'either = 'vanquished on the plaine', or = 'on the plain of his defeat'. (Kitchin.)
v. 4. Then afterwards; — 'it does not appear that this was the case. There are no relics of Asclepiodotus as Emperor. Hardyng calls him 'Duke of Cornwayle' (c. 56). In c. 57 he says he 'was crowned Kyng agayne'. (Kitchin.)
v. 5. Coyll; — 'Hardyng (c. 58) gives us this prince:
'For whiche duke Coyle agayne him rose ful hote,
The duke Caire Colun (that hight) Coylus,
Whiche cytee [now] this daye Colchester hight,
Then crowned was'. (Kitchin.)
v. 9. Coylchester; — 'Colchester is so called either from its older name Camulodunum (sic!), Camalo-chester, or more probably from the Latin Colonia, Colnchester. It was the first of the Roman colonies in Britain, and is mentioned by the name of Caer Colun, in Nennius. By the time of Boadicea there were three important Roman cities in Britain, Camulodunum, London, and Verulamium. So that 'Coylchester' existed long before Spenser's King Coyll the Second'. (Kitchin.)
LIX. Various readings: In Kitchin: v. 1. 'hither'. v. 3. 'agreement'. v. 6. 'prayse'. v. 8. 'dayes'. v. 9. 'layes'.
v. 2. Constantius; — 'Constantius Chlorus established his authority in Britain in A. D. 296, at the time of the overthrow of Allectus, but did not come into the island till rather later. He died at Eboracum (Everwyk, York) in 306, while on an expedition against the Picts.' (Kitchin.)
v. 4. 5. his daughter bright, Faire Helena, the fairest living wight; — 'Spenser attributes to her some of the qualities of the original Helena, the bane of Troy. Her origin seems to have been but low; nor is there any foundation for the legend adopted by Spenser from Hardyng, c. 59, 60, and Holinshed, Hist. Engl. 4. 28: 'His first wife Helen, the daughter (as some affirme) of Coell late king of the Britains.'

Faire Helena, the fairest living wight,
Who in all godly thewes and goodly praise
Did far excell, but was most famous hight .
For skil in musicke of all in her daies,
As well in curious instruments as cunning laies:

die schoene Helena, das schoenste lebende geschoepf, die in allen gottseligen tugenden und in
herrlichem ruhme weit hervorleuchtete; fuer die be-
ruehmteste aber von allen ihrer zeit wurde sie wegen
ihres musikalischen talentes gehalten, da sie eben-
sowohl kuenstliche instrumente spielte als sinnige lieder sang.

LX.

Of whome he did great Constantine begett,
Who afterward was emperour of Rome;
To which whiles absent he his mind did sett,
Octavius here lept into his roome,
And it usurped by unrighteous doome:
But he his title justifide by might,
Slaying Traherne, and having overcome
The Romane legion in dreadfull fight:
So settled he his kingdome, and confirmd his right:

Mit dieser erzeugte er den grossen Constantin, der
nachher kaiser von Rom war; waehrend er in seiner
abwesenheit darauf seinen sinn richtete, schwang sich
Octavius hier an seiner stelle auf den thron und bemaech-
tigte sich desselben durch ein ungerechtes verhaeng-
niss: aber er rechtfertigte seinen anspruch durch macht,
indem er den Traherne schlug und die Roemische
legion in grausiger schlacht besiegte: so ordnete er
sein koenigreich und sicherte sein recht.

LXI.

But, wanting yssew male, his daughter deare
He gave in wedlocke to Maximian,
And him with her made of his kingdome heyre,
Who soone by meanes thereof the empire wan,
Till murdred by the freends of Gratian.
Then gan the Hunnes and Picts invade this land,
During the raigne of Maximinian;
Who dying left none heire them to withstand:
But that they overran all parts with easy hand.

Aber in ermangelung eines maennlichen nachkommen gab er seine geliebte tochter dem Maximian zur
frau und machte ihn durch sie zum erben seines koenigreichs; bald befand er sich auch in folge dessen
im besitz der herrschaft, bis er von den freunden
Gratian's ermordet wurde. Waehrend der regierung
Maximinian's begannen dann die Hunnen und Picten
in dies land einzufallen; als er starb, hinterliess er
keinen erben, der ihnen haette widerstand leisten
koennen, so dass sie mit leichter muehe alle theile des
landes ueberschwemmten.

She was repudiated by Constantius when he was raised to the dignity of Caesar, because he wanted, for state
reasons, to marry Theodora, stepchild of Maximian.' (Kitchin.)
    LX.   Various readings: In Kitchin: v. 1. 'beget'.   v. 3. 'set'.
        v. 1. great Constantine; — 'surnamed Magnus, son of Constantius and Helena, born A. D. 272. He was
emperor from A. D. 306 to 337.' (Kitchin.)
        v. 4. Octavius; — 'not a historic personage, nor is Traherne. The legend is given by Holinshed, Hist.
Engl. 4. 29, and by Hardyng, c. 63, who calls Octavius 'Duke of Westesax', (Kitchin.)
    LXI.   Various readings; In Kitchin: v. 1. 'issew',   v. 9. 'easie'.
        v. 1. wanting yssew male; — 'Constantine, on the contrary, had four sons: Crispus; Constantinus II, 'the
younger'; Constantius II, and Constans. None of his daughters married Maximian: one of them was named Helena Favia
Maximiana, whence the error may have sprung.' (Kitchin.)
        v. 2. to Maximian; — 'there were two Maximians emperors: 1) Maximianus I, surnamed Herculius, whose
stepdaughter Constantius Chlorus married. He formed a close alliance with Constantine, and gave him his daughter Fausta;
but afterwards, intriguing against him in the south of France, he was ordered to choose the manner of his death, and
strangled himself, A. D. 310. 2) Maximianus II, who is also called Galerius. He was never on friendly relations with Constantine.' (Kitchin.)
        v. 5. Gratian; — 'he was not born till A. D. 359. Nor is there any foundation in history for this murder 'by
the friends of Gratian:' in the note on line 2 the manner of Maximian's death is mentioned; and it occurred forty-nine
years before Gratian was born.' (Kitchin.)
        v. 6. Then gan etc.; — 'the chroniclers are fond of these Huns. Geoffry of Monmouth, I. 11, tells us of
their entry into Britain under Humber their chief. The Scots and Picts were probably natives of Ireland'. (Kitchin.)
        v. 7. Maximinian; — 'it is not quite clear who this is; but Spenser probably meant Maximus, who in the
time of Gratian, was in Britain, A. D. 368, and remained there as general for several years. Fuller, Ch. Hist. 1, cent. IV,
§. 22, says he 'for a time valiantly resisted the Scots and Picts, which cruelly invaded and infested the south of Britain.'
(Kitchin.)

LXII.

The weary Britons, whose war-hable youth
Was by Maximian lately ledd away,
With wretched miseryes and woefull ruth
Were to those pagans made an open pray,
And daily spectacle of sad decay:
Whome Romane warres, which now fowr hundred yeares
And more had wasted could no whit dismay;
Til, by consent of Commons and of Peares,
They crownd the second Constantine with ioyous teares.

Die muedon Briton, deren kriegerische jugend durch
Maximian kuerzlich weggefuohrt war, wurden durch
entsetzliches elend und trauriges wohe fuer jene hei-
den zu einer offenen boute gemacht und zum taeg-
lichen schauspiel trauriger niederlage — sie, die die
Roemischen kriege, welche nun vierhundert jahr und
darueber gewucthet hatten, nicht im geringsten hatten entmnthigen koennen —, bis durch die zustim-
mung von volk und adel der zweite Constantin unter
freudenthraenen gekroent wurde.

LXIII.

Who having oft in butteill vanquished
Those spoylefull Picts, and swarming Easterlings,
Long time in peace his realme established,
Yet oft unnoyd with sondry bordragings
Of neighbour Scots and forrein scatterlings,
With which the world did in those dayes abound.
Which to outbarre, with painefull pyonings
From sea to sea he heapt a mighty mound,
Which from Alcluid to Panwelt did that border bownd.

Nachdem derselbe oft jene raeuberischen Picten
und schwaermenden Ostlaender in der schlacht besiegt hatte, hielt er lange zeit sein reich in frieden,
wenn er auch oft durch verschiedene grenzeinfaelle
von den benachbarten Scoten und fremdeu raeuberban-
den, von welchen die welt in jenen tagen ueberstroemte, beunruhigt wurde. Um diese abzusperren,
zog er mit muehsamen schanzgraeberarbeiten von
einem ende des meeres bis zum andern einen maechtigen damm, der von Alcluid bis Panwelt jene grenze
ausmachte.

LXIV.

Three sonnes he dying left, all under age,
By meanes whereof their uncle Vortigere
Usurpt the crowne during their pupillage;
Which th' infants tutors gathering to feare,

Drei soehne hinterliess er bei seinem tode, alle
minderjaehrig, in folge dessen ihr oheim Vortiger die
krone waehrend ihres muendelstandes an sich riss; da
dies die vormuender der kinder zu befuerchtungen

LXII. Various readings: In Kitchin: v. 2. 'led'.   v. 3. 'miseries'.   v. 6. 'foure'.   v. 8. 'till'.   v. 9. 'joyous'.
v. 8, by consent of Commons and of Peares; — 'a curious anachrouism'. (Kitchin.)
v. 9, the second Constantine; — 'Spenser must here mean Constantine the 'tyrant', who was raised to the
purple by the British legions (scarcely by Commons and Peares') A. D. 407. See Holinshed, Hist. Engl. 5. 1; Hardyng, c. 65:
'The Scottes and Peightes he venged and overcam.'
Robert of Gloucester says:
'þe Brytones nome þo Costantyn, and glade þoru all þyng
In þe toun of Cicestre crouned hym to here kyng'. (Kitchin.)
LXIII. Various readings: In Kitchin: v. 1. 'battell'.   v. 2. 'spoilefull'.   v. 4. 'sundry'.   v. 5. 'mightie'.   v. 9. 'bound'.
v. 2, Picts and swarming Easterlings; — 'the Picts and Northmen.' (Kitchin. — For Easterling
see Gloss.)
v. 4, bordragings; — 'Bordraging is an incursion on the borders of marches of a country'. (Todd.)
v. 5, scatterlings; — 'Scattered or dispersed rovers or ravagers.' (Upton in Todd.)
v. 7, pyonings; — 'Works of pioneers; military works raised by pioneers.' (Upton in Todd.)
v. 9, from Alcluid to Panwelt; — 'this is the 'Picts Wall' from the Forth to the Clyde. This wall is said
to have been built by Carausius, A. D. 285. There is not the slightest reason for thinking that Constantine had any hand
in it. 'Panwelt' or Panvahel on the Firth of Forth is Falkirk; Alcluid, often mentioned by old chroniclers, is at or near
Dumbarton, on the Clyde. This great wall can still be traced over a large part of its course. The chroniclers seem to
think there was only one wall; that from the Tyne to the Solway; the Murus Britannicus, called sometimes Severus', sometimes Hadrian's wall.' (Kitchin.)
LXIV. Various readings: In Kitchin: v. 7. 'Germanie'.   v. 9. 'safetie'.
v. 1. Three sonnes; — 'Constantius, who was dull of wit, and therefore made a monk; Aurelius Ambrose;
and Uther (afterwards) Pendragon. Hardyng, c. 65'.
v. 2, Vortigere; — 'Vortigern is a British king who is said by the chroniclers to have been the first to call
in the Saxons, through fear of the Picts and of other aspirants to sovereignty.' (Kitchin.)
v. 4. gathering to feare; — 'is: fearing the usurpation of Vortigere.' (Church in Todd.)

Them closely into Armorick did beare:
For dread of whom, and for those Picts annoyes,
He sent to Germany straunge aid to reare;
From whence eftsoones arrived here throe hoyes
Of Saxons, whom he for his safety imployes.

veranlasste, so brachten sie dieselben heimlich nach
Armorica. Aus furcht vor ihnen und wegen der belaesti-
gungen jener Picten sandte er nach Deutschland, um
sich fremde hilfe zu verschaffen; und bald darauf kamen
von dort drei fahrzeuge mit Sachsen hier an, die er
zu seiner sicherheit verwendete.

LXV.

Two brethren were their capitayns, which hight
Hengist and Horsus, well approv'd in warre,
And both of them men of renowmed might;
Who making vantage of their civile jarre,
And of those forreyners which came from farre,
Grew great, and got large portions of land,
That in the realme ere long they stronger arre
Then they which sought at first their helping hand
And Vortiger enforst the kingdome to aband.

Zwei brueder waren ihre fuehrer, welche Hengist
und Horsus hiessen, wohl bewaehrt im kriege und
beides maenner von anerkannter macht; diese zogen
vortheil aus deren buergerlichem zwiste, und eben
noch fremde, die aus der ferne kamen, wurden sie
immer maechtiger und erwarben grosse landstriche,
so dass sie bald staerker im reiche waren, als die,
welche zuerst ihre helfende hand suchten. und den
Vortiger zwaugen, das koenigreich zu verlassen.

LXVI.

But, by the helpe of Vortimere his sonne,
He is againe into his rule restord;
And Hengist, seeming sad for that was donne,
Received it to grace and new accord,
Through his faire daughters face and flattring word.
Soone after which, three hundred lords he slew,
Of British blood, all sitting at his bord;
Whose dolefull moniments who list to rew,
Th' eternall marks of treason may at Stonheng vew.

Aber mit hilfe seines sohnes Vortimer wurde er
wieder in seine herrschaft eingesetzt; und Hengist,
der, was geschehen war, zu bereuen schien, ward
wieder zu gnaden und neuer versoehnung angenom-
men durch seiner schoenen tochter antlitz und schmei-
chelworte. Bald nachher jedoch erschlug er dreihundert
edle von Britischem blut, wie sie gerade alle bei ihm zu
tisch sassen; wer die schmerzlichen denkmaeler davon
zu beklagen lust hat, kann die ewigen kennzeichen
des verrathes zu Stonheng schauen.

LXVII.

By this the sonnes of Constantine, which fled,

Waehrend dessen waren die geflohenen soehne Con-

---

v. 5. **Them closely into Armorick did beare;** — 'Holinshed, Hist. Engl. 5. 1: 'With all speed got
them to the sea, and fled into little Britaine, 'i. e Brittany or Armorica.' (Kitchin.)
v. 7. **straunge aid to reare;** — 'To his foreign troops.' (Church in Todd.)
v. 8. 9. **three hoyes Of Saxons;** — 'so Hardyng, c. 67:
'In shyppes thre arryued so there in Kent'.
Gildas, c. 23, says: 'Tribus ut lingua eius exprimitur Cyulis. ut nostra, longis navibus', i. e. 'three keels'.
(Kitchin.)
LXV. Various readings: In Kitchin: v. 5. 'forreiners'.
v. 2. **Hengist and Horsus;** — 'Saxon chiefs, according to the early historians. It is noticeable that their
names both signify 'horse' (cp. mod. Danish and Germ. Hengst, and Engl. Horse, Germ. Ross.) Historians are divided
as to the fact of their existence. Hengist is said to have established himself in Kent A. D. 454. Holinshed, Hist. Engl. 5.
2, 3; Hardyng, c. 67.' (Kitchin.)
v. 9. **enforst;** — 'ed. 1590 reads: 'have forst'. (Kitchin.)
LXVI. Various readings: In Kitchin: v. 7. 'bloud'.
v. 1. **Vortimere his sonne;** — 'a brave British prince who steadily and successfully stemmed the Saxon
incursions. This semi-legendary period is found at large in Nennius, c. 45—52; also in Holinshed, Hist. Engl. 5. 3; Hardyng, c. 67; Bede's Gesta Anglorum; Gildas; and William of Malmesbury.' (Kitchin.)
v. 5. **Through his faire daughters face;** — 'Rowan or Rowena, for love of whom Vortiger abandoned his
own wife; so restoring Hengist to favour. The chroniclers tell us she saluted Vortiger with the word 'Wassal', to which
he made reply (through the interpreter) 'Drink hail'; whence came those words into English speech as salutations.'
(Kitchin.)
v. 6. **Soone after which;** — 'They invited the British to a parley and banquet on Salisbury plain; where,
suddenly drawing out their seaxas, concealed under their long coats, they made their innocent guests with their blood
pay the shots of their entertainment. Here Aurelius Ambrosius is reported to have erected that monument of Stonehenge
to their memory.' (Fuller, Ch. Hist. I. cent. V. § 25.) This exact commentary on this stanza is, of course, of no historical
value. The Druid circles of Stonehenge were standing centuries before the period of this doubtful banquet and massacre.
See also Holinshed, Hist. Engl. 5. 5 and 8; Hardyng, c. 68 and 70.' (Kitchin.)

Ambrose and Uther, did ripe yeares attayne,
And, here arriving, strongly challenged
The crowne which Vortiger did long detayne:
Who, flying from his guilt, by them was slayne;
And Hengist eke soone brought to shamefull death.
Thenceforth Aurelius peaceably did rayne,
Till that through poyson stopped was his breath;
So now entombed lies at Stoneheng by the heath.

. stantin's, Ambrosius and Uther, aelter geworden, kamen hieher und erhoben starke ansprueche auf die
krone, die Vortiger ihnen so lange vorenthalten hatte:
dieser wollte der strafe entgehen, wurde aber von
ihnen getoedtet; und Hengist wurde auch bald zn
schimpflichem tode gebracht. Seitdem regierte Aurelius friedlich, bis durch gift seinem leben ein ende gemacht wurde; so liegt er nun zu Stoneheng auf der
haide begraben.

LXVIII.

After him Uther, which Poudragon hight,
Succeeding — There abruptly it did end,
Without full point, or other cesure right ;
As if the rest some wicked hand did rend,
Or th'author selfe could not at least attend
To finish it : that so untimely breach
The prince himselfe halfe seemed to offend ;
Yet secret pleasure did offence empeach,
And wonder of antiquity long stopt his speach.

Indem auf ihn Uther, Pendragon beigenannt, folgte
— Da endete es ploetzlich ohne punkt oder einen
andern angemessenen abschnitt, als wenn das uebrige
irgend eine muthwillige hand zerissen oder der autor
selbst wenigstens nicht haette abwarten koennen, es
zu beendigen: jenes so unzeitige abbrechen schien den
fuersten selbst halb und halb zu beleidigen; doch
ein geheimes vergnuegen liess den verdruss nicht auf-
kommen, und die bewunderung der alten zeit machte
ihn lange sprachlos.

LXIX.

At last, quite ravisht with delight to heare
The royall ofspring of his native land,
Cryde out: 'Deare countrey! O how dearely deare
Ought thy remembraunce and perpetuall band
Be to thy foster child, that from thy hand
Did commun breath and nouriture receave!
How brutish is it not to understand
How much to her we owe, that all us gave;
That gave unto us all whatever good we have!'

Endlich, ganz ausser sich vor entzuecken, den koeniglichen stammbaum seines geburtslandes kennen ge-
lernt zu haben, rief er aus: 'Theures vaterland, o,
wie gar so theuer muss doch die erinnerung an dich
und der bestaendige zusammenhang mit dir deinem
pflegekinde sein, das aus deiner hand die allen ge-
meinsame luft und nahrung empfing! Wie roh ist
es, nicht einzusehen, wieviel wir unserm theuern
vaterlande verdanken. das uns alles gab, alles gute,
was wir irgend besitzen'.

LXVII. Various readings: In Kitchin: v. 2. 'attaine'.   v. 4. 'detaine'.   v. 5. 'slaine'.
        v. 1. 2. the sonnes of Constantine, . . . Ambrose and Uther; — 'Ambrose, or Aurelius Ambrosius, a
semi-mythical character, 'is said to be extracted of the Roman race' (Fuller, Ch. Hist. I. cent. V. § 28), and is described
as attacking Vortigern in Wales, at his castle of Generen, where he set fire to his castle, and burnt him with it. He is
also reported to have been a great champion of the British race,' (Kitchin.)
        LXVIII. Various readings: In Kitchin: v. 7. 'him selfe'.   v. 9. 'antiquitie'.
        v. 1. Uther; — 'the great Pendragon (a title worn by British chiefs as defenders of their race), is said to
have kept up the strife against the Saxons, and to have been the father of Arthur. Cp. F. Q. Bk. I. VII. 31. Hardyng, c. 71:
        'His brother Uter at Caergwent was crouned   Of gold in goulis, wher so he gan to fare,
        In trone royall then fully was admit: And for he bare the dragon so in warre
        Twoo dragons made of gold royall that stound,   The people all hym called then Pendragon
        (That one) offred of his devout wit,   For his surname, in landes nere and farre,
        In the mynster there, as he [had] promit: Whiche is to say id Britayn region
        That other before hym euer in battaile bare   In theyr langage, the head of the dragon'. (Kitchin.)
        v. 2. There abruptly: — 'the plan which Spenser is working out does not allow him to go on any farther.
Otherwise Prince Arthur would learn his own parentage and dignities long before his time; for Uther is Arthur's father.
So he rends the MS. at this point abruptly.' (Kitchin.)
        v. 8. empeach; — 'Hinder, Fr. empêcher.' (Todd.)
        v. 2. royall ofspring; — 'the pedigree or descent of kings. This use of 'ofspring' proves that the sense of
Bk. I. VI, 30, 'ofspring auncient', is 'ancient descent' or origin; whence one has sprung'. (Kitchin.)

B. Spenser's Language Criticised.

Spenser had not only a deep knowledge of the English language that was spoken in his own century, he studied also profoundly that of his forefathers, even imitated it in his writings — therefore he has been ironically called 'the Gothic poet' [1] — especially in his Shepheards Calendar and the Fairy Queen, whereas the View of the State of Ireland is written in the language of the sixteenth century.

Before we begin, however, to explain the characteristic of Spenser's idiom, such as it is to be found out in the Cantos of the Fairy Queen, translated and commented by us, we ought to premise some general observations about the origin of the English language.

The family of the Indo-European languages is divided into six capital stocks: 1. the Indian, containing the Old (Sanscrit, Pali, Prakrit, Kawi) and Modern Indian languages; 2. the Iranian and Persian languages, containing the Zend and Ancient Persian, and of the modern languages the Modern Persian, the Armenian and those which are spoken in Afghanistan, Beludshistan, by the Kurds and by the Ossets; 3. the classical or Greek and Latin languages with their continuations, the Modern Greek and the Romance languages (French, Spanish, Portugese, Italic, Rhaeto-Romanesque, Wallachian); 4. the German tribe, divided into three capital branches: the High German, the Gothic-Low German, the Scandinavian; 5. the Sclavonian with the Ancient Prussian and Lithuanian; 6. the Celtic, now only preserved in Ireland, the Scottish Highland, Wales and Britany, divided into the Gaelic or Ghadelic, and the Welsh or Kymric.

To the Gothic-Low German branch there belongs first and foremost the Gothic, the oldest German language of which we possess written monuments. It is usually regarded as a particular branch of the German languages, but it is only a Low German language that, however, came down to us in a much older form than any other; it is, therefore, of incalculable importance for German philology. Without the Gothic, as Grimm says, it would only have dawned in German philology, never become daylight. Three other Low German languages appear in written monuments four or five centuries afterwards: the Old Saxon, the Anglo-Saxon, and the Ancient tongue of Friesland. The Modern English is a combination of the Anglo-Saxon with the French-Norman, often, however under the influence of the Celtic, Latin and Danish.

Comparing the Modern English with its two chief elements, we perceive that there gradually has taken place a considerable retrenchment in the words, and that the terminations of flexion have significantly diminished in number. This tendency of abridgement, however, is not peculiar only to the English tongue, but rather to all the Indo-European languages. For without mentioning that already the Latin tongue has shorter terminations than the Sanskrit, we also observe especially in the Romance languages many terminations of declension and conjugation to have wasted away by degrees and to have been supplied by prepositions and auxiliary verbs. The same difference is to be found between the Ancient and Modern Greek, between the Ancient Sanskrit and the Modern Indian dialects. That the case is the same with the German tongue, nobody will deny, who is comparing the Modern German with the Gothic. Notwithstanding the German language has preserved the flexion in many words, yet the Dutch dialect, employing almost but prepositions for expressing the relation of words, proves also that the German language has more and more diminished the number of flexions; the cause of which seems to be in the accent.

In the oldest Anglo-Saxon as well as in the German the root of the words is accented [2]),

---

[1] Bishop Hurd, for instance, calls this his 'Gothick style'. (Kitchin I, p. XVI).
[2] Cp. Rask, Grammar of the Anglo-Saxon Tongue, translated by Thorpe, p. 135 sq. in Willisius.

whence may be concluded that, in those times already, the terminations and prefixes have been pronounced more hastily and more weakly than the root. When the language had long time been in want of any cultivation, the syllables were gradually stripped of, the signification, the meaning of the word not being altered by it. On the one hand this was caused by the mixture of two different nations, endeavouring to speak as short as possible, in order to understand each other; on the other hand it was principally founded in the nature of the Anglo-Saxon language itself. To wit, before the junction of French and Anglo-Saxon the mass of forms had already been diminished, as we may conclude from early Anglo-Saxon writings, for instance from a homily written in the beginning of the thirteenth century [1]).

'Þanne hie mid here wise word turneden mannes herte fram corbeliche Þankis to hevenliche Þanke . . . from alle ivele lustes to luven God and heren him' — i. e. Cum per sapiens verbum averterent hominis pectus a cogitationibus terrestribus ad coelestiam cogitationem . . . a malis omnibus cupidinibus ad Dei amorem obedientiamque. [2]) — Only the letter e was left in the declension of the adjectives, and the plural dative of the substantives already finished in s, which formerly was peculiar only to the nominative. In like manner the French words and those of the other Romance tongues have been shortened by virtue of the accent. Thus, many consonants of the unaccented syllables disappeared or advanced more towards the syllable with the principal accent. As for instance the Latin words 'magistrum', 'sanguinem', have become maître', 'sang'; and often the last syllable of the Latin word being thrown off, the accent of the French word has come upon the ending syllable, as in 'cheval' — 'caballus'. Frequently as rest of a fuller termination has only remained the letter e, and this is, but in poetry, almost mute, as for instance in 'courage', 'aime'. In what manner the accent influences the Romance words, we may learn from Diez, Gramm. vol. I. p. 133 sq.[3]); only in accented syllables, however, may be perceived a certain norm in the alteration of vowels; as for the rest, there is the greatest capriciousness. Concerning the place of the accent, the Romance words do not always accent the root, like the German words, but that syllable which is accented in the Latin language; here the penultima has the accent, if it is long, if short, the antepenultima.

Although the English sprang likewise from those two languages, yet it has, in other respect as well as in the accent, almost exclusively followed the laws of the Anglo-Saxon tongue. For not only in the Anglo-Saxon words, but also in the French words generally the root is accented, as we may already see in the writings composed before Chaucer's time. But in what degree the words are contracted by the accent, becomes evident already by remarking that only the terminations of the singular genitive and of the plural nominative have been preserved, and that the final e, formerly being a termination of flexion, afterwards used to be pronounced only in rhythmical verses, in our days not at all. — The vowels of the unaccented syllables, as above said, vanished by virtue of the accent. From the same tendency of distinguishing certain syllables proceeded the protraction of the accented short vowels. Although we are not able to show, within which limits this prolongation took place in the Anglo-Saxon language, yet there is no doubt but that this prolongation of the chief vowels has been caused by former contraction [4]). In French nearly all short vowels are protracted in the accented syllables, unless two consonants were following [5]). The English has, in this regard, followed the French to a certain degree, since there almost all vowels are shortened

[1]) Cp. Wrigt and Halliwell 'Reliquiae Antiquae', vol. 1. p. 128 sq. in Willisius.
[2]) See Willisius p. 4.   [3]) See ibidem.
[4]) Cf. Grimm, Gramm. vol. I, ed. III, p. 32 in Willisius.
[5]) Diez, Gramm. vol. I p. 16 in Willisius.

before two consonants, lengthened, however, before one consonant which does not stand at the end of the syllable. Thus it seems that in English the quantity of vowels is principally dependent on the accent, though there may be some other reasons for its depending on the sound of the letters.

In no other language such a difference is between letter and sound, as in the English. This will appear according to nature, when we have an eye upon the origin of that language. Coming from two tongues which are subjected to so different laws, many sounds of the one language were naturally represented by letters of the other, and on the contrary, many letters of the one were pronounced with the sounds of the other language.

But in what degree has the English followed those two languages in letters as well as in sounds? As for the former, we observe that the Anglo-Saxon had two letters, which the Modern English is not possessed of (þ, ð), but wanted the letters j, k, q, v, z. The French and English alphabets do not differ at all from each other, except that in English the letter w is much more frequent. According to this conformity of the alphabets the orthography of the English words taken from French happens to be not so different from the primitive one as that of those borrowed from Anglo-Saxon, since here it was necessary to employ other characters. But as for the sound of the English letters, we shall not be at all surprised that here this language has followed the Anglo-Saxon, in as much as the spirit and disposition of these two languages are more harmonizing with each other.

There are three periods to be distinguished in the development of the English language, in the first of which the laws already appear that afterwards have been followed; the second period still fluctuates in these laws, the third, at length, shows perfect forms and is subjected to positively fixed rules. Spenser, as above said, lived in that time which separates the second period from the third, when neither a fixed norm existed by which the language went, nor, indeed, every rule wanted. We shall find, therefore, in his Fairy Queen much arbitrariness, many inconsequences not only as for the different editions, which, as we have seen, considerably vary; but even in the very same edition, for instance in the Tauchnitz edition CCCCC, is to be found a very great indecision in accent, orthography, rhyme, flexion a. s. f., so that it would require too much time in proportion to the profit accruing from thence, if we should sift and cite the passages we have gathered up. Be it, therefore, permitted to alledge only the most significant.

a. Mètre, Accent, Prosody, Rhyme.

The Spenserian stanza [1]) does not much differ from that of Ariosto and Tasso, save that Spenser adds to the iambuses of five feet still a ninth verse, an iambic trimeter or an Alexandrine. The cesure of this Alexandrine, however, is by no means always in the middle of the verse. If it were so, many words would be dismembered, as for instance:

I, 1, 35. II, 9, 18. 19. 20. 27. 35. II, 10, 1. 13. 14. 16. 18. 25. 32. 34. 37. 42. 44. 57. 58. 59. 63. 66. 68.

Or the personal pronoun would be separate from its verb, as in II, 10, 50;

or the preposition from the word governed by it, as in II, 10, 5. 19. 45. 47. 48. 54. 64.

But often it is after the second foot, as in II, 9, 60;

or after one foot and a half, as in II, 10, 20. 86;

---

[1]) See above p. 21.

or after three feet and a half, as in II, 10, 30. 40. 46. 60;
or after the first and the seventh half-foot, as in II, 10, 13.

Spenser's verses let some difference appear, sprung from the different nature of the English and Italian languages; for almost to every Italian verse a short unaccented vowel is added, so that the verse is composed of eleven syllables. Such verses are not to be found in the three first books of the Fairy Queen [1]), afterwards sometimes, yet mostly ending with a consonant, as in VI, 7, 41:

'For he was sterne and terrible by nature,
'And eeke of person huge and hideous,
'Exceeding much the measure of mans stature,
'And rather like a Gyaunt monstruous'.

Sometimes a syllable of the verse seems to be wanting, as in I, 1, 19, 4; II, 9, 25[2]).

The letter e abounds in Spenser; at the end of the word it is never pronounced, but is perfectly mute, as in our days. In the middle of some French words, however, it must be heard, where now it is either mute or shall only indicate that the precedent vowel has been protracted, or where it is not written at all. Sometimes it is marked by the diaeresis. We have found:

I: com-man-de-ment[3]) (2, 22). em-bra-ce-ment (2, 5) sa-fe-ty (9, 1).

II: a-gre-ĕ-ment (10, 59). Fa-ĕ-ry (9, 4). sa-fe-ty (10, 6). sa-fĕ-ty (10, 64). saf-te-ty (10, 1)[4]).

The licentia poetica being immense with the English, Spenser does not stand behind the boldest poets. Frequently mute syllables must be pronounced and sometimes, having the accent, become long; for prosody and accent coincide in English, as the accented syllable is long, the unaccented short [5]). Thus, for instance, the letter e in the termination of the preterite and of the passive participle often has become long [6]); often, however, it is not written at all [6]) or supplied by an apostrophe [6]). In prose this e is mute in most of words. Besides not only French words have been increased by a syllable, but also in other words the diaeresis has taken place, particularly in proper names.

Words being lengthened by the accent or the diaeresis:
I: compassion [7]) (3, 1). conscience [7]) (10, 23). counsell (1, 33). eventyde (1, 34). gorgeous (4, 8). often (1, 29). patience (10, 23). prayed (1, 29).
II: arrived (10, 64). Aurelius (10, 67). Cantium (10, 12). castle 9, 20). Christianity (10, 53). Claudius (10, 61). communed (9, 41). compressed (9, 45). Concoction (9, 31). conquered (10, 10). Constantius (10, 59). contention (10, 11). Corinĕus (10, 18). Digestion (9, 31). disthronized (10, 44). favoured (10, 56). fensible (9, 20). gathered, 10, 57). gracious (9, 20). honored (9, 6). knowen (9, 50). legion (10, 60). lived (9, 47). looked (9, 11). nation (10, 26). Octavius (10, 60). opened (10, 23). opinions (10, 51). passed (10, 58). passioned (9, 41). portions (10, 65). possession (10, 9). reason (10, 55). reckoned (9, 6). reckoning (10, 49). recovered (10, 44). seemeth (9, 42). speciall (8, 20). treason (10, 48. 66). worm-eaten (9, 57).

Many words have been lengthened by the epenthesis:
I: thorough (1, 32).
II: fier [8]) (9, 13). nouriture [9]) (10, 69). thorough (9, 23).

The following words have been shortened by the elision: [10])

---

[1]) Cp. Willisius p. 16.
[2]) But in Todd and Kitchin it does not want, for there we read 'seemed' instead of 'seemd'.
[3]) Cp. Willisius. [4]) Tauchnitz. [5]) See Wagner's gram. d. Engl. spr., von Herrig.
[6]) See Wagner § 963, n. 2. and below. [7]) See Willisius.
[8]) Cf. Willisius p. 20: I, 2, 17. Cp. A.-S. botm and bottom, blósma (bloosme in Spenser IV, 8, 2), blossom; sorh, sorwe, sorrow; búr, bowr, bower. [9]) Else usually nurture.
[10]) To wit concerning the pronunciation; as for the orthographical elision see below.

monosyllabic are:

I: heavens ¹) (7, 43). monethes ¹) (9, 15).

·II: seven (9, 12). wealthes (9, 53).

III: shallowes ¹) (4, 9).

dissyllabic:

I: adamant (7, 33). enimies (3, 36). gathred (1, 25). Morpheus (1, 36,. murmuring (1,. 41). perilous (7, 2). Scrazius (2, 20). sumpteous (4, 6). womanish (6, 10). yvorie (1, 44).

II: linage (10, 2). numbred (9, 6;. puissance (9, 14). suffred (9, 56). utterers (9, 25). venturous (10, 6). woudred (9, 59).

trisyllabic:

I: tumultuous (4, 35).

II: distempred (9, 1). impetuous (9, 14). remembred (9, 57). subtilly (9, 46).

quadrisyllabic:

II: continually (9, 46).

Even between two different words a contraction often takes place either by elision, then marked by an apostrophe ²), not only in examples as

II: th' achates (9, 31). th' antique (10, 36). th' other ;9, 22) etc.,

but also in such as

II: Aetn' (9, 29). Genuiss' (10, 52). t'avenge ³) (10, 35). th' hindmost ⁴) (9, 54). th' house ⁵) (9, 52). etc.;

or by synaeresis, as in

I: crimson ¹) (11, 3). many a ;1, 15. 17), méry Englánd ¹) (10, 61).. the Aegyptian (1, 21), visnomie ¹) (4, 11).

II: many a (9, 34. 35. 40; 10, 49). ·

III: power and ¹)⁵) (1, 12). ⸺

IV: many a ¹) (1, 19).

Neither lengthened nor shortened. but remarkably altered by the dislocation of the accent are the following words:

I: úncouth (1, 15):

II: ágainst (10, 32). Albány (10, 38). ántique (9, 45. 59; 10, 5. 36. 56). argúment (10, 3). brimstón (10, 26). Britáyne (10, 41). captív'd (10, 55). findíng (10, 6). foresíght (9, 49). fórlorne (10, 23). hewíng (9, 15). impórtune (10, 15). infiníte (9, 50. 56). Locríne (10, 14). óblique (9, 52). officés (9, 31). out-raígned (10, 45). poúrtrahed (9, 33 — twice). that⁶) (10, 16). the (10, 22). thencefórth (10, 49. 67). thousánd (9, 3;. till thát (10, 6). úncouth (9, 43). whilóme⁷)⁸) (9, 21; 10, 16). wíthout (10, 7. 54).

Many French words seem to have retained their former accent:

I: agony (10, 22). détestáble ¹) (1, 26). forrésts ¹) (2, 9). impercéáble ¹) (1. 17). perplexity (10, 22). persóns ¹) (10, 7). trespás (1, 30;.

---

¹) See Willisius.
²) In the very same word this expedient for shortening the verse is naturally often enough employed by Spenser, but with the greatest capriciousness. ³) = To avenge. ⁴) Before an aspirate h.
⁵) Not really a synaeresis.
⁶) Walker will accent this word only as demonstrative pronoun (Cp. Wagner). ⁷) or whylóme.
⁸) It is a matter of course, that Spenser shows the same inconsequence in the accentuation as in other points, for instance he has accented the first syllable in II, 9, 45; VI, 12, 32. (Cf. Willisius).

II: achátes (9, 31). Aegerié (10, 42). Armoríck (10, 64). centaúrs (9, 50). consórt (9, 35). couráge ¹) (1, 42). décretals (9 53). envíes (10, 21. 33). envy (9, 7). índecént (9, 1). isséwed²) (9, 17). Madáme (9, 37\. matcháble³) (10, 56). meláncholy (9, 52). perdíe⁴) (10, 48). periúred (10, 40). recórds (9, 57). succoúre⁵) (19, 19). tribunáls (9, 53). uságe (9. 54).
VI: courtesyes ¹) ⁶) (2, 16).
C. of Mut.:⁷) penánce ¹) (7, 22).

As for the rhyme, too, Spenser lays hold on the poeticál license to the highest degree. There rhyme together:
I: wound — sound (1, 9. 25).
II: againe — remaine (10, 32). agonyes — eyes, skyes (9, 52). appere — there (9, 52). auncestryes — enterprise, arise, skyes (10, 1). beare — feare, reare (10, 64). Caccily — supply (10, 34). cease — preace (10. 25). close — foes (9, 23). dames — hippodames (9, 50). diademe — eme (10, 47). diapase — base, place (9, 22). emperoure — powre, howre (10, 57). envies — infamies, victories (10, 21). floure — paramoure (9, 34). foeminine — divine (9, 22). fro — bestow (9, 28). heare — weare, rosiere (9, 19). heath — breath, death (10, 67). hould — could, would (9, 12). lies — fantasies, prophesies (9, 51). liv'd — depriv'd, surviv'd (9, 57). lov'd — proov'd, behoov'd, moov'd (10, 28) — remoóv'd, proov'd (10, 17). masculine — nine (9, 22). perdie — dy, flye (10, 48).⁸) privily — whereby, espy (9, 32). poure — succoúre, stoure (10, 19). devoure (9, 3). raigne — playne, slaine, soveraine (10, 58). receave — gave, have (10, 69). report — rote, wrote, note (10, 3). shew — hew, vew (9, 52). wals — picturals, tribunals, decretals (9, 53).

Spenser does, what even Walker is not allowing⁹) — he rhymes not only homonymous words with each other, as
II: raught — wrought (9, 19). wit — whit (9, 49). rote — wrote (10, 3),
but also words of the same orthography, and that not only as long as their meaning differs¹⁰),
I: traine (= tail) — traine (= snare) (1, 18).
II: rayne (= rain) — rayne (= reign) (10, 34).
else too:
II: wrought — wrought (9, 19).
pas — pas (9, 23).
In this place let us point to two passages, where, perhaps, alliteration was purposed by our poet:
I: 'In which that wicked wight his dayes doth weare'. (1, 31).
II: 'Nor wight nor word mote passe out of the gate'. (9, 25).

b. Orthography, Orthoepy. ¹¹)

First of all we must mention again that principally the orthography of Spenser is more inconstant and vacillating than that of any author in the fourteenth and fifteenth centuries. Not only

---

¹) Cf. Willisios. ²) Old-French i s s i r, Lat. axire.
³) The termination, at least, is French.— macá Ags. ⁴) See below the lexicogr, remarks.
⁵) Fr. sec oure. ⁶) Rhyming with e y es (see below.) ⁷) See above p. 19. 21. ⁸) See above.
⁹) See Wagner § 976.
¹⁰) 'Spenser (like Chaucer) often allows words exactly alike in form to rhyme together, as long as their meaning differs'. (Kitchin I, p. 166).
¹¹) Cf. Mueller, Loth, Maetzner etc.

the apostrophe, as above said, and the hyphen that will be talked about once more below, when we shall be treating of the compound words, are exposed to these fluctuations, as:

II: maister cooke (9, 31), but: high-way (10, 39);

not only we read now a e now æ, or o e and œ printed in the same edition, as:

I: Aegyptian (1, 21), but: Ægyptian (II, 9, 21);

II: Phœbus (9, 10), but: Phœbus (9, 48);

and the same word now written with a small initial letter, now, without any particular inducement, with a capital, as:

I: Faire knight (1, 27), but: Sir Knight (1, 33);

but there are, within this inextended fragment of the Fairy Queen, also several words spelt in a quite different manner, now so now otherwise:

I: eventyde (1, 34), but: eventide (II, 9, 16).

II: renowmed (9, 4), but: renownd (10, 11); forreigne (10, 35), but: forreine (10, 43); enemies (9, 12), but: enimy (10, 46).

Now we have to inquire, what sounds are represented by an orthography differing from the Modern English.

1. Vocalic Sounds.[1]

Sounds 23. 24. (as in father mannn.)

Hart (heart) I, 1, 3; II, 9, 42; 10, 14. 17. 25. 32. A. - S. heorte, hiorte, heort[2]. Goth. hairto; O. - S. herta, herte; O. - Fr. hirte; Dt. herte, hert, hart; L. G .hart; O. - N. hiarta; Sw. hjerta; Dau. hjorte; O. - H. G. herza; M. - H. G. herze; Mod. - H. G. herz. (Cp. cor, κέαρ, Skr. hrid etc.)

Maister (master) II, 1, 31; O. - E. maister; Fr. maître; O. - Fr. maïstre; It. maestro, mastro; Sp. maestro, maestre; Pg. mestre; Lat. magister; but it came into the German languages, too: meistar, meister, meester etc. A. - S. mäster, mägester.

Mervayld[3] (marveled) II, 9, 43.

Sounds 25. 26. (as in fall, jackdaw.)

Caudron (caldron) II, 9, 29. Fr. chaudron; It. calderone; Sp. calderon. Cp. Lat. calere; O. - Fr. caloir, chaloir.

Crall (crawl) II, 1, 22. Dt. krielen; M. - H. G. krabbeln.

Faund (fawned) III, 9, 36. A. - S. fägnjan[4], fagnjan, fahnjan. Cp. fain.

Nought[5] (now usually: naught) II, 9, 32. 43. 49.

Ought (now usually: aught) II, 9, 32. A. - S. â - viht, auht, âht[6].

Sounds 11. 12. (as in man, chapman.)

Barbican[7] (barbacan) II, 9, 25: Both formes are used in our days, too. In this word, which was in French 'barbacan', and in A. - S. also 'barbycan', the A. - S. sound y has become i[8].

Emong[9] [10] (among[11]), amongst, 'mong, 'mongst, mongst) I, 1, 32 (twice). O. - E. amang, amanges.

---

[1] The ciphers answer the system of Smart.
[2] Cp. deórling (A.-S.) and darling (E.); feórding — farthing.   [3] Cp. below.
[4] Cp. smael (A.-S.) — small (E.); waeter — water.   [5] See below the lex. rem.
[6] Cp. gánjan (A.-S.) — yawn (E.); brâd — broad.   [7] See lex. rem.
[8] Cp. þyane — thin; synn — sin; cyssan — kiss; lytel — little; cycone — kitchen.
[9] Cf. below the Prepos.
[10] Cp. ascjan (A.-S.) and ask (E.). The like: mentle — mantle; treppe — trap; þrescan — thrash.
[11] II, 9, 53.

A. - S. âmang, onmang c. dat. This proceeded from the A. - S. snbstantive gemang, mang; Mod. - H. G. menge, gemenge.

Hond[1][2]) (hand) II, 9, 60. A. - S. hand; Goth. handus. O. -, M. - H. G. hant, hand; O.-Frs., L. G., Dt., O. - S. hand; O. - N. hönd; Sw. hand; Dan. haand etc.[3]) [4]).

Menage[2]) (manage) II, 10, 37. ⎰ M. - L. managium; It. maneggio; whence, then, derived Fr. ma-Managed (managed) II, 9, 27. ⎱ nége.

But compare too ménage, mesnage, maison — M.-L. mansio. mansionaticum, managium. Scheler says: 'manage, maison, habitation, formé directement du vieux verbe manoir', lat. manere, demeurer. Ce subst. doit être distingué de mesnage, ménage, qui dérive de maison. Cf. Rapp. No. 171. 172. Wedgewood (2, 373) raises objections to a mixture between manége and ménage. Mueller thinks it comes from the O. - Fr. menage, mesnage, but has afterwards leant against manus, managium.' As for our two passages, he may be right.

Lond (land)[2][4]) I, 1, 3; II, 9, 60. A. - S. land, lond; Goth., O. - S., L. G., Dt., O. - Frs., Sk., O. - H. G., M. - H. G., Mod. - H. G. land (lant) — lond, lon, lan. It. landa; Fr. lande (steppe.)

Then (than)[5][6]) I, 1, 4. 13. 24 (twice); II, 9, 1. 3. 15. 24. 29. O. - E. then, thenc, in Orm thann. A. - S. Þonne, Þon; O. - S. than; O. - Frs., O. - Dt., Dan. dann; O. - H. G. danne, denne; M.-H. G. dann, denn; Goth. Þan, Þana. In Modern English then, than are separate forms.

Understond[2][7]) (understand) II, 9, 60.

Several words of French origin, in which an, i. e. a with the nasal sound, is spelt aun[8]).

II: Auncestryes (10, 1). braunch (9, 39; 10, 36). braunched (9, 19). chaunce (9, 36; 10, 8). chaunced (9, 59); chaunst (9, 60). chevisaunce (9, 8). displeasaunce (10, 28). entraunce (9, 11 — twice. 17). Fraunce (10, 11. 23). geaunts (10, 8). giaunts (10, 7). governaunce 10, 38). graunted (9, 20. 60). mischaunce (9, 8. 30). ordinaunce (9, 30). pleasaunce (9, 35). pleasaunt (9, 10). puissaunce (9, 4. 14; 10, 23). remembraunce (9, 56; 10, 69). semblaunce (10, 23). semblaunt (9, 2. 39). substaunce (9, 15)[9]). temperaunce (9, Motto). valiaunce (10, 38). variaunce (10, 38). viaundes (9, 27. 30).

Sounds 17. 18. (as in what, somewhat.)

This sound is in Modern English represented by the letter a only when a w precedes, nor have we found another manner of spelling in Spenser.

Words, lengthened by the epenthesis of one of these eight sounds we have not found in our Cantos, but such as are shortened by the apocope or by the syncope:

II: Aetn' (9, 29). Genuiss' (10, 52)[10]). gainst[11]) (10, 46. 57). mongst[12]) (9, 6; 10, 13. 27). un-wares (10, 54).

Sounds 1. 2. (as in gate, retail).

This sound is abnormally spelt in the following words, mostly[13]) of French origin; a great

---

[1]) Cp. oxa — ox; god — god; dropjan — drop; scohen — shot; morgen — morrow; folgjan — follow. The like: lang — long; wrang — wrong; fram — from; strang — strong; papig — poppy; wan — won. The like: hamm — ham; mann — man; habban — have; land — land.

[2]) Although we are here to pronounce ö in these words, because of the rhyme already (see the cited passages), notwithstanding they must be alledged in this place as they differ from the modern orthography â.

[3]) Lex. rem.
[4]) Cp. also Diez 199; I, 244. Diefenbach (vrgl. woerterb. d. goth. spr. 1851) 2, 126. [5]) Lex. rem.
[6]) Cp. also Koch 2, 426 sqq: Grimm 2, 740 sqq. [7]) See below the Verb. [8]) See Maetzn. I, p. 103.
[9]) II, 9, 46: substance. [10]) See above p. 93. [11]) See below the Prep. [12]) See above.
[13]) Save two words: rayne (=rain) and: streight (?).

many of them differ from the modern words only by spelling a u n instead of a n, or a y, e y instead of ai, ei:

I: Daunger (1, 31). disdayning (1, 1).
Mayle (mail. 1, 16). Fr. maille; It. Sp. Pr. maglia; Lat. macula.
Pray (prey. 1, 17). O.-Fr. preier, preer, p r a e r, p r a i e, preie; Mod.-Fr. proie; Lat. praeda, praedari.
Sayd (1, 12). straunge (1, 30. 31).
II: Apayd (9, 37). auncient (9, 59. 60. 57; 10, 36).
Ay de (aid. 1, 7). Fr. aider; older romanesque forms: ajude, ajue, aïue, atie etc. from the Lat. adjutum, adjutare, adjuvare [1]).
Assayle (assail. 9, 14). Fr. assaillir; Lat. assilire.
Attayne (10, 67). Britayne (10, 41). chaunge (9, 39. 40). claymd (10, 37). contayne (10, 34).
Couvaid [2]) (convey, convoy. 9, 32). O.-Fr. convoier, couvcier; Mod.-Fr. convoyer; Lat. con — viare=envoyer from inviare [3]).
Demayne (9, 40). detayne (10, 67). dismayd (9, 37). displayd (10, 50). enraunged (9, 26).
Fained (feigned. 9, 51) [4]).
Fayle (fail. 9, 14). Fr. faillir; Pr. faillir; It. fallire. O. - Sp., O. - Pg. fallir, falir (now: fallecer, falecer); Lat. fallere. [5])
Gaynd (10, 45). layd (9, 34). layes (10, 42). mayd (9, 41). mayn-land (10, 5).
Obay (obey. 10, 20. 49). Fr. obéir; Lat. obedire (audire).
Obeysance (9, 26); cp. abaisance. overlayd (9, 41).
Paynes (pain. 10, 14). . O.-Fr. paine, poine; Mod.-Fr. peine; It., Sp., M.-Lat. pena; Lat. poena; Gr. ποινή.
Paysd (10, 5) [6]).
Playne (10, 58). praysd (10, 5). prayses (9, 46; 10, 22. 56).
Raine (10, 33. 58). raigne (subst. 10, Motto. 61.) raigned (10, 13. 21. 27. 45). raunges (9, 29).
Rayne (rain. 10, 34). A.-S. rĕgn, rĕn, rĕgnan; Goth. rign; O.-S. regan etc.
Rayne (=reign. 10, Motto. 44. 67). raysd (10, 5). rayse (10, 56). remayne (10, 41). retaynd (10, 45). sayd (9, 3. 37). slayne (10, 67). Spayne (10, 41). straunge (9, 13. 33. 35. 40. 41. 54; 10, 15. 64.)
Streight (straight. 10, 37). See [7]) stretch. Cp. A.-S. streccan, pret. s t r e h t and strait, O. - Fr. estreit; Mod. - Fr. étroit; O.-E. streit, Lat. strictus. This A.-S. word and this French word were mingled with each other. The A.-S. verb s t r e c c a n was conjugated strehte, s t r e h t or streahte; s t r e a h t; the O.-E. verb strecchen s t r a u g h t e, straught and s t r e i g h t.
Sustayne (10, 43). unpraysed (10, 5).

Sounds 41. 42. (as in mare, welfare).

I: Faery (1, 3).
II: Affayres (10, 37). despayrd (10, 30). empayrd (10, 30). Faery (9, 8. [8]) 40. 60).
Faëry (fay. 9, 4). Fr. fée; Mod. - H. G. fee, fei; Pg.; Pr. fada; Sp. fada, hada; It. fata; Lat. fata.
Fayre (fair. 9, 2. 3. 24. 27. 38. 40. 41. 42; 10, 28. 42). and
Fayrely (fairly. 9, 24). O. - E. faeir; A. - S. faeger, faeigr; Goth. fagrs; O. - S., O.-H. G.

---

[1]) Cf. Diez 8; I, 11.   [2]) Lex. rem.   [3]) Cf. Diez 747; II, 438.   [4]) Lex. rem.
[5]) See our Dissertation on f a i l l i r and f a l l o i r.   [6]) Lex. rem.   [7]) In Mueller and Maetzner I, pp. 150. 333.
[8]) Todd has here: 'F a r y land.'

13

fagar; O. - N. fagr; Sw., Dan. fager, faver, feir etc.
Hayres (heir. 10, 28. 37. 42). O. - Fr. hoir, hier; Lat. heres.
Heyre (heir. (10, 61).
Payre (pair. 9, 30). Fr. paire, pair; It. pare; Lat. par.
Repayrd (10, 30). shayrd (10, 29).
Shayre ¹) (share. 10, 12. 28. 37). A. - S. scearu, scaru; scär etc.

Sounds 39. 40. (as in urgent, sulphur).

I: Durtie (dirty. 1, 15). O.-Scot. dryte; O.-N. drit, drîta; A.-S. drîtan.
Shepheard (shepherd. 1, 23). A. - S. scaep and heorde, heord.
Thurst (thirst. 1, 26). O. - E. in Orm þirrst, þirrstenn; A. - S. þyrst, þyrstan; O. - S. thurst etc.
Vertue (virtue. 1, 12).
II: Hard (heard. 9, 25).
Perle (pearl. 9, 19). A. - S. pearl; Roman. perla, perola, perle.
Styre (stir. 9, 30).
Vertue (virtue. 9, 3. 8). Fr. vertu; Pr. vertut, virtut etc.
Vertuous (virtuous. 10, 44).

Sounds 13. 14. (as in lent, silent).

I: Brest (breast. 1, 2. 20). A. - S. breost; Goth. brusts; O. - S. briost; Frs. briast, brast, brust, burst etc.
Enimy (enemy. 1, 27). frend (friend. 1, 28). least (lest. 1, 12).
II: Affray ¹) (effray. 10, 15) is antiquated. Fr. effrayer from the Lat. frigere ²) or frangere ³).
Assay ¹) (essay. 9, 42; 10, 3). The O. - E. form assaye has remained in several meanings; but, of course, the letter e has disappeared.
Enimy (enemy. 10, 46).
Foeminine (feminine. 9, 22) from the Lat. femininus, which formerly was written with oe like foemina, foetus, though all these words derive from a verb feo.
Freends (friends. 10, 13. 61). A. - S. freónd, friond, friend; O. - S. friund — from the Sanscrit root pri=to love.
Heven (heaven. 9, 7 (twice); 9, 22; 10, 2).
Hevenly (heavenly. 10, 3 twice).
} A. - S. heofon; O. - S. hebhan, hevan.
Imployes (employes. 10, 64). least (lest. 9, 30).
Mathusalem (Methusalem 9, 57). 1. Mos. 5, 21. מְתוּשֶׁלַח. מַת=man, mate.
Maydenhed (maiden head or maiden hood. 9, 6). Head O.-E. heved, haved. A.-S. heáfud, heáfod, heáfd, haefd, haeved, heófd. — Hood O. - E. hede, hed etc.
Outragious (outrageous. 9, 13).
Plesure (pleasure. 9, 54). Fr. plaisir; O.-Fr. plaisir, plesir. It is really the infinitive = placere.
Traveilers (travel(l)ers. 10, 39).
Weld ⁴)⁵) (wield. 9, 56; 10, 32).
Yit (yet. 9, 50).

---

¹) Lex. rem.   ²) Diez.   ³) Wedgewood.   ⁴) See above and lex. rem.
⁵) Only as for the rhyme it is to be read weld (ĕ).

Elision of the Letter e [1]).

I: Els (1, 19). elswhere (1, 21). hast (1, 27). lynage (1, 5). wastfull (1, 32).
II: Ay (always. 10, 40) dy (10, 48). fiersly (9, 14), somwhat (9, 36. 55). strauug (10, 15).
In many preterits and participles[2]), as:
I: Gazd (1, 26). mournd (1, 4). resolvd (1, 24). seemd (1, 6. 8. 10. 29). slombring (1, 36). threatning (1, 17). wondring (1. 13).
II: Accoyld (9, 30). admird (10. 3). annoyd (9, 14; 10, 63). auswerd (9, 43). apayd (9, 37). arayd (9, 19. 37). armd (9, 13). ashamd (9, 40). betrayd (10, 48). boyld (9, 30). cald (9, 31; 10, 27). claymd (10, 37). confirmd (10, 60). constraind (9. 36). crownd (10, 58. 62). declind (9, 55). deemd (10, 42). deformd (9, 13). defrayd (10, 49). despayrd (10, 30). disdaind (10, 18). dismayd (9, 34. 37). drownd (9. 36). dweld (9. 56). empayrd (10, 30). employd (9, 14). enjoyd (10, 14. 25). entertaind (9, 20). entring (9, 59). eschewd (9, 13). faynd (9, 44). flamd (9, 46). flattring (10, 66). immeasurd (10, 8). inquyrd (10, 27). joyd (10, 53). loathd (10, 9). measurd (9, 9). overflowd (10, 15). proportiond (9, 22). raignd (10, 50). raisd (10, 33). raynd (10, 27. 45). raysd (10, 5). reard (9, 29). refusd (10, 50). renownd (9, 11). repayrd (10, 30). requyrd (9, 25). resignd (10, 30). restord (10, 32). retournd (9, 15). reveald (10, 39). scord (9, 2). shayrd (10, 29). spard (9, 28). strayd (9, 19). subdewd (10, 41). surrendred (10, 27. 45). swarmd (9, 13; 10, 15). toyld (9, 30). turnd (9, 44). unmannurd (10, 5). unpraysd (10, 5). unproovd (10. 5). wandring (9, 24). warmd (9, 13; 10, 26). warrayd (10, 50). warreyd (10, 21).

Epenthesis and Suffixing of the Letter e[3]).

I: Arme (1, 1). certaine (1, 24). curbe (1, 1). dayes (1, 31). deepe (1, 1). displaide (1, 14). eftsoones[4]) (1, 11). entertainement[5]) (1, 35). fearefull (1, 24). fielde (1, 1). foule (1, 1). froe (1, 34). holinesse (1, 1). marke (1. 1). remaine (1, 1). shielde (1, 1). steede (1, 1). whilest (1, 13). wisedome (1, 13).
II: Affaires (10, 37). againe (10, 48). backe (10, 48). carcase (10, 43). chiefetain (10, 16). childe (10, 69). civile (10, 38). contayne (10, 34). craftsman (9, 41). duely (9. 25). fayre (10, 28). fearefull (10, 16). judgementes (9, 53). loe[6]) (9, 13). painefull (10, 63). perle (9, 19). poure (9, 3). ruine (10, 33). reaedifye[7]) (10, 46). shewes (9, 51). throwes (9, 8. 23). truely (10, 31). whome (10. 57. 62). woefull (10, 62).

Metathesis of the Letter e[8]).

I: Affraide (1, 16). amazde (1, 26). cride (1, 19). edifyde (1, 34). satisfide (1, 26). spide (1, 7). stolne (1, 2).
II: Allide (10, 52). bowre (9, 47). dide (10, 54). dyde (10, 32. 40. 53). elles (9, 32). flowre (9, 4. 18. 46). fortifyde (9, 26). howre (10. 57). justifide (10. 60). magnifide (10, 52). mollifide (10, 25). powre (9, 1. 3. 7. 20. 47. 57; 10, 57). spide (9, 10). supplyde (10, 51). tigre (9, 14). towre[9]) (9. 21. 45. 47). tride (10, 55). tryde (10, 31).

Sounds 3. 4. (as in me, defy).

In words, which, in Modern English, are terminating in y, Spenser usually has spelt ie, sometimes ee [10]).

---

[1]) Cf. what is above said about the elision and the apostrophe.
[2]) Those preterits or preterit participles which, moreover, have undergoue other alterations, will be placed among the irregular verbs.
[3]) Cf. above. [4]) Lex. rem. [5]) See above.
[6]) In Modern English this word is sometimes spelt in the same manner. [7]) Lex. rem. [8]) Cf. above.
[9]) II, 9, 21 towre rhymes with endure and sure. Cf. below. [10]) Often modestee; see below.

I: Bloodie (1, 2). bodie (1, 18). countrie (1, 31), enimie (1, 27). fattie (1, 21). filthie (1, 20). happie (1, 27). hoarie (1, 29). ladie (1, 4). lasie (1, 6. 12. 32). loftie (1, 7). mightie (1, 9). shadie (1, 7). sundrie (1, 15).

II: Albanie (10, 38). antiquitie (10, 68). beautie (9, 37). bountie (10, 30). Briƫannie (10, 39). easie (9, 33; 10, 61). Germanie 10, 64). happie (10, 27). lasie (9, 17). memorie (10, 50). mightie (9, 29; 10, 43. 63). miseries (10, 62). modestie ¹) (9, 43). perdie²) (10, 48). progenie (10, 36). safetie (10, 64). tributarie (10, 49). unworthie (10, 21). wearie (10, 30).

Other words:

I: Aegyptian³) Egyptian. 1, 21).
Bee (be. 1, 19).
Feends (fiends. 1, 5. 21).
Neerest⁴) (nearest. 1, 10). It comes from the A.-S. comparative form neára, neár; the positive was neah. Cf. nigh and ny⁴).
Nether (neither. 1, 24). O.-E. nather, neither; A.-S. nâƀer, nâhväƀer. Grimm says⁵): 'The Anglo-Saxon âvƀer, nâvƀer turned into the Old-English other and nother and in the Modern English either, neither.
Phebus (Phoebus. 1, 23).
Reed⁶) (read. 1, 21). O.-E. reden; A.-S. rêdan; Goth. rodjan; O.-N. raeda; Mod.-H. G. reden.
Spere (spear. 1, 11). O.-E. spere; A.-S. spĕre, spĕore, spiore; O.-Frs. sper, spire; O.-N. spior; Dan. spär; O.-, M.-H. G. sper; Mod.-H. G. speer; Kymr. yspêr; Gael. spâr; Lat. sparus, sparum.
Vele (veil. 1, 4). O.-Fr. veile, vaile (therefore vail in the Modern English, too); Mod.-Fr. le, la voile; Pr. vel; Sp. velo; It. velo; Pg. veo; Lat. velum.
Wrethed (wreathed. 1, 18). A.-S. vraeƀ, vrîƀan, vraeƀian, vrêƀan; O.-N. rîda, rîƀa; Sw. vrida; Dan. vride; O.-H. G. rîdan; M.-H. G. rîden, reiden; Mod.-H. G. raideln.

II: Aegerie⁷) (Egerie. 10, 42).
Aegles (eagles. 9, 50). Fr. aigle; It., Lat. aquila.
Aegyptian³) (Egyptian. 9, 21).
Agonyes⁸) (agonies. 9, 52).
Antiquitee (antiquity. 9, 60).
Appere (appear. 9, 52). O.-Fr. apparoir, appareier.
Bee (be. 9, 18. 37. 54; 10, 18. 24).
Bountihed⁹) (bountihead. 10, 2).
Breech¹⁰) (breach. 9, 30). Fr. brèche; A.-S. brice, bräc.
Cheare¹¹) (cheer. 9, 42; 10, 30). Fr. chère; O.-Fr. chière; Sp., Pg., Pr. cara.
Countrey (country. 9, 60; 10, 69). Fr. contrée; It. contrada; M.-Lat. contrata; from the Lat. contra. Cp. gegend, gegenôte, gegen.
Crueltee (cruelty. 9, 24).
Faryes (faries. 9, 60).
Feendes (fiends. 0, 50; 10, 8). A.-S. feónd (part. of feon=odisse); Goth. fijands; O.-S. fiond, fiund; Frs. fiand; D. vijand; L. G. viand, fjnd; O.-N. fiandi; Sw., Dan. fiende; O.-H. G.˙fiant; M.-H. G. vient, vînt, Mod.-H. G. feiand, feind.

---

¹) Often modestee; see below. ²) See above and lex. rem. ³) See above. ⁴) See below.
⁵) Gramm. 3, p. 55. 723. ⁶) Lex. rem. ⁷) See above. ⁸) See below. ⁹) See above, and below the lex. rem.
¹⁰) Now: ═ buttocks. ¹¹) Sometimes also in Modern English: cheare. — Lex. rem.

Heares[1]) (hair. 9, 13). A.-S. haer; O.-Frs. hêr.
Honny[2]) (honey. 9, 51). A.-S. huuig; O.-S. honeg, hanig etc.
Leyr (Lêar. 10, 27).
Memoree (memory. 9, 49[3]).
Modestee (modesty. 9, 18[4]).
Pearless (peerless. 10, 40).
Peares (peers. 10, 62[5]). O.-Fr. peer, per, par, pair; Mod.-Fr. pair ; Lat. par; O.-E. peer.
Pere (10, 33[6]).
Privitee (privity. 9, 44[7]).
Receave (receive. 10, 31). Fr. recevoir; O.-Fr. reçoivre, receveir; Lat. recipere.
Shene (sheen[k]). 10, 8). In Orm shene and scone; A. - S. scêne, scîne; Goth. skauns; O.-
Frs. scôn, skêne; L. G., D. schôn; O.-N. skion (?); Sw. skön; Dan. skiön; O.-H. G., O.-S. scôni;
M.-H. G. schoene; Mod.-H. G. shön. Cp. shine.
Steares[9]) (steers. 9, 13). A.-S. steór; Goth. stiur etc.
Succeded (succeeded. 10, 53). Fr. succéder; Lat. succedere.
Unclene (unclean. 10, 8). Clean: A. - S. claene; O. - H. G. chleini; M.-H. G. kleine; Mod.-
H. G. klein.
Unweldy[9]) (unwieldy. 9, 13).
Weld[10]) (wield. 9, 56: 10, 32). O. - E. welden; A. - S. gevyldan, geveldan and vealdan,
valdan; Goth. valdan, gevaldan; O. - S. waldan; O.-Frs. walda; D. welden; O.-N. valda; Sw.
välla; Dan. volde; O.-H. G. waltan, gawaltan; M.-, Mod.-H. G. walten.
Wene[11]) (ween. 10, 8). O. - E. wenen, in Orm wenenn; A. - S. vênan, vaenan; Goth. vênjan;
O.-Frs. wêna etc.
Yeeld (yield. 9, 38). O. - E. yielden, yelden; A. - S. gildan, geldan; O. - Frs. gelda, jelda; O.-
N. giulda; Sw. gälda, gälla; Dan. gielde; O.-H.G. geltan; M.-, Mod.-H.G. gelten ; Goth.
gildan.

Sounds 15. 16. or mute. (as in pît, sawpît, batt'le).

I: Battell (battle. 1, 3).
Certeine (certain 1, 24).
Soveraine (sovereign. 1, 2). O.-E. soveraine, soverejne, soferand; Fr. souverain; O.-Fr.
sovrain, soverain, suverain from the Lat. supra, superus.
Suddaine (sudden. 1, 12) ⎱ O.-E. soden, suddain, suddeine; O. - Fr. soubdain, sudain,
Suddeine (sudden. 1, 6) ⎰ sodain; Fr. soudain; Pr. subtan, sobtan, subitan; Sp. subitaneo;
It. subitano, subitaneo; Lat. subito, subitus (subitaneus, subire).
Traveiled (travel(l)ed. 1, 28).
Traveill (travel. 1, 34).
II: Batteile (battle. 10, 51. 55. 58. 63). Fr. bataille; It. bataglia — already in Adamantius Mar-
tyr: 'batualia quae vulgo battalia dicuntur.'[12]).
Batteils (see the precedent word; 10, 10. 16. 18. 33).

---

[1]) Viz. it rhymes with speares and steares; II, 9, 19, however, with weare and rosiere. Perhaps in II,
9, 13 those words shall be read spârs, stârs; in this case heares would belong to the chapter treating of Sounds 41. 42.
[2]) As for nn see below.   [3]) See above p. 100.   [4]) See above p. 100.
[5]) Peer is the verb appear mutilated. Cp. O - Fr. parer, parir, pareir, paroir; Norm. pérer.
[6]) See the precedent word.   [7]) See above p. 100.   [8]) See below.   [9]) Lex. rem.
[10]) See above, and below the lex. rem.   [11]) Lex. rem.   [12]) In Mueller.

Chevalrous (chivalrous. 10, 22). Chivalry: Fr. chevalerie.
Devonshyre (-shire. 10, 12). O.-E. shire; A.-S. scire, scyre.
Empeach¹) (impeach. 10, 68). It. impacciare; Sp., Pg., Pr. empachar; Fr. empêcher; Lat. impectare, impactiare — impingere.
Hether (hither. 10, 47. 52.²) 59). A.-S. hiser, hider; Goth. hidre etc.
Hetherto (hitherto. 10, 1). See the preceding word.
Mervayld³) (marvelled. 9. 43). Marvel: Fr. merveille; Pr. meraviglia; It., Sp., Pg. maraviglia; Lat. mirabilia.
Regesters (registers. 9, 59). Fr. régistre; It., Sp. registro; Pr. registre; Pg. registo; M.-Lat. registrum, regestorium, regestrum (regestum, regerere¹).
Soveraigne³) (sovereign. 10, 1).
Soveraine³) (sovereign. 9, 4. 6; 10, 2. 4. 14. 58).
Soveraintie (sovereignty. 10, 48).
Soverainty (10, 33). See the preceding word.
Thether (thither. 9, 10). O.-E. thider, in Orm þiderr; A.-S. þider, þyder etc.
Tirannize (tyrannize. 10, 57). Tyrant: O.-E. tyrant, tirant; Fr. tyran; O.-Fr. tiran, tirant; Lat. tyrannus. Gr. τύραννος.
Traveilers (travel(l)ers. 10, 39). A secondary form of travail; Fr. travail, travailler; O.-Fr. travciller; Pr. trebalhar; Sp. trabajar; It. travagliare etc.
Vermell⁶) (vermil. 10, 24). Lat. vermis, vermiculus; Roman. vermicular, vermiculate, vermil, vermeil, vermilion, vernin.
Villeins (villains. 9, 13). Fr. vilain.
Weeke (wick. 10, 30⁶).
Yf (if. 9, 3). O.-E. gife, gif, gef, if; A.-S. gif.
Yssew (issue. 10, 61). Fr. issue, p. p. of issir; Pr. eissir; It. escire; Lat. exire.

Syncope of the Letter i or y.

II: Companing (companying. 10, 8).
Hastly⁶) (hastily. 10, 52), a mutilation.
Perlous⁶'⁷) (perilous. 9, 17), a mutilation. Fr. périlleux; Lat. periculosus. Sometimes Engl: parlousʰ).
Renforstʰ) (reinforced. 10, 48).

Sounds 7. 8. (as in no, obey).

I: Approcht (approached. 1, 27).
Cole-black (coal-black. 1, 24).
Foming (foaming. 1, 1). A.-S. fám; O.-H.G. faim, feim; Skr. phêna; Lat. spuma.
Groning (groaning. 1, 25). A.-S. grânjan.
Lothsom (loathsom. 1, 14).
II: Approch (approach. 9, 17). Fr. approcher.
Coles (coals. 10, 33). A.-S. col; D. kole; Sw. kol etc.
Groning (10, 10⁹).
Hould (hold. 9, 12). A.-S: Ic heold.

¹) Lex. rem.   ²) In Kitchin.   ³) See above.   ⁴) Du Cange.   ⁵) See above,
⁶) Lex. rem.   ⁷) See above, and lex. rem.   ⁸) See below.   ⁹) See above.

Loth (loath. 10, 40). Scot. laith; A.-S. lâþ; O.-S. lôth, lêd; O.-Frs. lêth, lâth. Cp. Fr. laid.
Oth (oath. 10, 40). A.-S. âþ; Góth. aiþs; O.-S. êd etc.
Reproch (reproach. 9, 11). Fr. reprocher; Pr. repropchar.
Shew¹) (9, 3. 9. 20. 52). O.-E. shewen, in Orm schaewenn; A.-S. scavjan, sceavjan etc.

Sounds 47. 48. (as in more, therefore).

I: Foorth (forth. 1, 8). A.-S. forþ.
Uprore (uproar. 1, 5). Sw. uppror; Dan. uprör; D. oproer etc.
II: Affoord (afford. 10. 20). Likely the French afforer, afeurer; perhaps the A.-S. forþian.
Bord (board 10, 66). A.-S. bord; Goth. baurd etc.
Flore (10, 10). See the following word.
Floure (floor. 9, 34). A.-S. flor, flore; D. vloer; O.-N. flôr; L. G. floor; O.-H. G. fluor; M.-H. G. vluor; Mod.-H. G. flur.

Sounds 19. 20. (as in nut, walnut).

I: Bloud (blood. 1, 25). | A.-S. blôd (==blôs from blôvas); Goth. blóþ.   O.-H. G. pluot;
Bloudy (bloody. 1, 26). | M.-H. G. bluot.
Corage (courage. 1, 22). Fr. courage; O.-Fr. corage; Sp. corage; It. coraggio; M.-Lat. coragium (cor).
Encombred (encumbred²) 1, 22).
Floud³) (flood. 1, 20). A·-S. flôd; Goth. flodus; O.-S. fluod etc.
Mirrhe (myrrh. 1, 8).
Slombring⁴) (slumbering. 1, 36). O.-E. slomberen, slomeren; A.-S. slumerjan etc.
Sommers (summers. 1, 7). A.-S. sumor, sumer; O.-S. sumar, sumer; O.-Frs. sumur, somer; D. zomer; O.-N. sümar; Sw. sommar; Dan. sommer; O.-H. G. sumar; M.-H. G. sumer; Mod.-H. G. sommer.
II: Bloud⁵) (blood. 10, 66).
Bloudshed⁶) (bloodshed. 10, 49. 51).
Combrous⁷) (cumbrous. 9, 17). Cp. Fr. encombrer and Mod.-H. G. kummer.
Comenly (commonly. 10, 12).
Commun (common. 10, 69).
Demeanure (demeanor, — our. 9, 27).
Encombred²) (encumbred. 9, 51).
Fornace (furnace. 9, 29). Fr. fournaise; It. fornace; Sp. hornaza; Lat. fornax.
Nourse (nurse. 9, 48). O.-E. nourse, norse, nourice, norice; Fr. nourrice; Lat. nutrix.
Retourn or other forms of this verb (return. 9, 15. 34; 10, 11. 17). Fr. retourner.
Shonneth⁸) (shuns. 9, 40). Shun: O.-E. shun, shunt; A.-S. scúnian etc.
Sondry (sundry. 9, 48. 50; 10, 23. 37. 54. 63). Cp. Sunder — asunder — sundry. O.-E. sondres; A.-S. sunderjan, syndrjan, sundor, synderig etc.
Tonnell⁹) (tunnel. 9, 29). Fr. tonnelle.
Trompetts¹⁰) (trumpets, 9, 16). Fr. trompette.

---

¹) In these passages we have to read shu or shju because of the rhyme. In the following stanzas it may be read shu, as usually: I, 1, 19; II, 9, 51, 53.
²) Now, too, sometimes written with o.   ³) Sometimes also in our days floud.   ⁴) Cf. above.
⁵) In Kitchin. — See above.   ⁶) See above.   ⁷) Lex rem.   ⁸) As for th see below.   ⁹) As for ll see below.
¹⁰) As for tt see below.

Some words, in which instead of the termination o r , most usual in our days, is to be found o u r :

I: Conquerour (1, 8). Errour (1, 13. 18).

II: Conquerour (10, 4). Emperour (10, 15. 52. 57. 60). Treachetour [1]) (10, 51. 52). Victour [2]) (10, 23. 57).

The case is inverse in the following passages:

II: Favor (9, 6). Honored (9, 6).

Omission of the Letter O.

I: P o i s n o u s (1, 15) ==poisonous [3]).

II: A l s (10, 18) ==also [4])

Sounds 9. 10. (as in cube, usurp..

I: D e a w (dew. 1, 36). A.-S. deáv.

Dewly (duly. 1, 34 . Fr. dû; Pr. deut; Lat. debutus ·for debitus.

II: D e w (due. 9, 20. 25. 59; 10, 41. 45).

D e w t y (duty. 9, 28).

H e w [1]) (hue. 9, 3. 40. 52). A.-S. hiv, hiv, heov; Sw. hy.

I s s e w (issue. 10, 54. 61). [1])

I s s e w e d (issued. 9, 17). [4])

L e w d l y (lewdly. 10, 17). A.-S. laeved, laevd, leáved.

M o n i m e n t s (monuments. 9, 59; 10, 21. 36 [1]).

P u r s e w (pursue. 9, 9; 10, 18). Fr. poursuivre; O.-Fr. porsevre.

S u b d e w (subdue. 9, 9; 10, 13. 41. 54); probably from the O.-Fr. sosduire, sousduire.

S u r v e w d [1]) (surviewed. 9, 45). Cp. O.-Fr. vëue; Mod.-Fr. v u e from the part. v e u, vu, fem. v e u e, v u e of the verb v o i r, O.-Fr. veoir; Lat. videre [3]).

V a l e w (value. 9, 24). O.-Fr. value, fem. of the part. v a l u of the verb v a l o i r; Lat. valere.

V e w [5]) (view. 9, 3. 20. 40. 44. 59).

Sounds 27. 28. (as in pool, whirlpool).

I: D r o u p i n g [1]) (drooping. 1, 36). Cp. A.-S. drôf, drêfe; O.-S. drôbi; O.-H.G. truobi; Mod.-H.G. truebe.

T o o (to. 1, 10). A.-S. to; O.-S., O.-Frs. to, te, ti; the A.-S. to, in Orm t o, O.-E. to, separates afterwards in t o and t o o.

II: B l e w (blue. 9, 40). A.-S. bleoh (bleov, bleó, blió), blae.

L o u p [1]) (loop. 9, 10). Fr. loupe.

P r o o v' d (proved. 10, 27). Prove: O.-E. prove; O.-Fr. prover, pruver; Mod.-Fr. prouver; Lat. probare.

R e w [1]) (rue. 10, 66). O.-E. ruwen; A.-S. hreóvan; O.-S. hrëwan etc.

R o w m e (room. 9, 28. 47. 48. 53. 54; 10, 34). O.-E. r o w m e, roume; A.-S. rûm.

S h e w. See above p. 103.

T r o u p e s (troops. 9, 15). Fr. troupe, troupeau; O.-Fr. trope, trupe; Pr. trop; It. truppa; Sp. Pg. tropa; M.-Lat. troppus etc.

T r e w (true. 9, 3. 39. 52). O.-E. trewe, in Orm t r o w w e and t r i g g; A.-S. treóve; O.-S. triwi; O.-Frs. triuve, triowe, trowe etc.

[1]) Lex. rem.   [2]) In Kitchin.   [3]) See above.   [4]) See above.   [5]) Cf. Burguy III, 386.   [6]) See above.

Trewest¹) (truest. 10, 42).

Sounds 21. 22. (as in good, childhood).

We did not find any word in which these sounds have been altered, either orthographically or orthoepically.

Insertion of the Letter u.

II: Guilt²)³) (gilt. 9, 44).

Sounds 5. 6. (as in wide, idea).

I: Hy (high. 1, 8). A.-S. heáh; Goth. hauhs. (A.-S. secondary forms are: héag, heá, hèh, hig); O.-Frs. hâch, hâg.

Inquere⁴) (inquire. 1, 31). Lat. inquirere.

II: Clime (climb. 9, 21). O.-E. climben; Scot. clim; A.-S. climban³).

Despight²) (despite. 9, 10; 10, 56). Cp. O.-Fr. despiter, despire; Pr. despieg, despeytar; Lat. despectus.

Geaunts (giants. 10, 8). O.-Fr. gaiant; Mod.-Fr. géant; Pr. jaiant; Catal. gigant; It., Sp., Pg. gigante; Lat. gigas; Gr. γίγας, γίγαντος.

Nyc (nigh. 9, 13). O.-E. neigh, neighe; A.-S. neáh, nèh, nih; O.-Frs. nei; O.-S. nâ.

Very frequently the only anomaly is the letter i turning into y; in some of the following examples, however, the case is inverse:

I: Eies (1, 13). lie (1, 27). lion (1, 17). triall⁶) (1, 12). — tydings (1, 30). wyde (1, 34).

II: Aryse (9, 42). aspyre (9, 39). behynd (9, 38). cryme (9, 25). desyrd (9, 54). desyre (10, 22). devyse (9, 42). entyre (10, 31). flyes (9, 51). fyre (9, 30. 40). guyse (9, 31). hyde 9, 38). hyre (10, 12). inspyre (9, 30. 39). kynd (9, 31). lyes (10, 46). mynd (9, 31). pyonings (10, 63). requyrd (9, 25). requyre (9, 30. 39; 10, 12. 27). retyre (10, 22). syde¹) (10, 51). syre (9, 48; 10, 29. 31). tyme (10, 58). wyde (9, 25). ydly (9, 35). yvie (9, 24). yvory (9, 41).

Sounds 29. 30. (as in toil, turmoil.)

The letter i often turns into y, in one example (roiall) y into i.

I: Poyson (1, 20).

II: Adjoyning (9, 13). boyling (10, 26). foyle (10, 48). oyle (10, 30). poyson (10, 67). rejoyced (9, 18). roiall⁶) (10, 9). soyle (10, 9. 48). spoyle (10, 48). spoylefull⁷) (10, 63).

Sounds 31. 32. (as in noun, pronoun.)

Ou turns into ow; in one example (frounds) the case is inverse:

I: Arownd (1, 18). fowle (1, 22). shrowd (1, 6).

II: Bownd (10, 63). confownd (9, 15). fowle (9, 1. 11. 32). fownd (9, 35). fround (9, 36). grownd (9, 15. 41; 10, 11). howre (10, 57). lowd (9, 11. 25). prowd (10, 47). rownd (9, 15. 26. 32. 40). sownden (9, 16).

---

¹) See the preceding word.   ⁷) Lex. rem.
³) Cp. Diefenbach 2, 403; Weigand (Schmitthennors kurzes deut. woertb. 1853 ff.) 1, 438; Schmid (gesetze der Angelsachsen 1858) 603; Grimm Myth. 34.
⁴) Because of the rhyme this verb must be read with sound 3. Cf. above.
⁵) Cp. Maetzn. I, p. 347.   ⁶) As for II see below.   ⁷) In Kitchin.

14

2. Consonant Sounds.

Sounds 21, 22. (as in childhood,)
Omission of a Consonant.

We do not find any word in which these sounds have been altered, either orthographically or orthoepically.

d.

II: Kinred[1]) (kindred. 10, 35). It communicated with the A.-S. cynryn, cynren etc. It has been composed of kin and red — A.-S. ráed, réd; Mod.-H. G. rath (hebath etc).

Sounds 5, 6. (as in off.)

II: Ofspring[2]) (offspring. 9, 60; 10, 69). Of and off are secondary forms of the same word. A.-S. of, af, äf; Goth. af; Gr. ἀπό; Lat. ab[3]).

g.

II: Forrein (foreign. 10, 63. 65). O.-E. forein; O.-Fr. forain. It. foraneo, forano; M.-Lat. foraneus from the Lat. word foras. The letter g, in the Modern English, has been falsely inserted, as in sovereign too[4]).

Sovdraintie[5]) (sovereignty. 10, 48). See the preceding word.

Wagon (waggon. 9, 10). A.-S. vaegen, vaegn, vaen, a secondary form of wain[6]).

l.

I: Compeld (1, 5). expeld (1, 5).

Wel-nigh (well nigh. 1, 22). O.-E. wele; A.-S. vèl, veln; Goth. vaila.
II: Al (all. 9, 7). A.-S. eal; Goth. alls; O.-N. alr; Gr. ὅλος.
Cald[7]) (called. 9, 31; 10, 12. 27). Dan. kalde; Lat. calare; Gr. καλεῖν.
Dwell (9, 56); dwelt (10, 7); enrold (10, 4). exceld (10, 25). fild[?])(10, 21. 27. 32).
Hils (hills. 9, 45); A.-S. hyll, hill; D. hille, hil; Mod.-Frs. hel (cp. hele).
Kild[?]) (10, 21. 27. 32). rebeld (ibidem). roiale[8]) (10, 36). mervayld[?])(9, 43).
Skil (skill. 10, 59). O.-E. skile, skill; O.-N. skil; Sw. skjäl, skäl; Dan. skiel.
Til (till. 10, 62).
Vaut (vault. 9, 29). O.-E. vault; Mod.-Fr. voûte; O.-Fr. vaute, vaulte, volte; Pr. volta, vouta, vota; Sp. vuelta; O.-Sp. Pg. It. volta; M.-Lat. volth, voluta, volutio (volvere[9]).
Wals (walls. 9, 53. 55; 10, 46). A.-S. veall, vall; O.-S. D. wal; Dan. val; Lat. vallum.
Wel-nigh[?]) (10, 40).
Wild (willed. 10, 32).

Sounds 31, 32.

II: Comenly[10]) (commonly. 10, 12). dim'd (dimmed. 10, 43).

n.

II: Maner (manner. 9, 37). Fr. manière; It. maniera; Sp. manera; Pg. Pr. maniera from the Lat. manarius, manuarius.
Sternesse (sternness. 10, 7).

r.

II: Arayd (arrayed. 9, 19. 37). Array: O.-Fr. arroi, arrei, from the O.-Fr. roi; It. redo.

[1]) Lex. rem. and Maetzn. I, p. 440.   [2]) Lex. rem.   [3]) Maetzn. I, p. 400 sq.   [4]) Maetzn. I, p. 176.
[5]) See above.   [6]) Maetzn. 205.   [7]) See below.   [8]) In Kitchin: See above.
[9]) Burguy III, 396; Diez I, 445.   [10]) See above and lex. rem.

Debard,) (debarred, 9, 25). (ward ¹). (marred, 9, 43). stird ²) (stirred, 10, (35, (37).
s.

I: Glas (glass. 1, 35). A.-S. gläs; M.-H. G., Mod.-H.G., D. glas; Dan. glar, glas.
Gras (grass. 1, 20). A.-S. gras, gears, gärs; Goth. etc. gras.
Pas (pass. 1, 30. 34. 35).
II: Amis²) (amiss. 9, 58). carcase (carcass. 10,⁴43). witnes (witness. 10, 10).

I: Litle³) (little. 1, 14. 35). Old forms: lite, lytae, lile, lille; A.-S; lyt, lytel, litel; Goth.
leitils etc. Cp. λιτός⁴).

Other irregularities concerning the Consonants.

Doubling of a Consonant.

d.

I: Biddes¹) (1, 36). eye-liddes (1, 36). homebredd¹) (1, 31). mudd (1, 21). riddes¹) (1, 36). ycladd¹) (1, 1).
II: Dredd¹) (10, 52). ledd¹) (9, 28; 10, 29).

l.

Mostly at the end of the words:
I: Counsell (1, 33). cruell (1, 8). fearfull (1, 24). laurell (1, 9). royall (1, 5).
II: Babell (9, 21). bashfull (9, 41). civill⁵) (10, 38). compell (9, Motto; 10, 11). continuall (9, 54; 10, 30). counsell (9, 27; 10, 37). cruell (9, 15; 10, 33. 35. 43). damzell (9, 42). disloyall (10, 19). dolefull (10, 66). dreadfull (10, 60). equall (10, 1). fatall (10, 9). fearfull (10, 16). festivall (9, 27). finall (10, 13). immortall (9, 22. 56; 10, 4. 42). imperiall (9, 3; 10, 13). liberall (9, 20). lilly (9, 19). mortall (9, 3. 22. 48). painefull (10, 63). royall (10, 4. 35. 47). sinfull⁵) (10, 50). speciall (9, 20). spoilefull (10, 63). vessell (9, 30). virginall (9, 20).
In the middle of the words:
II: Elles⁶) (else. 9, 32).
Pollicies²) (policies. 5, 48. 53; 10, 39).
Pupillage (pupilage. 10, 64). Cp. Fr. pupille.

n.

I: Sonne (son. 1, 30). sunne (sun. 1, 32). winne (win. 1, 3). wonne (won. 1, 27).
II: Donne¹) (done. 10, 66). fennes (fens. 9, 16). honny⁶) (honey. 9, 51). shonnetti''y (shuns. 9, 40). sonne (9, 7. 11. 13. 20. 23. 34. 35. 41. 45. 46. 64. 66. 67). sunne (9, 7; 10, 2).

p.

I: Chappel⁵) (chapel. 1, 34). Fr. chapelle; It. cappella.
Entrappe (1, Motto). propp (1, 8). steppe (1, 13). worshippe (1, 3).

r.

I: Farr (1, 7). farre (1, 6. 31). firre (1, 9). forrests (1, 18). starr (1, 7). starre (1, 27). warre (1, 30).

---

¹) See below. ²) Lex. rem. ³) Maetzn. I, p. 269, and above. ⁴) II, 9, 58: little. ⁵) In Kitchin. ⁶) See above. ⁷) See below. ⁸) See below, and above; Alsp in our index with pp.

14*

II: Abhorre (10, 6). arre¹) (10, 65). farre (9, 4; 10, 4. 5. 65). forreiners (10, 65). forreyne (10, 26. 43. 48. 63). iarre (10, 65). outbarre (10, 63)·

s.

II: Ceasse (cease. 10, 52). Fr. cesser; Lat. cessare.

t.

II: Begott (10, 8). blott (10, 23). cittie (9, 48). fitt (10, 27). gnattes (1, 23). gott (9, 29; 10, 12). jett (9, 24). lott (10, 12). pitt (10, 11). pittilesse (10, 35). pitty (9, 21; 10, 37). satt (9, 35), Scottes (10, 29). sett (9, 22. 58). sitt (9, 85).

Other Irregularities concerning the Consonants.

c instead of k.
II: Besprincled (10, 10).

c instead of s.
I: Sence (1, 18).
II: Bace (9, 1). cace (9, 43; 10, 57). enchaced (9, 24). recompence (10, 23).

ch instead of c.
I: Christall (1, 34).

ck instead of c.
I: Magick (1, 36).
II: Armorick (10, 64). Celticke (10, 5). Musicke (10, 59).

ck instead of k.
II: Lincke (9, 18).

h inserted.
II: Unhable (9, 14. 58). Cp. Fr. habile.
War-hable²) (10, 62).

k instead of c.
II: Raskall (9, 15).

l inserted.
II: Salvage (savage. 10, 5. 7. 10. 25). O.-Fr. savaige, salvage; Mod.-Fr. sauvage; It. salvaggio, selvaggio, salvatico from the Lat. silvaticus³).

m instead of n.
II: Renowmed⁴) (9, 4; 10, 4. 36. 65). Cp. O.-Fr. renomer.

s instead of c.
II: Fensible (9, 21). fiersly (9, 14). forse (9, 55). prophesies (9, 51). redusd⁵) (10, 38). thrise (9, 5; 10, 45). twise¹) (9, 26; 10, 48).

s instead of z.
I: Lasie (1, 6).
II: Wisards (9, 53).

st instead of ced.
II: Shamefast²) (9, 43). shamefastness (9, 43).

---

¹) See below.   ²) Lex. rem.   ³) Cf. Burguy III, p. 339; Diez I, p. 364.   ⁴) See above.   ⁵) In Kitchin.

t i n s e r t e d.

II: Saftety ') (safety. 10. 6).

t i n s t e a d o f c.

II: Gratious²) (10, 39).

th i n s t e a d o f s.

II: Swarth³) (swart. 9, 52).

In the third singular person of the present tense⁴):

I: Brusheth (1, 23). creepeth (1, 36). doth (1, 23. 31. 32). draweth (1, 32). needeth (1. 26). wasteth (1, 31). weepeth (1, 8).

II: Doth (9, Motto. 1. 5. 14. 16. 42. 47. 56; 10, 1. 2. 14. 56). hath (9, 7. 34. 37. 41. 47; 10, 4. 23). seemeth (9, 42', shonneth (9, 40).

ve i n s t e a d o f ff.

II: Caitive (9, 13).

wh i n s t e a d o f h.

II: Whott (9, 29. 39).

s i n s t e a d o f s.

I: Raized (1, 18).

II: Advize etc. (9, 49). advizement (9, 9). damzel (9, 36). deviz'd (9, 46. 50. 59). rize (9, 59). wize (9, 12).

c. · Etymology.

As to forms and inflections we may notice, that Spenser's language does not much differ from that used in our days. Comparing, however, the following examples with the modern forms, we find that, in this regard too, the English language has more and more striven for brevity and simplicity, and that Spenser has followed very vacillating laws.

1. The Parts of Speech and their Inflection.

The Substantive.

In the declension of the substantives Spenser sometimes employs weak forms instead of strong ones:

I: Eyne ⁵) or eyen (eyes. 1, 14). fone⁶) (foes. 2, 23).

II: Fone (10, 10).

Very often the words ending in y do not change this letter into i in the plural number, though being preceded by a consonant, but preserve the letter y, which, now, is only the case in proper nouns ⁷)⁸):

II: Agonyes (9, 52). allyes (10, 38). auncestryes (10, 1). skyes (10, 1).

Other words terminating in y preceded by a vowel turn this letter into i:

I: Alleies⁹) (1, 7). eies (1, 13).

II: Daies (10, 59). laies (10, 59);

---

¹) See above. — Probably a misprint. The other two editions being at our disposition have not saftety: Todd has safěty, Kitchin 'For safeties sake.'
²) In Kitchin.   ³) Lex. rem.   ⁴) See below.   ⁵) See Willisius p. 28.   ⁶) But foes: II, 9, 10; 10, 54.
⁷) Cp. above and Maetzn. I, p. 216.   ⁸) But pollicies (II, 6, 48); fantasies (II, 9, 50).
⁹) See above.

Or they preserve *y*, but add *es* instead of *s*, as Moyes [1]) (10, 64). Other words with the termination *y* preceded by a consonant, turn it into *i*, but add only *s*: ... II: Enemis [2]) (10, 56). infancis (9, 57). propertis (9, 58). ...

Four times we have found bre th ren instead of bro th c r s, though: the poet intends to signify children of one family: ...
II: 9, 2; 10, 33. 45. 65 [3]).

Spenser sometimes preserves in the singular genitive the termination *es*, which, in the Modern English, is only used after a sibilant or after the palatal *ch*: ...
I: Aspes [4]) (5, 50). clothes [4]) (10, 39). heroes [4]) (11, 6). nightes [4]) (5, 23). worldes [4]) (9, 31). ... younges [4]) (5, 17). ...
II: Ladies (9, 2. 17). Lucies (10, 58). worldes (9, 47). ...

Often the apostrophe has not been employed [3]);
I: Princesse [4]) (5, 53).
II: Phoebus (10, 3). Princes (9, 59).

Sometimes Spenser makes use of the possessive pronoun, in order to express the genitive [6]):
I: Pegazus his kind [4]) (9, 21). — This man of God his godly arms [4]) (11, 7).
V: Sansfoy his shield [4]) (5, 5).

The Adjectives and the Adverbs.

There are no traces in Spenser of Anglo-Saxon forms in the declension of the adjectives; as for the comparison, however, some forms differ from those which the Modern English language uses [4]): *Etymology.*
I: Lenger (1, 22. 26). A.-S. lang; lengra; lengesta, lengsta [7]).
II: Lenger (9, 21; 10, 20). ...
IV: Fellonest [3]) (most: felon 2, 32). learnedst [4]) [3]) (most: learned 2, 35). most [5]) (greatest 11, 9).
warre [6]) (worse 8, 34). ...

Oftentimes Spenser vacillates between the French and the English manner of comparing;
I: More white [7]) (1, 4). whiter (1, 4 the foll. line).
II: More whot [9, 20]) ...

1. The Parts of Speech and their Number.

Once the letter *e* has not been elided [5]); Strange-er (in two different lines II, 9, Motto).
Many Adverbs deriving from adjectives are deficient in the termination *ly*.
II: Exceeding (4, 9) unwonted [4]) (4, 9). ...
II: Exceeding (9, 24).

In most words the loss of the final *e* explains the seeming use of adjectives for adverbs, since the latter, in an earlier period, were formed from adjectives by adding a final *e* [9]) ...
I: full (1, 4). wide (1, 23). ...
II: cleare (9, 4). constant (9, 6). easie (9, 33). lowd (9, 11). pittilesse (10, 35). right (10, 2). sondry (9, 48). vile (10, 18). whott (9, 29). wide (10, 2). wondrous (9, 54) ...
VI: Incontinent [4]) (6, 8). ...

The Number.

As for the numerals we did not find any abnormity in our stanzas, but Willisius [9]) tells ut that Spenser has preserved the Anglo-Saxon numerals in the following passages:

The same, which, in Modern English, is only [...]
that like the O.-E. like, has been employed by Spenser [...] in connection with this [...]

II. 10, 0.

The nominative, dative, and accusative of the second personal pronoun are:
thou, A.-S. þu, O.-E. thou, thow.
thee, A.-S. þē, þēc, O.-E. the, thee.
ye, you, A.-S. gē, O.-E. ye, yee.
you, A.-S. eóv, cóvic, O.-E. you).

As in the modern language the plural exceedingly prevails, it seems that Willisius[1]) is right telling us that Spenser makes use of the singular only when servants or friends are accosted, else employs ye and you. He cites V, 5, 29, where the mistress addressing the servant employs thou, the servant, however, you. We add:
Thee (I, 1, 19; II, 9, 5).

In the latter stanza, however, the lady first uses ye and then, accosting the same person, thee), and
I, 1, 31 the knight accosts the old man with ye, but the latter him with thee.

Concerning the difference between ye and you we have read the latter more seldom than the former, as nominative only, in the emphasis.)
II, 9, 43, where it is the antithesis of she;
II, 9, 8, where it is accompanied by an apposition.

Mostly it is accusative or dative: I, 1. 13. 31; II, 9, 6. 9. 42. Ye is always nominative:
I, 1, 19. 27. 31. 32. 33; II, 9, 2. 3. 6. 8. 9. 12. 37. 42. Sometimes we read yee), as in II, 9, 43.

It is a matter of course that the possessive pronouns accord with the personal pronouns as for instance; Thee — thy (II, 9, 5).

The pronoun self (A.-S. silf, sylf, sälf, seolf), is sometimes added to substantives without another pronoun):
II: Eden selfe) (12, 53).
III: Guyon selfe) (1, 6). Saxon selves) (3, 46).
Often it is separated from the pronoun):
I: Her selfe (1, 12).
II: Her owne self) (10, 54). Her selfe (9, 18; 10, 20. 54. 55). Him selfe (10, 49. 68). It selfe (10, 2). But:
II: Herselfe (10, 19. 54). Itselfe (9, 43; 10, 1).

The Anglo-Saxon pronoun hira (pl. gen.) is preserved by Spenser in her II, 7, 7.).
The pronouns, his, her, who, are referred by Spenser not only to persons and excellent animals, but also to things));
II: Eyen whom.) (4, 15). Towre whom on her bulwark) (8, 35), Yvie in his proper hew) (12, 61).
(V: It took his name) (1, 19).
Often which has been referred to persons): II, 9, 5. 19. 48. 52; 10, 20. 22. 24). 31.
Very frequently this pronoun is accompanied by the definite article, perhaps caused by the O.-Fr. liquels), the which: I, 1. 26. 36.; II, 9, 24. 34. 50. 56. II, 10, 10. 12. 41.

) Cp. above twist 2 thris. 2) Maetzn. J. p. 282. 3) Maetzn. III. p. 228. Cp. Maetzn. I, p. 234.
5) See John Wallis in Maetzn. J. p. 284, and above.) Maetzn. J. p. 290.) Willisius p. 29.
8) Maetzn. I. p. 291.) Often in our days too. (Maetzn. I, p. 291; III, p. 223). 10) Maetzn. I, p. 257.
11) Maetzn. I, p. 297. 12) Perhaps referred to blood.

The same, which, in Modern English, is only reinforced by self or very, or is preceded by that like the O.-E. ilke, has been employed by Spenser also in connection with this: I, 1, 33; II, 10, 9.

Often we read the same, where we should expect only the personal pronoun: I: 1, 4. 22; II, 9, 28. 31. 55; 10, 6[1]). 32. 57.

Instead of the ordinary expression some — others[2]) we often read: Some-some II: 9, 13. 50. 57. Some-some-some etc. — others some II, 9, 35.

The Article.

Frequently we read an instead of a before an aspirate h or before u preceded by a silent h:

I: An holy (1, 34).

II: An happy[3]) (10, 22). an huge (9, 30).

The Verb.

The third person, singular number, present tense, indicative mood very frequently ends in th instead in s[4]).

The termination en has been made use of by Spenser more frequently than in our times. For not only in the preterit participle and in the infinitive many verbs have this termination, but also in the plural number, indicative mood[5]).

Indicative.

I: Beene (1, 10).

II: Beene (9, 6. 37). doen (9, 45). liveden[6]) (10, 7).

Infinitive.

I: Vewen (1, 23).

II: Beene (10, 29). sownden (9, 16). taken (10, 37).

VI: Donne[7]) (10, 32).

Preterit and Participle.

I: Doen[7]) (4, 43).

II: Bene[8]) (10, 5. 8). doen (9, 11. 37). hewen (9, 24). overcommen (10, 32).

In forms where the Modern English language takes the sound t in termination ed, Spenser mostly also spelt this sound by the letter t, changing c before t into s[9]).

I: Accurst (1, 26). advaunst (1, 17). approcht (1, 27). chaunst (1, 27. 29). enforst (1, 7). enhaunst (1, 17). forst (1, 20). glaunst (1, 17). grypt (1, 19). knockt (1, 29). lookt (1, 16). nurst (1, 26). vanquisht (1, 27).

II: Abasht (9, 43). addrest (10, 31). chaste (10, 16). chaunst (9, 60). deckt (9, 46). disperst (9, 17). enforst (10, 65). exprest (10, 43). forst 9, 14; 10, 16). heapt (10, 63). laught (9, 35). lockt (9, 10). marcht (9, 10). plaste (9, 10. 32). polisht (9, 41). preacht (10, 53). prickt (10, 33). profest (10, 28. 31). ransackt (10, 40). ravisht (10, 69. recompenst (9, 55). renforst[10]) (10, 48). renounst (10, 52). stopt (9, 8; 10, 68). tuckt (9, 40). usurpt (10, 64). vauquisht (10, 18. 58). walkt (9, 7).

Often we read the preterit having ld instead of lled[11]):

II: Cald (10, 27) fild (10, 21). kild (10, 21). rebeld (10, 32). wild (10, 32).

---

[1]) Here we read that same.   [2]) For instance II, 9, 31.   [3]) Cp. Wagner p. 82.   [4]) See above.
[5]) Remainder of the Anglo-Saxon language. Cp. Maetzn. I. p. 317 sqq.
[6]) A later edition has lived then. Spenser seems to have thought this form too archaic. (Cp. Kitchin I, p. 222).   [7]) See Willisius.   [8]) I, 1, 23: bin.   [9]) See above.   [10]) = reinforced; see above.   [11]) See above.

' Sometimes the letter *s* has been elided before *r* [1]):

II: Encountred (10, 16. 18). murdred (10, 55. 61). surrendred (10, 20. 45).

Or there has taken place a metathesis of this letter [2]):

II: Dide (10, 53). stolne (9, 2).

In some participles an apocopy of the letter *d* seems to have taken place: Nominate (10, 38). rhyming with the adj. miscreate.

The syllable *ge* usually prefixed to the Anglo-Saxon preterit participles has been preserved by Spenser in the letter *y* [3]):

I: Yblent (2, 5 [4]). ycladd (1, 1). ydrad (1, 2). yplace [4]) (4, 23).

II: Ybuilt (9, 29). ycladd (9, 27).

The active participle often terminates in *and* or has the French termination *ant*:

I: Glitterand [5]) (4, 61). thrillant [4]) (11, 20). trenchant [6]) (1, 17).

III: Persant [4]) (9, 20).

Weakly are conjugated:

Abide; abid [7])·
Alight; alight [7]).
Arraught [8]) p. (II, 10, 34).
Beat; bet [7]).
Bestride; bestradd [7]).
Blend; blent [7]).
Bren; brent [7]). (II, 9, 29).
Brust; brust, brast [7]).
Cast; kest [7]).
Catch; keight [7]).
Deck; dight [7]).
Deem; dempt [7]).
Delay; delaid (II, 9, 8).
Dismay; dismaid (II, 9, 8. 34).
Display; displaide (I, 10, 14. 16).
Dispred p. (II, 9, 27).
Drent p. [7]).
Dreade [7]); drad [7]), dred (I, 1, 8), dredd (II, 10, 52), dreaded (II, 10, 1 [9]).
Find; fond [7]) (II, 9, 60).
Heap; hept [7]).
Hight; hight, hot [7]) (II, 9, 27. 31. 52. 59. 60; 10, 2. 16. 22. 33. 35. 46. 59. 65).
Hold; hild [7]).
Lead; lad, ledd [7]). (I, 1, 4; II, 9, 28. 33. 54; 10, 29. 62).

Lean; lent [7]).
Leap; lept (II, 1, 17).
Leave; leaved (II, 10, 31).
Meynt, p. [7])
Pitch; pight [7]).
Play; plaid (II, 9, 35).
Quoth (I. 1. 12. 30. 32).
Reach; raught [7]). (II, 9, 19; 10, 20).
Read; red, rad [7]).
Reave; reft, raft [7]) (I, 1, 24).
Ride; ridd, rad [7]).
Scrike; shright [7]).
Shend; shent [7]).
Shew; shewd (II, 9, 53).
Sigh; sight [7]).
Spread; spred (I, 1,· 7; II, 10, 10). overspred (II, 10, 2).
Sprent p. [7])
Strew; strowd (I, 1, 35).
Sweat; swat [7]).
Upstart, pr. (I, 1, 16).
Won; wonned (II, 9, 52).
Wont, pr. (I, 1, 34).
Yield; yold [7]).

Strongly are conjugated:

Awake; awooke [7]).
Bespeak; bespoke (II, 9, 43).

---

[1]) See above. [2]) See above and cp. Maetzn. I, p. 346. [3]) Cp. Maetzn. I, p. 328; Kitchin I, p. 250.
[4]) See Willisius p. 30. [5]) See Willisius p. 30; Kitchin I, p. XVII; Maetzn. I, p. 327.
[6]) Tauchnitz, Kitchin: trenchand; cp. Todd. [7]) See Willisius p. 30 sqq. [8]) Lex. rom.
[9]) In Tauchnitz by misprint dreadred; the other editions have dreaded.

15

Bid; bad (II, 10, 13).

Clyme: clomb; clombe [1]).

Drink; drunke; drunke [1]).

Drive; drive, drave; drive [1]).

Gin; gan (I, 1. 17. 21. 23; II, 9, 9. 11. 14. 36. 59; II, 10, 6. 9. 28. 30. 31. 33. 57. 58. 61).

Glide; glode [1]).

Hang; hong; hong [1]). (II, 9, 24; 10, 32).

Melt; molt; molten [1]).

Overcome; overcommen (II, 10, 32). A.-S. cumen.

Overromne (II, 9, 15).

Quake; quooke [1]).

Quoth (I, 1, 12. 30. 32. 33).

Ring; rong (II, 9, 25).

Rive; rive; riven, rive, rift [1]).

Shake; shoke, shooke [1]) (II, 9, 11).

Shape; shope [1]).

Shine; shone, shined [1]).

Shrink; shronk, shronk [1]).

Sing; song (II, 9, 35).

Sleep; slep, slept; slept [1]).

Smite; smott, smitt; smitt [1]).

Spring; sprong [1]) (II, 10, 8).

Sting; stong; stong [1]).

Stink; stoncke, stanke [1]).

Stryke; stroke, strooke, strake; stroken, stricken [1]). (I, 1, 24).

Swell; swollen, swolne (I, 1, 26).

Wex, wax; wax, wox, woxe. wext; woxen [1]). (II, 10, 17. 20. 30. 32 [2]).

Win; wan (II, 10, 61).

Wreake; wroke; ywrake, wroke, wroken [1]).

Write; writt, wrate; writt, writ [1]). (II, 9, 50).

Anomalous Verbs:

Bee [1]), been (ar I, 1, 7; are II, 9, 22); was; been bin, bee, bene (I, 1, 33; II, 10, 5).

Can [1]); couth, could; (I, 1, 8; II, 9, 46. 47. 50).

Eo; yod, yede; gone [1]).

May; mote, might, mought [1]) (I, 1, 16. 32. 33; II, 9, 2. 3. 5. 6. 9. 21. 23. 25. 42. 45. 49. 52; 10, 24).

Wot, wote, weete [3]); wist; (un) wist [1]). (I, 1, 13. 32; II, 9, 6. 9).

The Preposition.

Some prepositions in Spenser have different forms: [4])

Amiddes (I, 1, 36). II: amid (10, 5); amidst (9, 58).

Besides amiddes the O.-E. language had: amid, amyd, amydde [5]).

Emong (I, 1, 32 [4]). II: emongst (9, 52); mongst (9, 6; 10, 13. 27).

The most usual form in Modern English is among. The forms ending in st have, like amidst, against originated from ancient forms, as in the N-E. and Scot. dialects amonges, emonges, emongs, and have added an inorganical t [6]).

Gainst (II, 10, 46. 57); against (II, 10, 54 etc.).

Thorough (I, 1. 32. II, 9, 23); through (9, 8 [7]).

Twixt (II, 9, 22; 10, 24. 28. 29).

The usual form is betwixt, O.-E. betwix, betwixen, betwixt; atwix, atwixen, atwixt [8]).

Withouten = without (II, 9, 58).

From the modern language differs the use of the following prepositions:

Besides = near. (II, 10, 54) [9]).

For the sake (of [10]), that usually is employed with the Anglo-Saxon genitive or with the possessive pronoun. is sometimes construed by Spenser in the following manner:

For whose sweete sake (I, 1, 2). [11])

---

[1]) See Willisius p. 30 sqq.　[2]) II, 10, 30 wax impf. or inf. . . .? probably inf.
[3]) Lucas means, wot is the imperfect tense, but see I, 1, 13.　[4]) See above.　[5]) Maetzn. I, p. 404.
[6]) Maetzn. I, p. 404.　[7]) Cp. Maetzn. I, p. 402.　[8]) Maetzn. I, p. 406.　[9]) See Todd; Church.
[10]) Maetzn. I, p. 408.　[11]) Maetzn. II, p. 442.

For to c. inf.: Ready for to fight[1] (I, 1, 12; II, 9, 59).

In-stead[2]. In his sted (II, 10, 44), in his stead (II, 10, 58) is not unusual, but: In watches stead (II, 9, 46) = in the place of watchmen.

Roundabout usually is substantive, adjective or adverb, but preposition in II, 9, 7 (though divided into two words).

To is used by Spenser, as in German, before the word frend:
With God to frend[3] (I, 1, 28).
With Love to frend[4] (III, 3, 14).

Wanting. Maetzner does not mention wanting as preposition, though he enumerates concerning, touching, respecting, considering, regarding etc. among the prepositions. In I, 1, 32; II, 10, 61, however, it seems that wanting has thoroughly become a preposition.

Finally, a peculiarity of Spenser is his making use only of the form toward, not of towards, in our stanzas at least; the like only of the adverbs backward, forward (I, 1, 28).

The Conjunction and the Adverb except that of quality[4].

All with the subjunctive mood instead of although: All be they loth (II, 10, 40; III, 7, 9, [1]).
All so — as. (I, 1, 54; 2, 4[1]); II, 9, 21; 10, 22.) French: tout aussi — que.
Als = also[5].
As = as if: (II, 9, 11)[6]. (II, 9, 36: as if).
As that[7] = as: (I, 1, 30).
As well = as well as (II, 9, 31).
As yet (II, 9, 40).
Attone[8]), attonce = at once (II, 1, 42; 9, 28. 36; 11, 18. 22).
Before that[1]) (III, 9, 33).
Both - and eke[8]). Eke = also. A.-S. eac, subst. eaca, increase, and verb eácnian. (I, 9, 18; II, 2, 34; 4, 19. 44; 5, 8. 36; 9, 16. 36; 10, 28; 11, 3. 45.
But = quin (II, 9, 6).
But for = but for that, but inasmuch 'as. (II, 9, 58).
But if[1]) (III, 3, 16).
But that (II, 9, 40. 49).
Elles[5]) = else (II, 9, 32). Els[6]) (II, 8, 33; 9, 56; 10, 48).
Foreby[7]) (II, 10, 16).
For that (II, 10, 50).
Forthy (II, 9, 49).
Hereof (II, 9, 46).
If that = if[7]) (II, 9, 12; 57)
Least[5]) = lest (II, 9, 30).
Nath'lesse[8]) or Nathlesse = none the less. (II, 1, 5. 20. 22; 6, 24; 7, 45; 10, 57).
Ne = not (II, 9, 19. 57; 10, 2).
Ne — ne = neither — nor (II, 9, 47; 10, 5. 6).
Ne — nor = neither — nor (I, 1, 28. 35; 10, 48; II, 9, 19. 28. 29. 38. 49. 50. 56. 57; 10, 2. 20).

---

[1]) Cp. Willisius p. 34.   [2]) Lex. rem.
[3]) Kitchin (I, gloss.): = 'with God for a friend'. An O.-E. idiom, corresponding to 'to have one to my friend, to my foe'. Or frend may be a verb, = to befrend.   [4]) See above. Unusual Interjections we have not found.
[5]) See above.   [6]) Maetzn. II, p. 130.
[7]) Sometimes, like the French conjunction que that has been added to the particles. See also below and Maetzn. I, p. 415.   [8]) Lex. rem.

15*

Nether = neither (II, 9, 24).
Nor — nor = neither — nor[1]) (II, 9, 25).
Frequently the negative has been redoubled (I, 1, 22; II, 9, 21. 28. 29; 10, 35; III, 10, 25.)[2])
Now that (II, 9, 57).
Sith[3]) = since. A.-S. sibþan. (II, 9, 7).
Soone as = as soon as (I, 1, 15. 25; II, 9, 36).
Then[4]) = than (I, 1, 24; II, 10, 28[5]).
The whiles[6]) = the German derweilen (II, 9, 9. 30. 40. 43; 10, 48).
Tho[4]) = then. O.-E. þo, þa, þag; A.-S. þonne. (I, 1, 18; 8, 11; 11, 42; II, 1, 26; 3, 13; 5, 7. 23; 6, 38; 8, 27; 9, 30; 10, 21. 27. 30; 11, 42. 46; 12, 2. 26).
Til = till[7]) (II, 10, 62).
Till that[6]) = till (II, 9, 11; 10, 6. 32. 67).
Untill[9]) = until (I, 1, 10; II, 10, 15).
Untill that[8]) (II, 10, 15).
Whenas, whereas, instead of when, where (II, 9, 10. 14. 33. 60).
Whiles[10]) = while or whilst, is the plural of the substantive while[11]) (II, 9, 1; 10, 56).
Whilest (I, 1, 13; II, 10, 36. 47. 54). See the preceding word.
Whilst ever that[6]) (V, 4, 14[12]).
Whylome[13])[14]) (II, 9, 45; 10, 16).
Yet — but[15]) (I, 1, 2).

2. Formation of Words. ✗

There are some terminations which Spenser employs io order to form substantives and adjectives, and which, in the modern language, may be found but seldom or not at all. The terminations esse, ise, hed, dome[16]).

I: Covetise (4, 29). drowsyhed (2, 7). humblesse (2, 21). lustyhed (2, 3). richesse (4, 7). riotise (5, 46).
II: Nobilesse (II, 8, 18). III: Bountyhed (3, 47). IV: Feeblesse (8, 37). maisterdome (1, 46).
The prefixes for and to answering the German syllables ver, zer:
I: Forwandring (6, 34). forwearied (1, 32). forworne (6, 35).
III: Forhent (4, 49). forlent (4, 47). V: To-rent (8, 4).
Compare also the following words:
I: Dreriment (8, 8). hurtless (6, 31). VI: Griefful (8, 40); and these:
I: Outfound (12, 3). outwell (1, 21). upbrought (10, 4). uprose (12, 3).

In some words, however, it seems that in the modern language the usage of prefixes does not differ from the Old-English so much as in Spenser's language, especially in those words which, at the end of the first syllable, connect the letter s with another consonant, as in the following passages:
I: Scapt = escaped (9, 28). spersed = dispersed (1, 39). III: sdeigned = disdained (2, 40). Besides:

---

[1]) Cp. Wagner p. 411.   [2]) Willisius p. 34.   [3]) Lex. rem.; Maetzn. I, p. 414; II, p. 275.
[4]) Lex. rem. and above.   [5]) II, 9, 26 used in the ordinary meaning.
[6]) See below whiles and cp. above the which.   [7]) See above. Maetzn. I, p. 414. Till: I, 1, 11; II, 9,
32 etc.   [8]) See above.   [9]) Until: II, 10, 9.   [10]) Cp. above the whiles.   [11]) Maetzn. I, p. 414.
[12]) Willisius p. 34.   [13]) Maetzn. I, p. 380.   [14]) See above.   [15]) Maetzn. III, p. 364 sq.   [16]) Willisius p. 33.

I: Playnd = complained (1, 47). refte = bereft (9, 29). II: Fray (effrayer. 12, 40). spalles = espales (6, 29). III: Colled (acolla; 2, 34). gin = engin (7, 7). VI: Long = belong (2, 8).
Concerning the composition we cite the following passages:
I: Sweete-bleeding (1, 9). the vine - propp elme (1, 8).
II: Lively-head (9, 3). Babell towre (9, 21)
We should have expected a hyphen in the following compounds [1]:
I: Ocean waves (1, 32).
II: Beetle browes (9, 52). canker holes (9, 57). castle gate (9, 17). castle hall (9, 20. 21). castle wall (9, 11). commen wealthes (9, 53). conduit pipe (9, 32). craftesman hand (9, 41). great grandfathers (10, 4). hoarie gray (9, 29). kitchin clerke (9, 31). kitchin rowme (9, 28). lilly white (9, 19). maister cooke (9, 31). morning rose (9, 36). morning starre (9, 4). Ossa hill (10, 3). parchment scrolls (9, 57). poplar braunch (9, 39). purple pall[2]) (9, 37). rosy red (9, 41). silver sockets (9, 46[2]). yvie twine (9, 24).
One word is divided into two in the following passages:
I: No where (1, 23). with hold (1, 12). II: Ere long (10, 65). high-way (10, 39). no where (9, 38). war - hable (10, 62).
As for it self, her own self etc. see above.
Spenser contracts into one word:
I: Eventide (1, 23). eventyde (1, 34). eyclidds (1, 36).
II: Backgate (9, 32).
He has the genitive instead of the compound in: Queene of Faëry (II, 9, 4).

d. Syntactical Remarks.

It would be very interesting, to be sure, to inquire into several syntactical details of the Spenserian language, and we reserve this inquiry for a future time, now only citing the passages that may offer fulcrums to such an undertaking, and entering into particulars only for the most striking differences from the modern language.
The impersonal verbs were more frequent in Spenser's age than in ours, as for instance: Me chaunced I, 2, 35 = I chanced[3]).
Spenser very commonly omits the pronoun before impersonal verbs:[4])
Seemed in heart some hidden cáre she had (I, 1, 4.)
'Fayre damzell, seemeth by your troubled cheare,
That either me too bold ye woene . . .' (II, 9, 42.)
'Ah, Ladie', sayd he, 'shame were to revoke
The forward footing for an hidden shade'. (I, 1, 12.)
Now needeth him no lenger labour spend. (I, 1, 26.)
With holy father sits not will such thinges to mell. (I, 1, 30.)
Perhaps, the personal pronoun has been omitted: I, 22, 3, l. 3; II, 9, 23, l. 9.
'It' and the verb, perhaps, in: I, 1, 13, l. 2. 3.
Sometimes Spenser makes use of the verb 'to do' in order to express the meaning of the

---

[1]) See above.   [2]) But purple, silver are also adjectives.
[3]) Cp. Kitchin I, p. 163. — Maetzn. II, p. 30. — Above.   [4]) Willsius p. 32.

Latin verb 'efficere', as in: 'To do her die' (I, 8, 45. Cp. I, 8, 36; 10, 32)[1]. Besides we find this verb in:[2]

I, 1, 3. 4. 5. 6. 7. 9. 13. 14. 19. 21. 23. 26. 28. 29. 30. 31. 32. 34.

II, 9, Motto. 1. 2. 3. 5. 7. 9. 10. 11. 14. 15. 16. 17. 19. 20. 23. 24. 28. 30. 31. 33. 34. 35. 36. 37. 39. 40. 41. 42. 43. 45. 47. 48. 49. 52. 56. 58. 59. 60; 10, 1. 2. 6. 8. 11. 14. 17. 19. 32. 68 etc.

As for the use of Tenses[3] cp.: I, 1, 2. 4. 5. 22. 26. II, 9, 9. 15. 17. 19. 20. 23. 24. 27. 34. 37. 39. 46. 50. 52. 54. 55. 68; 10, 64. 66.

Moods[4] (except the infinitive and participle): I, 1, 10. 11. 19. 24. 26. 32. II, 9, 1. 3. 5. 6. 11. 21. 27. 32. 36. 39. 42. 55. 57; 10, 2. 3. 14. 20. 28. 43. 68.

As for the Infinitive[5] especially: I, 1, 3. 20. 22. 23. 26. 31. 33. 36. (bid Maetzn. III, p. 40). II, 9, 9. 11. (begin or gin Maetzn. III, p. 6). 12. 14. 21. 26. 28. 30. 31. 33. (Maetzn. III, p. 41. 42.) 35. 36. 39. 41. 42. 44. 48. 49. 56. 58. 59; 10, 3. 5. 6. 7. 9. 18. 20. 25. 27. 28. 30. 31. 33. 37. 39. 42. 49. 50. 57. 58. 61. 63. 64. 66. 69.[6]

Cases[7]: I, 1, 29. 30. 34. II, 9, 1. 3. 7. 8. 10. 12. 15. 16. 19. 20. 21. 35. 38. 39. 42. 43. 45. 46. 48. 49. 52. 53. 54. 56. 57. 60; 10, 6. 7. 8. 9. 11. 12. 13. 14. 16. 17. 18. 20. 21. 24. 30. 38. 44. 50. 57. 58. 60. 61. 62. 64.

Pleonasms: I, 1, 13. 14. 21.[8] 22.[9] 34. II, 9, 1. 25. 27.[8] 28. 42. 44. 47.[8] 54[8]); 10, 5. 11. 25. 37. 44. 45. 58. 64.

Polysyndeta: I, 1, 17. II, 9, 24. 27.

Asyndeta: I, 1, 17. 20. 21. 33. 34. II, 9, 16. 21. 22. 27. 33. 38. 41. 45. 50. 55; 10, 9.

Συνεκδοχή: I, 1, 8.

Anacoluthon: II, 10, 11. 19.

Chiasm: II, 10, 13.

Anticipation or Prolepsis: II, 10, 13. 50.

Construction κατὰ σύνεσιν: II, 10, 15. 49.

Zeugma or Syllepsis: II, 10, 21. II, 9, 52.

Ἓν διὰ δυοῖν: II, 10, 43.

As for the relative construction: I, 1, 11. 22. 26. 36. II, 9, 11. 60; 10, 13. 23. 30. 44. 49. 54. 59. 60. 63. 65. 66. 67.

Position of Words: I, 1, 3. 4. 5. 6. 7. 8. 12, l. 2.[10] 14. 16, l. 9. 18. 19. 20. 25, l. 2. 27[11]). 28, l. 6. 32, l. 9. 33, l. 3. II, 9, 4, l. 8. 6, l. 1. 7, l. 8. 8, l. 9. 13, l. 1. 16, l. 9. 17, l. 4. 20, l. 6. 21, l. 1. 22, l. 4. 5. 23, l. 1. 26, l. 6. 28, l. 5. 32, l. 6. 33, l. 1. 2. 36, l. 8. 42, l. 8. 49. 54. 6, l. 9. 7, l. 4. 27, l. 6. 52, l. 1. 54. 55, l. 9. 58, l. 1. 59, l. 4. 7.

---

[1] See Willisius p. 32 and below. [2] Cp. Maetzn. II, p. 54. [3] Cp. Maetzn. II, p. 87 sqq. 92 sqq.
[4] Cp. Maetzn. II, p. 109 sqq. [5] Cp. Maetzn. II, p. 157; III, p. 201. 209. 212. 296.
[6] Ought without to. See Maetzn. III, p. 6. [7] Cp. Maetzn. III, p. 1 sqq. 19. 25. 34. 50. 54.
[8] Cp. Maetzn. III, p. 105. [9] See above. [10] Cp. Maetzn. I, p. 197; II, p. 54.
[11] See Kitchin I, p. 167.

e. Lexicographical Remarks.[1]

A.

Aband II, 10, 65 = to abandon.

, This form of the word seems to indicate a modification of the derivation usually given — Fr. à ban donner, to put under ban. Low Lat. abaudonnare, to permit or forbid by public 'ban': thence Low Lat. abandonum, abandum, property used as a guarantee, i. e. over which one's own rights are given up. There is an A.-S. abannan, to proclaim, command; to aband may be a form of that word, with signification modified by the sense given to the ban in the middle ages. 'To put under ban' would be to hand a person over to destruction, to put all help out of his reach, to give him up. Levins (Rhyming Dict. 1570) has 'abandon, exterminare', so making it equivalent to banish.

About I, 1, 11 (abouts I, 9, 36), to the edge, or out of; A.-S. abútan, lit. around, on the outside. Or perhaps in this place, to the end. Fr. à bout.

Accoyl II, 9, 30 = to gather together to a place. It. accogliere, to collect together; Low Lat. accolligere; O.-Fr. acueiller. Or, to be in a coil, or bustle of business.

Achates II, 9, 31 = purchase of provisions. The fuller form of cate (cake), whence caterer, one who provides provisions for others. This form occurs in Chaucer Prol. 571. Speaking of the 'Maunciple, whose business was to provide food, he says, 'He wayted so in his acate'. Fr. achat, acheter, It. accattare, Low Lat. accapitare (ad-captare).

Advaunse[2]) I, 1, 17 = to lift up in front of one. Chaucer spells it avaunce. Fr. avancer, following the literal signification, 'to send to the van or front'; It. avanti, avanzo; avanzare, are used in the sense of gain, advancement, from Lat. ab ante. A derivation from Du. van, Ger. von, Eng. from, is attempted.

Advise II, 9, 38 (avize II, 9, 59; 10, 31) = to look at, see, consider, understand. Fr. s'aviser, avis, It. avvisare, Low Lat. advisare, avisare, advisum; O.-Fr. adviser, to turn one's glance upon a thing.

Advisement II, 9, 9 = consideration, cautious looking into a thing. See Wright's Bible Word Book.

Affray arch. like effray II, 10, 15.

Aghast I, 1, 17 = frightened, terrified (pret. of 'to aghast'); we now use only the adj. Chaucer uses the verb to agast —

'That me agasteth in my dreme (quod she)' (Legend of Dido, 246.)

Horne Tooke, Div. of Purley, part. I. chap. X., says Aghast, agast, may be the p. p. agazed — 'All the whole army stood agazed on him'. (Henry VI. 1. 1.)

But agazed, and Fuller's phrase (Worthies, Bucks) 'men's minds stood at a gaze', are erroneous as derivations. The Goth. us-gaisjan, to horrify, contains the root whence it comes, us being the Ger. aus, Eng. out, and gaisjan connected with Ger. geist, A.-S. gast, Eng. ghost cp. Sc. gousty, desolate.

Alabaster II, 9, 44. The accepted spelling in early times was 'alabbaster'.

Als II, 10, 18. = also. A.-S. calswa.

Amate II, 9, 34. To be or make stupid, from O.-Fr. amater, mater, to mortify, from mat, dull, faint. Ger. matt. Then: to keep company with, be mate to.

Amenaunce II, 9, 5 = carriage, behaviour. Fr. amener; Lat. ad manus.

Amis II, 9, 58 = in the wrong place (having missed his way) Not to confound with amis (I, 4,

---

[1]) Cp. Lucas; Kitchin gl.; Mueller; Nares, Johnson, Du Cange etc., and the Remarks above.   [2]) See above.

18) = amice. Lat. amictus — an oblong piece of fine linen worn by priests as a tippet to cover the shoulders and neck.

Annoy II, 9, 35; 10, 64. Subst. = annoyance, harm; verb = damage, harm. Queen Elizabeth herself uses this word, 'such snares as threaten mine annoy'. Ellis' Specimens of Early Engl. Poets, II, 136. Fr. ennui, It. annoio, connected with Lat. noceo.

Apayd. appaid II, 9, 37 = satisfied, paid, appeased (well or ill). So Rider's Dict. (1640) has 'well apaid, glad; ill apaid, sorie'. Fr. payer, It. pagare, Low Lat. appacare, pacare, to satisfy claims, appease. So in Chaucer, Persones Tale, we have: ·Of the which (i. e. by mercy etc.) Jhesu Christ is more appayed than of (i. e. by the wearing of) haires or of hauberkis'. See also Marchauntes Tale, 1146: 'God help me so, as I am evil apayd'. Not A.-S., but in common use in Chaucer and Wicliffe; a word that probably came in with the Normans.

Arraught II, 10, 34 (pret. to arreach) seized on by force[1]). Inf. is not to be found.

Aspine I, 1, 8 = aspen, aspic, asp. A.-S. äsp, äps. O.-N. espi. Mod.-H. G. espe[2]).

Assay — verb: II, 9. 42; 10, 3. 40; subst.: II, 10, 49 = to attempt, try. assail; an attempt. Fr. essayer; Low Lat. exagium, a pair of scales, a test, thence, a mark of full weight, stamped on loaves of bread, thence 'assay - mark' on metals up to standard, from exigere. (The It. assaggiare is a different verb from ad-sapere, to taste, savour; then to test, try).

Assott II, 10, 8 = to befool. Fr. assotter, sot, a fool, from a Low Lat. sottus, whose origin is not known (? sopitus, or from the same root with to seethe, sodden). This word was the soubriquet of one of the early French kings, 'Carolus Lottus', Charles the Simple. Spenser recognises this word as obsolete, as it is explained in the Gloss. to the Sheph. Cal., March.

Attone (atone[1]) I, 1, 18; II, 9, 28 = at once, Attonce II, 9, 36.

Avale I, 1, 21; II, 9, 10 = to fall, sink; dismount. Fr. avaller, from Low Lat. avalare, to drop down a river, or to descend from a hill; Lat. ad vallem, just as amount is ad montem. The O.-Fr. phrase would be à mont et à val, to amount and avale. O.-Fr. avaler (descendre aval), in Mod. Fr. = to swallow down. Cp. Chaucer, Tr. and Cr. III, 577, and Hamlet, 'vailed lids'.

Avize = advize[1]).

Ay II, 9, 53; 10, 40. = ever. Goth. aios. (Gr. αἰών, ἀεί; Lat. aevum); Icel. ey.

B.

Barbican II, 9, 25, a casemate, or advanced fort: also a watch - tower, or tower used for strength, and for watch and ward as well. In this passage 'within the barbican a Porter sate', (where Spenser is describing the human face, of which 'the Porter' is the tongue), it is clear that the barbican is not a watch - tower or high post, but rather a gateway. 'The porch' is the mouth: the 'barbican' within the porch, the teeth. Fr. and It. barbacano, Low Lat. barbacana. Du Cange says it is Arabic, and calls it 'propugnaculum exterius, quo oppidum ant castrum, praesertim vero eorum portae aut muri muniuntur'. Cotgrave says that 'Chaucer useth the word for a watch-tower, which in our Saxon tongue was called a burgh-kenning.' Halliwell and Wright (ed. of Nares' Gloss. 1867) say that it is a word derived from the Arabic, and properly signifies the temporary fortification of woodwork erected before a gate, when a siege is expected; but eventually it came to mean a permanent advanced fort. The Accademia della Crusca defines it as 'parte di muraglia che si fa da bosso a scarpa der sicurezza e fortezza'.

---

[1]) See above.   [2]) See Mueller and Grimm 3, 1157.

There is a fancied likeness between this sharp woodwork and the teeth. See Wedgwood, Dict. Balcony. He defines it as 'a mere projecting window from whence the entrance could be defended;' and derives it from the Persian bàlakhaneh, an upper chamber.

Bash; hence a bas h t II, 9. 43 from abace = abase, to lower. Low Lat. abassare (basis), It. abasso, abbassare; Fr. abaisser. Hence:

Bashfull II, 9, 41.

Befell II, 9, 17 = it was fitting, proper.

Beseme II, 9, 26. 38 = to suit, fit, to be seemly.

Bestedd I, 1, 24 = situated. A.-S. stede, place (as in homestead); more usually in an unpleasant sense; 'ill bestead'. So Chaucer, Man of Lawes Tale, 551.

Bestowe II, 9, 28 = to place (guests), to put them in their 'stow' or place: the usage remains in the phrase to 'stow away' — and in the names of certain towns. A.-S. stow, a place. Luke 12, 17, 'room where to bestow my fruits.' Hall, Edw. V, uses the verb as here: 'divers others, whiche were bestowed in dyvers chambers.'

Bery II, 9, 34 = a company (of ladies). Origin: Fr. bevée; It. beva. (Wedgwood I, 149): perhaps a contraction of 'bella vue' = a fine sight. Used of ladies and of birds; formerly of partridges, now only of quails. Shakespeare, Pope make also use of it, Milton too.

Bid I, 1, 30 = to pray. Ger. beten, A.-S. biddan. The subst. bead (A.-S. béd) probably means first a prayer, and then the measuring 'beads' on which prayers are told. Or bead may come from O.-E. bee (A.-S. béh or beág), a crown or ring. See Morris, E. E. Specimens, p. 415. Beadsman, properly one who prays. So in the Glossary published with the Shepheards Calendar we have this note: 'To bidde is to pray, whereof cometh beades for praiers, and so they say 'to bidde his beades', sc. to say his praiers.' In the Romaunt of the Rose, 7372, are these lines:

'A peire of bedis eke she bere,
Upon a lace, alle of white threde,
On which that she hir bedes bede'.

Blaser II, 9, 25 = one who blazes, or blazons forth, proclaims. A.-S. blaésan, to blow; Ger. blasen. So St. Mark I, 45, 'to blaze abroad the matter,' to blow it far and wide. So Sidney, Arcadia, II, has 'being blazed by the country people'.

Bord II, 9, 2 = to address. Fr. aborder. Probably in proper sense, to attack, used originally of tilting, from Low Lat. bohordicum, Fr. behourt, bohourt, a joust, tourney, whence bordiare, burdare.

Bordraging II, 10, 63 = border - raid; a ἅπαξ λεγόμενον. Spenser uses it of the incursions of the Scots into N. England, so that the word is probably only a corruption of 'border - raid.'

Boughtes I, 1, 15 = bends, folds; of a serpent's coils. Also written bight. A.-S. bugan; to bend, to bow. So in geogr. the Bight of Benin = the bend of Benin. Bough and bow come from the same root.

Bountihed II, 10, 2 = goodness (with Teutonic termination to a Latin word): bounty — It. bonjtà, bontà, Lat. bonitas; Fr. bonté.

Braunched II, 9, 19 = worked in branches (of an embroidered robe).

Britany II, 10, 13. 39 = Britain (Britannia).

Buss II, 9, 51 (elsewhere not used as verb).

16

C.

Caitive = mean, worthless, base, low. Fr. chétif, O.-Fr. chaitis, It. cattivo, Lat. captivus. The Low Lat. captivus bears the sense of 'vilis, contemptibilis'.

Can I, 1, 8 — see Gan.

Castory II, 9, 41 = a colour, pink or red; used, with 'vermilion', of a lady's complexion. The substance 'castoreum' is a medicine, taken from the beaver. The printers substituted the word 'lastery' in ed. 1590, shewing that they did not understand it. In Low Lat. 'vestes castorinatae' were luxurious robes, dyed red (?), as appears partly from Sidonius Apollinaris, Ep. 5. 7, where (speaking of the Gallo-Roman Christians) he says, 'incedunt albati ad exsequias, pullati ad nuptias, castorinati ad litanias; 'where, however, reference may be made only to the texture of the robes.

Cesure II, 10, 68 = a breaking off, as at the end of a chapter or a volume. Lat. caesura.

Cheare II, 10, 30 = countenance, manner, then cheerfulness. Then 'good cheer, entertainment, welcome'. Chiere is the face, or look, in O.-Fr. Cp. Cotgrave, chère, It. cera. (It may be related to Sanskr. cára, adj. = beautiful, active, 'mobile', which again may be related to Gr. κάρα, the person, the head).

Cheere I, 1, 2.

Chevisaunce II, 9, 8 = enterprise, achievement. Fr. achever, probably from chef [1]), Lat. caput; O.-Fr. chevisance, Low Lat. chevisantia, — 'pactum, transactio, conventio,' — and cheviare, O.-Fr. chevir, to agree, transact business. Hence the more common sense of to cheve, and chevisance, seems to be that of agreement, bargaining: as if it was connected with cheap. So Piers Ploughman. 'Chaffare and cheve therwith'; and again, 'Chaffared with chevisaunce, chevede selde after.' In Chaucer, an agreement for borrowing money, Schipmannes Tale, l. 347.

Cleep II, 9, 58 = to call. A.-S. cleopian. clypian. Hence 'clapper'. Cp. Du. and Ger. klappen, to sound, strike. Morris (Gloss. to Chaucer) adds Scot. clep, prattle, tattle. Bailey, Dict., gives Scot. clep as a form of claim, libel, or petition.

Clepe, II, 9, 32 p. p. cleped.

Combrous I, 1, 23; II, 9, 17 = troublesome, laborious, teasing (of gnats). Ger. kummern, It. ingombrare; Fr. encombrer; Low Lat. incumbrare, to overload with 'impedimenta'. (Not in sense of burdening, as in 'why cumbereth it the ground?' — Kitchin.)

Comenly = II, 10, 12 commonly.

Compacture II, 9, 24 = close knitting together; whence 'compact' for an agreement, which binds both sides closely. Fr. compacte, Lat. compactum, from compingere, which answers to Gr. πήγ-νυμι, ἰ-πάγ-ην.

Compel I, 1, 5 = to cite, call to aid. Lat. compellare, to call or challenge at law; a forensic term.

Comprise II, 9, 49 = to comprehend, understand. Fr. comprendre, Lat. comprehendere.

Consort II, 9,.35 (verb) = to combine; (subst.) = agreement, company; concert (of music) The modern spelling 'concert' does not prove any connection with certare; the word is probably rightly spelt 'consort', from consors, consortium, a companionship, not a rivalry.

Contrive II, 9, 48 = to wear out. Lat. contritum, conterere. (Jortin.)

Convey II, 9, 32 = to carry away. It. conviare; Low Lat. conveare, convehere. Used as a 'more decent term for to steal'.

---

[1]) Cp. Lafaye 'achever'.

Corse I, 1, 24. II, 9, 55 = the body. (Not dead body, but directly from Lat. corpus.) So Davies (of Hereford) writes, 'The mind with pleasure, and the corse with ease'.

D.

Dame = lady; from Lat. domina.

Date II, 10, 45 = given or assigned length of life. Lat. datum, the given time. The datum at end of epistles led to this use. So 'given under our hand'.

Debate II, 10, 58 = to contend, fight (in battle, not with words); Fr. débattre.

Decay II, 9, 48 = to perish; Fr. déchoir, Lat. decidere; subst.: = destruction, downfall, death.

Deeme = to judge. A.-S. deman. A doom is a judgment, favourable or unfavourable: doomsday, deemster. Goth. dôms: A.-S. dóm, Icel. dómr, all signify judgment. The Germ. termination — thum contains the same word, as the English — dom (koenig-thum, kingdom, etc.)

Delay II, 9, 30 = to temper, stop the course of. So Spenser seems to prefer to use it, cp. Prothalamium, 3:

'Zephyrus did softly play,
A gentle spirit, that lightly did delay
Hot Titans beames'.

And again, in the dedication to Sir Christopher Hatton, l. 11:

'May eke delay
The rugged brow of carefull Policy',

i. e. may smooth the brow. The word is used also = diluted. So' 'Vinum dilutum, lymphatum, ύδαρής. Vin trempé. Wine delayed and mixed with water'.

Demeyne II, 9, 40 = demeanour, bearing.

Depart II, 10, 14 = to part, divide. So in the Marriage Service, 'till death us depart'.

Despight II, 9, 11 — malice. O.-Fr. despit, Mod.-Fr. dépit; It. dispetto. Probably from Low Lat. despi-care, to despise, contemn.

Devise II, 9, 42. 59 = to guess at, discover; to write about, treat of. Probably related to A.-S. wísian, to shew, inform, lead; or wísa, a wise man. The word is used by early writers nearly in the same sense as to advise.

Dight II, 9, 27. 33. 40 = to dress, arrange. A.-S. dihtan, to set in order; possibly the same word as deck. Ger. dichten, dichter (the poet being the arranger?). Cp. Chaucer, Knightes Tale, 183.

Discure II, 9, 42 = to discover, disclose. (So recure in Spenser = recover). Fr. découvrir.

Dismay II, 9, 34 = to render lifeless. Perhaps from It. smagare, to be bewildered, to lose presence of mind. Sp. desmayo, a swoon.

Dismayd = faultily made, of ugly shape; 'some like to apes, dismayd.

Dispainted II, 9, 50.

Dispart II, 9, 23 = to divide.

Dispence II, 9, 29 = expense, outlay. Fr. dépense.

Dispred II, 9, 27 = to spread abroad.

Disthronise II, 10, 44 = to dethrone.

Doome II, 9, 48; 10, 60 = judgment (acquittal or condemnation). See under 'Deeme'.

Doubt I, 1, 10 = fear. It. dotta. In Low Lat. dubitare was used for 'to fear', as in the Acta Alex. III (1169), quoted by Du Cange, 'Ego neque vos, neque excommunicationes vestras appretior, vel dubito unum ovum'. Cp. Fr. redouter.

16*

Drapet II, 9, 27 = cloth. Fr. drap; Low Lat. drappus.

Draught II, 10, 51 = stratagem (?). From the verb 'to draw', in the sense of drawing persons away from the truth.

Drouping II, 10, 30 = drooping, fainting (with old age). Wedgwood 1, 494: 'To droop, Icel. dryp, driupa, to drip; driupi, driupa, to droop, hang the head, hence to be sad or troubled; driupr suppliant, sad; to droup or dronk to dare, or privily be hid.

Dyapase II, 9, 22 = diapason, the octave: διὰ πασῶν (χορδῶν).

E.

Eachone I, 1, 15 (as one word in Kitchin), each person. O.-E. uchone, echon.

Earne I, 1, 3 = to yearn; so earnest. A.-S. georne, geornian, cornoste; Ger. gern.

Earst, erst II, 9, 17 = the soonest, earliest. Superl. of ere. A.-S. ærest. O.-E. comp. erur. The word early is ere-lich.

Easterlings II, 10, 68 = men of the east ('austrasians'), used by Spenser of Danes, etc., after Holinshed (quoted by Richardson): 'Certain merchants of Norwaie, Denmarke, and of other those parties, called Ostomanni, or (as in our vulgar language we term them) Easterlings, because they lie East in respect of us'. (Hist. of Ireland, A. D. 430). Hence too, according to Camden, Remains ('Money'), comes the word sterling. 'In the time of K. Richard I. monie coined in the east parts of Germanie began to be a special request in England for the puritie thereof, and was called Easterling monie, as all the inhabitants of those parts were called Easterlings, and shortly after some of that country . . . were sent for to bring the coin to perfection; which since that time was called of them stirling, after Easterling'. Du Cange has both forms, esterlingus and sterlingus, and says it is used 1) of the weight of coin, 2) of its quality, 3) of a particular coin, 'denarius sterlingus'.

Edify I, 1, 34 = to build, used in its natural signification. Lat. ædificare.

Effraide I, 1, 16 = scared. Fr. effrayer.

Eftsoone I, 1, 11; II, 9, 11; 10, 64 (eftsoones) = soon after, forthwith.

Eke II, 9, 36. 60; 10, 7. 11. 23 = also (that which is added. A.-S. eacan, eac).

Eld II, 9, 56; 10, 32 p. p. of A.-S. yldan, to stay, continue, last; A.-S. yldo is 1) age, with no sense of oldness; 2) an age, = Lat. ævum; 3) old age. The English still retain the word in elder as distinct from older.

Elfe II, 10, 71 = a young fairy. Spenser himself explains the word as = quick, living: 'Elfe, to weet Quick'. A.-S. ælf. The word is found in Icel. Álfr; in Shakespeare, ouphes, Mids. Night's Dream. 4. 4 Chaucer uses the adj. of his own cast of countenance, in the Prol. to the Rime of Sir Thopas:

'He seemeth elvisch by his countenance.'

Tyrwhitt translates it as shy. Rather it is weird, scarcely human. See note to Book I, 1, 17. — II, 9, 60.

Els, else, elles II, 10, 48 = otherwise, elsewhere, sometimes, or perhaps = already.

Eme II, 10, 47 = uncle. Chaucer has it, Tr. and Cr. l. 629, 'If it so were hire em;' and l. 1159, 'and seyde hym, Em, I preye', etc. — the mother's brother, avunculus; and Hardyng, Chron. c. 42, 'Nemynus, theyr eme'. Somner says 'to this day so called in Lancashire.' Ger. oheim. Todd says it is still used in Staffordshire.

Empayr II, 10, 30 = to diminish. Fr. empirer, to make worse; pire, from Lat. pejor.
Empeach II, 10, 68 (verb) = to hinder. Fr. empêcher, O.-Fr. empescher, Lat. impedire. Subst. = hindrance.
Enchase (enchace) II, 9, 24 = to embellish, or to set in a chasing, or case. Fr. enchasser.
Enhaunce (enhaunse) I, 1, 17 = to raise, lift up. Fr. hausser, haut; so 'enhanced prices.' Lat. altus.
Enlumine II, 9, 4 = to illumine, make glorious.
Entertain II, 9, 6 = to take, receive (pay), an usage apparently peculiar to Spenser.
Entraile (entrayl) I, 1, 16 = entanglement, fold, twist. From to trail, to draw. Fr. entraille; It. intralasciare, to interlace.
Equipaged II, 9, 17 = equipped. Fr équipper; O.-Fr. esquiper; Low Lat. escipare, to fit out a ship.
Error II, 10, 9 = wandering, used in the Latin sense.
Engh I, 1, 9 = yew.
Evangely II, 10, 53 = Gospel. Fr. évangile; Low Lat. evangelium; Gr. εὐαγγέλιον.

F.

Fain = II, 9, 51. feign (feindre)
Fantasy II, 9, 50. = fancy. Gr. φαντασία.
Fare I, 1, 11 = to go. Icel. for, för; Ger. fahren; A.-S. faran, fœr, faru, a journey; whence 'to pay one's fare'. The English still use 'how did you fare?' as 'how went it with you?' and the E. fare (of food) is viaticum; so too farewell, ferry.
Favourlesse II, 9, 7 = unfavourable.
Fay II, 10, 42 = fairy. Fr. fée. Lat. fata.
Feasible II, 9, 21 = fit for defence. So there were regiments of volunteers in the French war called 'Fencibles'.
Fett II, 9, 58 = to fetch (older form of the word). Fett is usually the old p. p. A.-S. feccan, pret. feahte. In the English Bible (1611) it is a very common form of the word, as a p. p.; as, for example, 2. Sam. 9, 5; Jer. 26, 23; Acts 28, 13. Chaucer has it, Prol. 821; Knightes Tale, 2529.
File I, 1. 35 = to sharpen and smoothe; so Chaucer, Prol. 713, has
        'He moste preche, and wel affile his tunge'.
Shakespeare, Love's Labour's Lost, I. 1, has
        'His discourse peremptory, his tongue filed'.
Cp. Lat. linguam acuere; Fr. avoir la langue bien affilée.
For-, intensive prefix, utterly, quite. Ger. ver-, Goth. faur-. Cp. Lat. per-, Gr. περι-. Also used as an intransitive prefix; as for- break.
Foreby II, 9, 10; 10, 16 = forth by, hard by, near.
Forlorne (forlore I, 8, 39) II, 10, 36 = lost, left desolate, cast away. A.-S. forleóran, Ger. verloren, p. p. of verlieron, to lose.
Forthy II, 9, 49 = therefore. A.-S. forþi, forþig.
Forwasted I, 1, 5; II, 10, 52 = utterly wasted or ravaged.
Forwearied I, 1, 32 = utterly wearied, tired out.
Foy II, 10, 41 = tribute due from a subject to his lord. Fr. foi; O. Fr. fé; E. fee.

Foyle II, 10, 48 (verb) = to defeat, ruin. Cotgrave explains Fr. affoler as 'to foyle, wound, etc.; also to spoyle, ruine; also to besott, gull, befool'. (subst.) 1) = weapon 2) repulse.

Frame II, 9, 45 (subst.) = making, building. (verb) = to form, make, prepare (sometimes), perhaps to steady. A.-S. fremman.

Fretted II, 9, 37 = worked like lace - work; from 'frett' = to consume (as a moth a garment). A.-S. fretan, to eat up, gnaw, Ger. fressen.

G.

Gall I, 1, 19 = the bile. A.-S. gealla, yellow.

Game II, 9, 44 = sport, play. A.-S. gamian, gamen. The English still say 'to make game of a person.'

Gan, Gin ').

Gent II, 10, 52 = gentle, used of Prince Arthur, and therefore not of ladies only, though far more commonly of them.

German II, 10, 22 = brother (by the same father and mother). Lat. germanus. Also, all of the same germ, near of kin, and of the same blood.

Gest II, 9, 53 = adventure, deed of arms. II, 9, 16 = gesture.

Glusts I, 1, 1 = tilts and combats in the lists. Fr. jouster, It. giostrare (hence the English jostle) Low Lat. giostra; Mod.-Gr. τζουστρία.

Glistering I, 1, 14 = glittering. Wicliffe uses both glisnynge (Habak. 3, 11) and glitteren (Judg. 5, 31.). Du. glisteren, Ger. glitzen, glitzern, to glitter. (See Wright's Bible Word-Book).

Gobbet I, 1, 20 = a lump, piece, or mouthful; hence gobble. In O.-E. gobet, gobat, from gob, the mouth. Sir John Maundeville, speaking of the apples of Paradise, says, 'Cut them in never so many gobettes or parties'. Fr. gobbe, gobbet, gobine, gober etc.

Gorge I, 1, 19 = throat. Fr. gorge, Lat. gurges.

Governance II, 10, 38 = government.

Gramercy II, 9, 9 = many thanks.

Grayle ') II, 10, 53 = the holy grayle, graal, or grail, or sangrail, forms a peculiar element in Arthurian romance. There are two explanations of it. 1) That it is the very blood of our Lord; and that the word is misconceived from sanguis realis; sangreal, san-greal, thence saint-greal, thence holy-grayle. This opinion is not generally accepted. 2) That it was a broad plate or dish (a terrine, or turcen as the word is now absurdly spelt), on which the paschal lamb was said to have been placed, and off which our Saviour therefore ate at the Last Supper. Low Lat. grasale, a large earthenware dish said at table; O.-Fr. grasal, greil. Wedgwood says that 'grais or grès seems the Latinised forms of the Briton kråg, hard stone', crag, cp. the Provençal crau. It was said to have been brought to England by Joseph of Arimathea, as Spenser says; but after a while was lost. It then became the special 'quest' of the Knights of the Round Table; Lancelot, Galahad, Boort, and Perceval going forth and having divers adventures in the search. When Merlin made the Round Table, he left a special place of honour for it; and Sir Galahed was marked out by our Lord to be the honoured discoverer of the relic. It again disappeared, and was recovered by Baldwin, King of Jerusalem, who in 1101 sent it to Genoa: here it was kept in great state as the 'sacro catino', till it was transferred to the Imperial Library at Paris and placed in the Cabinet des Antiques in 1806.

') See above.

Greedy I, 1, 14 = eager; not here for food.
Guerdon[1]) II, 9, 6 = reward. Fr. guerdon; It. guiderdone, from Ger. wider, and don, a gift.
Guilt II, 9, 45 = guilded.
Guize II, 9, 31 = dress, apparel; appearance.

H.

Harbour I, 1, 7 = refuge, shelter; also written arbour; in Shepheards Cal. Ecl. VI, 19, it is spelt harbrough. By Chaucer herberwh. Ger. herberge, It. albergo, Low Lat. hereberga, alberga, whence Fr. auberge, a word of Teutonic origin, signifying a camp, or fortified quarters for a host, thence any kind of hospice, shelter, or inn. A.-S. here, army, and beorgan, to protect, shelter; whence here-beorgan, to harbour; hereberga, a station at which an army rested on its march.
Hardiment I, 1, 14 = hardiness.
Hastly II, 10, 52 = hastily.
Herbars II, 9, 46 = herbs. Lat herbaria. The word is probably peculiar to Spenser.
Hereof II, 9, 46.
Hew II, 9, 3. 40. 52; = face, appearance, shape, not colour. A.-S. hîw, form, or aspect.
Hight II, 9, 27. 31; 10, 22 = is (or was) called. (p. p.) II, 9, 59; 10, 16. 46 = called. Ger. heissen; A.-S. hátan (pret. hatte), to call, or to be called.
Hippodame II, 9, 50 = an imaginary monster.
Hospitale II, 9, 10 = a place of rest. Low Lat. hospitale, whence Fr. Hôpital, Hôtel, corrupted in England into a place for sick folk — though not so in Spenser's day; 'Christ's Hospital' for example. From Lat. hospes, a host or guest.
Hoye II, 10, 64 = a vessel, ship. The word still survives in the Dutch-built 'Billyb-hoy.'
Humor I, 1, 36 = moisture. Lat. humor.

I.

Immeasured II, 10, 8 = unmeasured, unmeasurable.
Impe I, 1, 26 literally a graft, or shoot; thence a child; always used by Spenser in a good sense. But Shakespeare uses it only in jocular passages, shewing that the word was becoming degraded. (Nares' Gloss.) A.-S. impan, to engraft, plant; Ger. impfen. Used of shoots of trees by Chaucer and Langland; Newton's Herbal to the Bible, A. D. 1587, has a chapter on 'shootes, slippes, young imps, sprays, and buds'.
Importune II, 10, 15 = strong, violent. Todd says, 'cruel, savage, as importunus'.
In I, 1, 33 = lodging, habitation; not hostelry. So in Gen. 42, 27. 'The word had not acquired the vulgar idea which it bears in modern language'. (Warton). Old Scottish inn, lodging. Cp. Inns of Court. In this sense it chiefly occurs in the phrase here used by Spenser, 'take up your in,' or in the corresponding expression 'to take one's ease in one's inn' = to be at ease at home[2]).
Incontinent II, 9, I = forthwith, without holding one's self in.
Inly II, 10, 40 = inwardly. A.-S. inlíce.
Inquire II, 10, 12 = to call.

---

[1]) See above.
[2]) See Nares' Gloss. under Inn, and Take one's ease.

J.

Jarre II, 10, 65 = a quarrel, variance, difference. We still speak of 'domestic jars'. The verb is still used of discordant sounds, 'a jarring noise'. A door ajar is one neither open nor shut.

Jeoperdie = danger, risk. See the Bible Word Book, on the verb 'to jeopard'. The derivations suggested are, Fr. j'ai perdu, I have lost (improbable); or jeu perdu, lost game (which is also doubtful, as it does not give the real sense of the word); and lastly jeu parti, which is probably right. Jeu parti means 'an even-game' an equal chance one way or other. Chaucer's forms of this word are jeopardye, jeupardye, jeupartye; the last two favouring this last derivation. Du Cange¹) says that jocus partitus is 'an alternative', which would be equivalent to O.-Fr. jeu parti.

Jolly I, 1, 1; II, 9, 28. 34 = handsome, pretty. Fr. joli. Also used in sense of 'true'.

Joy II, 10, 53 = to take one's pleasure, to enjoy. Lat. jocus, jocare, whence It. gioia, Fr. jouer, jeu.

K.

Keepe (keep) = heed, care; so Old-Engl. ne kepich, 'nor keep I', nor care I. See Morris, E. E. Specimens, p. 339, l. 110. A.-S. cépan, to take, hold. So Chaucer, Prol. 898, 'Of nyce conscience took he no keep.

Kinred II, 10, 35 = kindred.

L.

Lad I, 1, 4 = led, pret. to lead. A.-S. laédan, pret. lædde.

Lamp- burning II, 9, 7 = burning like a lamp.

Larum- bell II, 9, 25 = alarm-bell. Fr. à l'arme.

Lay II, 10, 42 = law. So in the Ballad of Sir Isumbras, 'I wedded hir in Godis lay.' So also Chaucer.

Leasing II, 9, 51 = a lie, falsehood. Spenser seems to make a distinction between a leasing and a lie; he classes both together under 'all that fained is', to which he adds 'as leasings, tales, and lies'. But the words are usually taken to mean the same thing. A.-S. leasung, from leas, false. Leasing seems to be connected with the Goth. liusan, to lose; Goth. laus (our loss, especially as a suffix, godless, etc.) means empty: so that leasings would be empty reports: while lie is connected with Goth. ga-liug, a false god's image, then, anything false. From liugan, Ger. luegen. — Latimer speaks of lease-mongers. Ps. 4, 2, 'seek after leasing.'

Leave II, 10, 31 = to give leave to, then, to take leave of = Fr. congédier.

Leman I, 16; II, 10, 18 = lady, lover. Minshew suggests Fr. le mignon = the favourite: others, the Teutonic laden, 'ladman' = to allure: others, leofman; but it is the Fr. l'aimant. (Henshaw).

Lend II, 9, 58 = to give, provide.

Liege = lord, master: the word is properly liege-lord: answering to liege-man. Low Lat. ligius, from ligo, I bind: hence liege = bound in feudal relations; usually of the inferior to the lord. See Du Cange¹), 'is dicitur qui domino suo ratione feudi vel subiectionis fidem omnem contra quemvis praestat'.

---

¹) Gloss. M. et I. Lat., s. v. Jocus.

List II, 9, 1; 10, 66 = it pleases (verb impers).
Livelyhead II, 9, 3 = livelihood; life, living vigour.
Loathly I. 1, 20 = loathsome.
Loup II, 9, 10 = a fastening, loop. Levins (Rhyming Dict. 1570) has 'loupe, ansa, capulum'.
Lout I, 1, 30; II, 9, 26 = to bow humbly. A.-S. lutan, to bow; Icel. laut. The word is still u-ed in N. England. See Morris, E. E. Specimens, p. 380.
Lug II, 10, 11 = a perch or rod of land (16½ feet).
Lust = desire, wish (subst. and verb). See 'list' above.
Lynage I, 1, 5 (lignage I, 9, 3) = lineage.

M.

Mace II, 10, 4 = sceptre. Such was the 'leaden mace in the famous apostrophe to Slumber in Shakespeare, Julius Cæsar, 4, 3; such too the 'mace' in the House of Commons.
Maine II, 9, 14 = force; in other passages = the high sea. A.-S. mægen, strength, mágan, to be able; whence may, might, as auxiliary verbs. Ger. macht from machen leads on to E. might (strenght) and connects the two. Icel. magni has the same sense.
Meed II, 9, 6 = reward. A.-S. méd.
Mell 1, 1, 30 = to meddle. Still used in N. England. Fr. mêler, O.-Fr. mesler, It. mescolare, Low Lat. misculare, dim. of miscere.
Menage II, 9, 27; 10, 37 = to wield (arms); in other passages = to guide, manage (a horse, a steed). Fr. manier, ménager; Lat. manu agere, to guide by hand.
Mickle II, 10, 59 = much. So Milton, Comus, 31:
'Of mickle trust and power'.
Sometimes spelt muchell, whence much.
Miscreate II, 10, 38 = wrongly created, bastard. Milton, Par. Lost, 2. 683, has 'thy miscreated front'. Spenser is charged by Addison with having coined this word; but; it existed long before him.
Moniment II, 9, 59 = records; in other passages = mark or stamp on gold. 'Veterum monumenta virorum', Virg. Aen. 3, 108.
Mortall I, 1, 15 = death - dealing. Lat. mortalis.
Mote = might, must, can, could.
Munifience II, 10, 15 = fortification. Lat. mœnia facere.

N.

Nath'lesse II, 10, 57 = none the less.
Needlesse I, 1, 11 = useless, unavailing.
Needments I, 1, 6 = necessary baggage, necessities for travelling.
Nephewes II, 10. 45 = grandchildren or their children, not in the modern sense of 'nephews'. Lat. nepos.
Nought II, 9, 32 = of no value. A.-S. na-with, no thing.
Nouriture II, 10, 69 = bringing up. Fr. nourir, Lat. nutrire. Usually 'nurture'.
Noyance I, 1, 23 = annoyance. Lat. nocere.
Noye = II, 10, 15 Noah.
Noyous II, 9, 16. 32 = harmful, noxious. So Chaucer, House of Fame, 66.

17

O.

Ofspring II, 9, 60; 10, 69 == origin. So used in Bk. VI, 30:
'To see his syre and ofspring auncient'.
And Fairfax (Tasso 7, 18):
'Nor was her princely offspring damnified,
Or ought disparaged by those labours base'.
Ordain II, 10, 18 = to arrange (battle). Lat. 'in ordines redigere'.
Order II, 9, 15. 28 (subst.) == rank (of army). Lat. ordo. (verb) = to arrange. So in Judg. 13, 12,
and Shakespeare, Richard II, 2, 2: 'to order these affairs'.
Ordinaunce II, 9, 30 = ordering, arrangement; in other passages == ordnance, artillery.
Outbar II, 10, 63 = to arrest, bar out.
Outwell I, 1, 12 = to pour forth, well out.
Overhent II, 10, 18 (pret. to overhente), to overtake. Levins has Hente, snach, eripere.
A.-S. hentan, which is connected with the English verb to hunt, as it signifies 'to make active
search for', then to seize. Possibly also with 'hand', with which one seizes: the prehensile
organ, pre-hend-ere. The Goth. has both words, handus, the hand, and hinthan (inf.
hunthun), to seize, catch, hunt (whence also Ger. hund, Eng. hound).
Oversee II, 9, 44 = to overlook, not to see.

P.

Palfrey == usually a led horse, ridden by a lady; but here it is the ass on which Una rides. Du
Meril suggests O.-Fr. vair (Ger. pferd), whence Low Lat. veredus, para-veredus, also
written palafredus, palafrenus, O.-Fr. palefroy, It. palafreno. There does not seem
to be any ground for the tempting derivation per frenum, bridle-led. The Low Lat. para-
veredi, 'equi agminales', were horses employed (says Du Cange) on cross-roads, or military
roads; as distinguished from the veredi, which were post-horses on the public ways or high-
roads. Not, orginally, a lady's led horse.
Paramour II, 9, 34 = a lover. Fr. par amour. Cp. Spenser's belamour.
Parbreake I, 1, 20 = vomit, that which breaks or bursts forth.
Passioned II, 9, 41 = affected with feeling.
Paynim II, 9, 2.
Payse II, 10, 5 = to poise, balance. Fr. peser, from Lat. pensitare. Spelt also peise, pease.
Perceable I, 1, 7 = penetrable, that can be pierced.
Perdy Perdie (Tauchn.) II, 10, 48 = par Dieu, an oath. Piers Ploughman, pardy, and Chaucer
pardé.
Perlous == perilous, dangerous. Shakespeare writes it 'parlous'; so Richard III, 2. 4. 'A parlous
boy: — go to, you are too shrewd'. Nares adds that a certain bathing-place in Islington,
now called Peerless-Pool, was originally Parlous-Pond, and thence corrupted.
Pictural II, 9, 53 = a picture.
Pitteous II, 10, 44 = feeling compassion, tender-hearted.
Plaste II, 9, 10 (pret. to place) = placed.
Platane I, 1, 9 = plane-tree. Lat. platanus.
Point = I, 1, 15. appoint. (subst.): see note on I, 1, 16.
Pollicie II, 9, 48. 53; 10, 39 == statecraft (in a bad sense, as opposed to law).

Pourtrahed II, 9, 33 = drawn, p o u r t r a y e d whence p o r t r a i t.
Preace II, 10, 25 (verb) = to press; (subst.) = crowd, press.
Prejudise II, 9, 49 = quick judgment (of the imagination).
Prick I, 1, 1 = to spur, to ride quickly. A.-S. p r i c c i a n, to p r i c k or sting.
Prime II, 9, 25; 10, 58 = morning; the spring-tide of life. A.-S. prím, Lat. p r i m u s. Its proper
sense is, of course, the first part of anything — of life, youth; of day, morning; of the year,
spring-tide. But more particularly, as still in French, the first canonical hour of the day.
Proper II, 10, 57 = own, peculiar. From the Lat. p r o p r i u m. So used by Shakespeare, Winter's
Tale, 2, 3:
> 'The bastard's brains with these my p r o p e r hands
> Shall I dash out'.

Pyoning, II, 10, 63 = work of pioneers, military works. Low Lat. p i o n a r i u s.

Q.

Quart II, 10, 14 = quarter. The French form, 'le q u a r t'.
Quell II, 10, 11 = to destroy (life), kill. Shakespeare uses the subst. in this sense, Macbeth, 1, 7:
> 'Who shall bear the guilt
> Of our great q u e l l?'

Quite I, 1, 30 = to requite, to return a salute, to repay; from Low Lat. q u i e t a r e, to still or
satisfy a debtor; hence to repay, also to free.
Quoth I, 1, 12. 13, etc. = said; from pret. of A.-S. c w e ꞅ a n, pret. c w æ d; Icel. kvaꞅ; Goth.
q i ꝑ a n, to say; cp. Lat. in-q u i t. In Old-English the usual form is q u a t h. It survives in
the verb to q u o t e.

R.

Rain = to reign.
Raught II, 9, 19; 10, 20 (pret. to reach, O.-E. r e c c h e) reached. Goth. rahton; A.-S. roécan, pret.
raéhte; Ger. r e i c h e n.
Read, Reed I, 1, 13. 21; II, 9, 2 = to know, declare; also, to advise.
Remdify II, 10, 46 = to rebuild.
Reare II, 10, 64 = to raise up, to take up or away. 'Spenser is said to be singular in so using it'.
(Nares.) Milton also has a peculiar use, Par. Reg. 2. 285: 'Up to a hill anon his steps he r e a r e d.'
A.-S. hréran, to move, agitate, raise.
Reave I, 1, 24 = to snatch away, p. p. raft; so to b e r e a v e, p. p. b e r e f t. Dan. r i v e, to tear,
to r i v e. Connected with r a m p, with rive, r a v i n e, and r a v e n (the ravenous bird). A.-S.
r e á f i a n, to rob; h r æ f e n, the raven; Dan. r a v n.
Recure II, 10, 23 = to recover. Lat. r e c u r a r e.
Regiment II, 9, 59; 10, 30 = government. Lat. r e g i m e n.
Relent II, 10, 52 = to give way to; to slacken, Fr. r a l e n t i r. Lat. l e n t u s.
Renforst II, 10, 48 = pret. to enforce, compel again (= re-forced, not re-in-forced); in other
passages = recovered strength.
Report I, 10, 3 = to carry off. Fr. r e p o r t e r.

Reselse II, 10, 45 = to be repossessed of, to have se is in of: 'to be seized of a thing' is still an ordinary law-phrase. Du Cange: Low Lat. res a is ire, 'iterum sa is ire', to invest again; also to possess again,' whence the word sa is it ia, sa is in e. That is probably derived from sa cire, to take as one 's possession (possibly a form of so ciare;) others say Gr. σακκίζειν, 'to bag.'

Retraitt II, 9, 4 = portrait, ret rate; in other passages = look, cast of countenance. It. ritratto.

Rew II, 10, 66 = to lament over, to pity.

Rid I, 1, 36 = to bring out, to remove. A.-S. hreddan, to rid, deliver. (Ger. retten, Dan. redde.)

Rise II, 9, 59 = to come (perhaps, used for rhyme-sake):
'There chaunced to the Princes hand to rize
An auncient booke.'

Rosiere II, 9, 19 = a rose-bush.

Rote II, 10, 8 = a musical instrument, here = a lyre; the ancient psalterium, with more strings and an altered shape: Du Cange explains it under Low Lat. ro cta. In the so-called letters of Boniface Abp. of Maintz (Epist. 89), we have, 'Cithara, quam nos appellamus Rottam'; and Notkerus on the 'Athanasian Creed', 'antiquum Psalterium instrumentum decachordum utique erat; ... postquam illud symphoniaci ... ad suum opus traxerant, formam utique eius et figuram commoditati suae habilem fecerunt, et plures chordas annectentes, et nomine barbarico Rottam appellantes.' Chaucer uses it, Prol. 236:
'Wel couthe he synge and pleyen on a rote.' Nares explains it as 'that which is now called a cymbal, or more vulgarly a hurdy-gurdy.' In present usage there is no relation between the clashing cymbal and the stringed hurdy-gurdy. Roquefort, Glossaire, supposes it to be a fiddle with three strings. It was probably used loosely for any stringed instrument. Hence 'to learn by rote' means to learn a thing so that one can say or sing it without book, as when one accompanies one's self with the guitar. Cf. the Latin 'rota', and the German 'herleiern', 'ableiern'.

Rout II, 9, 15 = a confused crowd. Chaucer uses it for a company, assembly. Levins (Rhyming Dict. 1570) has 'a route of men, caterva, turba.'

Rule II, 10, 20 = sceptre, management (?). Spenser's phrase is 'the rule of sway.' Cp. II, 10, 49.

Ruth II, 10, 62 = pity, sorrow; subst. of verb to rue, so ruthless. A.-S. hreówian, Ger. reuen, reue. Sidney, Arcadia, uses it of a sheep-dog, 'whose ruth and valiant might' (i. e. his pity for and defence of the sheep.)

S.

Sacred II, 10, 36 = accursed. Lat. sacer.

Sad I, 1, 2 = set, settled, firmly fixed, heavy; then sober, dark-coloured; then mournful. Properly the p. p. of the verb settan, to set, settle.

Salve II, 10, 21 = to restore the credit of.

Scatterling II, 10, 63 = persons scattered about, nomads. So in his State of Ireland, Spenser writes, 'gathering unto him all the scatterlings and outcasts.'

Scorse II, 9, 55 = exchange, barter. Derivation uncertain. (?) It. scorsa. The system of Exchanges, etc., was introduced into England from Venice and Rome; and it is probable that terms connected with exchange also came thence. The French la course used of the rates óf exchange in the precious metals is the same word. The verb 'to scorse' == to exchange, is very common in Drayton. Can the word be connected with the Low Lat. discussor, which meant a commissioner of finance, sent out to examine the taxes, etc. of the provinces? Or from discursus, discourse, interchange of money, as discourse is 'the coin of conversation'? See Wedgwood, s. v. Horse-courser, whence to course, to deal as a broker. Wedgwood connects it with the Fr. courtier, a broker, which comes from corrector.

Scrine II, 9, 56 = writing-desk. O.-Fr. escrin, Mod.-Fr. écrin, Low Lat. scrinium; shrine is the same word: connected with scribo.

Seemly II, 9, 23 = in seemly sort (adv.).

Semblaunt II, 9, 2. 39 = likeness, appearance; in other passages == phantom.

Serve II, 10, 55 == to bring to bear on an enemy; used of 'Bunduca' who gathered an army and 'served' it on the Romans. So a writ is 'served on' a person: so also artillery is said to be 'served.'

Shalres II, 10, 37 = shires, divisions of a country; from A.-S. scéran.

Shamefast II, 9, 43 = shamefaced = modest. A.-S. scaemfæst; it has no connexion at all with the face: cp. stedfast, fast in its place.

Shene II, 10, 8 = bright, clear; the same word with shine. Goth. skeinan; A.-S. scéne, bright, scíne, brightness, scínan, to shine; Ger. scheinen, Dan. skeinna.

Shroud I, 1, 6 == to take shelter (from a storm).

Silly I, 1, 30 == harmless, simple; thence foolish. A.-S. soél, time, luck, happiness; adj. soél, prosperous, good, ge-soélig, happy; Ger. selig.

Sink I, 1, 22 == hoard, deposit, first of treasure, afterwards of anything, fair or foul. A.-S. sinc, gathered treasure.

Sith II, 9, 7 = since.

Sly II, 9, 46 = subtle, clever; not in a bad sense, as now. O.-E. slegh means wise, and sleight is properly wisdom, prudence.

Sold II, 9, 6 == pay; whence soldier. Fr. solde, solder; Low Lat. solidus; whence O.-Fr. sols, Fr. sou.

Spill II, 9, 37 == to spoil. So in the phrase 'to save or spill.'

Spright I, 9, 36 = spirit.

Stead II, 9, 9 (verb) = to favour, so 'to bestead', to stand in good stead to one; (subst.) sted (II, 10, 44) = a place. Prompt. Parv., 'stede, place, situs.' So 'in my stead' is still used. A.-S. stede, place, as in home-stead, bed-stead, sted-fast, steady. Though the Danish sted-fader, stedbroder, etc. are connected with this word, the Engl. stepfather, etc. comes from another source.

Steare II, 9, 13 == bull, steer. Goth. stiur, Ger. stier.

Stir (styre) II, 9. 30 == to stir, move. spur on (== incitare).

Stole I, 1, 4 == a long robe; not the strip of black silk familiar to the English clergy. Gr. στόλος.

Stress II, 10, 37 = to distress; the Engl. use the subst. in 'stress of weather.' 'to lay great stress on.'

Successe II, 10, 45 == succession.

Sundry II, 9, 48 = separate, different. Goth. sundro, single; Ger. sondern, A.-S. sunder.

Surmount II, 10, 3 = to surpass.

Surview II, 9, 45 = to overlook (as a height does a plain). The modern word is survey.

Swart II, 10, 15 = black, swarthy. So Milton's 'swart fairy of the mine,' Comus, 436. Goth. svarts, A.-S. sweart, Ger. schwartz, Dan. sort.

Swarth II, 9, 52.

Sway II, 10, 49 = to resist with a swing. The English still speak of a 'tree swaying to and fro.' Cp. Shakespeare, Henry IV, 4, 1:
'Let us sway on, and meet them in the field.'
In other passages it is subst. and signifies swing, of the down-stroke of a sword.

Swayne II, 9, 14 = a young man, a youth, properly a labourer; from A.-S. swán, a herdsman, servant, connected with swincan, to labour, to swink; Dan. svend, youth, servant, journeyman; so in boatswain, coxswain.

T.

Then = than.

Thewes II, 10, 59 = manners: wherein Spenser differs from Shakespeare, whose use of the word is always physical and muscular, as in Hamlet, I, 3, and in Henry IV, 3, 2: 'Care I for the limbs, the thewes, the stature, bulk, and big assemblance of a man!' The additional notion of being strong, well-grown, goes with it, and makes it pretty clear that as Shakespeare uses the word it is related to thee = to prosper, thrive.

Tho I, 1, 18; II, 9, 39; 10, 21. 27. 30. = then.

Thorough I, 1, 32; II, 9, 23. A.-S. þurh, or þorh, Ger. durch. Connected with A.-S. duru, or þuru, a door, Ger. thuer. In Dutch, door is both door (subst.) and through (prepos). In O.-E. thorrucke is used for door. Chaucer, Person's Tale, has 'Ydlenesse is the thorrucke of all wycked thoughtes;' whence the word thorugh (through) comes directly. The adj. thorough has the same stem-meaning.

Thrist II, 10, 21 = thirst (by metathesis).

Timely I, 1, 21 = in their time: 'the timely hours,' the hours as they duly passed.

Tire (tyre) II, 9, 19. 40 = attire, head-dress. — Tier, a rank or row. Fr. tirer, to draw (I, 4, 35.) — Generally, though not always, applied to head-dress; cp. tiara. A.-S. tyr, a Persian head-dress. So 2 Kings 9, 30, Jezebel 'tired her head;' and Levit. 16, 4, 'with the linen mitre shall he be. attired.' Possibly connected with Ger. zieren. Attire in O.-Fr. is atour, attour, a woman's hood or head-dress. Low Lat. atorna, 'mundus muliebris.'

Toy II, 9, 35 (verb) = to play; (subst.) in other passages = sport. Richardson thinks from A.-S. tawian, to till, prepare (of hides, so Dan. tougo); Dut. toyen, touwen, to dress, ornament. But the word is really derived from the Ger. zeug, Low Ger. tueg, Sw. tyg, Dan. toï. It is used for the compound spiel-zeug, which answers to the English play-toy, or plaything. See Wedgwood's Dictionary.

Tract I, 1, 11 = trace, the footing of man or beast. Fr. trait, Lat. tractus, traho.

Traine I, 1, 18: = 1) train, anything drawn out in length; whence 2) = tail. Fr. trainer. 3) = trap, or snare. The English speak of 'laying a train to catch a person.' Lat. trahere.

Treachetour II, 10, 51 — in other passages Treachour. Nares says of this word, that it is not merely another spelling of traitor (traditor), but derived from an independent source. The word is often used by Chaucer, in different forms. Thus he has treccherie, trechoure, words closely related to the French triche, tricherie, the modern trickery (as of jugglers.) But there are other forms from which we can gather the origin of the word: treget, guile, craft, a juggler's trick, and tregetour, a juggler. Roquefort in his Dict. gives tresgier, an O.-Fr. word, meaning magic, juggling, which seems to be the furthest point to which we can trace the word. Spenser uses the word throughout in the sense of traitor, not magician or juggler.

Twain (twayne) II, 10, 28. 34. = two (almost obsolete).

U.

Uncouth I, 1, 15 = unusual, properly unknown; used in this sense by Spenser, Shepheards Calender, Ecl. IX, 60: 'In hope of better that was uncouth.' A.-S. uncuᵬ, from cyᵬan, gecyᵬan, to know; so O.-Eng. selcouth, seldom known, rarely known, uncommon. The later sense of awkwardness is a natural deduction.

Uneath II, 10, 8 = not easily, scarcely, with difficulty. A.-S. un-eaᵬe, uneasy; O.-Eng. une-eᵬes, with difficulty; Icel. auᵬ, easy, and unodi, uneasy: and in Scottish audie is an easy-going fellow. There is some doubt as to the usage of the word in I, 11, 4, 'and seemed uneath to shake the stedfast ground,' where some commentators suppose that it is a contraction for underneath.

Unfold II, 9, 39 = to discover.

Unkindly I, 1, 26; II, 10, 9 = unnatural, unlike their kind. — kind A.-S. gecynd, nature from cyn, kin, race.

Unmannerd II, 10, 5 = not cultivated (worked by hand). Manure is the Fr. manœuvre, Low Lat. manopera, mannopera, the work of the hand. The later use of the word = Fr. engraisser, is a corruption.

Unwares II, 9, 38 (adv.) = unexpectedly, catching one in an unwary state. A.-S. unwáres, from unwaér. Connected with it are the verb warnian, to warn (to make ware). and probably also ward, guard. Ger. warten. The earliest form of the word is seen in the Goth. dauravards, door — ward, door — keeper.

Upbray = to upbraid: A.-S. upabredan, upabregdan, to pull up, snatch up; abregdan, to twist out, draw out; connected with bredan, to braid. There is an Old-Eng. to braid = to reproach.

Upstart I, 1, 16 = started up.

Uptrain II, 10, 17 = to train up.

Upwound I, 1, 15 = knotted together, wound up.

V.

Valiaunce II, 9, 5; 10, 38 = valour; a Fr. form, vaillance.

Vantage II, 10, 65 = advantage.

Vaut = vault. Fr. voûte, Low Lat. volta, Lat. volutare, volvere. Connected also with A.-S. wealtian, to roll (?).

Vermell II, 10, 24 = red, vermilion coloured. So Ariosto, Orl. Fur., has 'vermiglie rose.' The word is derived from vermis, either because of the trailing, braided (wormlike) patterns, painted in dull red, with which MSS. were adorned. There was a part. vermiled, used not of colour but of form, in the translation of Phil. de Commines, 'vermiled with gold', i. e. with a pattern in gold running about all over it. Or it is from Low Lat. vermiculus, the worm which makes a red dye. Du Cange says (quoting a MS. of Gervasius, de Otiis Imperialibus) that in the kingdom of Arles and the sea-coast below is a tree of wonderful value. This is the vermiculus, with which royal robes are dyed. He says that the vermis (worm) punctures the leaves. This was known in the time of the later empire.

Vildly I, 1, 20 = vilely.

Villein II, 9, 13 = low folk, also with the sense of rascality. (So Chaucer has vilonye of what is unbecoming, low, Prol. 726.) Low Lat. villanus, a slave attached to a villa. See Du Cange, who defines them as 'qui villae seu glebac adscripti sunt.'

Virginal II, 9, 20 = pertaining to a virgin. So Shakespeare, Coriol. 5, 2: 'the virginal palms of our daughters.'

W.

Wade I, 1, 12 = to walk, or go. Spenser also uses the form to vade (III, 9, 20). The verb to wade, A.-S. wádan, did not at first necessarily signify walking through water, though A.-S. wád is a ford. Connected with Lat. vadere, vadum, where also the verb is used more generally, and the subst. signifies a ford. Low Lat. vadare, to cross a ford, is in its turn derived from vadum.

War-hable II, 10, 62 = fit for war (of the youth of a kingdom.)

Warray II, 10, 50 = to make war on, worry, and perhaps as harry (of an army). Connected with to wear, and war. Fairfax, I, 6, has 'The Christen Lords warraid the eastern land.' (A.-S. werig, weary?) To worow, in O.-Eng. = to strangle; as dogs worry a sheep. seizing it by the neck (Ger. wuergen); but this it not the original sense.

Warrey II, 10, 21.

Wastfull I, 1, 32 = wild. Mod.-Fr. gâter; O.-Fr. gaster, It. guastare; Lat. vastare, to spoil, devastate.

Weare I, 1, 31 = spend, pass (of time). Cp. Lat. phrase terere tempus; usually in a bad sense.

Weeke II, 10, 30 = wick (of a candle or lamp). A.-S. wecca.

Ween I, 1, 10; II, 9, 8 = to think, suppose. A.-S. wénan, to hope, expect; wén, hope, expectation.

Weet II, 9, 39 = to know, perceive. A.-S. witan, to know; Ger. wissen; akin to wise and wit; wote and wot are the present tense of this verb.

Weld II, 9, 56; 10, 32. = to wield, govern. A.-S. wealdan.

Welke I, 1, 23 = to fade, grow dim (of the sun in the west); cp. Ger. welken, to be welked or wrinkled: so Chaucer (Pardoneres Tale, 277), 'full pale and welkid is my face.'

Well = to flow down I, 1, 34.

Wend I, 1, 28 = to go. A.-S. wendan; Goth. vandjan, Ger. wenden, to turn or wind. From it comes the past tense went.

Wene II, 10, 8.

Western I, 1, 5. II, 9, 10 = west.

Wexe II, 10, 20 = to grow (wax). A.-S. weaxan, Ger. wachsen.

Whenas II, 9, 10 = as soon as ever; when.

Whereas = where.

Whiles.
Whyleme II, 9, 45; 10, 16 = formerly, some time ago. Morris says that '-um (A.-S. hwil-um) is an old adverbial ending, as seen in O.-E. ferr-om, afar; Eng. seld-om.'
Wield II, 9, 45 = to manage, guide.
Wight II, 9, 39 = a being, person, of either sex. A.-S. wiht, wuht. Levins has 'wight, a creature.'
Wimple I, 1, 4 (verb) = to plait or fold; in other passages (subst.) = neck-kerchief or covering for the neck; so distinguished from the veil. A.-S. winpel, O.-Fr. guimple, Du. wimpelen, perhaps Ger. wimpel, a pennon, flag; Low Lat. guimpa. In the dress of nuns it is the white linen plaited or folded cloth around their necks. When Spenser speaks of the 'vele that wimpled was full low,' he must mean that it fell low in folds like a wimple. So Chaucer writes of the Prioress, Prol. 47:

> 'Upon an amblere esely sche sat,
> Wymplid ful wel, and on hire hed a hat.'

In O.-Fr. guimple is a hood. It had been derived from vinculum, 'parce qu'on en lie la teste.'
Withouten II, 9, 58 = without.
Witt II, 9, 49 = mind, intelligence.
Wittily II, 9, 53 = sensibly. See 'Weet.'
Wizard II, 9, 53 = a wise man; used by Spenser in this place in its proper sense. It came to be appropriated to a man skilled in witchcraft and magic: answering to the female 'witch', who is also often called 'a wise woman.' A.-S. wicca is used of both male wizard and female witch; (possibly the Engl. wicked is the same word = one skilled in an unholy knowledge.) But, in point of derivation, wizard is from wisa, an honourable sage; witch from wicca. Milton also uses it in its earlier and better sense (though here the notion that the Magi were magicians may have led to the use of the word), Ode on the Nativity, 23:

> 'The star-led wizards haste with odours sweet.'

The name Guiscard is the same word; that being the nearest approach to wizard possible to Italian lips. Roger and Robert Guiscard, the Norman Conquerors of Sicily, were simply Roger and Robert the wisards, the Wise. Du Cange says 'eo cognomine vocatum Robertum Normanum ob vafritiem annotat Wilh. Gemet. 7, 3.' William of Apulia writes:

> 'Cognomen Guiscardus erat, quia calliditatis
> Non Cicero tantae fuit, aut versutus Ulysses.'

Wise II, 9, 42 = manner, way, guise. A.- S.wise, Fr. guise, Ger. weise. The English still have the word in likewise, otherwise. So Spenser uses guize I, 12, 14. Similarly, the word disguise means to dissemble in dress or manner, to strip off the usual guise or dress, and to wear another.
Wonne II, 9, 52; 10, 1. = (subst.) dwelling; (verb) to dwell. A.-S. wunian, to dwell. O.-E. woning dwelling; Ger. wohnen. From this comes (as a p. p.) the subst. wont, that which is usual customary; whence again a p. p. wonted. There are also a subst. wonne, a dwelling, and the verb neut. he wonts = is accustomed.
Worshippe I, 1, 3 = honour, reverence. Cp. 'with my body I thee worship.' Now used properly of God alone. A.-S. weorð-scipe.

Wot (wote) I, 1, 8. 32 — see 'Weet.'
Woxe II, 10, 17 pret. to wax.')

Y.

Y- as a prefix, denotes the past part., and answers to the Mod. Ger. *ge-*, and partially to the Ger. and Eng. *be-*, as *be*-sprent, *be*-loved, etc. It is descended from the Goth. *ga-* (as in *ga*-kannjan = *be*-kannt machen, to make *be*-known.¹, A.-S. *ge-* prefixed to imperfects, as well as to p. p.: hence in O.-Engl. the prefix *i-*, as in *i*-brent, burnt; *i*-writen, written; this was also written *y-*, as by Spenser, though the use of the form was probably almost obsolete in his day. Traces of it may still remain among us, as in the word *a*-go (= agone, *y*goe, *y*gone, p. p. of 'to go'), *a*-fraid (p. p. 'to fray.'), *a*-ghast (terrified). But modern etymologists object to this claim of relationship, and hold that this *a-* is 'in', or 'on', as in the case of *a*-foot, *a*-hunting, *a*-talking. It is, however, tempting to think that in some cases the *y-* has been retained in the common speech.

Ybuilt II, 9, 29 = built.
Yclad (ycladd) I, 1, 7; II, 9, 27 = clothed.
Ydrad I, 1, 2, p. p. of to dread. Cp. A.-S. adraédan, pret. adred, to dread, fear; O.-Engl. adrad. Cp. Sidney's Arcadia, II., to make all men adread.'
Yfere II, 9, 2 = in company, together. A.-S. ge-fera, a companion; from feran, to go.

f. Synonymous Words.

Compare:

1. Vale I, 1, 21; II, 9, 10.
   Dale I, 1, 21; II, 9, 10.
2. Bear I, 1, 2. 6. 9; II, 9, 2. 4. 19; 10, 35.
   Wear I, 1, 2. 31; II, 9, 19; 10, 39.
   Wield I, 1, 5; II, 10, 2. 39.
4. Knight I, 1, 1.
   Sire II, 9, 11. 48.
5. Train I, 1, 18; II, 9, 19.
   Tail I, 1, 16. 17.
6. Mudd I, 1, 21.
   Slime I, 1, 21.
7. Brood.
   Impes I, 1, 26.
   Progeny II, 10, 22. 35.
   Issew II, 10, 61.
8. Well I, 1, 27. 33.
   Right I, 1, 33; II, 9, 17. 36. 40. 55;
     10, 2. 23.
   Very I, 1, 29.
   Greatly II, 10, 53.

All II, 10, 55.
Quite II, 10, 69.
9. Parentage II, 10, 27.
   Sire II, 10, 22. 31.
10. Native land II, 10, 69.
    Country II, 10, 69.
11. Shortly II, 10, 33. 44. 52. 54. 58.
    Late II, 10, 38.
    Earst II, 10, 38.
12. Fealty II, 10, 37.
    Foy II, 10, 41.
13. Rule II. 10, 45. 46.
    Raign II, 10, 58.
14. As befell II, 9, 17.
    As became II, 9, 28.
    As beseemed II, 9, 26. 38.
15. Force I, 1, 3; II, 9, 14; 10, 18.
    Strength I, 1, 27; II, 9, 57; 10, 39. 46.
    Might I, 1, 32; II, 9, 46; II, 10, 2. 8. 35. 56.
    Power I, 1, 7. II, 9, 1. 3. 7; 10, 54. 57.

¹) See above.

Puissance II, 9, 14.
Maine II, 9, 14.
16. Field I. 1, 1; II. 10, 43.
Giust I, 1, 1.
Encounter I, 1, 1.
Batteill II. 10, 10, 18. 55. 58.
Stoure II, 10, 19.
Fight II, 10. 16. 35. 56.
Debate II. 10, 58.
Fray II, 10, 10.
Contention II, 10, 11.
Bloodshed II. 10, 49.
Assay II, 10, 49.
17. Realm II, 10, 65.
Regiment II, 9, 59.
Empire II, 10, 5. 61.
Rule II. 10, 20. 34. 41. 49. 66.
Kingdom II, 10. 34.
Crowne II, 10, 64.
Government II, 9, 59.
18. Leman I, 1, 6; II, 10, 18.
Soveraigne II, 9, 4.
Liege II. 9, 4.
Lady.
Princesse II. 9, 5.
Madame II, 9, 37.
Dame II, 9. 44.
19. Reward.
Meed II, 9, 6; 10, 12.
Recompence II. 10, 23. 40:
Guerdon II. 9, 6.
20. Crave I, 1, 3; II, 9, 60.
Earne I, 1, 3.
21. Prick I, 1, 1.
Ride I, 1, 3.
22. Constrain I, 1. 6.
To be fain I, 1, 6.
Enforce I, 1, 7.
23. Vanquish II, 10, 58.
Conquer II, 10, 10.
Slay II, 10, 10.
Defeat II, 10, 10.
Foyl II, 10, 48.
Overrun II, 10, 61.
Sway II, 10, 49.

Withstand II, 10, 61.
24. Pleasure I. 1, 8.
Delight I, 1, 10.
25. Perill I. 1. 12. 24.
Danger I. 1, 12.
Jeopardy II; 10, 17.
26. Den I. 1. 13. 15. 16.
Cave I, 1, 11.
Hole I, 1. 14.
27. Hideous I, 1, 16.
Vile I, 1, 13.
Ugly I, 1. 14.
Lothsom I, 1, 14.
Filthie I, 1, 14.
Foule I, 1, 14.
28. Earth.
Ground.
Soyle II, 10, 9.
29. Shore II, 10, 10.
Coast II, 10, 6.
30. Gest II, 10, 12.
Deede II, 10, 21.
31. Part II, 10, 14. 39. 54.
Quart II, 10. 14.
32. Portion II, 10, 14. 39.
Lotte II. 10, 29.
33. Eke.
Also II, 10, 41.
34. At last I, 1, 11.
At length I, 1, 11.
35. Man.
Creature.
Body.
Wight I, 1, 6. 32; II, 10, 8. 59.
36. Mightie II, 10, 4. 10. 16.
Stout II, 10, 34.
37. Wize II, 9, 12.
Manner II. 9, 13.
38. Stocke II, 10, 9.
Line II, 10, 9.
39. Called II. 9, 31.
Hight II, 10, 16.
Cleped II, 9, 32. 58.
Named II, 10, 6.
40. Sage II, 9, 47. 48. 54.

18*

Wise II, 9, 47. 48. 54.
41. Leasing II, 9, 51.
Tale II, 9, 51.
Lie II, 9, 51.
42. Room.
Chamber II, 9, 50. 51. 55. 57.
43. Thoughte II, 9, 51.
Fantasie II, 9, 51.
Device II, 9, 51.
Dream II, 9, 51.
Opinion II, 9, 51.
44. Mad II, 9, 52.
Foolish II, 9, 52.
Sad.
Solemne.
45. Seem.
Appere II, 9, 52.
46. Chronicle II, 10, Motto.
Regesters II, 9, 59.
Decretals.

Rolls II, 9, 57.
Records II, 9, 57.
47. Holy I, 1, 34.
Sacred II, 10, 39.
48. Entertainement I, 1, 35.
Feast I, 1, 35.
49. Ste(a)d II, 10, 44.
Roome I, 10, 60.
50. Picture II, 9, 2.
Retraitt II, 9, 4.
Pictural II, 9, 53.
51. Defence II. 10, 15.
Munifi(c)ence II, 10, 15.
52. River II, 10, 16. 19.
Stream.
53. Flight II, 10, 16. 55.
Chace II, 10, 57.
54. Wex II, 10, 17. 20. 30. 32.
Grow II, 10, 54.

Conclusion.

Gathering up the consequences of our dissertation we find in the first place confirmed what was above said about Spenser's b i b l i c a l a n d c l a s s i c a l l e a r n i n g as well as about his pre-dilection for A r i o s t o. The notes of the second part of the precedent treatise are filled up with such passages as must have been known to Spenser:

Of the Bible: cp. above ·p. 29. 30. 31. 32. 34.
    39. 49. 58 etc.
Of Virgil p. 30. 46. 55. 60. 64. 66 etc.
of Curtius p. 46 etc.
of Arrian p. 46 etc.
of Lucretius p. 30 etc.
of Statius p. 31. 32. 39. 46 etc.
of Ovid p. 32. 37. 56. 63 etc.
of Plinius p. 32 etc.
of Lucan p. 60 etc.
of Claudian p. 56 etc.
of Seneca p. 41 etc.
of Horace p. 31. 41 etc.

of Hesiod p. 34 etc.
of Mela p. 37 etc.
of Macrobius p. 37 etc.
of Homer p. 35. 37. 41. 55. 57. 64 etc.
of Aristophanes p. 41 etc.
of Cicero p. 41. 49. 57 etc.
of Tacitus p. 41 etc.
of Plato p. 48. 49. 50. 55 etc.
of Herodot p. 49. 57 etc.
of Propertius p. 60 etc.
Of Ariosto: p. 31. 39. 63 etc.

Herewith, then, are connected our poet's so called L a t i n i s m s, respectively his Grecisms and Italianisms. For it was impossible that a writer of such keen sympathies as Spenser should avoid the influences of those books which he regarded as his models. He has borrowed not only many passages from them, but his imitations extend also to single words and constructions, as for instance:

'Threatning her angry sting' I, 1, 17.
'Edifyde' I, 1, 34.
'Overrun to tread them' II, 9, 15.
'In batteil well ordaind' II, 10, 18.
'Nephewes'.= nepotes II, 10, 45.
'Richesse to compare' = divitias comparare I, 4, 28 [1]).
'Relate' = referre, reducere III, 8, 51 [1]).
'Invent' = find = invenire III, 5, 10 [1]).
'Evil heare' = male audire I, 5, 23 [1]).
'To shew the place' I, 1, 31.

Moreover we find that, particularly in Book II Canto X of the Fairy Queen, Spenser has made a large use of English authors, of historians as well as of poets, especially of Chaucer.

And thus, we come to speak of the called Archaisms of Spenser. At first sight the chapters treating of the accent, the orthography, the etymology, and before all that one which treats of the lexicography offer very numerous Old - English or Anglo - Saxon elements.

The like for his Gallicisms you may compare those chapters, and here it is very interesting to trace the gradual assimilation of French words with the English language. Thus in edition [2]) 1590 we have 'ferse', in 1596 'fierce'; 'perse', 'persaunt' are nearer the French origin than 'pierce', 'piercing'; 'richesse', 'noblesse', 'humblesse', are words not yet digested by the Modern English; 'renverst', 'esloyne', 'covetise', 'pourtrahed', 'journall', (for 'daily'), are all French forms; 'insúpportable', 'spirítuall', 'the tigré cruél', are all in pronunciation nearer the French than the English.

We find, therefore, in Spenser not only such words as now are obsolete and were so already in his own age, or words with an obsolete meaning, but also such as have never been used by any other author, such as are quite different from those used in Old - English as well as from those of the modern language, as for instance:
'entertain'. 'herbars'. 'miscreate' [3]).

Also other peculiarities are to be found in Spenser's idiom. It may be mentioned that there sometimes seem to be traces of his Irish sojourn in his works, as for instance:
'trenchand' (see note ad I, 1, 17.,
Curious similes, as in II, 9, 35, note.
Cumbrous sentences, as in I, 1, 26, note.
Sometimes he plays upon words, as in
II, 10, 26: 'wealth they forth do well'.
He is fond of proverbs:
'Louting low' I, 1, 30.
'Night gives counsell best' I, 1, 33.
'The way to win is wisely to advise I, 1, 33.

---

[1]) See Willisius p. 32 sq.
[2]) Cp. Kitchin I, p. XVII.
[3]) See above.

'When the oyle is spent The light goes out' II, 10, 30.
Love is not where most it is profest' II, 10, 31.
Finally we are obliged to mention his principal f a u l t s pertaining to style. With these must be classed his frequent reiteration and wearisome verbosity, especially when he chances to praise Queen Elizabeth and her pedigree.

II, 9, 3 etc.
Not fitting comparisons, as in II, 9, 30.
Tautology II, 9, 51.
Idem per Idem II, 10, 4. 8.
Anachronisms II, 9, 20. 21.

E r r a t à.

Pag.	4 l.	1	from below	read	Demogeot.	Pag.	43 l.	12	from above	read	diesem.
„	4 „	12	„ „	„	gesch.	„	52 „	3	„ „	„	der Aetna oder
„	4 „	16	„ „	„	form.						flammende . . .
„	4 „	17	„ „	„	sprache.	„	52 „	11	„ below	„	is said.
„	5 „	3	„ above	„	numerous.	„	57 „	5	„ above	„	Ascending.
„	9 „	29	„ „	„	continues.	„	57 „	16	„ „	„	Griechen.
„	9 „	17	„ below	„	Colin.	„	63 „	10	„ below	„	accumulatur.
„	12 „	10	„ above	„	gave.	„	70 „	11	„ above	„	Manild.
„	12 „	11	„ below	„	had.	„	110 „	7	„ „	„	the.
„	14 „	19	„ above	„	him.	„	111 „	13	„ „	„	the.
„	14 „	24	„ „	„	eius.	„	112 „	5	„ below	„	kild.
„	19 „	8	„ „	„	matters.	„	120 „	8	„ „	„	aut.
„	21 „	17	„ below	„	above.	„	130 „	11	„ above	„	Outwell.
„	24 „	6	„ above	„	dissatisfy.	„	130 „	12	„ „	„	snatch.
„	39 „	17	„ below	„	πνεύματος.	„	130 „	19	„ below	„	public.

Schulnachrichten.

I. Lehrverfassung.

Prima.

Zweijähriger Cursus. Ordinarius: Oberlehrer Dr. Krahmer.

1. **Religion:** Lectüre des Römerbriefes und des Johannes Evangelii. Wiederholung von Evangelium, Spruch und Lied nach dem Bibelkalender. 2 Std. Director.
2. **Deutsch.** Die zweite klassische Blüthenperiode. Lectüre prosaischer Abschnitte von Lessing (Laocoon), Schiller (Das Erhabene und Schöne), sowie Lectüre des Nathan von Lessing und der Iphigenie von Goethe. Freie Aufsätze. 3 Std. Director.
3. **Latein.** Verg. Aeneis lib. I und II. — Curtius lib. III und IV. 3 Std. Dr. Krahmer.
4. **Französisch.** Racine's Athalie und prosaische Abschnitte aus Herrig. Freie Aufsätze, Exercitien, Extemporalien, grammatische Wiederholungen und mündliche Vorträge. 4 Std. Dr. Lambeck.
5. **Englisch.** Shakespeare's Richard II. und prosaische Abschnitte aus Herrig, sonst wie im Französischen. 3 Std. Dr. Krahmer.
6. **Geschichte und Geographie.** Neuere Geschichte und geographische Wiederholungen. 3 Std. Dr. Krahmer.
7. **Physik.** Akustik in Wiederholung und Optik. 3 Std. Dr. Schütte.
8. **Chemie.** Mangan, Zink, Cadmium, Kupfer, Quecksilber, Blei, Silber, Gold, Platina. 3 Std. Dr. Schütte.
9. **Mathematik.** Stereometrie. Wiederholung der Progressionen, Zinseszins und Renten-Rechnung. Arithmetische Reihen, Entwicklung von a^x, log. x. 2c. Wiederholungen aus den Gebieten der Mathematik an zahlreichen Aufgaben. Häusliche Arbeiten. 5 Std. Dr. Schütte.
10. **Zeichnen.** Freihandzeichnen nach Vorlagen und Gyps, Linear- und Planzeichnen; Schatten-Constructionen und axometrisches Zeichnen. 3 Std. Müller.
11. **Singen.** Die Schüler dieser Klasse bilden mit den besten Sängern der anderen Klassen (II—V) den ersten Sängerkreis und singen Motetten, 4stimmige Choräle, Volks- und andere Lieder. 2 Std. Dornhecker.

Ober-Secunda*)

Einjähriger Cursus. Ordinarius: Dr. Schütte.

1. **Religion.** Das Leben Jesu nach den vier Evangelien und die Apostelgeschichte, sonst wie I. 2 Std. Director.
2. **Deutsch.** Lectüre von Gedichten, besonders von Klopstock und Schiller. Poetik, freie Aufsätze. 3 Std. (Dr. Lübke.) Dr. Jock.

---

*) Die Trennung der Secunda in eine Ober- und Unter-Secunda ist zu Michaelis eingetreten; nur in der Physik blieben die Klassen vereinigt.

1

3. **Latein.** Ovid Metam. lib. VI, 314—411; 675—721. lib. VII, 1—370; 404—700; 753—Ende. Sallust. Catilina. Tempus u. Modußlehre. Exercitien und Extemporalien. 4 Std. (Dr. Lübke.) Dr. Fock.

4. **Französisch.** Ségur, histoire de Napoléon lib. III, lib. IV chap. 1—5; lib. XI und lib. XII. chap 1—4. Grammatik nach Ploetz, Cursus II. Lect 58—70 und Wiederholungen aus früheren Abschnitten. Exercitien und Extemporalien. 4 Std. (Dr. Lambeck.) Dr. Lübke.

5. **Englisch.** Lectüre aus Herrig. Grammatik nach Foelsing 2. Theil. Exercitien und Extemporalien. 3 Std. Dr. Krahmer.

6. **Geschichte und Geographie.** Mittlere Geschichte bis zu den Kreuzzügen. Europa. 3 Std. (Dr. Fock.) Dr. Krahmer.

7. **Physik.** Ruhe und Bewegung, gleichförmige und ungleichförmige Bewegung, Akustik, Wärmelehre, Meteorologie. 2 Std. Dr. Schütte.

8. **Chemie.** Oxydations- und Verbrennungs-Erscheinungen, demonstrirt an Metallen und an Wasserstoff. Verbindungen des Wasserstoffs mit Phosphor und den Salzbildern. 2 Std. Dr. Schütte.

9. **Mathematik.** Algebraische Constructionen, Kreisberechnung; Wiederholung der Trigonometrie, Stereometrie. Arithmetische und geometrische Progressionen, Gleichungen 2. Grades. 5 Std. Dr. Schütte.

10. **Naturbeschreibung.** Demonstration ausgewählter Pflanzenfamilien. (Passow.) Mineralogie. 2 Std. Director.

11. **Zeichnen.** Zeichnen nach Gyps, die Säulenordnungen, Projectionszeichnen. 2 Std. Müller.

12. **Singen** wie I.

Unter-Secunda.

Einjähriger Cursus. Ordinarius: Oberlehrer Dr. Schütte.

1. **Religion.** Das Leben Jesu und eingehende Besprechung ausgewählter Evangelien, sonst wie I. 2 Std. Director.

2. **Deutsch.** Lectüre Klopstockscher und Schillerscher Gedichte. Das Wichtigste aus der Metrik, Declamirübungen, freie Aufsätze. 3 Std. Dr. Lübke.

3. **Latein.** Ovid wie II A. Caesar bell. gall. lib. V und VI, 1—20. Tempus- und Modußlehre. Exercitien und Extemporalien. 4 Std. Dr. Lübke.

4. **Französisch.** Ségur wie II A. lib. III, IV, V und VI, 1—8. Grammatik nach Ploetz, Lect. 39—57. Exercitien und Extemporalien. 4 Std. Dr. Lambeck.

5. **Englisch.** Lectüre aus Herrig und Lübeking. Grammatik nach Foelsing 2. Theil Exercitien und Extemporalien. 3 Std. Dr. Krahmer.

6. **Geschichte und Geographie.** Geschichte des Mittelalters bis c. 1400. Die außereuropäischen Erdtheile. 3 Std. Dr. Fock.

7. **Physik** wie II A.

8. **Chemie.** Sauerstoff, Wasserstoff, Kohlenstoff, Schwefel, Phosphor. 2 Std. Passow.

9. **Mathematik.** Algebraische Constructionen, Kreisberechnung, Progressionen, Trigonometrie, Logarithmen, Gleichungen 1. Grades. 5 Std. Dr. Schütte.

10. **Naturbeschreibung.** Botanik. Mineralogie. 2 Std. Passow.

11. **Zeichnen** wie II A.

12. **Singen** wie I.

Ober-Tertia.

Einjähriger Cursus. Ordinarius: Oberlehrer Dr. Fock.

1. **Religion.** Lectüre ausgewählter Abschnitte des Matthäus, Geographie von Palästina, das christliche Kirchenjahr, Lied und Spruch wie II. 2 Std. Dr. Fock.

2. **Deutsch.** Wiederholung der Satzlehre, Elemente der Metrik. Declamirübungen und Aufsätze. 3 Std. Dr. Fock.

3. **Latein.** Caesar bell. gall. lib. III, IV, V, 1—15. Erweiterung der Casuslehre. Exercitien und Extemporalien. 5 Std. Dr. Fock.

— 3 —

4. **Französisch.** Thierry, Guillaume-le-Conquérant chap. 140—Ende und chap. 1—40. Grammatik nach Ploetz, Cursus II, Lect. 1—36. Exercitien und Extemporalien. 4 Std. Dr. Backe.

5. **Englisch.** Lectüre aus Lübecking. Vollendung der Formenlehre nach Callin. Exercitien und Extemporalien. 4 Std. S. Dr. Krahmer. W. Dr. Backe.

6. **Geschichte und Geographie.** Deutsche Geschichte bis c. 1740. — Deutschland, besonders Preußen. 4 Std. Dr. Fock.

7. **Mathematik und Rechnen.** Gleichflächigkeit, Aehnlichkeit. — Proportionen, Potenzen und Wurzeln, Gleichungen 1. Grades. — Wiederholung der bürgerlichen Rechnungsarten. 6 Std. Passow.

8. **Naturbeschreibung.** Das natürliche Pflanzensystem. Deutsche Wirbelthiere. 2 Std. Passow.

9. **Zeichnen.** Freihandzeichnen nach Köpfen im Umriß und mit Schattirung; Anfänge im architectonischen und geometrischen Zeichnen, perspectivisches Zeichnen. 2 Std. Müller.

10. **Singen** wie I.

Unter-Tertia.

Einjähriger Cursus.*) Ordinarius: Dr. Lüdke.

1. **Religion.** Das 2. Hauptstück. Evangelium, Spruch und Lied nach dem Bibelkalender 2 Std. Dr. Lüdke.

2. **Deutsch.** Die Satzlehre. Erklärung und Erlernung ausgewählter Gedichte. Declamirübungen und Aufsätze. 3 Std. Klinke.

3. **Latein.** Lectüre des Nepos: Hannibal, Cato, Atticus, Lysander, Alcibiades. — Miltiades, Themistocles-Pausanias. 5 Std. Dr. Lüdke und Brügmann.

4. **Französisch.** Michaud Iᵉ croisade chap. 3—12. Grammatik nach Ploetz. II. Cursus. Lectüre 1—20. Exercitien und Extemporalien. 4 Std. Dr. Backe und Lorenz.

5. **Englisch.** Die Elemente dieser Sprache nach Callin; Exercitien und Extemporalien. 4 Std. Dr. Lüdke und Dr. Backe.

6. **Geschichte und Geographie.** Brandenburgisch-preußische Geschichte. — Europa. 4 Std. Dr. Krahmer, Dr. Fock und Klinke.

7. **Mathematik und Rechnen.** Kreislehre. Die 4 Species mit algebraischen Zahlen. — Zins, Mischungs- und Gesellschafts-Rechnung. 6 Std. Director, Passow und Lorenz.

8. **Naturbeschreibung.** Pflanzenfamilien des natürlichen Systems. — Gliederthiere. 2 Std. Passow und Lorenz.

9. **Zeichnen.** Freihandzeichnen von Gesichtstheilen und Köpfen, einfache Gypsornamente. Vorübungen im Linearzeichnen, perspectivisches Zeichnen. 2 Std. Müller.

10. **Singen** wie I.

Quarta A.

Einjähriger Cursus. Ordinarius: Dr. Lambeck.

1. **Religion.** Lectüre des Lucas. Die 5 Hauptstücke, Spruch und Lied. 2 Std. Brügmann.

2. **Deutsch.** Lectüre aus Masius und hieran der einfach erweiterte und der zusammengezogene Satz, sowie die Satzerweiterung. Declamirübungen, Aufsätze und Dictate. 3 Std. Dr. Lambeck.

3. **Latein.** Lectüre des kleinen Herodot X, XI, XII 1—10. Die wichtigsten Regeln der Syntax der Casus, mit Ausschluß des Genitiv und Ablativ. Exercitien und Extemporalien. 6 Std. Dr. Lambeck.

---

*) Das Pensum dieser Klasse ist so bemessen, daß dieselbe von fleißigen und fähigen Schülern in einem halben Jahre durchlaufen werden kann. Die Klasse war im Sommer in 2 Coetus geschieden, welche nur in der Religion, Geschichte und im Zeichnen gemeinsam unterrichtet wurden.

1*

4. **Französisch.** Grammatik nach Ploetz, Cursus für Quarta. Lectüre der zusammenhängenden Lesestücke. Exercitien und Extemporalien. 5 Stb. Klinke.

5. **Geschichte und Geographie.** Griechische Geschichte bis zum peloponnesischen Kriege, römische bis zu Caesar's Tod. — Die außereuropäischen Erdtheile. 4 Stb. Dr. Karmohl.

6. **Naturbeschreibung.** Pflanzendemonstrationen, das Linnéische System. — Wirbelthiere. 2 Stb. Passow.

7. **Mathematik und Rechnen.** Elemente der Planimetrie, Dreieckslehre, Viereck. — Einfache und zusammengesetzte Regeldetri, Gesellschaftsrechnung, Decimalbrüche. 6 Stb. Lorenz.

8. **Zeichnen.** Modellzeichnen, Ornamente im Umriß und in Schattirung, Constructionszeichnen mit Anwendung des Reißzeugs. 2 Stb. Müller.

9. **Schreiben.** Deutsche und lateinische Schrift nach Vorschriften, Schnellschrift nach dem Dictat. 2. Stb. Müller.

10. **Singen.** Die Sänger dieser Klasse und die weniger geübten der III A B. der IV B. V A und V B bilden den 2. Sängerkreis, singen ein- und zweistimmige Choräle und lernen die gebräuchlichsten Dur- und Moll-Tonleitern. 2 Stb. Dornhecter.

Quarta B.

Einjähriger Cursus. Ordinarius: Dr. Backe.

(Diese Klasse ist der Quarta A coordinirt; hier wie in Quinta B und Sexta B beginnt der Cursus zu Michaelis.)

Die Pensen und Stunden sind dieselben wie in IV A. Die Vertheilung der Lectionen war folgende: **Religion** Brügmann; **Deutsch** und **Latein** (Weller, X—XV) Dr. Backe; **Französisch** (Lübecking VII, 2—3) Dr. Lambecd; **Geschichte** und **Geographie** Herbst; **Naturbeschreibung** Passow, dann Dr. Bergholz; **Mathematik** und **Rechnen** Gentzen; **Zeichnen** und **Schreiben** Müller; **Singen** Dornhecter.

Quinta A.

Einjähriger Cursus. Ordinarius: Herbst.

1. **Religion.** Biblische Geschichten A. u. N. Testaments nach Zahn, die 3 ersten Hauptstücke mit Erklärung, Wochenspruch und Lied. 3 Stb. Brügmann.

2. **Deutsch.** Lectüre aus Masius, an derselben der einfache und einfach erweiterte Satz. Uebungen im Lesen und Erzählen, Declamirübungen, Dictate und kleine Aufsätze. 4 Stb. Herbst.

3. **Latein.** Die unregelmäßigen Formen in Declination, Comparation und Conjugation, die Pronomina, Zahlwörter, Präpositionen, die verba deponentia, defectiva und anomala. Anfang der Weller Lectüre. Extemporalien und Exercitien. 6 Stb. Herbst.

4. **Französisch.** Die Elemente dieser Sprache nach Ploetz, Cursus für Quinta. Exercitien. 5 Stb. Herbst.

5. **Geschichte und Geographie.** Griechische Sagengeschichte. — Allgemeine Geographie von Europa. 3 Stb. Dr. Karmohl.

6. **Naturbeschreibung.** Beschreibung ausgewählter Pflanzen und Thiere (Vögel und Fische). 2 Stb. Gentzen.

7. **Rechnen.** Bruchrechnung in benannten und unbenannten Zahlen. Decimalbrüche. 4 Stb. Gentzen.

8. **Zeichnen.** Formenlehre und Darstellung geometrischer Figuren mit Zirkel und Lineal, Ornamente nach Wandtafeln. 2 Stb. Müller.

9. **Schreiben.** Uebung im Schön- und Schnellschreiben nach Vorschrift. 3 Stb. Müller.

10. **Singen** wie IV.

Quinta B.

Einjähriger Cursus. Ordinarius: **Brügmann.**

(Quinta A coordinirt.)

Die Pensen und Stunden sind dieselben wie in V A. Die Vertheilung der Lectionen war folgende: **Religion, Deutsch, Latein Brügmann; Französisch** Lorenz, dann **Brügmann; Geschichte und Geographie** Lorenz; **Rechnen** und **Naturbeschreibung** Gentzen; **Zeichnen** und **Schreiben** Müller; **Singen** Dornhecker.

Sexta A.

Einjähriger Cursus. Ordinarius: Dr. **Karmohl.**

1. **Religion.** Biblische Geschichten A. u. N. Testaments, die 3 ersten Hauptstücke, Wochenspruch und Lied. 3 Stb. Herbst.
2. **Deutsch.** Die Wortlehre und der einfache Satz. Uebungen im Lesen, Erzählen des Gelesenen und Declamiren. Dictate zur Befestigung der Orthographie. 4 Stb. Dr. Karmohl.
3. **Latein.** Regelmäßige Declination, Comparation und Conjugation. Mündliche und schriftliche Uebungen im Uebersetzen. 8 Stb. Dr. Karmohl.
4. **Geschichte und Geographie.** Griechische Sagengeschichte. — Allgemeine Uebersicht über die Erdoberfläche. 3 Stb. Dr. Karmohl.
5. **Naturbeschreibung.** Beschreibung ausgewählter Pflanzen und Thiere (Säugethiere, Reptilien). 2 Stb. Lorenz.
6. **Rechnen.** Die 4 Species mit einfach benannten Zahlen. 4 Stb. Lorenz.
7. **Zeichnen.** Formenlehre und Darstellung einfacher Linienverbindungen; Einfache Ornamente. 2 Stb. Müller.
8. **Schreiben.** Deutsche und lateinische Schrift in Buchstaben, Wörtern und Sätzen. 3 Stb. Müller.
9. **Singen.** Gehör- und Treffübungen. Einübung von einstimmigen Volksliedern und Chorälen. 2 Stb. Dornhecker.

Sexta B.

Einjähriger Cursus. Ordinarius: **Klinke.**

(Sexta A coordinirt.)

Die Pensen und Stunden wie VI A. **Religion** Herbst, dann **Klinke; Deutsch** und **Latein Klinke; Geschichte** und **Geographie** Dr. Karmohl, dann Gentzen; **Naturbeschreibung** Lorenz, dann Dr. Bergholz; **Rechnen** Gentzen, dann Dr. Bergholz; **Zeichnen** und **Schreiben** Müller; **Singen** Dornhecker.

Den Turnunterricht ertheilte Herr Riehl in Gemeinschaft mit Herrn Gentzen. Im Sommer turnte die gesammte Schule in 2 wöchentlichen Stunden, im Winter in je einer Stunde.

Tabelle zur Vertheilung der Lehrgegenstände an die einzelnen Lehrer.

Sommersemester 1871.

Namen.	Gegenstand.	I.	II.	III. A.	III. B. coet. 1.	III. B. coet. 2.	IV. A.	IV. B.	V. A.	V. B.	VI. A.	VI. B.	Sa.
1. Dr. Braudt, Director.	Religion	2	2										
	Deutsch	3											
	Mathematik					5							12 Std.
2. Dr. Krahmer, Oberlehrer. Ordinar d. I.	Latein	3											
	Englisch	3	3	4									
	Geschichte u. Geogr.	3				2							18 „
3. Dr. Schütte, Oberlehrer, Ord. d. II.	Physik	3	2										
	Chemie	3	2										
	Mathematik	5	5										20 „
4. Dr. Fock, Oberlehrer, Ord. d. III. A.	Religion			2									
	Deutsch			3									
	Latein			5									
	Geschichte u. Geogr.		3	4	2								19 „
5. Passow, ordentl. Lehrer.	Mathem. u. Rechn.			6	6								
	Naturbeschreibung		2	2	2		2	2					22 „
6. Dr. Lüdke, ordentl. Lehrer, Ord. d. III. B, coet. 1 u. 2.	Religion				2	2							
	Deutsch			3									
	Latein			4	5								
	Englisch					4							
	Geschichte				2	2							20 „
7. Dr. Laubed, ordentl. Lehrer, Ord. d. IV. A.	Deutsch						3						
	Latein						6						
	Französisch	4	4					5					22 „
8. Dr. Backe, ordentl. Lehrer, Ord. d. IV. B.	Deutsch							3					
	Latein							6					
	Französisch			4	4								
	Englisch				4								21 „
9. Herbst, ordentl. Lehrer, Ord. d. V. A.	Religion										3	3	
	Deutsch								4				
	Latein								6				
	Französisch								5				
	Geschichte u. Geogr.							4					22 „
10. Brügmann, ordentl. Lehrer, Ord. d. V. B.	Religion						2	2	3	3			
	Deutsch									4			
	Latein					5				6			22 „
11. Geuhen, ordentl. Lehrer.	Naturbeschreibung								2	2			
	Mathem. u. Rechnen							6	4	4		4	22 „
12. Dr. Karmohl, ordentl. Lehrer, Ord. d. VI. A.	Deutsch										4		
	Latein							4			8		
	Geschichte u. Geogr.							3			3	3	22 „
13. Alluse, ordentl. Lehrer, Ord. d. VI. B.	Deutsch			3	3							4	
	Latein											8	
	Französisch					5							
	Geschichte u. Geogr.												23 „
14. Lorenz, wissenschaftl. Hülfslehrer.	Französisch				4					5			
	Naturbeschreibung				2						2	2	
	Geschichte u. Geogr.									3			
	Mathem. u. Rechnen					1	6				4		27 „
15. Müller, Zeichenlehrer.	Zeichnen	3	2	2	2	2	2	2	2	2	2	2	
	Schreiben						2	2	2	2	3	3	26 „
16. Dornhecker.	Singen				in 2 Abtheilungen zu je 2 Stunden						2	2	6 „
		32	32	32	32	32	32	32	31	31	31	31	

Tabelle zur Vertheilung der Lehrgegenstände an die einzelnen Lehrer.
Wintersemester 1871/72.

Namen.	Gegenstand.	I.	II. A.	II. B.	III. A.	III. B.	IV. A.	IV. B.	V. A.	V. B.	VI. A.	VI. B.	Sa.
1. Dr. Brandt, Director.	Religion	2	2	2									
	Deutsch	3											11 Stb.
	Naturbeschreibung		2										
2. Dr. Krahmer, Oberlehrer, Ordinar. d. I.	Latein	3											
	Englisch	3	3	3									18 „
	Geschichte u. Geogr.	3	3										
3. Dr. Schütte, Oberlehrer, Ord. d. II, A.B.	Physik	3	2	2									
	Chemie	3	2										20 + 5
	Mathematik	3	5	5									
4. Dr. Frod, Oberlehrer, Ord. d. III. A.	Religion				2								
	Deutsch		3		3								19 + 5
	Latein		4		5								
	Geschichte u. Geogr.				3	4							
5. Passow, ordentl. Lehrer.	Chemie			2									
	Mathem. u. Rechnen			2	6	6							22 „
	Naturbeschreibung			2	2	2	2						
6. Dr. Läßle, ordentl. Lehrer, Ord. d. III. B.	Religion			2									
	Deutsch			3									
	Latein			4									20 + 4
	Französisch		4	5									
	Englisch			4									
	Geschichte			2									
7. Dr. Lambed, ordentl. Lehrer, Ord. d. IV. A.	Deutsch				3								
	Latein				6								22 „
	Französisch	4	4		5								
8. Dr. Bade, ordentl. Lehrer, Ord. d. IV. B.	Deutsch					3							
	Latein					6							21 „
	Französisch			4	4								
	Englisch			4									
9. Herbst, ordentl. Lehrer, Ord. d. V. A.	Religion						3						
	Deutsch					4							
	Latein					6							22 „
	Französisch					5							
	Geschichte u. Geogr.				4								
10. Brügmann, ordentl. Lehrer, Ord. d. V. B.	Religion				2	2	3	3					
	Deutsch						4						
	Latein						6						22 „
	Französisch						5						
11. Gentzen, ordentl. Lehrer.	Geschich.e u. Geogr.									3			
	Mathem. u. Rechnen					6	4	4					21 „
	Naturbeschreibung					2	2						
12. Dr. Marmohl, ordentl. Lehrer. Ord. d. VI. A.	Deutsch							4					
	Latein							8					22 „
	Geschichte u. Geogr.				4		3	3					
13. Minke, ordentl. Lehrer, Ord. d. VI. B.	Religion								3				
	Deutsch					3			4				
	Latein						5		8				22 + 3
	Französisch												
	Geographie					2							
14. Lorenz, wissenschaftl. Hülfslehrer.	Geschichte u. Geogr.								3				
	Mathem. u. Rechnen					6			4				15 „
	Naturbeschreibung								2				
15. Müller, Zeichenlehrer.	Zeichnen	3	2	2	2	2	2	2	2	2	2	2	26 „
	Schreiben								2	2	3	3	
16. Dornhecler.	Singen	in 2 Abtheilungen zu je 2 Stunden.									2	2	6 „
17. Dr. Bergholz, cand. prob.	Rechnen							2			4		8 „
	Naturbeschreibung										2		
		32	32	32	32	32	32	32	31	31	31	31	

II. Aus der Schul=Chronik.

Das Schuljahr begann am 18. April mit der Einführung der Novizen. Im Laufe desselben wurden einzelne Lehrer und Schüler durch längere oder kürzere Krankheit von der Schule ferngehalten. Vier Schüler (von denen 2 längere Zeit schwer erkrankt darnieder lagen) verloren wir durch den Tod. Am 15. April starb der Unter=Tertianer Paul Mie aus Stralsund, am 21. Juni der Quintaner (B) Carl Durow aus Stralsund, am 26. Januar 1872 der Unter=Tertianer Curt Lambeck aus Thorn und am 28. Januar der Unter= Secundaner Carl Lembke aus Stralsund. Alle vier Schüler, mit denen die schwer gebeugten Eltern manche theure Hoffnung begruben, geleiteten die Klassenlehrer und die Mitschüler zu Grabe.

Am 6. Mai pflanzte die Schule in Gemeinschaft mit dem Gymnasium und der Gewerbeschule eine Friedenseiche. Eine besondere Friedensfeier veranstaltete die Schule am 16 Juni, den Schluß derselben bildete unser Spaziergang nach Devin.

Die Hundstags=Ferienschule fiel, geringer Betheiligung wegen, dies Mal aus.

Am 26. September wurde unter Vorsitz des Herrn Provinzial = Schulraths Dr. Wehrmann die Abiturienten=Prüfung abgehalten. Der Abiturient Helmuth Kneisler erhielt das Zeugniß der Reife unter Erlaß des mündlichen Examens.

Das Winterschmester begann am 10. October. Mit diesem neuen Schulabschnitte war es möglich ge= worden, die bis dahin noch vereinigte Secunda auch räumlich zu scheiden Die größere Stundenzahl wurde durch Uebernahme von Mehrstunden Seitens einiger Collegen der Anstalt gedeckt. Für die beiden unteren Klassen wurden in einem Gebäude des Stadtbauhofes zwei Zimmer hergerichtet, ein Nothbehelf, der nach der nunmehr beschlossenen Erbauung eines neuen würdigen Realschulgebäudes, hoffentlich von nicht langer Dauer sein wird!

Am 23. Februar veranstalteten unsere Schüler, wie sonst, eine Abend= Unterhaltung. Vortrag von Dichtungen in den in der Anstalt gelehrten Sprachen wechselten mit Musikstücken für Clavier und Saiten= Instrumente. In einer besonderen Abtheilung wurde der „Anacker'sche Bergmannsgruß" von der Chor=Klasse ausgeführt. Die Einnahme — 59 Thlr. — wurde, nach Abzug der Kosten, — 39 Thlr. 10 Sgr. — mit 19 Thlr. 20 Sgr den hiesigen Armen zugewendet.

Bei der Geburtstagsfeier Sr. Majestät des Kaisers und Königs wird Collega Passow die Fest= rede halten.

Die Versetzungs = Prüfungen werden wir in den beiden letzten Schulwochen halten. Das mündliche Abiturienten = Examen ist auf den 25. März angesetzt worden. Tags darauf schließt die Schule mit der allge= meinen Censur.

III. Verordnungen der Behörden.

1. 28. October 1871. Gemäß einer Allerhöchsten Ordre vom 5. Mai 1870 wird vom 1. April 1872 ab die Zulassung zur Portepeefähnrichs = Prüfung von der Beibringung eines von einem Gymnasium oder einer Realschule erster Ordnung ausgestellten Zeugnisses der Reife für Prima abhängig ge= macht. Diejenigen jungen Leute, welche, ohne Schüler eines Gymnasiums oder einer Realschule 1. Ordn. zu sein, ein solches Zeugniß erwerben wollen, haben sich einer Prüfung bei einer der ge= nannten Anstalten zu unterziehen. Bei den Realschulen 1. Ordn. besteht die schriftliche Prüfung in einem deutschen Aufsatz, einem französischen und englischen Exercitium und mathematischen Arbeit; mündlich wird bei denselben in der lateinischen, französischen und englischen Sprache, in der Geschichte und Geographie, in der Mathematik und den Naturwissenschaften geprüft. Das Maß der Anforderungen ist das für die Versetzung nach Prima vorgeschriebene.

2. 31. October 1871. Der vorgeordnete Herr Minister verfügt, daß hinfort die Aufnahme der Knaben auch von der Beibringung eines Attestes über die stattgehabte Impfung resp. Revaccination abhängig zu machen ist.

3. 27. Januar 1872. Das Königliche Provinzial=Schul-Collegium genehmigt den Eintritt des ordentlichen Lehrers Brügmann in das bürgerschaftliche Collegium.

4. 3. Februar 1872. Dieselbe Behörde fordert die Einsendung von 345 Exemplaren des Programms.

5. 16. Februar 1872. Der Hochedle Rath genehmigt den Ausfall der öffentlichen Prüfung für dieses Jahr.

IV. Statistische Nachrichten.

Die Namen der Lehrer sind in der vorstehenden Tabelle verzeichnet.
Die Gesammtzahl der Schüler betrug im Sommersemester 348, im Wintersemester 344. Dieselben waren in den Klassen vertheilt:

Semester.	Kl. I.	II. sup.	II. inf.	III. sup.	III. inf. coet. A., coet. B.	IV. A	IV. B.	V. A.	V. B.	VI. A.	VI. B.	Summa.
Sommer 1871.	11	47	39	30	29	35	34	29	25	39	30	348
Winter 1871/72.	15	14	31	44	50	40	24	35	30	36	25	344

Zu Ostern 1871 und im Laufe des Schuljahrs 1871/72 verließen 49 Schüler die Anstalt. Unter denselben befand sich ein Abiturient:

No.	Namen.	Geburtsort.	Alter. Jahre.	Auf der Schule. Jahre.	Davon in I. Jahre.	Prädicate und Bemerkung.	Beruf.
	Michaelis 1871.						
37	Helmuth Kneisler	Ueckermünde.	18 9/12	3½	2	gut bestanden, von der mündlichen Prüfung dispensirt.	Baufach.

Die übrigen Schüler gingen ab aus:

Secunda.

Carl Appel (Landmann), Hermann Babe (Kaufmann), Wilhelm Bergholz (Buchhändler), Paul Biengräber (Kaufmann), Otto Heinzelmann (Buchhändler), Emil Lubnow (Kaufmann), Wilhelm Müller (Kaufmann), Bernhard Picht (Kaufmann), August Schmidt (mit den Eltern nach Metz), Otto Seehas (Soldat), Joachim Stahnke (Subalterndienst), Franz Tiburtius (Landmann), Carl Trommer (Cadettenhaus), Albert Müller (Subalterndienst).

Ober-Tertia.

Rudolph Crotogino (Privatunterricht), Paul Jahnke (auf eine andere Anstalt), Magnus Pahlmann (Soldat), Carl Probst (Soldat), Emil Wadzeck (auf eine andere Anstalt).

Unter-Tertia.

Erich Baier (Landmann), Robert Fehlhaber (Kaufmann), Otto Fischer (Kaufmann), Robert Franz (mit den Eltern nach Metz), Max Hoffmann (auf eine andere Anstalt), Robert Holtz (Landmann), Oscar Jahnke (auf eine andere Anstalt), Eduard Klammer (Kaufmann), Wilhelm Möller (Landmann), Friedrich Wasow (Müller), Hans Wadzeck (auf eine andere Anstalt), Otto Wewetzer (Privatunterricht), Johannes Wilken (Seemann).

Durch den Tod verloren wir 3 Schüler, die anderen 13 verließen die Anstalt aus Quarta A. u B.: 7 (2 Privatunterricht, 1 auf eine andere Anstalt, 2 wegen Umzug der Eltern [Metz], 2 Kaufmann); aus Quinta A.: 1 Privatunterricht; aus Sexta B.: 5 (auf andere Anstalten, darunter 1 nach Metz).

Themata für die Abiturienten-Prüfung.

Deutsch. Welche Vortheile und Annehmlichkeiten haben die Küstenbewohner von der Nähe des Meeres?
Französisch. La période palatine de la guerre de 30 ans.
Englisch. Exercitium (der große Brand in London).
Mathematik. 1. Wie weit sind zwei durch ein Thal getrennte Bergspitzen A und B von einander entfernt, deren Höhe über dem Standpunkt C im Thal bezüglich $a = 200$ m und $b = 150$ m betragen, wenn die von C aus gemessene Elevation der Spitze A $\alpha = 8^0 35'$ und die der Spitze B $\beta = 10^0 20'$ und die Projection des Winkels A C B $\gamma = 140^0 46'$ beträgt? — 2. Aus einem gegebenen geraden Kegel, dessen Höhe h ist und dessen Grundkreis den Radius r hat, soll derjenige gerade Cylinder geschnitten werden, dessen Volumen ein Maximum ist. — 3. Um den Mittelpunkt einer Hyperbel mit den Axen 2 a ($= 6$) und 2 b ($= 8$) ist ein Kreis geschlagen, welcher durch die Brennpunkte geht; wie groß ist das Rechteck, welches durch die vier Durchschnittspunkte beider Curven bestimmt wird? — 4. Zwei Körper bewegen sich von 2 Punkten, deren Entfernung $d = 1190$ m ist, in entgegengesetzter Richtung gleichzeitig auf einander zu. Der eine legt in der ersten Minute $a = 20$ m, in jeder folgenden $b = 10$ m mehr als in der vorhergehenden zurück, der andere in der ersten Minute $c = 90$ m, in jeder folgenden $f = 8$ m weniger. Nach wie viel Minuten treffen sie zusammen? —
Physik. 1. Von einer horizontalen Metallplatte springt eine senkrecht auf sie geworfene vollkommen elastische Kugel mit einer Geschwindigkeit $v = 10,9$ m empor; wann fällt sie wieder auf die Platte zurück? Wie ändert sich aber die Sache, wenn in der Höhe $h = 2$ m über der Grundfläche eine zweite horizontale Metallplatte angebracht ist, gegen welche die Kugel anstößt? — 2. Zwei Lichtquellen, von denen die eine dreimal stärker leuchtet als die andere, sind 12' von einander entfernt; es soll der geometrische Ort für alle diejenigen Punkte bestimmt werden, welche von beiden Lichtquellen gleich stark beleuchtet werden und in einer Ebene liegen, welche durch die Verbindungslinie beider geht.
Chemie. 1. Die Thonerde. — 2. Wie viel Kalialaun und wie viel kohlensaures Kali gebraucht man, um 100 gr. Thonerdehydrat darzustellen, und wie viel Kohlensäure wird dabei frei? —

V. Vermehrung der Lehr-Apparate.

Die **Lehrer-Bibliothek** unter Aufsicht des Dr. Lübke erhielt als Fortsetzung: Langbein, Archiv; Herrig, Archiv; Stiehl, Centralblatt. Außerdem: Darwin, Abstammung des Menschen; Wüstemann, Goethe's Goetz; Lewes, Geschichte der alten Philosophie; Barden, quadratische Gleichungen; Teuffel, Studium; Banke, die deutschen Mächte und der Fürstenbund, Ursprung des 7jährigen Krieges; Schoemann, griechische Alterthümer; Bormann, Erziehung und Unterricht; Riede, Erziehungslehre, Wartenien, christliche Ethik; als Geschenk vom Königlichen Provinzial-Schul-Collegium: Wangemann, Otto Büchlein; Histoire générale du moyen age p. C. O. Des Michels, 2 vol. vom Artillerie-Lieutenant Herrn Ascher. — Die **Schüler-Bibliothek** erfuhr eine Vermehrung von 58 Bänden An Geschenken erhielt dieselbe: Geschichte des Agathon von Wieland, 3 vol. vom Primaner Kuird; Orelli, Unterhaltungen vom Unter-Tertianer Kosbahn. — Die **Hülfs-Bibliothek** erhielt 30 Bände von Schulbüchern und an Geschenken von den Quintanern Berg, Insel, Kraaz, Martens, Mielordt, Picht, Rickmann, Tiede je ein Buch, Faeck und Wolter je 2 Bücher

Für den **geographischen** Unterricht wurden beschafft: Karte von Deutschland und Palästina von Raaz.

Der **physikalische** und chemische Apparat unter Aufsicht des Oberlehrers Dr. Schütte wurde vermehrt um: Influenzmaschine mit Nebenapparaten, zwei Geißler'sche Röhren, phosphorescirende Röhren.

Die **naturhistorische Sammlung** unter Aufsicht des Realschullehrers Bassow erhielt an Geschenken: Hausmarder vom Kaufmann Herrn Zoellner, mehrere Orthoceratiten vom Bürgermeister Herrn Francke, 38 oesterreichische Mineralien von Herrn Milosch aus Siebenbürgen, Epheustamm vom Herrn Steffen, Schlange von Herrn Nitz, Seenadel von Herrn Müller, Bernstein von Herrn Lucke, Lava und Bernstein vom Secundaner Potenberg, Fledermaus vom Ober-Tertianer Tode, 2 Mäuse vom Ober-Tertianer Kellmann, Dompfaff vom Ober-Tertianer v. Homeyer, Schlange vom Ober-Tertianer Gronow, 2 Schafhörner vom Ober-Tertianer Pieritz, Eberzahn und Hummelnest vom Ober-Tertianer Kühlbach, Hausratte vom Unter-Tertianer Genschow, Dornhai und Seestern vom Quartaner Engel, Eichhörnchen vom Quartaner Wurmsee, Thurmschwalbe vom Quintaner Niemann.

Die **Sammlung der Zeichnungen** und Modelle unter Aufsicht des Zeichenlehrers Müller erhielt einige Modelle.

Die **Sammlung der Noten** unter Aufsicht des Gesanglehrers Dornhecker wurde vermehrt um: 40 Exemplare zu Dornhecker's op. 12, 70 Exemplare zu Taubert op. 152, Heft 2; 50 Exemplare zu Dornhecker Psalm 100; A. Tottmann op. 5 und 9.

Allen freundlichen Gebern wird hiermit der herzlichste und ergebenste Dank gesagt.

Verzeichniß der in der Anstalt gebrauchten Lehrbücher und Leitfaden.

I. **Religion**: Bibel, 80 Kirchenlieder, Bibelkalender, Richter Lehrbuch. **Deutsch**: Viehof. **Latein**: Livius, Curtius, Virgil. **Französisch**: Herrig, Athalie und Horace. **Englisch**: Herrig, Macbeth, Caesar, Richard II. **Geschichte**: Pütz. **Physik**: Müller-Pouillet. **Mathematik**: Kambly.

II. A. und B. **Religion** und Deutsch wie I. **Latein**: Ovid, Caesar, Sallust, v. Gruber. **Französisch**: Ségur, Ploetz. **Englisch**: Herrig, Lübecking, Foelsing. **Geschichte und Geographie**: Dielitz und Daniel. **Physik** wie I. **Mathematik**: Kambly Trigonometrie und Stereometrie.

III. A. **Religion**: Bibel, 80 Kirchenlieder, Bibelkalender. **Deutsch**: Mager 2. Theil. **Latein**: Caesar, v. Gruber. **Französisch**: Thierry, Ploetz. **Englisch**: Lübecking, Callin. **Geschichte und Geographie**: Dielitz, Daniel. **Mathematik**: Kambly.

III. B. **Religion** und Deutsch wie III. A. **Latein**: Nepos, Ostermann. **Französisch**: Michaud 1e croisade und Ploetz. **Englisch**: Callin. **Geschichte und Geographie**: Mathematik wie III. A.

IV. A. und B. **Religion** wie III. A. **Deutsch**: Masius. **Latein**: Herodot, Ostermann. **Französisch**: Lübecking und Ploetz. **Geschichte, Geographie und Mathematik** wie III. A. **Naturbeschreibung**: Passow. **Rechnen**: Foelsing.

V. A. und B. **Religion**: Zahn, bibl. Geschichte, sonst wie III. B. **Deutsch** wie IV. **Latein**: v. Gruber, Kuhr. **Französisch**: Ploetz. **Geographie**: Daniel. **Naturbeschreibung** und Rechnen wie IV.

VI. A. und B. **Religion, Deutsch, Latein, Rechnen** wie V.

Atlanten: Liechtenstern und Lange oder Sydow. Karte von Alt-Griechenland und Alt-Italien von Kiepert. —

Die öffentliche Prüfung fällt mit Genehmigung des Hochedlen Raths für dieses Jahr aus. —

Das neue Schuljahr beginnt Dienstag, den 9. April. Die Prüfung neuer Schüler findet für die einheimischen Mittwoch, den 27. März, für die auswärtigen Montag, den 8. April, früh 9 Uhr im Locale der Anstalt statt. Bei der Anmeldung sind das Tauf- (Geburts) Zeugniß, das Impf-zeugniß und ein Abgangszeugniß der früher besuchten Schule mit zur Stelle zu bringen.

Die Unterrichts- und Prüfungs-Ordnung vom 6. October 1859 setzt in §. 2 fest: Der Eintritt in die Sexta erfolgt in der Regel nicht vor dem vollendeten neunten Lebensjahre. Die zur Aufnahme in die Sexta erforderlichen Kenntnisse und Fertigkeiten sind: Geläufigkeit im Lesen lateinischer und deutscher Druckschrift; eine leserliche und reinliche Handschrift; Fertigkeit, Dictirtes ohne grobe orthographische Fehler nachzuschreiben; Sicherheit in den vier Grundrechnungsarten mit gleichbenannten Zahlen. In der Religion wird einige Be-kanntschaft mit den Geschichten des A. und N. Testaments, sowie (bei den evangelischen Schülern) mit Bibel-sprüchen und Liederversen erfordert.

Bei der Aufnahme von Schülern, die nach Alter und Vorkenntnissen in eine höhere Klasse als Sexta eintreten zu können erwarten, ist besonders darauf zu achten, daß sie im Wesentlichen das Maaß von Kennt-nissen mitbringen, welches sie befähigt, mit den länger auf der Schule unterrichteten Schülern gleichen Schritt zu halten.

Dr. Brandt.

www.ingramcontent.com/pod-product-compliance
Lightning Source LLC
Chambersburg PA
CBHW021115020726
47500CB00003B/769